The Adjudicator

Also by Susan Daitch

L.C.

The Colorist

Storytown

Paper Conspiracies

Fall Out

The Lost Civilization of Suolucidir

White Lead

Siege of Comedians

THE ADJUDICATOR

A NOVEL

SUSAN DAITCH_

TITLE

GREEN CITY
BOOKS

Green City Books, Bend, Oregon

Published 2025

Paperback ISBN: 9781963101058

Printed in the United States of America

LCCN data has been applied for.

This book is for my extraordinary cousins
who live on two continents and several islands:
Aviva, Barbara, Karen, Lata, and Radhika.

DEDICATION

The wisest thing in the world is to cry out before you are hurt. It is no good to cry out after you are hurt; especially after you are mortally hurt. People talk about the impatience of the populace; but sound historians know that most tyrannies have been possible because men moved too late. It is often essential to resist a tyranny before it exists. It is no answer to say, with a distant optimism, that the scheme is only in the air. A blow from a hatchet can only be parried while it is in the air.

—G. K. Chesterton, *Eugenics and Other Evils*

Culture spawns the terms of its own rejection.

—Raymond Williams, *Marxism and Literature*

Evolution wants to make things better. It doesn't care about suffering.

—Leor Kauffman and Joe Egender, *Unnatural Selection*

Descartes offered, but did not endorse, the idea that the body is a ship, and the self resides in the body, the way a pilot resides in a ship. Hume advanced the idea that there is no self, that what we call the self is, in fact, just a bundle of perceptions, feelings, and ideas. Contemporary cognitive science combines these two ideas in a most awkward synthesis: we are the brain which is in turn modeled not as *a* self, but as a vast army of little selves, or agencies, whose collective operations give rise to what looks, from the outside, as a single person.

—Alva Noë, *Learning to Look: Dispatches From the Art World*

To what extent is the human genome predictive of the future and how much of it is random, how much of it is chance, fate?

—Siddhartha Mukherjee

Alfred Ploetz was a German doctor, an early advocate of eugenics and ideas about racial purity. His name sounds like a cartoon name, like Frau Farbissina from *Austin Powers: International Man of Mystery*, who was in turn based on Mel Brooks's Frau Blücher in *Young Frankenstein*. It may be pronounced "pletz" but it's hard to look at without thinking *plotz*. My mother and her friends often discussed situations where they were plotzing or could have plotzed, a common Yiddish word which meant to burst, to collapse from surprise, embarrassment, horror, but like many Yiddish words, has a comic current running through it.

Plötz (German):

1.*
from *plötz*, a nickname for someone thought to resemble the fish, or a metonymic occupational name for someone who caught or sold these fish.

2.*
variant of Plotz.

3.*
from an altered and shortened form for the Slavic personal name *Blogumil* (from *blogy* 'good,' 'rich,' 'happy').

ONE

When I ride the subway, I like to stand in the front window, the absolute front, so I can see down the long tunnel, at least as far as sporadically placed lights provide illumination. As I travel underground, I need a sense of distance—that assurance that there is a way out if one is needed, because every once in a while, there is a mechanical malfunction: signal, rail, human error, fire, body on the tracks, pump failure, or water pours in (a particular nightmare). You need to know, or have some idea, how you can get out, especially with thousands of people stampeding behind you, as if Godzilla was down there munching on the rear of the train, making his way to the front. If I turn around and look at fellow commuters holding their water bottles advertising their gym or radio station or coffee cup, scrolling through messages, reading news feeds, playing Dragon Krush or Creepsville or whatever, I feel the walls close in, as if the shaky metal capsule is heading to the center of the earth. I envy their calmness, their oblivion. As I look down the tunnel, I imagine being like one of those long-gone Wave Pilots of the Marshall Islands interpreting the motion of the ocean as it rocked their canoes traveling hundreds of miles between coral islets, archipelagos, and atolls. I recognize and register every swaying movement of my commute, acknowledging curving track and change of speed. I know what is customary and what could signal a problem. It remains to be determined what use this information could be put to.

There's another reason I prefer to look down the tunnel rather than face my fellow passengers. Unbeknownst to them, they're a riot of sensations, a bombardment of throbbing, itching, twisting. I feel the constriction of a hoodie tied too tightly around a child's head, string digging into neck, the jab of an umbrella through the toe of a rubber boot, the drumming of fingers against a pole. It's an old man playing "I Wanna Be Sedated," eyes shut as if the metal subway pole were an electric guitar and it's 1978, which is way before even he was born. Why I feel what they are feeling used to be called mirror touch synesthesia, but no one has tangled neural pathways anymore. No one sees sounds or tastes colors or gives graphemes personalities. If folks at work knew that somehow those genes snuck through, and as a result I struggle with the anomaly of a premotor cortex gone kablooey, I'd lose my job, and that would only be a best-case scenario. To the question, no longer used, Do you feel me?, my answer is always, Yes, I can't not.

That morning, the conductor draped his jacket over the window, so instead of the tunnel, all that could be seen was quilted lining and seams. This happens sometimes. Once a conductor taped a newspaper page over the window, and I read the funny pages between stops. This could be interpreted as an aggressive gesture on the conductor's part, though he or she might just want privacy, and has no idea who Zedi Loew could possibly be, or why she, above all other passengers, really needs to see and assess what lies ahead. That day, the conductor, apparently a young man, was singing "Sloop John B" at the top of his lungs. I looked around, but nobody smiled; earbuds and headphones blocked the sound. "This is the worst trip I've ever been on," he repeated over and over. Since I couldn't post myself as lookout for tunnel collapse, of which the odds are small anyway, I opened my book and began to read.

The Shadow Prince troubles me. It's the true story of a prince, Eugene, born in 1600 something, whose brain is completely out of sync with his body. A great military strategist but a hunchbacked dwarf, rumored to be queer—in love with another prince. His mother was a great beauty, sort of, depending on who was looking, but rumored to be a sorceress. Is physiognomy destiny? How can a particular physicality enable a particular personality, like a trellis the

personality grows over and takes the shape of accordingly? For the prince's mother, Olympe, yes, alluring to some, a witch to others. The body she inhabited was money in the bank. For her son, the prince, no. He was supposed to be a monk, his deformities and proclivities hidden away, but he said, screw you, buddy, and he led an army that kicked the Turks' asses out of what was then some idea of Europe.

If the prince was born today, none of these contradictions would manifest themselves in any way, shape, or form. Pangenica, Inc., and concerns like it, locally and globally, turn parents' desires into offspring. If, for example, parents might want the next Prince Eugene, they come to us requesting a boy or girl with a military bent. We analyze their genetic codes. (If they want such a child, they probably already have such a background. It's already in their genes, so a martially inclined offspring makes sense. Their wishes don't come out of nowhere.) The parents' genetic codes are stitched, snipped, adjusted, so that the requested talents, proclivities, drives, height, coloration, etc. are all within government guidelines, and the future soldier is created. We adjust skills for marksmanship, courage, foolhardiness, risk-taking non-aversion, tendency to resolve conflict by violence, but not by tyranny (that's a tricky one but not impossible). There are no more hunchbacks, no more sexual peculiarities as determined by ruling AX-RT 6703, originally Vatican-approved in some districts, but long since altered for greater flexibility. Homosexuality, for example, is off the taboo list.

We practice eugenics locally and globally. The word used to have a comet's tail of bad news attached to it, but let me explain.

If everyone is genetically engineered, there are no more hunchbacks, psychopaths, no physical deformities, no or limited mental anguish insofar as genetic engineering can exert control. Environmental circumstances aren't within our purview. There were doubters who feared so-called designer babies would turn out to be just bland, boring cookie-cutter humans. Nature pokes an oar in from time to time. Statistics show that the same number of geniuses occur whether naturally (as in the past) or engineered (now), and there are fewer deranged, miserable people, which, to most citizens, is a desirable outcome.

People used to debate the dangers of genetic alterations. What if mistakes are made, and a super-predatory animal, some kind of marine organism that could be as small as a virus, destroys every living thing in the ocean? Even destroying a majority of things, or even some lesser percentage than the majority, is catastrophic. We are careful. This hasn't happened over the years, so I expect odds are it won't in any overreaching way. The rogue genes for rapaciousness, for tyranny, seem to be gone, along with narcissism and obsessive-compulsive syndromes. In the past, jumping genes were a source of fear and caution, perhaps over-caution. Whoops, signs of schizophrenia, didn't see that coming. Parents requested Einstein but got Mad Ludwig instead. We check and double-check every step of the way, so this won't happen, and it never has, therefore the company states with confidence that the jumping gene anxiety turned out to be baseless.

Couples pick up their infant(s) nine months to the day after their forms have been approved. They stand in line with fellow prospective parents at one of the local incubatoria or at Pangenica itself, if they're in the tri-city area. (Originally the centers were all pastel-colored and filled with anodyne music, meant to be soothing and welcoming, but after a number of years, this design was completely altered. All music ends up meaning something, dislodges some memory, and furthermore, around the clock, repetitive sound can be oppressive, so now the centers are white and silent.) Parents' DNA is checked and double-checked to be sure no one is given the wrong child. Some are nervous, but all are clearly overjoyed and readying their phones and cameras. Unlike the old days, there are no tragic surprises. Ever. We all know that humans used to be born like any other mammal, by random, haphazard sperm meets egg, and you really had no idea what kind of person would emerge. Humans blundered along for hundreds of thousands of years, maybe. Now the nature of creating humans is about equality. No one is necessarily considered enormously more beautiful or intelligent or capable than anyone else. Engineering, of this kind, is about leveling the field.

A few generations ago, you would hear about outliers in remote mountains, jungle, desert, a South Pacific archipelago—those who had babies the old-fashioned way, but now that's impossible. Reproductive systems with their fallibilities, lethargic sperm, acidic fallopian tubes, ducts that twist and self-seal, eggs that would turn out not to have all their marbles, the multitude of formerly moving parts are no longer functional. The chanciness and risks of millennia have been eliminated. Globally, if these outliers were discovered, the penalty was death, not just because it's illegal, but because of the risk of contamination, of scrambling a carefully curated gene pool.

Mutations still occur from time to time, so the earth's population isn't entirely uniform, but there are no extreme cases of physical or mental aberration. When they do appear, they are a reminder of natural chaos, entropy cleansed by death. Exerting control over haphazard outcomes was a good choice in an age of chaos when mutations—following periods of increases in radiation—intensified, though the debilitated tended not to reproduce. And now here we are, on a planet where only animals are left to their own devices, so what passes as human knows how things used to be done, reproduction-wise, and is very glad this is no longer the case. It's what separates us from animals. There are benefits to this system.

Advantages: fewer doctors. People get sick in mild ways, get colds or have accidents, but there are no more major diseases like cancer, no autoimmune or hereditary diseases, no dormant genes for illness waiting silently to be turned on and then get to work with corrosive intent. People just peter out, die of old age for the most part. Crime is down. Wars tend to be about information, attention spans, client bases, technological innovation, and aggression takes other forms, such as computer hacking, theft of resources, identities, but not termination of lives, at least not immediately. Doctors now mostly work as geneticists, administrators of palliative, end-of-life care, or mitigating trauma in the case of accidents. There are downturns in other professions as well.

So, it's difficult to imagine an era when bodies arrived on the planet with physical disabilities and unpredictable mental impairments. We have all kinds of images for that unfortunate period, but a picture of literal daily life when one was so hobbled, for this, the characters in whatever film runs in my head as I read, these characters eventually straighten out, and they're just like everyday walking-around people here. My imagination fails. I shut *The Shadow Prince* and put it in my bag.

At the first stop after the train emerged from the tunnel, a man got on wearing only a T-shirt, shorts, and flip-flops. It had been raining while he waited on the platform, a pleasant early-morning rain, and he had no umbrella. I could feel the wet cotton of his T-shirt clinging to my shoulders, and my fingers tensed as his did around his phone. He was oblivious to the fact that everyone could hear him, or maybe he just didn't care. "It's people like me who get the short end of the stick every time," he rasped, "while the others make a bundle."

His sense of not knowing everything there was to know about one project after another, not getting the inside information, and so consistently shuttled off to schmuckdom, it sounded like a finely tuned story of which the speaker had no doubt whatsoever. Had his genetic code with markers for innocence and credulity soured into gullibility? I don't think it quite works that way. He was just a guy who was continually snookered, it sounded like. I appreciated the desire to stand in the rain, preordained or not.

Though rush hour trains were crowded, my commute took me away from the center of the city, and eventually as the train emerged above ground, apartment buildings gave way to clusters of office buildings. Pangenica was a large complex of glass buildings and labs, an office park with a view of the bay and the ocean beyond it. The sea was reflected in all those glass surfaces, giving an impression of the infinity of the ocean, but also during the day, one couldn't see in, manmade structures disappeared in the reflection. Looking north from my office, there was the illusion the Arctic was just over the horizon, if the world were flat and there were no obstructions in the way. That the company was located just outside of the city and in this environment, was meant to imply not just cheaper real estate, but that we operated within a natural ecosystem whose rules dominate, and we were helpless to alter them in a serious way, but in fact, we did exactly that with great seriousness. It was our theology, a given and accepted set of circumstances that determined how people entered the world, who those bodies were and, odds are, who they will become.

I swiped my ID through the turnstile, which voiced *Z. Loew*, chirpy style, and once past security, I stopped at the ground floor café to get coffee. Those who work at the café are the teenage children of employees, working temporarily, and they are friendly and unhurried, leaning against counters, tapping on their phones. I took my coffee up to the roof garden, lush with jade-colored grapevines, varieties of tomatoes last seen at Marie Antoinette's Petit Trianon, baby teardrop eggplant that could fit into a child's palm, flowers of all kinds. Other glass towers have similar gardens, and you can see them ringing the office park like a standing henge of glass creatures, the ocean reflected in their bodies, all sprouting wild green plant hair. Only a natural disaster, hurricane or earthquake, could reunite aerial plants with the valuable real estate below. On the other hand, let's say a series of explosives leveled the office park, so that the plants could reclaim the ground, and the landscape might, then, become truly a park, but then the saltwater of the ocean, sandy soil, and mineral air would be just as lethal as if all the humans vanished, and there was no one left to flip the irrigation switches that kept all the rooftop gardens flourishing.

At Pangenica, the rooftop garden is also harnessed experimentation. There are golden peaches that smell like roses and roses that have no smell detectable to humans, only to bees and hummingbirds. This strain of the plant is utilitarian, but still a rose is a rose, or at least looks like one. If you looked over one edge along the wall that faced away from the sea, there was an escalier espalier, a vertical garden constructed from apple, magnolia, and lemon trees, as well winter jasmine and juniper. When new saplings, the branches of the escalier espalier had been tied to a trellis, more like a ladder than an actual staircase, but as the limbs grew, guided by the wooden structure, the trees absorbed the trellis. (Is this a kind of plant cannibalism?) Whether or not you could actually climb the staircase to cut or prune or harvest would depend on the strength with which the whole shooting match was affixed to the concrete, glass, and steel that made up Pangenica. I don't know how this part of the garden was cared for—perhaps by gardeners posted on cherry pickers, though I never witnessed any caretakers attending to the vertical plants. This was one of the few wild-appearing parts of the entire Pangenica campus.

Under a seedless pomegranate tree, I saw a man staring out at the ocean, and I asked if I could join him. The tree was pruned, so its branches formed a dense canopy, and the fellow shrugged—do what you want—then he reached up, picked a pomegranate, cut a hole in it with a jackknife, and tipped the fruit back like a bottle in order to swallow the liquid inside. I had a pen that had run out of ink and considered doing the same by stabbing one of the low-hanging pomegranates I could reach. This was something my mother would do, and I would have if I were alone.

A few feet from a northern-facing corner of the roof, a massive elm was fenced off. Due to a planning error, it had been planted too close to the edge, and the landscape architects had also failed to take into account that the tree would grow beyond normal range projections, in fact, it had been bred to be larger than average, and was now in danger of toppling in the wind which was stronger at elevations. The giant elm, related to the Camperdown variety, felled due to the Dutch virus and predatory beetles, swayed and creaked, its roots tangled and exposed, rebelling, bursting from the box meant to contain them, growing over the surface of the dirt hauled up to its aerial plot. The man threw the pomegranate over the edge, ducked under the preventative wiring surrounding the tree, put his hand on the trunk, and looked up into what was left of its crown, the nests of unknown birds, the marks of insects who were all causing the destruction of their home, then he hoisted himself up to a lower branch. I could feel the rough bark crumble against my palms, smell the decaying wood. The elm's naturally contorted limbs had grown lopsided and leaned precariously, and I felt the soles of my feet accommodate the angle of the branches he climbed, slip, then regain balance. The bark was riddled with holes and cracks, dead branches, though still thick, were brittle and liable to snap off under his weight. What was known: anti-fungal genes were developed years ago, but something had shifted. Elms were again prone to diseases, phytoplasmas invaded the tree's vascular system, microfungus that arrived with invasive beetles, a feasting clattering mass, delivering spores that got into cracks and holes made by sapsucker woodpeckers.

"Why are you climbing?" I yelled up, but he couldn't hear me, or just didn't feel like answering. From that height, you could see further to some of the distant islands, I guess that's why he climbed the off-limits elm, but the wind was picking up. "The tree's going to fall on you," I shouted. He told me to get lost.

"I'm just looking around. Nothing is falling anywhere."

"Yeah, but it could and looks like it's going to any minute." Rows of red pineapple, prickerless and overripe, bowed on their stalks and imploded with the force of the hard rain. They had been bred to be too thin-skinned. Aloe and radishes with shallow root systems were no match for the rain, and they became airborne, their exposed roots like raw unruly white hair. The saguaro, on the other hand, hid deep radicles, bred to withstand jungle levels of precipitation running down its ribs and dripping from its spines. The sky was having a manic episode of which it would remember nothing, and it couldn't care less. I stayed on the roof until the man urged me to get to my desk several floors below, that he wasn't aiming to be impaled by a dying tree. I was afraid as soon as I was out of sight he'd fall or jump, so I stood at the door watching from an angle; he couldn't see me. For those minutes, his nerves were jangling, firing in all directions, as if he had already sat on a branch that would give, shirt and hair blowing every which way in the wind, then he steadied himself and inhaled. It was okay for me to leave. I tossed my coffee cup into a bin, walked downstairs to the lower level, then took an elevator to the fifth floor where my office was located, in Adjudications.

Adjudications, a small, quiet department, was set up in anticipation of problems. In the early days, there were concerns about control and the unknown. How can you be sure the boy will only grow to six-three and not six-eight, or that the extra inches won't appear concentrated in his neck and not generally distributed? A race of giraffe-humans wouldn't be a desirable outcome. (Some believe the giraffe was an evolutionary mistake. The idea that nature makes no mistakes, these advocates say, is a myth propounded by those who've never thought about earthquakes or volcanoes, or who think about aberrations and natural catastrophes as correctives.) Also, the gene for height could be connected to diminished hearing or a compulsion for counting steps. Traits don't exist in isolation, but are connected to other attributes and debilitations, impossible to sort and isolate. The example was given, if you change one word in *Moby Dick*, just one word but wherever it appears, would you still have the same book? What if you changed *whale* to *mouse*? What then? You've only changed one word, but the whole book would be affected.

But the early days are behind us, and now errors are so few, staff has been drastically reduced, and I, too, am in danger of losing my position. My office was cluttered with screens, papers, books from other eras that I find useful from time to time. The Law Library at Pangenica is extensive, and I have a habit of not returning things on time. I cleared some space and turned on a screen connected to the building's roof cam, but I couldn't concentrate. The man had seemed to be climbing down, but was he really? The tree appeared half-uprooted and teetering on the verge of being blown away altogether. I could hear the wind whipping around the building, even in my remote Adjudications wing. I decided to go back to the roof, walked to the bank of elevators, pressed the up button, and after a few minutes, a down elevator opened its doors. I didn't want that one, but noticed the man in the back of the crowded car. I was really embarrassed and hoped he hadn't seen me. Too late, he had. A woman sneezed, moved back, and stepped on his toes. I felt her heel coming down on the place where joints meet, but the stranger would never know I experienced what he was feeling. The doors closed. I stood in place for a few minutes until I felt like my own red-faced self, then returned to my desk.

An alert scrolled across my screen reminding us about Pangenica's continually updated security system. It's nice to be reminded, but we also knew it was continually vulnerable to hacking, and to hack one strand of DNA is possibly to disrupt all in a chain reaction that could set off who knows what. The company relies on the fact that there are no madmen left to flip that switch—or at least so far. This could be blissful naïveté, not a trait that's found in abundance in corporate headquarters and labs, but we generally go with it. DNA is valuable. It's the ultimate bio-identifier. Stolen DNA would enable the thief to plant someone else's identity at a crime scene, or anywhere at all for that matter. It happens, but most of the complaints that cross my desk are about the odd mutation. Persnickety parents who think their son or daughter's eyes aren't quite identical, not quite as good in math as we'd come to expect, better at speed skating than hockey: "That's not what we most specifically requested, please see the answer to 27B on our InTake forms." But most parents don't want to admit something is amiss. All's good here, thanks for asking!

Adjudicators aren't lawyers. I went to law school, but didn't take the bar exam, because I absorb the anxiety of everyone around me, and knew in advance I'd sit in my chair for however many hours, miming a test taker, but unable to get my brain to analyze questions of whether the evidence favored a verdict of intention to commit fraud or not. My mother had discouraged me from law school, because by then she was unemployed and viewed the law with skepticism, an endeavor at odds with mirror touch. The two could not co-exist. Be a doctor, a trauma surgeon, she wrote. Accidents happen. You would have a purpose then. I tried to explain to her that way lay paralysis as well. I would feel the loss of limb, the blow to the head. That would make you a world-class care provider, she insisted, but all I could envision was a world of pain. There's no avoiding that, my mother said.

At law school, I had done well in the class about fraud, attending an optional lecture at the Museum of Hoaxes on the Report from Iron Mountain, a document published in 1966, authored by a think tank that never existed. It's real author was Leonard C. Lewin. It warned of the economic and cultural dangers of prolonged peace. The book was intended as a joke, but some people took it seriously, as the urgent call to keep the bogeyman of a military industrial conglomeration alive and well. Later it was picked up as truth by conspiracy theorists unpersuaded by the original author declaring Iron Mountain was pure invention. He sued publishers of a bootlegged edition for an undisclosed sum. If you have an interest in fraud, my professor said, you might consider a career as an Adjudicator, and so I did, but with Adjudications, they find *you*, and so when tapped on the shoulder, I said sure.

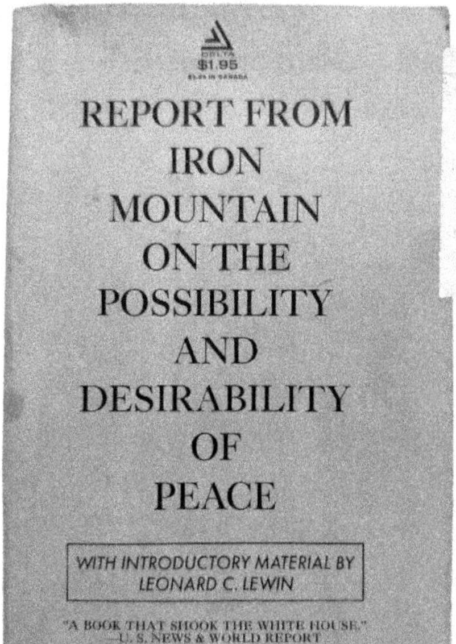

Being an Adjudicator generally meant a quiet life, though like any occupation, it had its share of fatalities. I sat in my office reading files, consulting records and law books, occasionally going into the field, doing impersonations when called for, and then handing my findings to teams of Pangenica litigators.

The thing about Adjudications was that no one can know you're an Adjudicator. The decisions our small department made were, when Pangenica was founded, considered potentially critical to the continuation of the whole engineering and design project. It was dangerous work. Adjudicators investigating reported cases of madness and physical deformities ran the risk of being killed in the field by either the anomalies who wished to stay as they were, or by parents who wanted to protect their accidentally defective offspring. At the same time, leakers or Adjudicators who made mistakes were sent to locations known as Orientation Sites from which you didn't return to your previous life, and it was possible you wouldn't return to any location at all. The exact coordinates of the Orientation Sites were not known. It has been suggested that O. Sites are nothing more than the evolution of what used to be called Nachtnebel Operations or Foggy Nights Ops—detention centers, no bail, no court, no trial. The state and its corporate arms, of which Pangenica is but one, work hand-in-hand to keep all interlocking parts running efficiently. Some O. Sites have been privatized, one reads, but no one knows for certain. Adjudication steps away and has no jurisdiction, once files are handed off.

TWO

Adjudicators are the first step in a process, and litigants approach with caution because quibbles have been known to reveal larger problems, missteps, miscalculations, to say nothing of outright fraud and chicanery, in which case the disappearachniks take over cases, and of this, for the most part, we do not speak. So, Adjudications is a gamble—not for the risk averse. But we do adjudicate fairly, and if oversight, breach of contract, or catastrophic error are found, large settlements may be anticipated on the part of the petitioner, therefore, some are willing to risk it, therefore, much of what Adjudicators need to develop is a nose that is sensitive to fraud.

It was inevitable that some working outside our department would detect a bit about what we did and who we were from time to time, but communications were so closely monitored, and the eject chute was such a final exit, no one (or few) took the risk of acknowledging the precise nature of what the fifth floor was actually engaged in. By the time I signed on, the Adjudications Department was quiet, edging toward archaic. Who cared what we did? But still, the penalty for revealing the particulars of individual cases was severe. When I got on the elevator, an Accent Precisionist from Crafted Identities might know who I was, but a lab technician, a genome analyst, would not.

When I returned to my desk that morning, there was a green plastic folder embossed with the Pangenica globe logo that hadn't been there when I left the night before. It had been placed between a copy of Patent Law, 2084 and a report from the International Bioethics Conference, Detroit, 2028. The file's contents were paper, and paper files are almost, but not entirely, nonexistent at Pangenica. Most, though not all, cases sent for my review and investigation, are delivered as file attachments of some kind.

I turned off the lingering roof cam, set my screensaver to Escher mode, stair climbers going nowhere logical, and picked up the file, clearly years old, a cold case, but there it was on my desk, and I had no choice but to read it. The folder contained a suit being brought against Pangenica by a woman named Singe Laveneer. Singe's name at birth had been Cygne, swan, but had been mispronounced and transformed into a nickname that stuck, though in the attached photograph, she did have a very long neck and a beaky nose. In the report's introduction, Singe recalled her first appointment at the company, filling out forms, interviews, medical tests, reviewing family histories. All that was reasonable and customary, done just like everyone else. Singe and her husband looked through their genetic lineages and picked out existing traits, writing proposals for new ones, a time-consuming process, and you have to be thorough, no skipping questions, or your application will bounce back. It's a real time commitment. There are 21,000 genes, and going through all of them and their possibilities takes months, years even. Some people hire a professional gene agent (Agenet is a popular company with a good record.) to do the forms for them. This is risky, to leave these decisions to someone else, but it's pretty much taken for granted. What is desirable among the plethora of desirable traits is pretty much all that remains in the human genome anyway: desirability. The penalties are severe for fucking up, so no commissioned agent, who is paid handsomely, would want to risk it. Singe cannot be excused for hiring someone sloppy. She and her husband hired no outside agency. They did all the forms themselves, all blood and other samples came from her and her husband. Their meticulousness could not possibly be in question. In terms of the introductory questions, everything in the file checked out. I turned to the section that explained her issue in detail.

Singe Laveneer
Case #78136 Confidential Pending Adjudications

In essay format, please give the Adjudications team any relevant background information that may or may not have appeared on your InTake forms, facts and/or data you would like Adjudications to be particularly aware of.

I work as a museum ethicist. My manifesto is simple: every object on earth should be repatriated to its location of origin, and I spend much of my time debating curators and museum directors who take issue with the idea that every statue, every column, every frieze and ritual object should go back to wherever these things have been taken from. My husband was a translator of legal documents. Though we separated when my daughter was two and we rarely saw him, when she was ten, her father disappeared entirely.

Tell us about your child beginning with the day you picked up your infant from Pangenica.

Picking up a child at a Pangenica Center is couched in such terms as to portray that moment of picking up as a twinkling of pure joy, and in many ways, it is, but I confess I also had waves of dread. You know those machines that are supposed to comfort and relax animals on the way to the slaughter? That's how I felt, like I was in one of those chutes, no matter how much I tried to reason my way into joyousness, I kept cycling back to calamity. No one who goes through the exhaustive application process of forms, physical and mental examinations, questionnaires, and general paperwork all to qualify to be parents—no one who signs on can entertain a shred of second thoughts—but as I backed our car into the allotted parking space between two white lines, for an instant I thought, what if I drove away? Has anyone ever done that, and if they did, what would happen to the baby left behind? I was told doing the unthinkable, which this action surely would have been, is known as postpartum depression, a genetic predisposition that was not considered a trait worth eliminating, since no one gives birth anymore, though it does seem to pop up from time to time.

But I didn't drive away. We got out of the car, tapped the Ingot app at the entrance, followed the pink and blue arrows to our assigned waiting room where we collapsed into squishy plush chairs along with other adults, all waiting as if about to be born or reborn ourselves. Humming "My Favorite Things," repeated use of hand sanitizer, folding gum wrappers into tiny origami cranes, these were some of the ways my fellow prospective parents betrayed their anxiety. After a short wait, our names were called, and we entered the Delivery Room where one of the Pangenica Facilitator Tots, an adult dressed as a nurse just off her break and smelling of cigarette smoke, handed me a swaddled creature, the weight of a house cat. There was much oohing and aahing, holding up of phones, but I was afraid to look at her with the team of Tots and Deliverers crowded around waiting for our overjoyed reaction as they must do every fifteen minutes, as families come and go. As soon as we were back out on the sidewalk beside the parking lot bordered by native grass, birch trees, and rows of potted mums, I pulled back the pink blanket, looked at her red screaming face, and fell totally in love. My husband and I went in one door, then exited via another, and life was forever changed.

So, we brought her home and learned that Patricia, nicknamed PomPom, was the child who never slept. We tried playing recordings of night sounds, crickets and owls, the sound of rain; we sang lullabies in languages known and unknown, driving around town in the middle of the night, giving her minute baby-sized doses of Dormazin. Her eyes would follow me around a room with such attentiveness, I melted. She was mine, and I was hers. One hears stories of infuriated, sleep-deprived parents who get angry at sleepless children, who bang their adult hands on beds and walls and tables. Yes, I was dismayed by her sleeplessness, but when her pediatrician wanted to up her dose of Dormazin,

I flushed the sweet-smelling liquid, dropper and all, down the toilet. Was she okay? I didn't know, but we would manage. I held her until she stopped crying, and I would settle for a cessation of the waterworks even if there was still no sleep. Had we forgotten to answer a question on InTake forms about sleep patterns? Of course, no such question exists. Who would sign up for insomnia? We started to have nagging doubts about something gone wrong, you know, those *m* words: mutant, mutation*, mutable, oh my! Meanwhile, I dreamed of sleep: a luxurious state of no consciousness that, for the first year of PomPom's life, was unattainable, eyes shut for more than a few minutes was a concept that lay just out of reach.

PomPom was late for two major developmental milestones: walking and talking, but when she did figure out she could let go of the table and stand alone, the clock sped up, and in an instant, she wasn't just toddling along but running like a baby gorilla, jumping, spinning until she dropped on the ground, watching the sky whirl overhead. In fact, repetitive motion was a problem, and at times, there was no off switch. I had to hold her to get her to stop moving, and then she began to speak, and that too, for a while, was a torrent of information. PomPom didn't ever sputter words in baby gibberish. Once she started talking, she spoke in paragraphs.

At about age four, PomPom described to us what sounded like a state of boundless excitement, like a delicious tickle at the back of the throat. Was she describing euphoria or happiness? The bubbling effervescence lasted a moment, then it passed, and her moods began to darken and sour. She became withdrawn, and even in kindergarten, a child was either her friend or a social pariah.

Around age six, she began what she called her experiments. Too young to write, she drew recordings on pieces of paper. Pulling up plants to see what was underneath, dumping out an Ant Farm, putting a goldfish in a shallow dish to see if it would acclimate, would its eyes rotate to one of its flat sides?

In your own words, please describe your child's problem or set of problems. Include when you began to realize or sense that there might be an issue with your offspring.

Even when Patricia was not a little cuddly PomPom anymore, the nickname stuck. PomPom grew up to be quiet, reserved, guarded, always in front of one kind of screen or another, but then everyone was. Snapping off, screen going to black, or suddenly something harmless like *Animal Planet* would appear when an adult walked into a room – every kid did that, no cause for alarm. PomPom worked at school with drive and obsession, but also, this was a way to isolate herself from other people.

I began to detect a thread of hauteur in PomPom's self-isolation, that she consistently looked at others with scorn. As she grew, her personality turned vinegary, bitter, sarcastic, and I was often at a loss in terms of how to deal with a child who, every day, seems to act more and more like a stranger in our midst. PomPom expressed little responsiveness for anyone or any circumstance. What little she was able to convey was mixed at best, but unalloyed empathy was the attribute we had most wanted and underscored in the essay portion of our application forms. When I suggested PomPom should turn off her screens and get out more, PomPom sneered at me: you're the one who's alone.

Attachment of subfile by Plaintiff. Exhibits A through D

Let me go back to the beginning, PickUp Day. The moments before we were called into the Delivery Room I met Dinah McCall and her husband, and we struck up a conversation. Our appointments were registered at the same hour, though with different staff, but once our names were called, as we each walked through different doors to pick up our respective infants, we exchanged numbers and contact information.

Over the course of the first year of being new parents, Dinah and I became friends. Discovering we lived in the same neighborhood, we shared babysitters, went to the playground together, to the zoo, the circus, puppet shows. When the children turned five, they went to the same school.

Dinah is critical to my case, so I have attached a photo. As you can see, she had a perfectly symmetrical face, the kind you could tell would never be tattooed or pierced in any way – no embellishment or alteration of any kind, now or in the future. A frank, this-is-good-enough-for-me, this-is-all-I-need sort of expression. During those years, Dinah had a life of unruffled satisfaction: a nice house, a husband, a meteorologist whose income was somehow higher than expected, two accomplished children whose pictures and cute activities were spread across social media in a breadcrumb trail of muted bragging.

My doubts about my friend began small, playground small. In meanness, Dinah followed the pack, but left to her own devices, she took the act of exclusion to carefully choreographed heights. There was one mother whom Dinah seemed to take particular pleasure in singling out. The odd man out was a lone mom who giggled too loudly, worked erratically as a substitute teacher, tended to lose track of time in such a way that imposed on the patience of others. Dinah engineered baroque means for freezing the woman out. Barely saying hello on the street when the other woman had slowed to stop, accelerating the exclusion to the point where Dinah would make sure the newcomer was subtly barred from outings, parties. "Sorry, dear, no room on the park bench." Did I speak up? No, I did not. I was having a difficult time at my job, I'd been accused of using the words *plunder*, *steal*, *loot* like weapons, sizzling with acid, even more so than they would ordinarily have been. I was called an Originist, a term that conveyed respect and derision simultaneously.

Before my husband and I separated, when he didn't come home for unaccounted hours, Dinah made me feel that she was on my side in the narration of the injustices I felt at work and at home. If donations were running dangerously low, or if I was slighted at a conference,

Dinah reassured me that those who stood in my way were morons. So despite my doubts, the friendship was maintained over the years, though sometimes I felt like a total coward, accepting drops of "you're really okay" or "you're absolutely right. You did the right thing, Singe," and never calling her out for her disgust and impatience with other people who offended her just by walking the earth.

Dinah's son, Clayton, like PomPom, was reticent, not exactly phobic, because no one is anymore, but he seemed happiest when left to himself playing computer games. As Clayton grew older, he developed a preoccupation with the Fermi paradox, a difficult-to-argue-with stop sign in your face when thinking about the possibility of extraterrestrial life. There are so many galaxies, Clayton would explain to his mother, planets spinning around stars, billions upon billions in the knowable and unknowable universes, so you would think the odds are good that life exists on at least one of them, and had evolved to be like life on our planet, dependent on freely available oxygen and carbon. Enrico Fermi, one afternoon while walking around Los Alamos with another physicist, said that if that were so, then where is everybody? He had all kinds of reasons we're rattling around a vacant old void. We're alone in the universe. Ain't nobody here but us chickens. Get used to it. Our aloneness in the universe terrified the boy.

Clayton was determined that his life's work would be to find evidence that Fermi was wrong. We're not solo. He read old NASA SETI files, stayed up all night listening to recordings made centuries ago of interstellar space sounds, as if he could detect some loophole, wormhole, some sound that could be subject to a different interpretation, an indication that life or a life produced those radio frequencies. Those scratchy blips were something, not random nothing.

At first Dinah found his interest charming, evidence of intellectual precocity, evidence he was like his father looking skyward, only concerned with more than just weather forecasting, until his conversations began to slip from interest to obsession. Perhaps life is out there, but whoever or whatever has chosen not to transmit to us, she would plead. "Okay, Mom, maybe their math is different from ours, but the laws of physics would be pretty much the same," Clayton argued. Dinah proposed that perhaps intelligent life occupied a virtual environment, and they were all around us, just undetectable, but watching us as if we're microbes squirming on a slide under a giant microscope lens. Clayton thought she was making fun of him and retreated from her even more. Dinah, not normally someone easily cowed by anyone, least of all a child, became afraid of setting off his anger, and ceased engaging with him on the subject of life elsewhere. Clayton grew so sensitive, the word "alone" couldn't even be used in his presence. Evidence had to be out there, even if communications were received millions of years after they were sent. He couldn't build his own personal LIGO detector, so he read, studied, bored his classmates till he was aware they'd begun to shun him. The sublunary world for him was material nothingness, of minimal interest beyond the practical.

Around this time, I received a note from an art teacher expressing concern. PomPom accidentally cut herself with an X-acto knife, Clayton grabbed his hand in pain, but if another child did the same, he had no reaction whatsoever. When Clayton was sick and threw up, so did PomPom, but she didn't when any other child was sick, and in fact, PomPom would ridicule the ill child, holding her nose, mocking the dry heaves. I knew the teacher disapproved of my Originist position regarding museum acquisitions, so I dismissed her note as professional animus, and resented her intimation of some kind of perversion of two thirteen-year-olds. She even suggested there was some kind of psychosomatic dissonance like anorexia between the two of them, that their bodies didn't match their minds' perceptions of who they were. One could get disappeared for less, and I responded to her with an angry eaeroscript that she

LIGO: Laser Interferometer Gravitational Wave Observatory

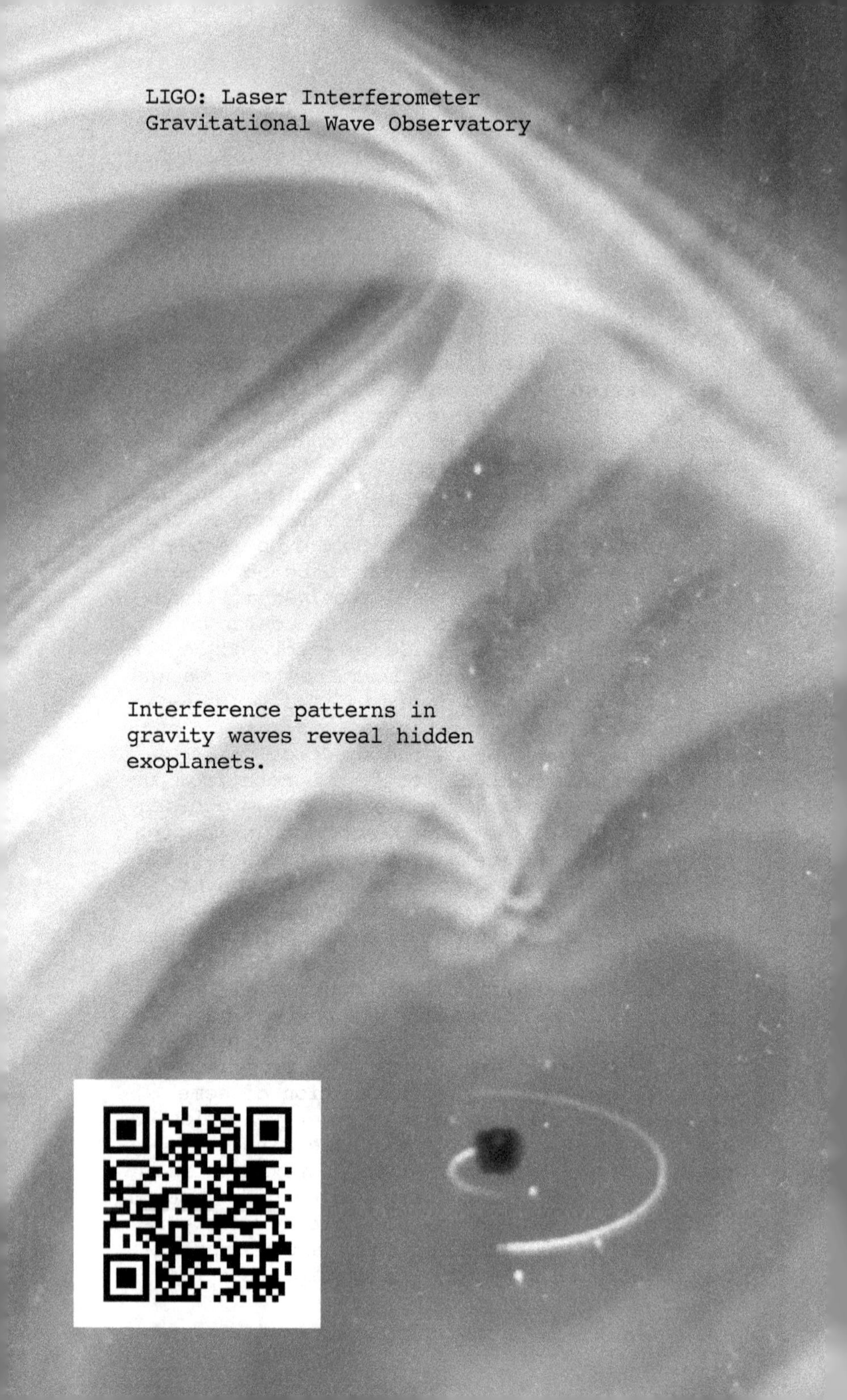

Interference patterns in gravity waves reveal hidden exoplanets.

should keep her theories to herself, and in no uncertain terms, piss off.

As the children entered high school and friends began to enter the zone of hookups, this was a turn of events Clayton felt he could witness if he had to, but could in no way participate in. Dinah sensed his isolation, though she didn't know the half of it. Clayton was a stranger to her, but she reasoned most kids are strangers to their parents. We all had secret lives, she would say, adults, parents, teachers, all knew nothing about us. That part of childhood, she believed, was a country whose borders they were barred from crossing. It would blow over, and so she confided to me about Clayton's research and night terrors that the Fermi paradox was accurate and true. I interpreted her troubled confidences as yet another example of Dinah's bragging about her kids: look, he's reading about astrophysics, and he's barely fourteen.

Dinah was often uncontainable, the kind of person who was said to be without boundaries, though over time, she did seem to respect her son's, perhaps because she was afraid of him. She was never at a loss for friends and always surrounded by a group of some kind, whether at the gym or volunteering at an animal shelter. She met people on planes, in lines, in waiting rooms, as she had met me. People were drawn to her, and though many were called, not all were chosen. She was fierce about those who, for whatever reasons, fell below her exacting standards in dress, speech patterns, food they chose to eat in her presence. Indication of her son's isolation was troubling to her, that in a room full of children, he'd stand as close as possible to an exit every time, while in a parallel situation she would smile, survey the group of strangers, and plunge right in. Her husband had a brother who had a similarly reclusive personality. The brother died in a car collision when he was fifteen, so memories of him were sketchy, but it was enough to assume that an ember of Clayton's personality was somehow like that of his long-gone teenage uncle. Fixedness of purpose must be allied to the desire to fly solo in ways that hadn't been foreseen.

One night Dinah rounded the corner into her street to see police cars and an ambulance parked in front of her house. Clayton had fallen through the ice that had covered a pond behind their house. His body had been discovered by a neighbor as it surfaced and drifted close to an iceless shore.

It was considered an accident, and as awful as it was, at first Dinah needed this to be true, saying that though shocked, her son had a curiosity about life in the water in all seasons: How did fish survive freezing temperatures, what happened to marine mammals, why does river ice crack? But he knew the surface was beginning to thaw, and I wondered if his stepping onto that thinning sheet hadn't been the result of some mechanism of hopelessness that should never have made an appearance in Clayton's DNA. Depression was supposed to be gone forever, still, it was reported from time to time, and many cases are, of course, unreported, as all anomalies are swept under the rug. No one would really want to admit that mistakes happened in the lab or random mutations or misfires still exist. We hide these conditions because we believe they are small and hideable.

But Dinah saw no evidence of profound despair or any mental impairment in the boy. I consoled her as best I could, and among the solace I offered was that it was admirable Clayton was consumed by something he was obsessed with proving wrong, that we aren't rattling around the universe all by our lonesomes. She shouldn't blame herself. He was a great kid. I wasn't sure I was very comforting, but was at a loss as to how to be in face of such a terrible death.

Then I had an image, not of the dead boy, but of myself posting photographs of artifact after artifact with bullet-like captions. Let me tell you, I am unflinching in my belief that all art should be repatriated to its country of origin. My colleagues, reporters, whoever, would challenge me by insisting that in many cases, objects and art might be safer in museums. So many things, if returned, would be destroyed, stolen, or at the very least, not maintained. I felt, well, that's part of their history, then, but at the time, very few agreed with me.

Chacmool. Origin: Chiapas. Private collection, Atlanta.

Simurgh. Origin: eastern Persia. The Metropolitan Museum, New York.

Gate of Ishtar. Origin: Babylon. The Pergamon Museum, Berlin.

When were you first made aware that there was a problem with your child? Please be as detailed as possible.

I believe a different scenario led to Clayton falling through the ice, something more dangerous than a random, but ultimately lethal, mutation for severe depression.

People aren't always careful. Children certainly are often careless. One night after PomPom had gone to bed, I found a phone that belonged to neither of us, as far as I knew. It was a metallic blue device and had been left behind some bottles of homeopathic medicines that had sounded promising but remained untouched, forgotten, veering toward their expiration dates. By scrolling through it, I learned the blue phone did belong to my daughter, and the bit of metal and plastic that could fit in the palm of one hand unfolded before me like a twentieth-century paper atlas of a toxic wasteland of contempt. My daughter was a psychopath with a spreadsheet. Texts and posts unspooled before me in a fury of creative malevolence. Then I looked at two files of films labeled Clayton #1 and Clayton #2, one several years earlier than the other.

Clayton #1 PomPom and Clayton were old enough to have phones and go places without an adult accompanying them. Here were scenes of which I had no knowledge. The children had been close friends, closer than I realized. There was footage of them on an inflatable raft going further out into the lake than they should have, Clayton stole his mother's car keys, and PomPom drove the retrofitted Buick to a Qwik Mart where she pocketed a couple of bottles of Tasty Brew that they drank, cracking up and pretending to be drunk, or maybe they were. They spied on Clayton's neighbors who appeared to be wealthy Dormazin addicts with a habit of falling asleep naked in their outdoor hot tub. In this folder there were years of texts, continual, as if they were, indeed, siblings, or in love. If you didn't know, and just happened to read these, it could have been one or the other or both.

Clayton #2 This collection of clips was shot by Clayton and sent to PomPom. She was with a group of friends in different locations: a hall, or concert, or on the street. She would glance at him, then turn her back. At first there was no sound, but it was clear she was cold-shouldering the boy. Then the sound came on. Clayton was a fountain of facts: Our solar system is 4.5 billion years old. The universe is 13.8 billion years old. Any entity out there with some form of rocket technology and colonialist ambitions would have found us by now. PomPom grew irritated and told him little green men saw him, turned around, and went back to Mars as fast as they could.

Dinah's hair was falling out due to chemotherapy. PomPom referred to her as *your mother, Baldy*. She accused Clayton of being manipulative, so people would feel sorry for him. I couldn't believe this was my daughter. I felt nauseated. Then she said, "You have something that belongs to me, and I want it back."

Clayton recorded the breadcrumb trail of his pain and humiliation and sent it back to her like people who record noisy neighbors and blast their noise back at them. That PomPom kept the recordings meant she thought of his pain as her success, her cackling at his anguish.

The next morning, I confronted PomPom. Gripping the blue phone as if it were electrocuting me, causing excruciating pain yet unable to drop it, I held it above my head out of PomPom's reach. I demanded PomPom's other phone, as well, but I might as well have been talking to a wall. She coldly refused to surrender any of her electronics, not even concerned enough to argue as she left for school. With money from babysitting and dog walking she would get another one, easy. They're cheap. Fuck you, bitch, she might have well said, and maybe she did for all I know. I don't remember exact words at this point.

Before the end of the day, I had PomPom's laptop hacked, and by going into her history, I uncovered the news that my daughter was a prolific cyber-bully who threw her acid anonymously under pseudonyms. The names of some of the targets were known to me, but others who lived in other parts of the world were strangers, as they must have been to PomPom. Something about her prey irritated her. Selected for a reason, they were obsessives, maybe in their own private way, the targets were pretenders, isolated people she felt it was her job to deflate. Her barbs, her sarcastic taunts, were so caustic and precise. One of the victims I knew well: Dinah's son, Clayton. When Clayton posted about the discovery of ice on a planet that revolved around a distant star, PomPom answered, who the fuck cares?

When she got home from school I confronted my daughter again, and this time, PomPom, round face twisted into cold fury, elevated the crime of spying into her private actions as a felony far more offensive than the *possible* misdemeanor of what she insisted were her harmless truthful posts and responses to people I didn't even know. I threatened to turn off her phone and everything else that connected PomPom to her targets, but we both knew that was impossible. These were needed for school and were an integral and inseverable part of daily life.

PomPom did look like me, and photos included will confirm this without a doubt. I watched her at the mall, at a local amusement park, at a school concert. I recognized her but didn't recognize her, certain she had been an invisible hand that gave a powerful shove the night Clayton stepped into the ice.

I want to offer a digression at this point. We had wanted our daughter, our only child, to be like an aunt from many generations back, who died in a typhoon-induced deluge because, even after making it to safety, she'd gone back to help others and disappeared, believed to have been swept out to sea. As you will see in our forms, this was a trait we specifically asked for, and it was present, in a minor way, in ourselves. My ex-husband and I used to volunteer to clean plastic trash from beaches, help rebuild a town destroyed by a mudslide, protest the treatment of animals at a local university lab. I'm an independent contractor who works gratis for my clients, but must therefore raise money via donations, which means I need to spend a fair amount of time attending dinners, fundraising events, parties, conferences of one kind or another. I have to get along with people, or at least try to. PomPom only befriended people to size them up and ultimately ice them out.

This is what I think: Something was interchanged during the early hours after or even just before the sperm met egg in a Petrie dish in a Pangenica lab, the combo that was supposed to result in PomPom. I don't know exactly what that something was, but I want answers.

Question: what if I am someone else? How do I know I'm me and not someone else?

One afternoon I got into an argument with the ossuary custodian of a natural history museum in a city I won't name. I was called in to discuss the provenance of a funerary object made from human bone, bits of Japanese pottery, Russian coins, and glass beads from Venice. The object had belonged to a tribe who had no surviving members by the twentieth century but had lived on the Aleutian Islands, and had contact with fishing and trading vessels from around the world. Who should it be returned to, he asked? What if an object is an aggregate, and picks up accretions from other locations and cultures, in which case, who can claim ownership? There could be multiple sources, like a human with a cadaver tooth implant or someone else's heart or liver, the metal from hip and bone replacements. Where's all that supposed to be returned to? To say nothing of blood transfusions. The ossuary custodian was an oppositional provocative asshole, and I said statuary are not people, but his accusations gave me an awful realization about PomPom and Clayton. When their DNA was assembled, some parts must have come from a foreign source, impossible to parse out with certainty and confidence.

Why am I pursuing this matter? I was just a person trying to do my job as a professional museum ethicist, but then the lawsuits began, and so I am no stranger to litigation. Bomb throwers are made, not born.

How is the issue currently affecting you and/or your family?

I began to spend hours in the city's planetarium and space museum, staring at asteroids, spherules, droplets of silica that result from meteorite impact, projections of Magellanic clouds, clusters of stars called globules because they look like clusters of cells, as if with all this looking I could reach some kind of understanding of what I believed was my real child's obsession, drifting from the present to objects of antique astro-technology, from astrolabes that charted the stars to orreries, models of planets mechanically driven by clockwork, wound with a key, brass and geocentric, planets revolved around the earth, a blue glass ball. The sun was gold, the moon half-ebony, half-ivory, Mars was red jasper, Mercury was yellow tiger's eye, Jupiter and Venus were silver-plated, but that's all folks, as yet no far-out Pluto, not exactly a planet anyway, or

Neptune either. For the men, and it was always men as far as is known, who made these instruments, the clumsy telescopes and oversized computers that would follow in the coming centuries were unimaginable. One had belonged to Prince Eugene of Savoy, made by English clockmakers. I was also fascinated by a giant pitted black rock displayed on a massive plinth, lit from above, this I would stand in front of for quite a while. A meteorite the size of a small bus could not be returned to the star it broke off of. The source was unknowable and why would anyone even bother? How is consciousness like a piece of a star?

It wasn't as simple as a personality switch, but the two children experienced the world very differently. PomPom suffered the world as Clayton ought to have. Clayton had the sensory/intellectual encounters but exhibited PomPom's responses and vice versa. It wasn't as if Clayton ate sushi and PomPom tasted salt and vinegar, but more like Clayton interacted with a child who threw up during band practice, while PomPom, who was not present, bullied not just Clayton, but the vomiter, as if they've exchanged skins, a perverse kind of non-empathy empathy.

So, it wasn't just that their personalities had been switched but their consciousnesses, how they experienced the world—or how they *would* experience the world if consciousness acts, in part, as a kind of filter or lens dropped over the eyes. Clayton was meant to experience the world through the scrim of hypercriticality, PomPom by single-minded obsessiveness.

I am known for endorsing the idea that objects should be returned to their place of origin with no allowance for mitigating circumstances, even if place of origin was under water (as in the case of Venice, both Californian and Italian, Mumbai, Rio de Janiero, Buenos Aires) or reduced to rubble, nothing left (the case of Kyiv, Grozny, Aleppo, Kirkuk). Paintings, sculpture needed to be submerged under the waves or left on a pile of landfill garbage. Could the same be done with consciousness? But the boy who stepped through ice was no more. No exchange was possible, even if he hadn't died, no medical procedure existed to change them back.

Assuming consciousness has a genetic component, how experience is responded to, how interpreted: PomPom's meanness, I insist, wasn't a personality trait, but a feature of her consciousness responding to an environment and people in it, and so things that made her sound hypercritical—apparently ordinary events, observations, and circumstances—turned into psychological irritants.

I mourned Clayton anew because his passing marked the death of some part of myself I couldn't quite identify. I kept a picture of him on my phone, a picture taken at about four years of age, smiling, sharing ice cream with PomPom, so if my daughter searched my phone, she would never suspect I had doubts: It's only a picture of her with a friend. Well, it might seem a little odd, but then PomPom is in no shape to check my phone these days.

I contemplated my own exit, plastic bag over head, pills lifted from friends' and acquaintances' bathrooms, but putting such ideation aside, what I want now is an accounting for the switch. What happened? Pangenica needs to track what led to their uncorrectable mistake. I'm not suing. I don't want the corporation's money, but what happened to me should never happen to anyone else. Pangenica needs to look into what went so terribly wrong.

The file ended there.

I examined the photographs included. Dinah McCall had large brown eyes, straight dark brown hair cut in a lob, didn't particularly look like anything, short nose, a smile that said to the photographer she had nothing to hide or be afraid of, as far as she was concerned. PomPom did not look like her in the least and bore a strong resemblance to Singe. The girl's face was like her mother's, but an expression of openness and curiosity in one turned into sourness in the other, the look-what-I-found expression of the mother evolved into a sarcastic eye-rolling grimace in the daughter, an air of being steamed in vinegar.

One of my law professors once asked the class to imagine brain transplants were legal and somewhat commonplace, like heart or liver or lung transplants. They can be done on an outpatient basis. This kind of surgery opens up a boatload of questions, among them: how much of character, of psyche, personality, history, is based on what we look like? At first, we believed what he was proposing was physically impossible, that this was just a thought experiment, but no. The surgery had been seriously considered in cases of certain diseases (which no longer exist) or effects of accidents that ravage the body but leave the head and/or brain intact and fully functioning. It was done with mice and possibly, it was suspected, in a Sino territory with a Russo-Ukrainian candidate. So, if there is a problem, who sues, the head or the body? Though Singe's daughter looked like her parents, she had been given the wrong head.

Doesn't everyone feel, at some point, they've been given the wrong head or woken up on the odd morning and not completely recognized themselves in the memories of what they may have done the night before? I'm not even talking about being drunk. Did I really tell the driver in a red baseball hat who stole my parking space that he was an anoid? Did I seriously think of going home with that person? Did I rob that bank? No, it had to have been someone else. Am I a voice box, possessed, in a fugue state, using some hidden attic part of my cortex previously unknown and mostly unused? Is someone else's sense of things suddenly running the show?

We ask ourselves questions like these, and then, if consciousness can be altered, saved, or, like gravity, is it something that can be measured and recorded, but remains unstorable? If it is possible to warehouse consciousness, who gets what transplant? Most people have no qualms about their consciousness. They might want to change certain personality traits, rid themselves of obsessions, anxieties, acquire confidence, but consciousness isn't, ordinarily, something to be traded in. How do you assess if you have a crappy one? No one ever says my consciousness is riddled with holes, blind spots, recurring numbness, I would very much like a new one, please.

Is there a genetic component to consciousness that can be replicated and downloaded, DNA-style, at some point in the future? Fade out. Fade in. Centuries roll, and that future is now. Somewhere in Pangenica's labs, Singe was convinced, a mistake was made, and Clayton and PomPom's consciousnesses had been switched. She wanted to prove her replacement theory had the strength of absolute fact. How to even do that?

Had Singe completed the formal inquiry process, I know the argument the Litigation Department would put forth in terms of Clayton's risky behavior that led to his death. Pangenica attorneys would make a case that Dinah had serious lapses of judgment as a parent. As unfortunate as they were, there were warning signs in Clayton's behavior, and Dinah should have heeded the signs if she wanted to avoid tragedy. If the rogue gene existed, perhaps ineluctably tied to another more dominant and desirable trait that Dinah had checked off on her forms (Exhibit D), such as night vision, sense of direction, or ability to focus, Litigation had the means to make that case. The switch that activated that gene for risk (tied to curiosity, say) could have stayed dormant, but Pangenica Litigation would state it was flipped by Dinah's parenting, a combination of suffocating demands, blindness, and laxity, combined with the social atmosphere of the school, all resulting in making Clayton's life unbearable. Nonetheless, there was no evidence in the file of exactly what kind of a parent she had been or that Singe was willing to throw Dinah under a bus to make a point. Stick to the ruling; it was an accident. End of story.

There were a few specific personality traits for which the debate about heritability had come up with no definitive answer, but no case challenging Pangenica, nor any other corporate entity, over these traits had ever succeeded, and I wondered if Singe didn't want confirmation that her monstrous child wasn't as genetically laced to her as she had assumed. What she said in the file I held before me was that she wanted to make sure what happened to her family never happened to anyone else. But vital parts of the file were absent.

Redactions were to be expected, but there were also pieces of information, normally part of any inquiry, that were nowhere to be found. A hand-drawn asterisk after the word *mutation* should have led to a footnote at the bottom of the page, but there was none. I turned over page after page of the file, but no footnote connected to that asterisk.

A note clipped to the file folder said that Singe's husband, Mr. Laveneer, translated sketchy documents related to the impossibility of global consensus on controls of medical technology, the weaponization of pathogens, the introduction of artificial intelligence into non-brain organs (a self-correcting heart, more efficient filter-capable lungs), the elimination of malarial mosquitoes that would disrupt a food chain. Goodbye frogs, then goodbye sentient *Homo sapiens*. Something is always happening somewhere in the world. Or at least that's the risk, the danger—inevitably so. There may appear to be a global consensus or agreement, but in a lab somewhere in Yekaterinburg . . . Yeah, yeah, I used to hear about that in law school. What else can you tell me? Otherwise, Mr. Laveneer was barely mentioned in the file, and there was no picture of him among its pages, but I made a note to look him up in Pangenica's database. Even if he was deceased, he might well have been a contract worker for the company, but a quick search yielded little more than digital dust.

Singe was the author of the document, but she appeared as a free-floating entity with no address, like a person from another century, a time when to find someone you had to have a telephone book made up of white and yellow pieces of paper, often hundreds of pages long. I'd never been given a file with zero contact information.

Also missing were copies of Singe and her husband's application to Pangenica. Copies of application forms are not easily available. Once submitted, parents do not retain copies, they are not able to, the software has been designed that way. One cannot obtain application records under the Freedom of Information Act such as it was, but in my job in Adjudications, I'm usually allowed access to these forms, and given the nature of the case, both Singe's and Dinah's should have been in the file, but they were not. I thumbed through every paper in the folder. There was nothing that resembled Pangenica application forms. I laid out each page on the floor, thinking that perhaps the application forms had been printed out in some unusual way, so in looking for a certain graphic, a certain font, if it wasn't what was customary, my eye could have missed it, but no, even in the oddly-shaped photographs and folded-over essays, there was nothing that resembled the application or even the by now discontinued and revised InTake forms.

I scraped up what digital detritus there was about Singe Laveneer, which, as with her husband, was close to nil, and not useful, then put the file aside. It was impossible to work further, and I had other cases that morning that presented solvable problems. A family wanted to copyright two rare but related traits they possessed: acute hearing, almost as good as bats, and a form of savantism, an uncanny ability to play music from memory, even long, complicated compositions, even after only having heard a particular piece once, timed footage included. This was their third petition. I buried myself in intellectual property law until late in the afternoon when the Director of Adjudications, Altner, called me, wanting to know the status of the Singe file.

"It's unworkable, full of holes and errors. No InTake forms, and that's just for starters."

"Go up to Admissions for non-digital paperwork."

The Singe Laveneer inquiry, as far as I could tell, was unlikely to go anywhere, but I had a patent case with a court date next week, and told Altner that the Laveneer file would have to wait.

"Patents are not permissible. Whoever these plaintiffs are, their lawyers are wasting our time and their client's money. The Laveneer case needs to be fast-tracked and wrapped up."

"There's quite a bit missing."

"So, find those bits. This is what you're good at: going through pockets, shaking out books, catching slips in alibis."

Okay, boss, whatever you say, I didn't say.

If Singe had disappeared (of her own volition) and not *been* disappeared, then she was in danger of *being* disappeared, and so hopped off the radar, since she'd filed her case, doomed to go cold anyway. Altner might have been making a show of just-find-the-girl, when, as the years passed, Singe figured it was better not to be so easily located. She would go into hiding when, and at such time as, a straightforward Adjudicatory Complaint transitioned to high crimes and felonious activity. If Singe can't be found, she must be in hiding, therefore, her actions have shifted from the legal arena, where there is only an occasional necessity to be a little cagey as to one's whereabouts, to full-blown no-fucking-way-am-I-going-to-give-you-my-exact-coordinates. Treacherous ground to find yourself navigating.

Somewhere in the city (or in a city), Singe Laveneer patrolled storage facilities, offsite warehouses, sub-basements, taking pictures of canoes from East Timor, snake goddesses from Crete (even the Edwardian-era fakes), *Entartete Kunst* Kandinskys from Amsterdam circa 2013, but she was also hiding, because you can't even hint Pangenica created zygotes with so much as a whisper of malfeasance and expect to carry on as if no biggie, sorry 'bout that, my mistake, let's let bygone be bygones, and Singe didn't sound like a *let's let bygones be bygones* kind of gal. Pangenica wouldn't let that one slip, even if she became as contrite as a penitent at Herod's Gate. I wouldn't be the only one trying to determine Singe's coordinates, and she probably knew that. She wasn't going to be easy to locate.

Singe and I might have this one thing in common, except I was hiding in plain sight, trying to blend in, mirroring the normal, and, as far as my job was concerned, also mirroring the slightly and criminally off when called upon to do so. An inkling of suspicion could take this form: Why is Loew so good at her job, so skilled at subterfuge and double simulation? Takes one to know one. If you can find the needle that is Singe, there must be something wrong with you, but if you don't find her, the penalty will look like this: Someone will ask you for directions in a parking lot, then force you into their car, someone will hustle you off a train that's empty in the middle of the day because other passengers have been paid off to not be there at that moment, a knock on the door when you happen to have the music turned up, so, unlucky for you, the neighbors won't hear a scuffle. Adjudicators aren't entitled to say, I'm going to pass on this one, I prefer not to, thanks very much for the privilege of serving you, but no. I clipped a binder clip to the edge of my desk and hung my headphones from it, then unsnapped, and put them on my head. I would have to pay a visit to Admissions.

THREE

Admissions at Pangenica had a double meaning. *Admission* both in the sense of an entrance portal but also confession in terms of sheer information. At one time the processing conditions of the Admissions Records had been a flood of activity. Photographs of the early days showed a vaulted hall the size of a hangar where you wouldn't have been surprised to see clerks in eye shades and ink sleeve protectors rolling documents into a system of pneumatic tubes or box-shaped computer terminals, glowing blue screens. Some division employees looked like they slept on the premises. But those days are past. Now, the Admissions Records requires only one person to find and hand over records.

The department was on the second floor, had its own security system, and you were cleared by degrees as you walked through a series of sliding doors. A number of wings had a similar arrangement, and when I had to go to one of them, I was often afraid of being trapped, the door behind me closing and the next not opening, and though it should have been reassuring, the sliding doors were glass, you could be seen banging on them, even if you weren't heard, there was something about being suspended in one of these glass boxes, the potential for it, that was often cause for anxiety. I hoped someone would be headed to Admissions at the same time I was, and that way, if trapped, I would have mirror touch access to their feelings, and with any luck, my fellow traveler would be calm.

On my way to the second floor, I stopped to get a coffee out of a vending machine that was known to dispense scalding hot coffee, black, in a thin, lightly waxed paper cup that I had no intention of drinking. Admissions was run by Vy Sapper. It is worth noting that not all parents want their children to be body builders or supermodels. Some aren't picky about physical attractiveness, find such questions a mark of superficiality, and leave a certain amount to chance, although this is generally discouraged. Vy had sharp features, a hatchet nose, and a face that said the school of hard knocks was somewhere behind her. I admired her *I don't give a shit* attitude, but I didn't want to mirror Vy, her blinking and finger tapping, nervous undercurrents, her worry that she might not be doing or saying the right thing. Scalding brew doesn't one hundred percent deflect, but it's better than nothing.

At the end of the series of doors, Vy came into view, feet on her desk. I'd never seen her on the commuter train, so I assumed she lived in the other direction, further out on the elongated island that was the home of Pangenica. She never ate with anyone or conversed in the elevator or on the roof, but could often be seen using the company gym. There was a man who was chummy with her, a guy who worked in Crafted Identities, and on a couple of occasions, I saw him hand her a shopping bag of clothes to be donated or used. I had no idea what happened to our used returned identities, so why not give them away? As far as I knew, working in Admissions, there was no requirement to ever be anyone else. Vy was always Vy, as far as I knew. She had a way of barely looking at you from behind aviator glasses, hair cut asymmetrically, probably self-administered, silvery nail polish, as if her hands were metal. When I exited the last set of sliding doors, Vy was playing a Metroidvania game. Every time I'd had to go to Admissions, Vy was playing a Metroidvania game. Like Adjudications, Admissions was a necessary part of Pangenica, but we were all slipping down the slope of outdatedness, and some of us felt occasionally like less than whole-hearted corporatitioners, while others cracked on with zeal in an effort to signal they still had to matter. I wasn't sure where Vy fell on this spectrum.

"Singe Laveneer," I said, hands on the counter, nothing to hide here. "I need her InTake forms that would include DNA records." Behind her desk were the stacks, corridors of files stretching as far as the eye could see. The majority of Admissions Records were digitized, but some were kept on paper.

"*L'avenir*, Laviner, would rhyme with Diviner, Avelar, Avatar, Kevlar." She leaned over to lace up a platform boot before lifting her feet from her desk, then walked to the counter that separated petitioner from the stacks as if she had all the time in the world. Nothing going on in Admissions that was urgent. Vy repeated those names as if a way of accessing the file lay in the words hidden in the name.

"No. Laveneer as in *surface*, not as in *the future*." I spelled it out for her, and she typed into a computer.

"Nothing digital. This one's on paper. Your Director was right. Aisle nine, row seventeen. I'll need the ladder." She unlaced her boots, put them on the counter, then disappeared into the stacks. Admissions archives were stored in locked, compressed, rolling stacks on rails that were motorized, but gizmos like steering wheels were attached to the sides of the shelving, so they could also be moved manually should the need arise. They extended as far as the eye could see. This part of the second floor was cantilevered out beyond the boundaries of the building. A strong wave would wash Admissions out to sea.

When Vy returned, she was empty-handed.

"For this file you need Q clearance. It's not even here. It's in Archives and Records."

"I don't have Q clearance."

"Well, you're out of luck then, aren't you? Can't help you, sorry. I can tell you this, the place where the file should have been, where the system told me it was, wasn't alphabetically accurate. Its alleged position was on a shelf beside some old twin studies."

"What are twin studies doing in Admissions?"

"Those twin studies that leveraged prediction, reduce chance? Applicants reference them all the time."

“So, the file was in place, and then someone moved it to Archives and Records.”

“Looks like it, doesn’t it? I’m not the only one with a key to this office, but it’s not like they’re given out like security IDs. The Director of Admissions has the other one, but doesn’t give it out.” Vy’s interest in the file ended there. Those above her could do what they pleased, as long as the information was somewhere identifiable, she had no stake where papers might be relocated. “Can I see what you do have?”

I handed her the file.

“There’s no signature here. Your Director needs to sign off on all queries. I couldn’t give you the file, even if it was here.”

I hadn’t noticed there was no signature on the top sheet, which was the query registration form. There’s generally no critical information on the registration sheet, so most of the time I just skipped the page, turned it over, and began. I could keep working on the case, but without a signature from the Director of Adjudications, pertinent files, like the InTake forms, wouldn’t be accessible. Then again, I didn’t seem to be getting those anyway, so I let that detail go. Vy Sapper couldn’t let it go, it was more than her job was worth. No signature. No access. She told me to come back when I had it, though it would save everyone a lot of time if I got Q clearance and went right to the source. That was never going to happen. I thanked her and left the way I’d come in.

FOUR

Back at my desk I typed in:
Clayton McCall, deceased.

ACCESS DENIED

Of Dinah McCall and her family, all kinds of data was available, but DNA records and InTake forms were not. This was not by itself unusual. DNA data was like gold in Fort Knox, not available for the download with a casual click. Adjudicators had some access, but not everyone's InTake forms were retrievable by Adjudications, and all this could be explained by one person.

Director of Adjudications Altner was a stooped guy with a shaved head and crooked nose, given to spasmodic movements due to a car crash that had caused nerve damage, and so signaled he was not always in control of the length of his body. He was in chronic pain, which I felt in my spine, so I made an effort to stand up straight as soon as I saw him, like a soldier in the presence of a commanding officer, but I had to be careful not to be too dramatic about it, that sudden ramrod spine could look ridiculous. I paused at his door, knowing that as soon as I knocked and opened, Altner's eyes would move up and down my body. I knew he would do this as soon as I opened his door because he always checked out women no matter how many times he saw one in the office, and if I wasn't careful, my eyes would involuntarily do the same raking motion, too, and the danger was continual that Altner would begin to realize I was mimicking him, and he would begin to wonder why. At first, he might have thought it was some kind of tic, but no one has tics anymore, not really, so hand on doorknob, I would try to focus on a spot on the wall, just above his head, but you can only do that for so long. Breathe in. Breathe out. Another possible situation: if the Director was looking down at me with irritation, I became annoyed with myself, imagining even greater incompetence, and given the right props, I would have engaged in the self-flagellation that he seemed to want to inflict on me. But what really took me off-balance was when he was clearly sizing me up, that gaze creeped me out no end, and peculiarities of mirroring turn you inside out. If I absolutely had to go to his office, I tried to leave as soon as I could. I'd already been in his office once that morning.

I hesitated at the threshold, but once Altner looked up and saw me, I had no choice but to go in. He was wearing mirrored sunglasses, which unnerved me. Was he onto me? Were the glasses a way of signaling, let's see what you do now? He might have been hungover, nothing more serious than that, but Altner had never been seen in an intoxicated or drugged state. He unfastened his cufflinks, little gold double helixes, and dropped them into an ashtray, then rolled up his shirtsleeves, as if to signal he was the only one in the vicinity actually working, though, in fact, the Director of Adjudications had developed the art of doing nothing, or as little as possible, into a science, and true to form, said zilch as long as he could get away with silence. That was what Altner did, let you do all the talking, and it felt so easy, so possible, to say the wrong thing without knowing why or how you tripped up and said too much. His office, too, was pillared with books and folders, but it was neat and orderly, as if any one of the piles could turn animate and tell you how wrong you were, look here at *Frankenstein v. Frankenstein 2121*, there's a long precedent for these decisions, how could you not know?

I explained the gaps in the file, that the case didn't appear to actually be a lawsuit, more a request for information, a clarification of what happened when two babies were born within minutes of one another about twenty years ago, and the registration page needed to be signed. Adjudication is about appearances, throwing a bone to the disgruntled. Though we do catch cheats, part of the role of Adjudications is to make plaintiffs feel they are being heard when, in reality, not much may be done for actual grievances.

Altner was silent, waiting for me to keep talking. I aimed my cataract of words in his general direction, and when he answered, his manner of speech was hard to interpret. Altner was from one of the conglomerate metropoli, Slavtown Ciudad Medina, an ocean away, and was adept at accent gymnastics with a voice that could span several social classes and districts depending on who he was talking to and what kind of point he was trying to get across, or authority he was trying to exert. His voice and tone could swoop between condescension, sarcasm, to the feigned ignorance of someone who worked at the lowest level of the organization. The accent conveyed: you figure it out, that's what you're being paid for, or what the fuck, smartypants?

"Can you obtain the original applications for me? I'll need their forms and don't have authority to get them."

"I'll look into it."

This meant he wouldn't do anything. He flipped through the file, tapped some keys on his computer, then signed the top sheet. "Another attempt to squeeze a payment from the company. The board of directors wants this file resolved and closed as soon as possible."

I knew what this meant. Every so often, a random case is selected for overview. The board didn't really give a shit. It's just a form of unpredictable surveillance to keep Adjudications, an increasingly sleepy department, on its toes, but this file with its typed complaint and stapled photographs looked like it had been dropped on my desk from a junked airbus. Nothing but the land of conjecture, as far as I could see. It was like half an overheard phone conversation, while the other half was lost in the atmosphere. You only knew what you'd heard. The rest was inaccessible.

"You need to find the woman who initiated the inquiry." He thumbed through the pages as if reading them for the first time. "Singe."

He wasn't telling me anything I wasn't completely aware of already, but the file didn't contain any way to find or contact her.

"She doesn't seem to want money, only a clarification."

"They all want money, Loew. You can appreciate that." He handed the folder back to me. If Altner spoke from experience, these were experiences he didn't talk about. His ability to parrot speech served him well back in his early days in the field. He could become anyone. I'd heard a story about him when he worked as an Adjudicator on the other side of the ocean. He and a co-worker were investigating the captain of a luxury cruise ship, one of those behemoths that are bigger than some inhabited islands. They were hired as entertainers. His colleague did stand-up comedy while Altner gave instruction in ballroom dancing. Apparently, this was something he also had some talent for.

Both men had grueling schedules, but at the same time, they were gathering evidence about a claim by the ship's captain about children who may or may not have existed. One night, the two undercover Adjudicators were supposed to meet on an upper deck to compare notes. Altner was dancing with a woman who claimed to be a former girlfriend of the captain's. In her suite, lime chiffon dress and clattering violet shoes fell to the floor. Altner thought he would learn something, but only discovered the woman was hard up for cash, and she dissolved into tears. By the time he got to the deck, the comedian was gone, not in his room, didn't appear for his show the next night, and was nowhere to be found. He was somewhere in the sea, many nautical miles behind them, fallen or pushed overboard. Swallowed, gone. That was the story. Altner could no longer work in the field after that incident, and became a consultant who transferred to the other side of the ocean as soon as a position opened up, and never went back to Slavtown Ciudad Medina.

"Find the two mothers. Interview the daughter, too. Get saliva samples to Lab C in the Bringates Pavilion. DNA should be archived, but let's be sure everyone is who they claim to be. Clarify to this Singe: What she's implying isn't possible, and she should continue her work in—" He glanced at the screen. "Museum sub-basements. How's your mother?"

"Still on her island. Thank you for asking."

"If she ever wants to come work for us, in a consulting capacity, my door is always open."

Yeah, consulting. I wanted to say, are you serious? My mother, trail of past addictions still burned into her mended brain, can barely speak two coherent sentences. His phone rang, and that was the end of our discussion.

As I walked back to my section, I passed L. J. Morris, junior archivist, loitering at the desk of a litigator. L. J. was sometimes known as El Jay or just Morris, but never Leo which was his actual first name. I could hear them talking about the World Cup, about the recent Republic of Senegal versus Japan Archipelago game. Morris's hand lingered on the lawyer's shoulder. The litigator, Smith, reached over and adjusted Morris's tie. Morris made the same adjustment to Smith's tie, though neither needed it. Hands rested longer than you might think was necessary. The two stood very close, flirting openly.

This should have been hot office gossip, especially because Smith was married to another man, and in the company hierarchy, a litigator is far above a junior archivist in station, but no one even looked up from what they were doing, for the most part. Waves of tolerance wash over the glass walls of Pangenica: Whatever makes you happy, by and large, it's your beeswax. One of the reasons for this ethos might be because so much is already known about us, before we're even born, when we're just ink on an InTake form.

And if there were cameras watching, we didn't even think about them most of the time. So, while Morris and Smith could stick a thumb in the camera's eye, I positioned myself in such a way so that when I maneuvered the Singe file into my bag, the gesture was, I hoped, out of view from any recording device.

Paper files weren't supposed to leave the floor. It would be easy to photograph pages and send them anywhere, if not for the cameras whose placement and vigilance, in this instance, I had to acknowledge. Most of our records were in a file system designed so they could only be forwarded in limited circumstances, and therefore, lockages were supposed to be in place, but for all its constantly updated and reinforced mirror domes, strategically placed cyber black holes, and moats with no drawbridges, security couldn't be relied on to infallibly keep up with shadow armies of hackers, agile and working with deadly accuracy, thoroughly anonymous.

The hacking of a corporation's files may sound like an ordinary and antique threat, but for Pangenica, holes in security could lead to tampering, which would be catastrophic. If genetic codes, individual patternings, could be interfered with, the peril of havoc and genetic bedlam was nightmarish. Once disrupted codes were established, the damage to a population could be irreversible. If it weren't for the International Genetic Counsel Agreement, warring nations could, in theory, alter the genetic codes of a given country to ensure future generations would die out of heritable incurable disease or grotesque deformities and madness. There was a precedent for meddling, dating back to the early days of DNA investigations. In an effort to find and isolate how genes direct specific traits, Christiane Nüsslein-Volhard and Eric Wieschaus working in Heidelberg in 1979 created fruit flies with legs growing out of their heads where antenna ought to have been, heads and tails reversed, as well as other mutations, not yet chimeras, though those would come. Their experiments were in no way arbitrary grotesqueries. By fiddling with genetic material, something about the blueprint process was learned, how proteins and enzymes could be marshaled to generate specific alterations and possible cures. To get there, monsters were created, but the door to the possible was opened. It didn't matter that the road to cure was paved with monstrosities. They were only fruit flies, after all, no big deal. Specks squashed in a blink.

The IGCA didn't mean the world could breathe a collective sigh of relief. There were nations who'd never signed the accords, rogue states, gangs, warlords with access and technical know-how, and if it was not within the grasp of reasonable, democratically governed populations to interfere and transform DNA, then geneticists could be kidnapped. (A Dr. Goldberg, for example, known as the creator of the Goldberg Variations, came to an end at the hands of such a group. The procedure he designed was not so much named after him, but because the process he engineered involved complex crossing over of genetic material, just as hands perform complicated crossing over when playing the Goldberg Variations. Dr. G. and his family were killed because he refused to cooperate with his kidnappers who were never identified, but it was suspected that the conspiracy had been hatched poolside by futures traders, or was connected to shorted stock, or linked to a massive Ponzi scheme that backfired. Whatever the scheme had been, the extortion, had it been successful, was expected to net millions, if not billions, instantly.) How to keep data safe? Pangenica and other corporations looked back to an age of paper clips and rubber bands. Fear of hacking was so extreme that some companies, ours included, took to storing high-risk records on paper in fire-retardant plastic-based folders.

Singe's case was isolated, so to think of her situation, as she presented it, as the work of a rogue hacker, a culprit somehow looking for a way to wreak havoc, made no sense. If so, there would be more queries like hers, but the file was a solitary one, a single complaint by a single mom. Even the missing forms, had they been in place, wouldn't have marked the file as a document that needed that caliber of security. But it existed only on paper. What I knew (one thing): Occasionally, there were abnormalities, physical or mental symptoms that were only discovered years later, but historically, these irregularities were benign and easy to dismiss. Being prone to migraines, for example, isn't the worst thing in the world. There's a remedy.

I stared out the window, at a loss as to how to proceed. Then I remembered Otto Crackhour, a long shot, but still, he worked with the same material as the lab technicians, and did what they told him to, so he knew things, sort of.

Otto Crackhour, or Crack, known mainly by his last name, doesn't look like an Otto, a George Grosz cigar-chomping john. More pencil-man than tank-like, he created animations of DNA and RNA that prospective parents could click on, animations that demonstrated how we do what we do. At least that's what he was hired for. Since the Flock Act, even schoolchildren know where babies come from, and so for seminars launched on the net, hits have plummeted. Who needs them, the thinking goes.

Transparency is a word used so often, I have to say, I'm quite sick of it, and often I've noticed people say *transparent* when they mean opaque to the point of total solidity. At any rate, everyone knows they are pre-configured—not born, as they'd been in the past. Everyone sees these animations in Sex Ed classes in high school. (Why is it still called *Sex Ed*? Sex, untethered from procreation, can only be about pleasure and maybe power, as well, but never about putting together another human being.) The result was that Pangenica had less and less need for his services, and Crack, like many of us, was very much afraid he'd be let go. He used to dream of spiraling helixes split and rejoined, the bars meant to represent genes changing color as diseases, according to voiceover explanations, were not just corrected, but eliminated. The sugar phosphate backbone is silver and swirls like twists of linguine in boiling water, the ladder bars of nitrogenous bases are blue, green, red, and yellow. Animated scissors snip, bars are replaced with other bars—indigo, olive, cerulean, and zip back together, realigned.

Crack animated specific traits on dancing genomes, but even though he was a hired hand who did what he was told, sometimes he turned up unexpected bits of data, so I made my way through the warren of carrels, walking toward the elevators to get to his floor.

When I was a few feet from the bank of lifts, someone tapped me on the shoulder from behind, and I jumped. It was Morris holding one of those grabbers, rubberized jaws at the end of a pole for grasping objects on high shelves or in hard-to-reach places.

"What's in your bag?"

"What are you talking about?"

"Citizen's arrest, sweetheart."

He was smiling, but it was considered part of his job as junior archivist to keep order in terms of the physical objects under his purview. Morris had unlimited opportunities to learn what was where, who'd done the ordering of which books and documents, and why. He was a kind of mobile librarian, running between Archives and Records, retrieving, returning, and remembering.

"There's nothing in my bag. You want to take a look?"

"If you don't mind."

My flamingo-colored bag was made of a material called vegan leather, which is another word for plastic, or so my mother claimed. She had found it when she used to scavenge in the city, and it was so large, I considered it my portable office. The file was partly obscured by a flap of torn lining, pushed to the side by my Pangenica water bottle, *The Shadow Prince,* a half-eaten bagel, a couple of expired metro passes, and balled-up tissues that might have had some space left on them to blow your nose. Morris didn't want to use his hands, so he poked around with the grabber. He squinted his eyes, miming a face that indicated he found the contents disgusting in the extreme, and I countered by bugging my eyes out, so I looked like something along the spectrum that ran from innocent to surprised. Had he used his actual hands and opened his eyes, he would have found the file, but he didn't, and I watched him shrug at the way I was wasting his time, then he carried on distributing and collecting from the desks of Adjudications.

I continued to the elevator, but I needed to stay hyper-aware of the gestures and expressions of those around me. A woman entered the car on the third floor, talking into her phone, rolling her eyes. I did the same. She glared at me, and so of course, I glared back. People got on and off, but once the elevator descended to sublevels below the ground floor, I was the only passenger, and from there I made my way to Crackhour's funhouse film studio.

FIVE

What I knew about Crack: When he was younger, before he became an animator, Crack had been an underwater photographer, swimming with a team under polar ice, taking pictures of life below. Diving under a roof of solid polar sea ice required calm and focus, the inability to panic, to keep track of time because your oxygen supply was finite, and when you felt almost weightless, and just a little further out was a pink jellyfish that looks like a baroque parachute, it's easy to lose any sense of time, but oxygen and light batteries will run out. That's a fact. Crack described how visibility in clear blue water went on for what seemed like infinity, but was really about a quarter of a mile, still under water, that's quite far. Everywhere he looked, he saw a range of blues or greens he didn't know existed. The ocean floor was littered with crystals like an ice garden, and creatures who looked like extraterrestrials crawled and swam.

After several years, the foundation that funded his team terminated the project. Human diving was expensive: long-distance flights, underwater cameras, housing facilities that needed to be constructed over Arctic diving holes, insurance, and that's just for starters. He was replaced by underwater drones who, unlike humans, didn't rely on oxygen and would not become dinner for leopard seals. The exhilaration of deep-sea dives was over, and he learned a new skill from an uncle who animated molecules. It meant sitting in front of a screen for long hours, but it was a job. First hired by Krisper Images, Inc., Crackhour had explained the name was a variation on CRISPR: Clustered, Regularly, Interspersed, Short, Palindromic, Repeats. I know, I said, I work in the business, how could I not know?

Crack's domain wasn't actually a film studio in the twentieth-century sense, though there were references to archaic forms of animation and Claymation classics on the walls. Stills from *Fantasia*, *Jason and the Argonauts*, *Prince Achmed*, and other cartoons were mixed with pictures from his polar expeditions. They were shingled on two partitions like a crime scene tableau and analysis posted in a police detective's office. How is a giant squid connected to Bugs Bunny? What does a narwhal have to do with Speedy Gonzales? Old arcade game machines had an area to themselves, since he had no place else to put them, and no one seemed to notice or care that he stored them at work. They flashed lights and played crash and siren sounds. There was also a Zoltar, a fortune teller in a closet-sized box, that I turned around when I walked in, so it faced a wall. Crack didn't notice, but the Zoltar, years of grime in the folds of his old metal turban and long goatee, spooked me out no end.

Crackhour's life, as far as I knew, revolved around his job, which he took very seriously, as flimsy as it was. He didn't come across as a cheerleader for the company, he just wanted his little piece of heaven, even if it only came in pill form.

There was another issue with Crack. I enjoyed hearing about his dives, but because his descriptions were so precise, his breathing would change as if he were underwater, and I would feel my breathing change, too. When he described the relationship between distance swum, remaining oxygen, and time to get back to the surface, I felt asphyxiated, even if we were sitting on the roof, I was sitting at the bottom of an ocean of air. My lungs struggled, oxygen was running out, I had miles to go and wouldn't make it. It looked like a panic attack, but wasn't exactly, and in this way, Crack learned my secret, but didn't tell me, not at first. What he did was he watched me at the movies, watched how I couldn't control my facial expressions. If the face on the screen was frightened, I looked terrified. If the actor expressed shock, I'd look startled, too. He used these observations, he figured some things out, and then, one time, when

I was in Crack's studio, he insisted we watch porn. He made it sound like I didn't have a choice, so I said okay, and he watched me watch the screen, and then I realized he knew. Crack was the only one in Pangenica who understood that I felt what he felt, his touch was my touch. So I had to be careful around Crack, the man who knew too much.

The funhouse was dark, illuminated only by the glow of a few screens, even the arcade machines were unplugged. Crack was lying on the floor, eyes shut, asleep. I sat cross-legged beside him, so my right knee grazed the side of his chest and said his name in a very low voice, because I didn't want to jolt him awake. Mirror touch blurs boundaries between the self and others, and skin is no border fence. The pressure on your skin becomes the pressure on my skin, the taste of melting butter in your mouth— I taste that, too.

What your cells telegraph to your brain also telegraph to mine in the same instant. Double your pleasure, double your fun. I touched his shoulder, trying to feel as lighthearted as Morris running his hand across the litigator's back, as if cameras hadn't yet been invented, and who cares anyway. Crack woke up, put his hand on my knee, not totally aware of who I was just for a disoriented minute before everything in the funhouse settled back into place. Pressing on my leg, he sat up, then stood. The moment passed, and I told him I needed to ask him some questions for which he probably had no answers, but I wasn't sure, at this point, who else to ask.

He was semi-conscious and not immediately ready for a serious conversation. I was glad he was awake because Crack was addicted to Dormazin, a pill that causes the user to sleep for a short, concentrated period of time. Depending on the strength, with Dormazin, you can sleep for two hours as if you've slept for eight, one for eight, one for four, and so on. Dormazin are blue, of course, but color-coded ranging from ice blue (I don't need so much) to midnight blue (concentrated evil: sixteen for one). They are also known as Z-titans or noddies on the street. Highly addictive, one of the side effects, over time, noddies hit your linguistic centers and one word accordions into many similar sounding words, and finally the addict becomes psychotic. How did I know this? Not because of synesthesia. I don't absorb the effects of drugs other people take because my mother was a Dormazin addict and suffered the effects of longtime use. Propensity for addiction had never been entirely eliminated, and Dormazin use was restricted, but Crack couldn't live without it. How he arrived at such a state, I never knew, only that he always had a bottle on him. I had to provide the pills for my mother, because she lived in isolation. It was not a task I enjoyed, but she couldn't live without them, and no matter how graphically I described her state to him, he remained undeterred, always claiming he had his usage under control.

Crackhour was fully awake, but had a bedroom eye look, and I was afraid he would ask me to watch porn with him, or rather he would watch me watch it. Crack wouldn't say this as a threat, but sometimes it felt like one, or close to it, and that's part of the excitement for him. I could say no, and sometimes I did, but it nagged at me that Crack knew I'm an anomaly, and he could tell the wrong person, not even intentionally—it could just slip out, "You know, Loew in Adjudications, she has mirror touch, yeah, it's really cool." So, every once in a while, I let him watch me.

He asked me why there were two of me until his eyes focused, and given my particular kind of synesthesia, this was a bit of a joke. If I'm with someone else, in a way, I am doubled. Crack once asked if I'd ever knowingly met a fellow citizen with mirror touch, comparing the event to being in a mirrored elevator or a Yayoi Kusama *Infinity Mirror Room*. The answer is no, I haven't, and the idea makes me feel weightless, as if floating in one of those simulated spaceships in which there is no gravity.

When he seemed alert, I asked if he knew where some specific traits were on the genome? Not all of them, but were there any he did know?

"The level of animation I do never gets that precise." Crack gestured into the air as if showing which trait is where on an invisible chromosome. "The films, the bits, are like advertisements, public service announcements, none of it is diagnostic. They're mostly like cartoons. Sorry. I follow directions, follow the script and the images sent from the labs. I barely know what any of it means." I'd seen some of his animations, the protein that cut DNA metamorphosed from a pumice-like blob into a pair of scissors.

"Ask someone in the labs."

I didn't have that level of security clearance. The actual brass tacks of what happened in the labs was off limits as well as uninterpretable. I could walk through a LIGO detector and recognize steel vacuum tubes, wingnuts, and screws, but have no idea how it actually measures gravitational waves from cataclysmic events that happened in impossibly distant time and space. Two black holes collided 1.3 billion years ago, and we're just getting the news now. I don't understand how we know what we know. Pangenica's business model, its success, relied on the isolation of information. Either based on level of clearance or job in the labs, you either had access or you didn't.

I can't just knock through the swinging doors, provided I could replicate some technician's security iris scan, suit up, and walk up to *Doctor X* or *Y* and ask, "Say, what about the gene for obsession?" Not obsessive-compulsive, that's extinct, but let's say a trait that's adjacent to compulsion. The precise location of genes is Q clearance stuff. Goldberg and his family were killed for less. It's like D Day is approaching, you're an Allied soldier, and you walk into the German headquarters in Normandy and say, "Could you show me your plans, if you don't mind, old boy?" They aren't going to answer my questions. No chance.

"You can find them in the cafeteria. Just ask."

"Even if I had authorization, for what I need to ask about, no one will talk to me. There have to be other ways to make inquiries."

“Everybody thinks their parents made mistakes when they filled out their request forms.”

“But this is a parent. Parents don’t usually think they made mistakes. They used to, historically speaking, but not anymore.”

Singe Laveneer wanted to prove that consciousnesses were switched. How can you even do that? We can edit for every physical trait, also cognition and behavior, but not consciousness because no one really knows what it is, whether any feature of it could be inherited, and if so, where would you find the state of consciousness, where would that be on the genome? What parts of the brain are essential for consciousness? I was at a loss.

Crackhour’s job wasn’t yet obsolete, but it was close to forgotten, and though there were cameras in the basement funhouse, there were only two of them placed in ceiling corners, easily evaded. I held his head in my hands and whispered so even the cameras wouldn’t pick up what I was about to say—that I wanted to photograph the file, but didn’t want to be seen doing so. He showed me how to move, where to stand, so then I stood in that corner of his studio, photographed every page of the Singe file, and sent it to myself, labeling it *ConSwitch,* a bunch of dead ends that were supposed to point to a plaintiff who claimed to want no money at all.

SIX

Since I had no address for Singe, no electronic eaeroscript notation, no social media, and the personal coordinates she wrote in the file were obsolete, I made inquiries at the Metropolitan, the Tate, the Pergamon, the Louvre, on and on, but no one knew how to find her, nor did they seem to care. Directors, curators all answered me, sometimes politely, sometimes not mincing words at all, letting me know Singe was a pain in the collective museum ass. If she were returned to place of origin, Pangenica, that would be a fitting outcome. Altner insisted she was still alive, and though I was skeptical of his certainty, could find no obituaries or missing person notices, nothing to indicate she was deceased. As if her daughter's electronically fueled personality had burned her, Singe was somewhere, but glided just above the earth, leaving no footprints. I did find PomPom, and that was easy. PomPom had been in an accident, and wheelchair-bound, lived in an institution where she could be taken care of. Lazarus House, Rehab and Development, Inc. was about an hour northeast of the city.

I couldn't go into the facility as Zedi Loew from Pangenica. Oh, excuse me, miss, your mother thinks you're some kind of bad seed, and we're trying to sort out what, if anything, happened in the lab before you were born. So, I became Jane Ames, complete with a false ID. Security had the machinery to produce these in a blink, no trouble at all if the case demanded it, and this one did. Green light from the Director was on file. No need for further bureaucratic okay. I had an interview on the eleventh floor with Security, Crafted Identities subdivision.

Crafted Identities put together IDs, clothing, props, histories. Their inventions, their imaginary citizens, may have had some basis in actual walking-around humans, businesses, institutions, and as far as my experiences with Crafted I, they were pretty much reliable, but it would only take one loose screw to put the person working incognito at serious risk. I could picture someone getting the brilliant idea of, say, let's make her an escape artist. You think the person she's investigating will test her? Lock her in a chained, weighted trunk, and sink it in the river? What are the odds? Slim to nil. It's a cool identity. Let's do it! They chuckle as they try out names. WTF. This thought kept me up the night just before I had to assume a character and go into the field. You had to trust them. Everyone in Crafted Identities, those you saw and those you didn't, worked in a lab of sorts, creating their own genomes for folks who existed and those who didn't. A woman who would barely acknowledge me if I ran into her in a hall or the café, gave me accent training and had me repeat my character's story until memorized and offhand-sounding. I'd work with her, then a package would arrive on my desk with everything I needed. Crafted Identities was supposed to be a highly trained department, but for all anyone really knew, the creators might be a bunch of half-drugged or drunk guys whooping it up in a less visible or accessible part of the eleventh floor, and in this annex or half-wing, they'd create characters. Initially, Crack had a more romantic view of the department, that they were like Charles Dickens collecting names from Highgate Cemetery then inventing characters, but Crack never had to rely on their services, so what did he know?

People who worked in Crafted Identities tended to be remote, humorless, chilly, professional. They were men and women in suits, dark glasses, polished shoes, notators of gestures, how a person gives away origins, say you're from East Jesus without telling me you're from East Jesus. They have feelers out for when a subject is being less than truthful, and so has to be corrected, and their eye for sartorial detail, for accent fluctuation has to be perfect, because these builders of secret personal histories have to instruct a Pangenica employee if they have to, for whatever reason, pass as someone else. What was your local newspaper, your grandmother's wartime hiding place, your father's attempt at building a backyard rocket, where were you during the great earthquake of '89? They gave you an identity, but you never knew anything about the worker drones of Crafted Identities. You could imagine department meetings where identities were fabricated, debated, details added, finessed, deleted as absurd, contradictory, not able to endure the test of time or intense interrogation, but really no one outside the Crafted Identities department knew what went on there. It was said they could change anything but a person's DNA. Odds are they weren't party-house good-time Charlies.

Before his fling with the litigator, Morris had been involved with a man who worked in Crafted, and when the man disappeared, Morris was disconsolate. He missed work, and when he returned, was silent, looked sleepless, had dark circles under his eyes. It was said that if you worked for Crafted Identities, you had a job for life, but even if no one could quit or be fired, they could be disappeared. When people disappeared, you didn't speak about them, and sooner or later even their names were forgotten.

By Wednesday, I had my new identity and an appointment at Lazarus House for the next day.

Across the airshaft, a man and woman argued, as they often did, accelerating into ever more vociferous fuck yous. They sounded like dueling lawn mowers. As far as I could see or hear, they never came to blows, though this didn't mean such occurrences never happened. If I heard the sound of a slap, I would have felt it. I shut the window and began making coffee.

While it was brewing, I put away pictures of my mother, Dot, who lived in a lighthouse. Also in the drawer were pictures of my former husband who recorded migratory bird songs and lived who-knows-where. Their images were more at home in the drawer than on a desk or wall. While rehearsing my character, I needed to eliminate as many external signs of Zedi Loew as possible without going overboard;

the kind of cleaning that total erasure required would take days, and where would I put everything? The lamp whose base was a reproduction of a raptor skeleton, the law journals, a copy of *An Actor Prepares,* these were all part of an immovable layer of what appears as disorder, but is really a kind of organization, clear to me at least. I've been waiting for my former husband to pick up the raptor lamp, and in the meantime have been using it to hang from the raptor's scapula and radius earrings that look like rhinestone orreries, emerald (green glass) cascading teardrops, resin pearls cast in the shape of miniature marshmallows. These are part of my repertoire of characters' trappings when needed for use.

Among the first things I do in order to prepare is spray the air and myself with a strong perfume from a collection I keep in a shoebox on a closet shelf. The glass bottles are small, some smooth, some faceted, but none of them would I, as myself, ever wear. They range from expensive to dollar store. There's nothing like Golden Delicious (knock off) or Subterfuge X ($10.99 in a black and silver box) to get into character.

I studied acting under a disciple of the get-completely-into-character method. The classes were painful but necessary for my job, paid for by Pangenica as a company benefit. For group scenes, like sports teams, I was always the last one picked. In the end, I'm decent enough but wouldn't win any awards, though my livelihood, if not my life, depends on these deceptions from time to time when I have to go into the field for cases. Mirror touch can take me out of character, so it's something I have to watch for. For example, one investigation led me to a couple who claimed Pangenica never delivered, that their application had gotten lost, and it was the company's fault. I rang their bell, posing as an exterminator in a green jumpsuit, carrying a cannister of insecticide and a bag of glue traps. The couple were very talkative, let me into their house. "Oh, a woman exterminator, cool." They wondered how I got into that occupation, and I had a ready answer. It was a family business. Okay, fine, this made sense to them. In this role, I should have had no fear of rats, and ordinarily I don't, but once we got to the kitchen, one ran across the floor, a skinny gray one, sort of a cross between a snake and a rat, and the woman in her terror backed into the corner edge of a kitchen counter. I grimaced in pain as the point of the Formica stabbed flesh and muscle. Her face was like a cartoon mask of panic, and I knew mine had become a mirror image of it. I had no control over my facial expression. When she ran out the back door, I tried to follow her. Her husband, now suspecting I was no vermin hunter, twisted my arm behind my back. Mirroring his clenched teeth, his anger, I was able to break free of him, and once out in the wilds behind their house, discovered they had three children stashed in a treehouse, homeschooled, kept in secret, delivered by a rival but equivalent company to Pangenica years prior. The lawsuit was a con to bilk the company out of millions.

But my favorite impersonage by far was Isla Fentster, a mapmaker who used words like *gnomonic, orthographic projection, azimuth, bathymetric, cartouche*. She wore an Irma Vep–style black jumpsuit and carried a satchel that held all kinds of equipment: vernier scale, collapsible telescope, waterproof compass, cameras, lenses both telephoto and for closeups. Satellites couldn't go everywhere, couldn't register precise details, only coordinates, so this identity required a considerable amount of travel. I rappelled down ravines, climbed rock formations and deforested slopes, sighted deer scuttling away when a branch snapped underfoot. The job, one of my first, was time consuming, a months-long assignment, no quick in-and-out. As I enjoyed being Isla Fentster more and more, Zedi Loew receded. It wasn't even a contest.

There were maps that charted the spread of epidemics around the world, density of airline travel patterns, light pollution, the migratory paths of birds. (My former husband, who was not former at the time, drew a map on Isla's leg.) I mapped networks of highways, canals, mountain trails, and said things like, "He who maps owns the world." Alone, I repeated names that rolled off the tongue: Molokai Fracture Zone, Charles-le-roi, Guinea Bissau.

Maps of the past were the easiest, no leaving home for those: the advance of the Conquistadors, of Genghis Khan, number of drones over the Tigris, movements of the Red Army, appearance of oil fields in deserts that thrived then vanished. Or a map in which each country was boiled down to one event: Waterloo, Hiroshima, Partition. There were problems Fentster couldn't solve—for example, when three countries claimed a particular region or city. What to call it? Which led to another map to be constructed of shifting language patterns, as some died (Judeo-Persian, Abkhaz, Walloon) and others severed ties with their origination (Articia, McMurdoon), becoming distinct with their own grammars, syntax, vocalizations. Traveling from accent to dialect, then disappearing altogether. *Sayonara*, old buddy.

I kept Isla's costume and papers, though I was supposed to return them to Crafted Identities. In fact, I kept her ID card declaring membership in a mapmakers union, headquartered in a place I never heard of. It was in my wallet, though I never took it out again. I was so absorbed in my role that I didn't pursue Fentster's colleagues, the plaintiffs, the ones I was meant to be investigating, and so the case was not a success for Pangenica, and I nearly lost my real job. It didn't matter how good I was at being Isla Fentster, the litigants won their case, something that rarely happened.

Jane Ames, my character for that day, was an ordinary insurance claims adjuster. Wearing black browline glasses with tinted lenses, a houndstooth viridian and brown checked suit, dark orange five-inch heels, sunbursts of rhinestones were clipped to my ears, she would be a quick in-and-out. Jane walked with confidence, unleavened by the knowledge she wasn't really very good at her job, clothing adhering to her body in a way that meant she'd be noticed in a way I am not, ordinarily. Someone who is used to being noticed, who expects it, even when she slips on a banana peel, saying the wrong thing or forgetting names she should have remembered. Jane spoke with a West Coast accent, she surfed in Malibu, drove up Highway 1, drank martinis in Big Sur, lost a house in a forest fire. I practiced in front of a mirror until it was time to run out the door and catch the train to a suburb I'd never heard of.

SEVEN

The view from the commuter train: Automotive centers and warehouses gave way to industrial parks, which melted into blocks of small aluminum-sided houses side by side, stucco rowhouses painted banana-peel yellow, blue, watermelon, but then the houses grew larger and further apart. Lazarus House was in a suburb outside a wealthy commuter town. The institution had a long-distinguished history as a rehab facility for those for whom there wasn't really any hope of rehabilitation. Most patients would never leave. LHR & D, Inc. occupied a large, red-brick Queen Anne with a wraparound porch. The original house, so storybook sweet, now served as a reception area. Modern additions, residential and hospital-like treatment wings, sprouted from it, white spider legs grown from quaint thorax, like the mutants engineered in Heidelberg in 1979. Serene but uninhabited gardens lay between buildings connected by concrete paths, all wheelchair accessible.

An aide, who introduced himself as Chester, met me at the front desk, welcomed me to the Home, and brought me to PomPom's room. As we walked from wing to wing, he described the car accident from years ago in terms of the damage it did, leaving his patient paralyzed from the neck down and unable to speak, but apart from the brain's inability to command motor function, it was, otherwise, in tiptop shape, this they knew. Given Singe's account of PomPom, I wasn't sure that particular tiptop brain should be given a microphone of any kind, and ought to be left bouncing around her cortex with no way out, but Lazarus House had developed an alphabetical system based on interpretation of blinks. Once she had a language, the barest glimmer turned into raging activity, torrents of verbiage at times. Chester would be my translator. I pretended I knew nothing.

PomPom was in her chair facing a window looking at the network of concrete paths just outside. Chester turned the chair around and said to her, "You have a visitor, Jane Ames, from Porphirion Insurance Company, let's say hello."

I would have to take her hand, she was unable to extend her arm on her own, but when I reached out, she blinked furiously, and Chester interpreted: "Keep your hands to yourself!"

Since she had no feeling or sense of touch below her neck, much was not possible: no pain or pleasure, but still desire and fear, memory of sensation, maybe. Because of her immobility, PomPom's room should have been a sea of calm for me. She couldn't feel a thing; therefore, I couldn't feel a thing either. But even a hobbled tormentor who took pleasure in torment is still a tormentor, and feeling what she felt was not pleasant. I anticipated there would be little to mirror, that she experienced nothing visceral on the spectrum from anxiety nor elation, so I would feel nothing, but PomPom was irritated, angry, I could tell. If she could clench her fists, she would have. There are times when being a recluse seems like a viable option, to live in a place or situation when I wouldn't have to endure this kind of pain, mortification, shame on behalf of someone else, and this was such a moment.

Gene therapy can restore some movement, but the accident had been so severe PomPom's spine was shattered, and no functionality could be restored. There is a suite of 116 genes called chatterbox genes, influenced by a master switch gene, *Foxp2*, thought to have coevolved to give humans language. It was put into mice, and you might think presto, the rodents stood on their hind legs and launched into grammatical speech, but no, only baritone squeaks, that is to say, their sub-sonic vocalizations were altered, but their neuron activity in the language centers of the brain now resembled those of people with language disorders which no longer exist, unless you count the brains of Dormazin addicts. My mother might be Exhibit A. At any rate, not good if you're human, but for a mouse, it's a step up.

Where did the word *chatterbox* come from? The visual is a box with a mouth, blah, blah, blah. I looked it up. First used in 1774, a few decades after the passing of the Shadow Prince. Who were the blabbermouths of his era, the folks of whom it could be said loose lips sink ships?

Jane Ames crossed her legs, and jiggling her foot, let it slip from a five-inch heel. A repetitive gesture, I realized too late, would be provocative, even unkind to the paralyzed PomPom, and so tried to remain as still as possible for the duration.

"This woman has some questions about your accident, PomPom, pumpkin."

PomPom looked like a blocky version of her mother. Confined, immobilized, her body fit the chair, legs dangled, though restraints were fitted to the side of the chair, perhaps meant for an earlier occupant. Her attendant stood by, never fidgeting or reacting at all, just interpreting.

Was it viable to say her head had consciousness, but her body no longer collected sensory impulses? Hair hung limply around her face, but there was nothing vacant about PomPom's eyes. They were a sharp means of assessment and communication, all she, whose fingers had been so acidic and so dexterous on a keyboard, had left. She wore a hospital gown with owls printed on it, pink socks, and black running shoes, though she wasn't running anywhere. Someone had put gold heart-shaped earrings in her ears, as if she were still twelve years old, the sentimental nature of which might have enraged the girl Singe had described as someone who would never wear hearts or flowers, but PomPom was powerless to reach up and remove them. "The crash accident happened ten years ago, asshat. What the fuck?" Chester faithfully interpreted. It was difficult to know if *asshat* was directed at him or at me.

"I'm sorry, but your case has been reopened." Jane Ames smiled. "I just have a few questions."

Review questions about the accident served as a sort of entrance ramp to get to my real purpose. I started with an inquiry about the driver. If the police investigation had been unable to identify the driver of the vehicle that ran over her, it was unlikely PomPom knew and hadn't told them. How would she know and why would she withhold that information? I wanted to appear a neophyte claims adjuster given a reassessment of a case Jane Ames hadn't read up on, so asked a bungling, stupid question. The driver ran a light. There were cameras everywhere. Why were they never caught?

"Do you have any idea, PomPom?"

"Ask Clay Town," Chester said.

"Who's Clay Town?" As if I didn't know.

"My friend who fell through ice."

"Well, we can't ask him then, can we?" Jane Ames used a kind voice, trying not to sound condescending. PomPom looked up at the ceiling as if to signify either Clayton was somewhere in the cumulus thunderheads, or I was a dodo, or both. "That's not possible, dear. You think he knew the driver?"

Dear? I realized too late the mistake in that word, whether Jane Ames would have used it or not. It's impossible to blink sarcasm, but PomPom would say nothing more. She glared at me. Minutes passed, or seemed to, and there were no blinks to interpret.

"I will need a saliva sample." There was no point in waiting for her to say something. I unsnapped my bag and removed swabs, glass tube, plastic gloves.

"Well, that's not happening." PomPom blinked and clenched her jaw.

"The insurance company needs DNA?" Chester was on the ball.

"It's a normal procedure to verify identity."

"I'm afraid I can't force her, not legally."

I cut straight to the real reason I, underneath the Jane Ames exterior, had made the trip and, as Jane Ames, asked her how we could contact her mother?

"How the fuck should I know?" Chester looked directly at PomPom and pronounced without affect.

"Does she ever visit?" I needed to ask questions that wouldn't anger her, and the subject of her mother was a minefield.

Standing slightly behind the chair, Chester grimaced and shook his head. This was a question that should not have been asked. In the silence, I looked around PomPom's room. There were books whose pages someone would have to turn for her, photographs of the façade of a Syrian caliph's palace from the Pergamon Museum in Berlin, the *Mona Lisa* in the Louvre, Aku Aku statues and the Elgin Marbles from the British Museum. Why these images? What did all these things have in common? They were all objects Singe had campaigned to be returned to their places of origin, even if those countries no longer existed. The *Mona Lisa* had been bought by Francis I of France from da Vinci's assistant and heir, Salai. It was, and had been, in France entirely legally, though there wasn't much of the painting left, despite the conservators' best efforts. By the time France was divided into Provincia Nostra Gaulle to the north and Lascaux-Massailia to the south, ancient pigments had darkened until barely anything remained to be seen of the woman whose portrait this had been, just a blackened rectangle with the slightest gleam of collarbone and blue lake in the background, but that hadn't stopped Singe. The Elgin Marbles and the Gate of Ishtar had been in their respective European museums for so many centuries no one really cared anymore. What had historically been a country known as Athenios had been absorbed by the Balkan Federation, and Indo-Mesopotamia was mainly uninhabited desert and a few isolated oilopoli, drilling and refinery stations, manned by a minimum number of engineers to keep facilities functional. No one was asking for the Gate or the Marbles to be returned. Singe's campaign to repatriate regardless of circumstances had made her a laughingstock, a source of joy for her daughter. At her direction, Chester would have found, cut, and pinned these up. He was an extension of her body, her will, her consciousness.

"What can you tell me about Clay Town? Why would he have known the driver?"

No blinking. No answer.

Then: "Clay Town was an asshole."

Did PomPom know some bit of her should have belonged to Clayton, the itchy sneer at the sight of someone wearing a buttercup yellow dress, the snarl directed at a classmate who brought in day-old cupcakes, who only got colored pencils as a present, who gave her a book she didn't want, so she gave it back? Meanwhile her erstwhile forced-upon-her childhood friend experienced the aching of his spine as he stared at the sky as she was meant to. Perhaps she had begun to suspect there had been some kind of switch, she couldn't put a finger on it, couldn't quite articulate, but that's why she hated him. She knew she should have been him. Now her spine was as numb as his. I wanted to ask her but couldn't. How did it feel to suspect your mother wasn't entirely your mother?

She was blinking like crazy, but Chester had stepped behind the chair, so he couldn't see her face. I didn't know if this was deliberate or he planned to push her somewhere. He stroked the top of her head and her hair, a gesture of kindness, trying to calm her, though I wasn't sure PomPom could accept anyone's kindness. I felt badly for Chester who seemed like a sympathetic person, a mouthpiece for someone else's consciousness, pushing his own aside, at least while he was on the job.

One of the indignities PomPom suffered was the elimination of privacy. Her body was no longer her own, she had no control over its functions. Despite the open window, her room suddenly began to smell like crap. Her shit and piss went somewhere in the chair. It must have been like sitting on a perpetual toilet. PomPom had no sense of feeling, so didn't know when she'd have to go; it all fell into a compartment in the seat and her ass had to be cleaned a few minutes later. Did she have a sense of smell? Her nose worked, she could breathe, so I would guess, yes. She knew exactly what was going on. The smell got worse. She blinked that she was less than a brain in a jar. No brainer.

"It's time for you to leave."

I hadn't gotten anything resembling what I needed, information that could lead to Singe and some idea of who PomPom was, but I suspected that for both PomPom and Chester, who would have to lift and clean her, the interview was over. Jane Ames stood, kept hands in pockets, breathing through my mouth. I said goodbye, it was nice meeting you—though nice wouldn't have been the first word to come to mind when thinking about our interview.

"Toodle-loo, motherfucker," said Chester as PomPom.

Chester then turned his back to PomPom, but while he was telling me he would show me out, since Lazarus House was a labyrinth of wings and annexes, PomPom rang a buzzer that was attached to her chair. It was an annoying sound. If it irritated Chester, he was polite and patient, at least while I was still standing there. He turned, looking straight at PomPom's reddening face.

She blinked, "Look up Porphirion. My mother's insurance company was Dometop. I remember because they paid for some things but not everything. My mother called the adjuster the Dometop Majordomo. No one ever said anything about any Porphirion."

Chester took out his phone and tapped a few keys, said, "It's a real company, PomPom, angel cake, don't be silly. Your mother may well have changed insurance. People do that all the time."

"If she changed companies, then Porphirion would know where she lives, and this dumbass would have no reason for being here."

“Not necessarily. She could have moved.” There was annoyance in Chester’s voice. Perhaps she made him look up mindless impulses all the time, and he was getting tired of it.

“Show me the screen.”

“Honey, I just *X*-ed out of it. I’ll show you when I get back from seeing our guest out.”

“*Honey*, my ass.” Chester dutifully repeated PomPom’s words as if she were actually speaking, though there was no need for me to know her remarks to him.

“Show me the screen.”

The room was small, and Chester was standing near the door, so he could reach over and open it, but could still see enough of PomPom’s face to say, “Don’t leave me sitting here in my own crap.”

He pronounced the words, then completely turned his back to her as he held the door open for me, so there would be no more interpreting blinks. Was PomPom so humiliated that the indignity of Chester cleaning her in front of me didn’t even register? Since she was feeling nothing, I felt nothing, but she knew what had happened to her, and what the remedy had to have been. Chester almost pushed me into the hall, shutting the door on his patient.

“She gets these fears into her head every once in a while, having to check everything. Some days I do what she wants, sometimes I have to skip it. You know, her wants, it’s like seeing an avalanche coming your way. *Look up this. Look up that.*”

As we walked down the hall, I could hear a buzzer going off from one of the rooms. Whether or not it was PomPom’s was difficult to know for certain, but Chester ignored the sound, saying, “You must have a train to catch.”

When we got to reception, I tried to stall Chester, to keep him talking. There was something else I wanted to know. Lazarus House was not cheap. Someone was paying for PomPom to reside there year after year with her own private aide. Singe didn’t appear to have those kinds of resources, so I asked Chester if I could speak to someone in billing. He said this was confidential information.

"Of course it is, but in terms of the claim being investigated, Porphirion needs to know."

"I'll speak to Accounts and send you the information."

I gave him Jane Ames's card, j.ames@Porphinc.com. "Please," I said, "as soon as possible."

"J dot ames at poor fink," Chester repeated. He'd see what he could do, no promises, nice meeting you, apologize for PomPom's testiness. That's who she is. I'm used to it. Then the aide disappeared back to his post to deal with his patient.

What did they talk about during those long hours of consciousness, PomPom blinking, Chester speaking, sitting in front of her? He could put his hands on her if he wanted to, but she would feel nothing. She referred to herself as a brain in a jar, and Chester knew the contents of that jar. He was the one I should have been speaking to, but if he discovered Jane Ames didn't exist, I would never have the opportunity to talk to him again. Chester was the only person who knew what was brewing inside PomPom's jumbled amygdala, the Dalai Lama of synapses and neurons. PomPom's existence, her consciousness, wherever it came from, only rendered expansive by her thoughts.

In what way was PomPom's consciousness only partial (because most of her body was inert)? If a living sentient body, as a vector for environmental stimuli, is nonfunctioning, is consciousness any less? Can it be disembodied, or nearly so, and still be operational? If sleeping is an unconscious state, and a person can only be awakened by having their body touched, shaken, but they, like PomPom, have no sensation below the neck, then the body is a tripwire to alert consciousness, maybe, and in PomPom's case, it wouldn't work. For me, a crowded train or sidewalk or even being in a room with one person in pain, is a riot of sensations. For PomPom everything is nothing, no sensation at all.

No brain. No consciousness. Does consciousness transcend its container, or could it leak? Why does the brain get all the good stuff, asks the heart and nerve endings. No claims by bile ducts or intestines. What about a partial brain, one that is not all there?

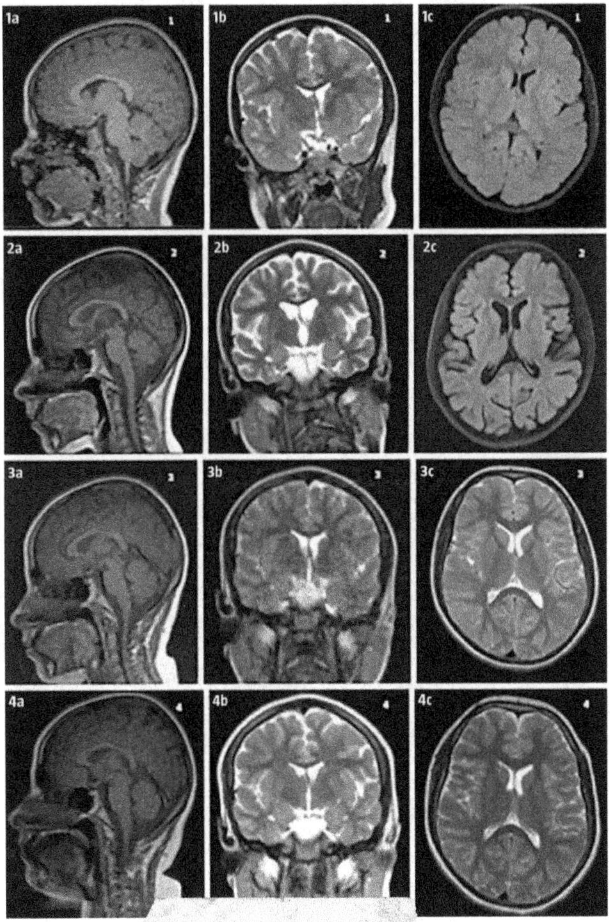

EIGHT

The cab back to the train station was taking forever to arrive, and I was nervous. I read Lazarus House promotional brochures as I waited.

Providing alternative modes of mobility
Offering hope for those with spinal injury
Throwing out a lifeline to those adrift

Reception had positioned wood and metal don't-get-too-comfortable chairs and couches against walls. Decorative pots of parrot tulips were lined up along the front desk. I couldn't sit anyway and wanted to be close to the door as I strained to hear the possible sounds of someone running down the hall to stop Jane Ames from leaving. The receptionist scrolled through whatever was on his phone, ignoring me, which was just as well. A security guard back from her break tossed out a cup of coffee and stood in the doorway. Had she been on a break or had she been called to keep the woman who had just visited PomPom from leaving the premises? If Chester looked up Porphirion before he cleaned PomPom, enough time had passed to call security. But that didn't mean he wouldn't check after he cleaned her, and how long would it take to do that? Again, I wondered if Identity Crafters allowed for online checking? Was there a site with actors standing by in case of phone calls? Would he show her the screen if she asked again, as soon as he got back and finished wiping her ass, and if so, was there a real Porphirion somewhere? Had Crafted Identities set up a dummy website? Maybe. I had no idea. Crafted Identities had a reputation for being scrupulous, but they did screw up on occasion, and for all I knew they spent their free time throwing darts at the company logo. If they hadn't created a site and a viable phone number, then what?

If Lazarus House discovered there was no Porphirion Insurance, that I was an imposter, a threat to the facility, an infiltrator, there would be both known and unknown consequences. If the facility had anything to hide—money laundering, human trafficking, experimental medicine of the most wacko kind—they might jump the gun, not realizing those activities were no concern of mine. A visitor who wasn't who she claimed to be asking questions about a long-term patient whose benefactor paid high-end bills and trusted LHRC for a level of security—that would raise alarms. It was a violation of the terms of my contract as an Adjudicator to identify Pangenica when in the field. To do so would undermine the reputation of the company. Information related to Adjudication cases is highly restricted. For our own safety, much of how we do business depends on confidentiality, on the inner workings, as I understand them, not to be exposed, so by law neither myself nor the corporation can discuss cases. The privacy of anything that touches on genetic coding is so vital, its position has been compared to tons of nuclear waste buried in a mountain, fathoms deep, but still so radioactive you die from exposure just rock climbing on the surface. Get near coding and you're liable, as if contaminated by that truth, for those secrets.

Trust relies on security, and parentage is a fundamental building block, deeply personal, private, and in protected hands. If I told Lazarus my real identity and purpose, whether voluntarily or by coercion, Pangenica would first claim no knowledge of me, then have me transported. When I signed my employment contract, I knew that if the Confidentiality Clause was, even if only perceived to have been violated, the result would be catastrophic. Chester, somewhere in the facility cleaning shit, then reaching for his phone, whistling while he worked, thinking about what he'd do when he got home, take a shower, meet friends, get drinks, go dancing, then tap, tap into his phone, P-O-R-P-H-I-R-I-O-N, and I have a one-way ticket to Orientation Site Panopticon Palookaville.

Orientation Sites could be almost anywhere: the basement of an abandoned warehouse, a fork in a subway tunnel leading to a never-used station, a windowless airplane hangar at the edge of what you thought was a commercial airstrip in the middle of a desert, a corrugated metal structure at the end of a decomposing pier. All appear accessible to a random explorer, but you can't get in or out. I could already feel the brutalities inflicted on men and women whose cells would be adjacent to mine, the endless stream of water as lungs fill, the electric shocks, the repeating loop of jingles from the era of lithium batteries.

Outside, in whatever city, I'd be erased: She never worked here. Everyone from the accent coach at Crafted Identities to Crackhour would say the same thing. They would have no other choice, and after a while, they'd forget, and it would be true. Who? Zedi Loew, rhymes with slew or Loew rhymes with toe? Never heard of her.

The brochures bragging of pacific vistas had little in common with the stark halls and gray-green carpeting I'd just walked down. Lazarus House promised a kind of tranquility that turned unimaginable as morning wind rattled the windows of the original house, and chimes hanging on the front porch went berserk. Impossible to wait outside in the pouring rain, but then, someone was running down one of the corridors. I could hear rapid footsteps getting closer. Few people on the premises could actually run, putting one foot as quickly as possible in front of the other, eventually out of breath. Chester was one of the few potential Road Runners, legs spinning like wheels, holding up his phone, sprinting while calling the police: here on false pretenses, a danger to the community, threatening fragile patients, explosives wired to wheelchairs.

A car was turning onto the long drive. I ran outside holding Jane's orange high heels, running down the paved road. Despite the driver looking at me like I was a lunatic,

I slammed the door shut, and as the towering brick house with its many modernist wings receded, I twisted around, looked out the back window, expecting to see PomPom's private aide shouting at the car, waving his hands, an image that would verify my narrow escape, but there was no one on the steps of Lazarus House. It was possible the unseen runner wasn't Chester at all. I would never know and stared at the scenery, the Victorian houses and farm stands giving way to a small town. A storm was starting to pick up, wind coming from the southwest, blowing across the Sound.

And then the rain let up enough so that a few blocks from the station, I got out of the cab, walking around nearly empty streets, looking for a place to get a cup of coffee, finding a bodega, lottery and cigarette signs plastered over its storefront. Bodegas had disappeared from the city but taken root in surrounding towns and small metropolises. I got a regular coffee that tasted of cinnamon and sugar, though I'd put none in, and stood in the drizzle till it was almost time to get to the platform. In the station bathroom, I took off the glasses, stepped out of the orange heels and suit, changing into black pants and an olive shirt that needed to be ironed.

My phone vibrated, nearly falling off the edge of the sink. A text from Altner, he wanted an update. This kind of hovering oversight wasn't the D of A's style, which, in my experience, was consistently detached, as if to say, and to say at every opportunity, this is not my bailiwick, so you do it. I texted back I was making progress, though I certainly was not.

Once on the train, I opened *The Shadow Prince* and continued to read. The prince escaped Paris at night and made his way east, arrayed in women's clothing, a dwarf Hercules dressed like Athena, people would come to say of him. The prince slept in an alley, awakened by a sword at his throat, yet he ducked and parried. Now outnumbered, he's nimble and knows an entrance to a tunnel under the Bastille, little more than a rathole, and he escapes only to be cornered when he emerges. This time, the little man is beaten, robbed down to his clothing, and there he is naked, left for dead. The king sent his men to bring little Hercules back, and his close getaways kept me completely absorbed, even when I transferred from the commuter rail to the subway in order to get back to work, even when the subway stopped in the middle of a tunnel, and the conductor said train traffic ahead, or signal malfunction down there somewhere, which is just another way of saying no one gives a shit, you're underground, you're not going anywhere. Get used to it.

NINE

The remains of a smoked salmon sandwich lay in front of one of Altner's screens. Capers rolled onto its wrapping paper. He waved me to a seat before taking another bite, onion crunching in his teeth, but was careful to swallow before he began to speak. Pouring a finger of whiskey into his coffee, he then turned his screen to face me.

Security footage of a tall thin man, very short hair, getting out of his car, walking across the Pangenica parking lot all unspooled with black-and-white clarity. Raincoat flapping in the breeze, one hand keeping his porkpie hat on his head, he walked up to the building, passed through various security portals, no problem with iris or hand scans. The interloper had trouble moving through narrow spaces, but knew his way around the facilities. When he took off his raincoat and draped it over his arm, he was wearing a suit and tie, a pipe sticking out of one pocket, but otherwise he was a real neatnik, as were many of the technicians employed by Pangenica. Altner focused in on the tie, which had the atomic pattern of electrons circling a nucleus. The man entered one of the lab floors, hurrying past rows of giant glass boxes full of arrays of plates, themselves an array of divots filled with cells, past spectrophotometers that analyzed molecules according to how much light was absorbed by certain color compounds, bottles of solutions, shelves for gel electrophoresis, centrifuges, things as ordinary as a pile of used Eppendorf tubes, and Bunsen burners crusted with who-knows-what. From there he walked through an automation room, past equipment whose names were unfamiliar to me, mechanical arms that moved fragile embryos by day were now motionless in the middle of the night. He walked through endless corridors of shelf after shelf of embryos in their Phytosacks, a plant-based transparent, expandable encasement that enlarges as the embryo does. Nourished by steady infusions of Phytobase, the fetus, when ready, can kick out of it or use its head to pierce its housing. In some cases, a sterilized scalpel may be used if the child is in distress or just isn't making it through. This procedure is called the Julian Incision, after the doctor who developed it.

Endless hallways were always dark. You made your way through them using only a narrow pen light picked up wherever you entered and surrendered for sterilization and subsequent reuse when you exited. The Phytosacked were organized by sex, race mixture, final destination, and name of parents, as well as own name, if it had been assigned early on. The incubatoria shelves were mounted on what looked like conveyor belts, as each child in a sack became an hour older, it would move to the next slotted location, and its heart and other bodily functions would be monitored. Medical intervention would be summoned if necessary, though this was rare. Pangenica babies were perfect babies.

The man arrived at another door-lined hall and with a key card, walked into an office. A poster behind the desk looked like an abstract design made of railroad ties, like a map of a subway system, a polymerase chain reaction (PCR)

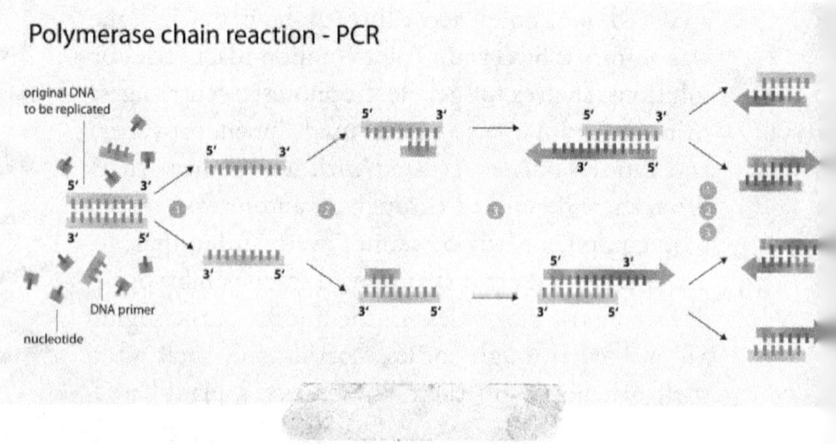

diagram from the early days of gene editing, a technique that was used in making copies by heating and cooling strands of DNA.

He wasn't supposed to be in that office. I knew this because Altner's heart rate was increasing, and I held my breath in order not to mirror his accelerated breathing. Feeling around under his desk, the man extracted a file taped to the bottom of a drawer. Then he leaned back and forth in a swivel chair, back and forth, as he went through its pages, stopping to write in a notebook he had with him. So far, the man seemed preternaturally calm for someone who was trespassing. The director zoomed in for a closeup of the document. It was the Singe file. I could see the photographs of the parties concerned clipped to the folder, but I was less interested in the papers than in the man's hands, which had begun to shake. Altner thought it was an issue with the recording, and he wanted me to focus on the file, so he zoomed in even closer. The man clenched his fists for a few seconds to control the tremor, then continued to write notes. I clenched every fiber of my arm muscles to control my own mirror shaking. The Director noticed.

"Are you okay?"

"I'm getting a cold."

"Stay out of the rain and go to Health Services for a flu shot."

Altner sped through this part, which must have gone on for some time, then finally, the man put some of the papers in an inner pocket of his raincoat, shut the office door, testing it to be sure it was locked, returned to the elevator, and Altner stopped the tape.

"That's Arthur 'Art' Waxman." He pointed to the man frozen at the elevator. "A lab technician who quit last week to take a position at Iridium Labs, a prosthesis research company. His security protocols had not yet been switched off, so he was still able to enter the building, though no longer working at Pangenica."

Before I could say the odds were good that someone in security was no longer working here either, Altner confirmed this was the case. Because of this footage, there had been multiple firings.

"But Waxman must know he was being filmed."

"He doesn't care. Why should he? He thinks he'll never be back."

The Director took another swallow and explained. Waxman was working on the connection between neurons and body movement, how those signals traveled from the idea of walking across a room to actually putting one foot in front of another. What does figuring out how the premotor cortex sends signals to legs and arms have to do with the Singe file?

Altner restarted the security footage. Waxman exited the elevator on our floor, made his way to Adjudications, and left the file on my desk.

He passed me a piece of paper, a receipt for a dinner, with an address and number written on the back. It had been an expensive dinner for at least two people. The handwriting wasn't Altner's, whose perpendicular loops and stems quavered. This writing slanted sharply, as if the writer was in a hurry.

"You'll have to ask him."

He poured another finger or so of whiskey into his coffee. There must have been very little coffee left in the cup, but even if there had never been any caffeine in it to begin with, the Director seemed his usual slightly unfocused, but in fact taking-in-everything self.

What he told me about Art Waxman: He was a solo child refugee from GorodEndoCittì, a megapolis that was firebombed in a territorial dispute between GorodEndoCittì and GorodEndoStadt. Such disputes are rare, don't receive a lot of attention, and are often considered fake news feeding the deep-fake industries, but Waxman's story has been verified by multiple sources. The day before hostilities began, his mother found him a place on a twentieth-century ocean liner that could pretty much stay afloat and propel itself forward most of the time. It tended to list to the starboard side no matter how passengers were distributed on and below deck. Denied entry at several ports, when Waxman finally arrived in our city, he suppressed his accent and presented himself as a lifelong citizen, trying to blend in to the extent he was able, but no one can truly ever fly under the radar altogether. He isolated himself in the study of protein coding as related to motor control, but he eventually abandoned that line of inquiry for what's known as the missing heritability problem, subjects one would think no one would have any interest in, but then his work came to the attention of Pangenica, Department of Incongruities and Heritability Fractures.

Of course, his history was known to us, and he should have been denied entry when a child. Despite GorodEndoCittì being reduced to cement dust and pit fires, his DNA, as he surely knew, was archived and not going up in smoke, so his reinvention of himself could only be skin deep. You can only fool some of the people some of the time. Waxman probably knew Pangenica was fully aware of his real identity, and when he was of no further use, he would have a date with a disappearachnik, but he would continue hopping from shadow to shadow as long as he could. He may have overestimated his value on the navalny-oppenheimer score matrix, as people are wont to do. We all have a tendency to overvalue ourselves from time to time, and the visibility and good intentions we think will save us. No such luck. Waxman had a daughter with a woman who had been disappeared. He had little contact with the daughter who, now an adult, lived in ShaharQalaUrbs and worked at Equigenica, a rival company we don't talk about.

Morris entered the office carrying a volume of bound records, which he then held out toward the desk. The

Director tried to stand to take the book from him, but fell back in his chair. I felt the tingling of nerves as he swayed, the pressure of ankle bone against the edge of shoe as he tipped to the right, almost falling to the floor as equilibrium evaded him, and he collapsed into his chair. Morris acted as if nothing were out of the ordinary. While I tried to stay in my seat, Morris ignored Altner's lost balance, saying brightly, "The records you asked for."

I took the cardboard-bound ledger from him, tempted to open it for just a moment, before I passed it on to crumpled Altner, but I was only a conduit, and had no business cracking the binding. When Morris was gone, Altner reminded me the Laveneer file needed to be resolved by Monday morning.

As I walked back to my desk, I passed Morris stacking law books on a cart, and I asked him what he had handed to the Director? The archivist was trained to be discreet about requests but often was not.

"Some shit from Accounting," he said.

"It seemed important."

"It is. Your boy Altner is in hot water. Have you ever noticed there are no pictures of his family on his desk or on his screens?"

No, I hadn't. Who even cared?

Morris seemed to have a periscope that looked into other people's houses, apartments, or offices. He could tell you an odd fact about someone out of the millions of facts that existed: what they read, watched, their financial bits and pieces, what they ate, their private conversations. He knew the sites they visited more than once, texts deleted, ads clicked on, or at least it seemed as if he did, and he would just toss a piece of secret salvage out from time to time. It put you on edge, on notice: What did he know about you? What spiders did he launch from his handheld device that wiggled in, broke down walls, had a look round, then reported back? Or maybe nothing at all, and he was just the archivist who knew things because of this job. I had no idea how he knew what he knew, only that he did. His new boyfriend was the archivist for the Department of Evolutionary Engineers, the chief executive officers, the ones who made decisions about applications, which traits should be amplified, which should be permanently off the table. Their directives were sent to the labs, not so much sent as coded in, so there couldn't or weren't supposed to be any errors. You rarely saw them, so the new boyfriend probably didn't know Morris flirted with Smith when the opportunity arose, or maybe he did if he watched camera footage. Hard to say. I never met him. Evolutionaries, evolutioneers, had private elevators in a separate building.

I collected Jane Ames's clothing to return to Crafted Identities, but before I could leave, a notice popped up on my screen that a severe storm warning had been issued, and everyone was advised to leave before hurricane-level wind and rain hit the coast. Crafted Identities was closed. Message from Crack to meet him on the roof to watch the tempest sweep in. It was something we did when the opportunity presented itself, watching the ocean spin out of control from the roof of a tower of labs.

I grabbed a yellow-green rain slicker that I kept rolled in a drawer, tucking the plastic jacket under my arm so the color associated with caterpillar innards wouldn't necessarily be identifiable as a raincoat, because I didn't want any questions about where I was going, as I threaded around a pattern of desks and cubicles, mostly empty. Nearly everyone was in the process of leaving, though the workday was almost over. Some were more nervous than others. So far, no typhoon had ever leveled the office park, and there was no reason to think business wouldn't go on as usual in the place for absolutely ever, but we could watch and imagine someone turning up the volume, pressing fast forward, shaking the snow globe till the thing cracked open and water, the Empire State Building, King Kong, and plastic snow fell on whatever there was to drift toward, something we would call the ground.

Rain seemed heavier as soon as I stepped onto the roof, but it felt cool, like taking an outdoor shower. The remnants of the Camperdown tree were gone, uprooted and blown over the edge, wind just calm enough for me to walk around for a few minutes. When I was thoroughly wet, I unfurled my jacket, put it on, and buried my hands in its deep pockets, but then the wind and downpour picked up again, and the roof wasn't draining fast enough. My shoes became soaked as water rose to my ankles. The wind made ripples across this miniature lake while actual waves in the distance turned into white caps. Plants and trees swayed in the wind, some toppling, even rolling over the edge. Trails of dirt, aerial spirals like little tornadoes of potting soil, leaves, twigs, branches, dead birds. Rain made wind patterns visible, ghosts of crazy energy—you can't see me, but I know you're here. I tried to figure out what direction the wind and rain were coming from, but air currents and bursts of rainwater were everywhere, as if the elements couldn't make up their minds, and so the roof was in chaos. In a few days, it would be someone else's job to right the planters; repot seedlings, flowers, trees, and vines; collect the plant life that had scattered to who-knew-where. This would be urgent because interbreeding of plants outside Pangenica's control can cause genetic bedlam in the plant community and must be controlled. I looked over the espalier escalier. It remained intact, sheltered by a wall and the angle of the adjacent building. That there was no one on the roof didn't bother me. At times like these, it was one of the few places of complete emptiness and silence in all of Pangenica, and even my synesthesia was quieted. When ocean waves became the size of a small apartment building made of green-black glass and cameras were torn from their posts, one nearly beaning me on the head, it was time to go inside. Where was Crackhour?

I pulled at the handle of the door that led to the stairs. It was locked. I kept pulling, hoping something would give, that the door would fly off into the wind, but it wasn't budging. Panes of glass from the greenhouses shattered and flew into the air. Trees on land were bent, stripped, uprooted. I tried ducking under a redwood table that was bolted in place, but there was no way any human grip could withstand gale-force winds.

A tin potting shed creaked on its moorings a few yards from the bulkhead, the sealed entrance to the stairs. The shed door came off in my hands, but I made it inside, thinking it would give me a few minutes before it, too, flew off the roof. The enclosure smelled of mold and wet soil, and things had been dumped in it, forgotten things. In the clutter, there was barely enough room to sit on the floor cross-legged. There were out-of-date kits for testing pH levels of soil and sodden wicker trellises, bottles of blue-green growth solutions that looked poisonous, and empty spray bottles. Beside a pile of trowels and shovels were seed catalogs and other paper rubbish. Wedged into the pile was an old biology textbook. I turned pages as I waited for either rescue or to be blown out to sea, less panicky because there was no one nearby panicking, so I looked at archaic diagrams of neurons and mitochondria as if I had all the time in the world, though I knew I certainly did not. The neural map of the brain looked like a guide to a mountain range rolled into something that resembled a ball. I tore out those pages, folded them, and put them in my pocket.

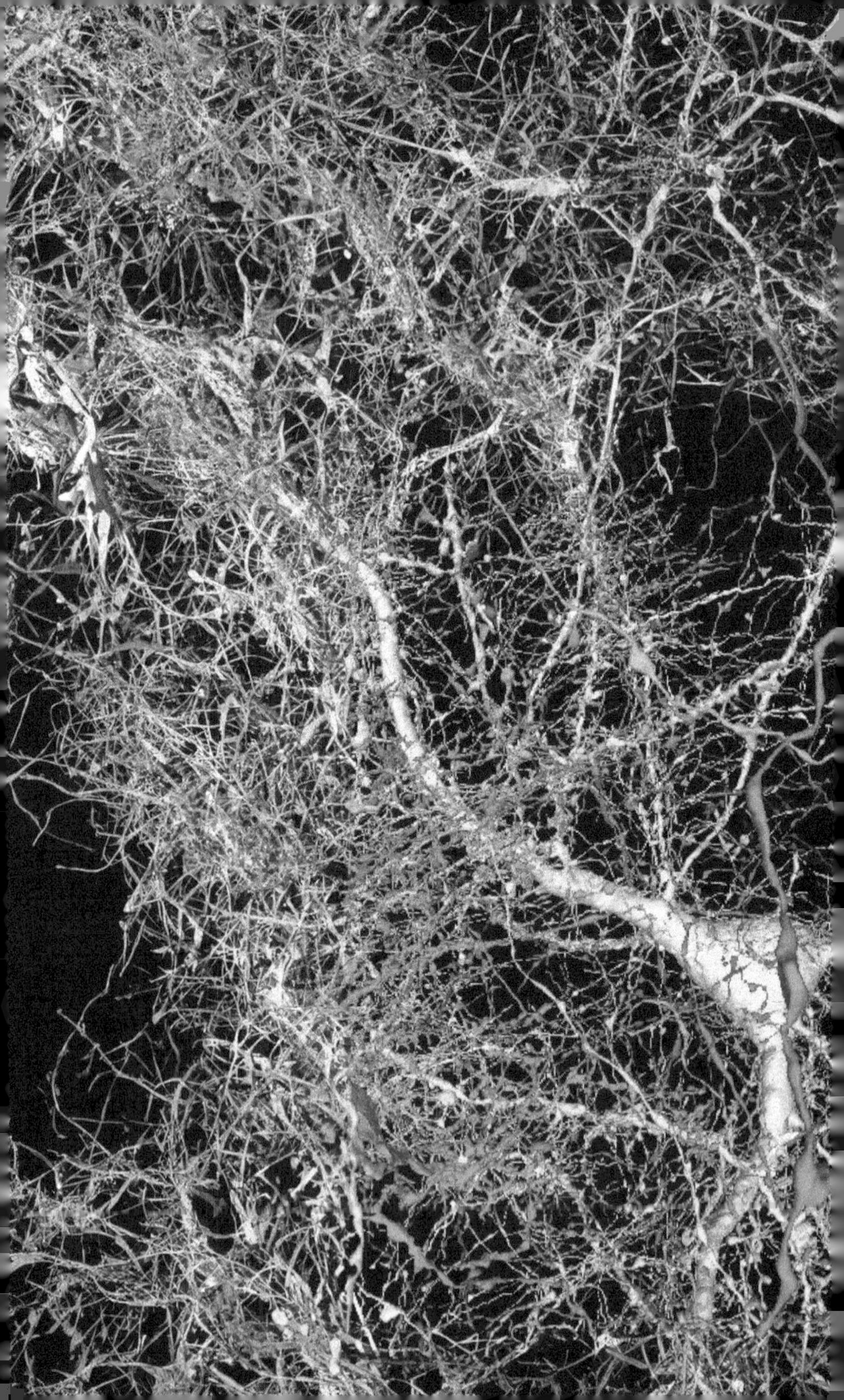

Wind ripped a piece of the shed roof off. I would be in the air next. I wanted a storm-chaser moment, like the ecstatic lost who take their clothes off in the snow, who will be overcome by freezing temperatures because they can no longer tell up from down, gravity no longer making sense.

The rest of the roof followed the first piece, and chunks of corrugated metal scattered. Not just roofing material but bottles, papers, and dirt became aerial. The door at the bulkhead opened and a man appeared wearing a black trash bag with slits sliced open for his head and arms. I just made it to the threshold before the older trees became airborne, but the man holding the door while his trash bag suit was whipped by the wind looked really annoyed. He was just checking doors and only found me by chance. The door locked automatically when there were severe weather conditions. This was a new regulation to prevent accidents, people being blown off the roof, in the event of a major surge, which this was, though no one had told me about the new policy, enacted because cameras had picked up unlawful activity on the roof.

We walked down the stairs to the elevator, and he peeled off his trash bag and threw it in the garbage can near the bank of lifts. His uniform bore the stencil: Security, Physical Plant Division. He appeared to be what he said he was.

TEN

I found Crack in the lobby sitting in the café drinking coffee, feet up on the opposite side of the booth. He looked surprised to see me. Where were you? Didn't you get the emergency alert that all roofs were locked and off limits during the storm?

I'd received no alert, I was certain. I'd gotten the storm warning, but nothing about roof access or any other change to building protocols. Crack unzipped his olive Pangenica hoodie. Pangenica hoodies were distributed free from time to time; I had a small stack of them. He looked as if he were only waiting for the rain to stop, of course, he didn't think I'd really go up to the roof while a hurricane level something was brewing, it was predicted the wind and rain were going to be that level of disaster.

I had a sense of betrayal, because he hadn't come up to the roof even though he claimed he thought I wouldn't be up there due to the lockdown. Let me say in my defense, I'd been living solo for so many years, and would sometimes ventriloquize the people I'd been, my assortment of Crafted Identities, a review of my favorite performances. Here's Isla Fentster talking to Jane Ames as if they're two action figures held by a child imagining a conversation. How are you? Not bad. And yourself?

When Crack appeared with his tales of calving icebergs and the midnight sun, he offered a little bit of effervescence to an otherwise dull office landscape, so I looked forward to meeting him on the roof, and felt stood up, stuck in the gale, while he was listening to the rain from the safety and comfort of the café, probably scrolling through pictures of his ex-wife who he stalked from time to time. He had told me how they met. He talked about her often.

After a life underwater, Crack's job—sitting in the darkened room at Krisper—made him restless, and the woman sitting next to him tapped keys with a similar kind of impatience. They knocked wheeled office chairs and laughed at animations of mutants gone haywire before they were completely deleted. When summer arrived and they'd been working together a few months, he took her diving, not to the Arctic, but someplace tame. Even though he was a pro, submersion was not calming to her, and she saw sharks and stingrays where there were none. He would pull her to the surface, pointing out the boat and the direction of the shore. It made Crack feel like he could do something useful for someone in an obvious personal way, and she seemed to enjoy being with him on land, if not underwater. The woman who became his wife animated viruses, headache-inducing neon green balls sprouting suction cups on stems.

How can a person be like a virus? A virine presence implies infection, something that infiltrates a host, exploits the safe haven to reproduce, then exploding in numbers, takes over, becomes the ruling class, though she wasn't like that, not totally, but sometimes, he thought, there were similarities. He once posed the question to me, do viruses always wear bad hats? If you got rid of all the viruses in the world, the ocean would be unregulated. Bacteria, unchecked, would go to town, and the ocean would become a soup of malaise. Crackhour's wife left him for a wealthy fellow, someone in development or futures, or both, he wasn't sure, and never really wanted to know, but someone with money he didn't have. She felt the poverty of his house with its mismatched chairs, sloping floor, air conditioner held together with duct tape, and was now living in a house with a view of vineyards, redwood trees, palms, cacti he imagined, on another coast. I wanted to tell him the duct tape didn't bother me, but there was also the fear that none of this should matter when his job could become as archaic as typewriter repair.

Once she left, he became obsessed, picturing her fingers tapping on a phone, leaving lipstick stains on a coffee cup, drawing cilia-like appendages on the one-celled creatures that swam from one side of her screen to the other. I'd heard all about it, and wanted to tell Crack he needed to think about ridding that virus from the ocean that was what was left of his consciousness, but I never did. Despite his preoccupation, I enjoyed going down to his sub basement once in a while, and now that I'd been stood up on the roof, I left it at that, that I hadn't gotten the phone alert that he and everyone else had. Crack finished his drink, and we got up to leave. The storm was fierce, but we could still drive away, or so we thought.

The ground floor was mostly empty, defended only by guards with nothing much to do that evening except sit in the café, helping themselves to day-old pastry and endless coffee concoctions. All the teenage workers had evacuated with their parents. During what was categorized as a severe weather event, uncontainable and unstoppable, the guards were only marginally useful, bound to be caught up in disaster, not rescue, and for the most part, and they knew it. Unauthorized people could be kept off the premises, but not catastrophic levels of wind and water.

Our steps tapped on the floor as we made our way to the front of the ground floor. I'd never seen Pangenica so empty. One of the guards sat alongside the conveyor belt that led to an X-ray machine, a feature of the metal detector at the entrance. When he saw us, he stood, adjusted his khaki Level Eight jacket, globe logo stenciled on the back. Eight was near the bottom of the security ladder, a lower-level guard. His pants were tucked into his boots. Style of pants were one of the few sartorial choices the guards had. They could be baggy, and so when tucked into boots they looked like genie pantaloons, or they could be tight, as his were, and I could feel the belt buckle cutting into my waist, the inseams leaving marks on my inner thighs. My butt ached from sitting on the stool near the machine with no one coming in for hours, though many left. He had been studying a screen, then he stood up, bullet-shaped and solid on his feet, and waved us over. Until the cameras were blown down to the shore and into the Atlantic, I was recorded somewhere yelling, pulling at the door, hiding under a picnic table. He had seen all of it, and he put his hand on his high-powered taser, then asked, as if he didn't know, why we were still in the building? Didn't we know the office park was in the Red Zone, mandatory evacuation? He turned his ID badge over, so his name wasn't visible. I only caught his last name, Debonis. His eyes were red-rimmed, white-blond eyelashes like bits of straw, and he swayed a little when he stood, so I did, too.

"No one could be so deliberately moronic," he said as he demanded to look in our bags. "Empty your pockets." His voice was quiet and soft, and he dumped the contents of our bags on the paused conveyor belt, examining everything down to our keychains, sunglasses, lipstick, ticket stubs, and contents of our wallets, then he tossed the textbook brain map pages into a bin, saying, who saves that shit? He looked at our phones and whatever other devices he found, whispered for our passwords which he claimed he, as security personnel, had the right to, then he repeated them out loud, slowly, carefully, with a very slight lisp, and when he spoke in this way, the tip of my tongue touched my front teeth. He stood opposite us, so we couldn't see what he was reading, then he held up his own phone and took screenshots. My fingers twitched. There were cameras in the lobby. He didn't seem to care.

His fingerprints should have signaled that he was unauthorized to be on my phone. Flipping through Adjudication files isn't like scrolling through infinite saveds looking for a discount car wash code. I tried to control the tapping of my own fingers, but he noticed and asked me if I was nervous.

"No. Why should I be?"

Debonis twitched and when I twitched, too, he suspected I was mimicking him, I could see it in his face, and that only goaded him in a way he couldn't articulate. He didn't understand motion echolalia was involuntary, and we could stand like this for hours, like facing mirrors.

"You were on the roof, girlfriend, you no longer get to say what is and isn't beyond limits." The guard put a foot on the edge of the conveyor belt and leaned in toward me until I could see the border of his beard and shaved cheek. I wanted to take a step back, but I was up against a wall already.

While the paper Singe file was in a locked desk drawer, the copy I'd mailed to myself was labeled ConSwitch, *con* as in consciousness, containment, concomitant, constabulary, contusion, contravene, consensus, continent, consonant, con anything, you name it. I assumed I'd be the only one who would ever see it, but when Debonis said the name, it sounded like an invitation to three-card monte, like who are you fooling, buried in the notches and seams of invisible computer code, you've got something to hide, Ms. Adjudicator, and even if I'm just a guard with my hand on the metal detector switch, I know one or two things that you do not.


```
What I am suggesting is that during
the first phase of assembling the cells
that were to become PomPom and Clayton,
a mistake was made. I am not seeking
reparations per se but am requesting
clarification, and the records of how the
editing and selection process took place
after our applications were approved, and
the creation of our children began.
```

The guard read out loud, but whether he understood or cared about what he read, I couldn't tell. With a shrug and an eye roll, his attitude seemed to be: In your self-important saved files and texts, the markers of identity, notating the pre-eminence of bits and pieces that declare the twisted ladders you people get paid to snip and re-glue are in some way vital, pretending what you do matters when in fact, everyone is a done deal, so why bother to pay people like you, while in the meantime some of us have real jobs, sticking our necks out here on the ground floor, standing next to radioactive machinery for hours at a time, looking at the innards of bags and cases as if lives depend on our vision, paying attention, not sleeping in front of the screen, detecting the cancer cells, the clusters of danger, because, in fact, lives do depend on us, the ones you don't even say hello to, or say hello to as if saying hello means you're a decent human. Ha ha. He took more screenshots, then put his hand on his taser again. As far as I knew, the guards had never used their weapons within Pangenica. What would he do now, fire into the wind and rain?

Debonis looked at Crack's lagoon-colored hair and my imitation Breakfast at Tiffany's necklace. With the tap of a finger he could summon a disappearachnik, maybe two, one for each of us. He steps back from the X-ray machine. Nothing to do with him. Just reporting suspicious activity. Long drive into the night in separate cars. Doors locked. No possible exit. No way to absorb the driver's calm business as usual nerve endings. The ride will end at a Nachtnebel site. No case to be made for Debonis making a mistake. No opportunity to plead the file was really nothing, and this is most likely a lie anyway. Foggy Night sites are a one-way queue for death row.

Debonis was not finished with us. He issued a warning to step further back and reminded us that I had been on the roof during a weather event, endangering not only my own moronic self but others as well. Then he held up Crack's old Gaiawe phone and asked if I'd been jilted in the hanky-panky department. WTF? Debonis grinned, turning the phone around so we could see what he was scrolling through: pictures of a woman getting out of a car, going into a diner with a man who was not Crackhour, the two of them seen through a window. Crack shrugged, those were old pictures of friends. The pictures on his phone, is that what he did in his spare time? He could pretend he was engaged in private investigations for a third party, but he wasn't an impartial hired witness, he was stalking someone who didn't want anything to do with him.

"I don't know who this person is, but I'd say, Mr. Crackhour, someone is following this woman around, and that someone must be you because the pictures don't look like they were sent by anyone, they're sitting here in a file, boring a hole into your phone. Did she know she was being stalked by someone, hiding in the bushes, the trees, behind a mailbox, possibly? Well, here, look at this one, maybe she sees the photographer."

He tapped some numbers, showed us that he'd sent our files to himself, then tapped some more numbers and began to speak into his phone. I'm not sure the guard was actually making a call. His voice sounded as if there was no one on the other end, as if he was faking a conversation, but I couldn't be sure. It sounded as if he was informing someone to expect copies of the files, and that person or agency or voicemail would be very glad to receive them. Putting the phone in a back pocket, Debonis let us know we were detained, as if the other person or agency he may or may not have been talking to had so instructed him, then he turned his back to us and joined two other guards, a man and a woman, sitting in a booth in the nearby café. His job was done, and Crack and I were left standing by the metal detector.

The two other guards wore bottle-green uniforms, a level below Debonis. One was razor sleek, the other clunky, and they glanced our way from time to time, while sharing a giant Dagwood Bumstead sandwich.

"If the generators go on the fritz," the woman said, pointing at the refrigerated display cases with a French fry, "all this shit will go bad, so we might as well eat it."

We stood in place idling and frustrated and trying not to show one another that we were actually getting nervous. Depending on who the guard sent the files to, we'd be arrested in a matter of minutes, but no one appeared either from within Pangenica or just outside in the parking lot, ready to transfer us to the land of Nachtnebel that no one returns from. I pulled the biology textbook pages from the trash: a map of a fruit fly brain, 100,000 neurons buzzing around in a space the size of a poppyseed alongside images of human hemispheres colored like wads of chewed gum, tangles of asymmetrical connectivity. The storm surge was letting up slightly, there would be a lull, then it would pick up again, and this pattern could repeat for weeks—problems compounded by areas covered in concrete, asphalt, and buildings, so no water could be absorbed, and flooding was a constant danger even when the rain stopped. There was nothing for it. Crack looked at his retrieved phone, but Debonis spotted him as he turned to pick up a fallen piece of crumb cake.

"I didn't say you could look at your phone, did I?" The two other guards continued to eat without looking up.

Debonis moseyed back over as if he had all the time in the world, and when he was inches from Crack, he grabbed him by the front of his Pangenica hoodie. Crack was the taller of the two, but he probably never had cause to swing at anyone. I couldn't even imagine it.

Taken by surprise, he shoved the guard onto the conveyor belt. I'm not sure if this move was accidental or intentional, but the jarring motion of his fall set the conveyor belt in motion. Debonis's arms and legs waved to recover his balance and regain the floor, but as he moved toward the X-ray, he was like a turtle on its back. The guard's torso blocked the opening to the actual machine, limbs tangling with the strips of felt that hung from the opening. I could feel the pressure of the edges of the machine against the backs of my thighs, and pain radiated out from my spine. Debonis was angry, but also terrified he'd be sucked into the apparatus butt first, and I felt this, too. He twisted his head around, my neck torqued, and he looked at me with hatred. I didn't hate Debonis, but mirrored his facial expression, and felt the acid of this humiliation. It wasn't a pleasant sensation by any means, and I just wanted to run into the parking lot and into the rain, but I was bent over in the same *V* shape as the stuck Debonis, except he was lying on the conveyor belt, while I was doubled over into the same shape, just standing on my feet. He thought I was making fun of him. I wish that was true, but nothing could be further from the truth. Because he couldn't move into the X-ray bed, the machine generated alarms, getting the attention of the other two guards. Crack grabbed me and pulled me out the door. The guards barreled toward us, scattering lettuce, tomatoes, salami, and unidentified food in their wake. A taser sliced my leg, but we'd already run halfway across the parking lot, and in the darkness and rain, it stung, but I kept going. Crack, they never hit at all.

ELEVEN

You could never take your eyes from a rear-view mirror, but if a disappearachnik had your vehicle on their screens, you couldn't ever really escape or transform the moving dot that you now were. There might be roadblocks for them in the form of power outages, car breakdowns, battery slow death, but sooner or later, most living things are one hundred percent findable.

Since our sprint to the car, Crack had become agitated, and so I became jumpy. His eyes bugged out a little from the pressure, and I felt my lids open wider. His face reminded me of watching someone watching a movie, maybe a horror movie. A character goes into the basement after hearing a noise, the faint sound of footsteps or breathing when they thought they were alone—always a bad idea, by the way, don't ever go into the cellar alone. He told me to stop mirroring him, but I couldn't, and he knew it. He was going to change his name, move south, and become a diving instructor. I'd never seen him on edge like this. If I could calm him, I would calm myself, and I had my own reasons for anxiety. I had no alternative profession waiting for me somewhere, and as an Adjudicator, you can't just disappear at will. You can be *made* to disappear, but you can't evaporate and then reconstitute yourself someplace else. Adjudicators know the inner clockwork of Pangenica, the mistakes, the half-assed attempts at extortion, or what will be framed as such, the consequences of hidden children, or of offspring who never sprang. It's thought to be a job for life, which, when you pass your exams, is both the good news and the potentially bad. You can't resign, but can be retired if your memory begins to fail, or you suffer a catastrophic accident, or succumb to an unpreventable non-genetically controlled illness. When you're younger you think: Great! I love my job! I can work forever, never imagining how you might feel when you have doubts, or when you're just plain tired, and you never imagine you'll be given a case that will cause you to end your days in a Nachtnebel.

Crackhour's car was made of parts from several different eras: button locks, exterior fins, bench seats, built-in door ashtrays that flipped out, and a working lighter. We hydroplaned through flooded roads, and I hoped, as I always did when he was behind the wheel, that he hadn't taken a Dormazin, a delayed-action one, at some point during the day and forgotten he'd taken it, which would not have been unusual in advanced or even semi-advanced addiction. Crack suddenly conking out, snoring at the wheel of his whack car, wasn't a scenario I expected I would live through. He drove down the gabion-lined highway until we were about an hour out from the office park, we could see just off the road a large donut wearing a top hat, monocle, and cane, the sign of a Donuts of Distinction, a chain that was open round the clock. Inside a lone employee wearing a top hat and a shirt printed with a tuxedo jacket was wiping down a counter. Donuts of Distinction had borrowed its logo from a twentieth-century company called Mr. Peanut. Across the parking lot from the D of D was Mr. Levant's Route 57 Fine Dining, and next door to it was a motel whose *No Vacancy* sign blinked with ambivalence, at least the *No* did, so it was unclear whether rooms were available or not. Crack pulled in, parked, and threw his Pangenica hoodie into the backseat and changed into an identical one, minus the insignia, threads hanging from where it had been snipped away.

Mr. Levant's silver-sided diner served a combination of East and West Atlantic food common to many diners on the outskirts of the city. Revolving displays of olives, purple-black or sprinkled with slivers of chili peppers, but also buttery pies loaded with mountains of Technicolor fruit: ruby-colored cherries, midnight blueberries, apples tinted green to indicate sourness. The owner served us tiny glasses of arak, gratis, he said, on such a night.

Enveloped by the warmth of the diner, the storm was outside and we would be okay for the moment, and we ordered Turkish coffee, which came with curls of lemon peel floating on the surface.

I tried to keep his fears from becoming mine. Maybe they should have been, but they weren't. Nobody at Pangenica cared if Crackhour followed his ex-wife, but if they knew I'd made a digital copy of the Singe Laveneer file, I'd be dog food at an Orientation Site. Disappearachniks wouldn't have to waste personnel or resources to torture me, I could absorb torture from sounds alone. The ConSwitch file, that title behind the Singe case, was just a column of type on a screen to Debonis, and there was a possibility it was just a game to him, the ability to threaten. The voice of reason said I had to keep working while I still had a job—to close the file and collect a paycheck. At least I had to keep up the pretense that I didn't do anything so very wrong, or at least that's what I was telling myself. If I stopped looking for the plaintiff, it would be an admission of my own guilt. Then Crack lowered his head, put a hand on my shoulder, his mouth to my ear.

"There's someone at a table behind us, someone I see in the elevator from time to time."

I thought we were alone at Mr. Levant's, but there was a man in the booth visible only to Crack from where he was facing.

"Someone from Pangenica is here?"

Crack nodded. "We have to leave."

I turned around, trying not to stare, but to get a decent look at the lined gaunt face, thick black-framed tinted glasses, yellow-gray hair sticking straight up. He stared into the rain, focused on the parking lot as if glued to the window. Yes, I'd seen him, it was the man who gave bags of clothes to gaming addict Vy in Admissions, but I doubted he could identify me or Crack, or would have any interest in doing so. Mostly, it's safe to say, at Pangenica, we don't notice others all that much. People look at devices, strangers don't interact because there is an atmosphere of not wanting to engage, because why bother? We are bundles of data, saleable or locked up, and if you can be looked up, it's not entirely known what rises to the surface, so what's the point?

"He works in Crafted Identities." When I'd seen the man, he was usually carrying books flagged with markers, always different books, and most of them, I noticed, had illustrations of people, not photographs, on their covers, so I assumed they were stories he mined for cataloging personality traits. He could have been the behind-the-scenes author of Ames or Fentster, for all I knew, but he never looked at me in the elevator, or if I passed him in a hallway, and I only noticed him because I had weekly, sometimes daily, dealings with his department.

Mr. Levant changed the music to Rosemary Clooney, shouting over the counter that he liked the old stuff, especially on a night like this, then he disappeared into the kitchen. "Black Coffee" filled the diner. I tried to change channels from Crack's anxiety and impatience to Clooney in an empty recording studio somewhere. I knew nothing about the audio technology of her time, so I made it up. I closed my eyes and sang into an air microphone.

I stretched out each molasses syllable. Crack wasn't captivated by my lip-syncing, but his breathing did become steadier. He was plotting his getaway, filling his oxygen tanks, testing his buoyancy compensator, getting his fins and diving suit out of storage, calculating he had about forty minutes of oxygen at a sixty-foot depth.

The man from Crafted Identities had stopped reading and was looking out the window watching seagulls dive into dumpsters placed near the blinking sign. A loud electric-blue plaid jacket that I hadn't noticed before was folded and placed on the table.

"Singe couldn't care less what anyone wore." I tipped my head in the direction of the table behind us. "While PomPom experienced someone who wore the wrong shoes as a deeply defective person, Clayton, like Singe, never noticed what anyone was wearing and didn't care." The children experienced notions of taste completely differently, but she was trying to justify her daughter's behavior as something beyond her control. It wasn't about snobbery but sensory irritation, like finding certain smooth textures itchy. Still, you wouldn't want to be stuck in an elevator with someone like PomPom.

Once again Crack looked over my shoulder at the man whose jacket would glow in the dark.

"Say she's right, and PomPom is Clayton, and Clayton was PomPom or some part of them was interchanged. Let's say this vinegar has consciousness." He picked up a fluted glass bottle with a picture of grapes; each grape had a smiling face, not a care in the world. "The vinegar is sophisticated. I'm not talking about general awareness of phenomena but specific and individual. It experiences the table as the ascetic acid that it is, not as anything else. Its consciousness is vinegar consciousness. It's pretty aware of the coldness of glass, the stability of the table, the vertiginous nature of being tipped over. Salt, on the other hand"—he picked up a saltshaker—"suffers from less awareness, not even aware of the chaos of grains tumbling over one another. Salt consciousness might be on the comparable level of an amoeba. It is the one-celled paramecium of condiments. Its sensory abilities and processing are limited."

“Crack, it’s just salt.” He was starting to sound like he’d stepped out of archival footage from the 1970s, people tripping and talking about expanded consciousness and the cosmos. If I didn’t know better, I’d think he’d dropped acid while I was on the roof, the real reason he never came up. Doorness had become a fluid concept.

“Vinegar is aware of the threat of being consumed, of losing its identity when combined with olive oil, ground pepper, lemon juice, maybe a little honey and spices. Salt is a little dim. For salt it’s all a jolly good time. Shake me on food. What do I care?”

He knocked the vinegar into the saltshaker as if to say you can do whatever you want to it, the salt won’t talk.

“But suppose they can switch consciousnesses. Vinegar starts to behave like it’s salt, granular and dumb, and salt like vinegar, liquid with the ability to burn the inside of your nose if you inhale too much, too close.”

Mr. Levant appeared with sticky squares of basbousa smelling of orange flower water and almonds. He removed the sentient vinegar. Crack fell silent, looking at his reflection in the window, then began to describe how, when he traveled to diving jobs, he wouldn’t always know where he was when he woke up.

“A few days in a motel room on a Pacific island, then a room somewhere on the Aleutian chain, then Baffin Bay. We expect to wake up in the same place, sort of like instinct, not even really a conscious thought, but then you wake up in an unfamiliar place, a hotel after a long trip or a series of motel rooms, which one is it? Consciousness may mean *aware*, but how aware? The moments between a dream and fully waking when you’re in a mishmash of consciousnesses until you settle on one image, cognition of who you are. At the moment of waking, there are two consciousnesses, before one gives way to the other. A photograph of a polar bear means home. A mass-produced painting of Inuit fishing through a hole in ice means a motel room. But it takes a few seconds or minutes to remember which is which.”

Or imagine the cortex itself is like a hotel and some other consciousness has rented a room for a night. A hotel is a temporary home. It's like a home but isn't. So, perhaps the same can be said of that state Crackhour described. Some other consciousness rents a room for a period of time, you think it's home, but it really isn't, not quite. Except what Singe proposed had happened to the two children was permanent.

Part of the rationale for his polar dives was to explore how life clung on and even thrived in harsh conditions, similar to what might be found on other planets. That was the point, or one of them, how in extreme heat and extreme cold, you still found microscopic animals throwing parties on underwater volcanic vents, sulfide chimneys, home to tube worms as long as cars, blind crabs, micro-shrimp who can withstand high temperatures and intense pressure. He nodded, of course, you know that. I nodded, too, because he did. The vents were called Godzillas, and they spewed boiling hot water, grew and collapsed, then started over. There were pictures of Godzillas in Crack's office, as well as some of the animals, benthos, creatures with no backbones, who thrived on the heat and pressure of the vents. In close-up pictures, they looked like monsters with outsize claws, thousands of legs, appendages with suction features in brilliant golden yellows, oozy coral, fresh blood red, though the colors were unreadable in their native environments because the creatures lived in places where no sunlight ever made it that far down. Perhaps Clayton, when he fell through the ice, thought if the lake were far deeper than anyone realized, if he fell far enough, he would hit a volcano in the middle of the limnetic zone, the middle of the lake that gave way under his feet.

PomPom became a bat, he said, but I thought he said *brat*. No, *bat*, he insisted, and I asked what he meant. He explained that we, as humans, can't experience the world the way bats do. We can never have a bat's consciousness, use sonar, know what it's like to hang upside down, have webbed wings, fly around caves at night. But PomPom, because of the switch, or what Singe claims was a switch, suffers the world as a bat, as Clayton.

In a way, by being, as PomPom put it, less than a brain in a jar, due to the accident, her consciousness, her experience of the world is diminished. Does consciousness only work in the present? How can consciousness be hereditary if it's about being alive, experiencing the world as it spins around you? Crack had no answers.

A car drove up to the diner, turned into the parking lot, and a woman got out, as if we'd summoned her from the dark. She struggled against the kind of wind and rain where you would expect someone to burst into a room, currents of air and water powering behind them, but the woman entered quietly, her silvery raincoat dripping, her inside-out umbrella soundlessly disposed of in a bin by the door. She had feathery greenish-blue hair, brown at the roots, oversized men's shirt hanging over black tights, silver rain boots.

Her clothes said she was ready to party like it's 1999, but her expression was serious. I just saw her for a few minutes as she walked past our table. She smiled at someone who could only have been the man in the booth.

I scrolled through my phone to find the picture of Singe and held it up to Crack who had a better view of their table, but her back was to him. Not clear, hard to say. Mr. Levant brought her a glass of arak, and Crack said they appeared to be ordering food. I told him I was going to ask if I could borrow their sugar dispenser. The one on our table had run out. So that's what I did, strolling past casually, I asked, and of course, the man said, yeah, take it, no problem. He didn't even look at me, and as I reached for the jar, I considered, for a second, knocking over one of the glasses of arak. That would give me more time to get a better look at her face, but she put her hand on the glass, impossible to spill. I returned to our table with inconclusive results. We needed more data.

Then Crack said he'd amble in the direction of the men's room and try to offhandedly look her way without appearing to stare. I watched him move past their table, head swiveled, then he realized the men's room was somewhere else altogether and had to reverse his steps. I ordered two more Turkish coffees and noticed he'd left his phone on the table.

It was unlocked, and I admit, I waited a few minutes, then I looked. A text appeared that was only an emoji, a face, hands over eyes, one peeking through, from someone named PartayGrl. The ceiling fan reflected in its black glass was hypnotic, so I held it in my hand for longer than I should have. I heard footsteps behind me and spun the thing on the table, as if bored, waiting, a tapping fingers kind of gesture, as if I was certainly not the kind of person who snooped.

He didn't think the woman was Singe, she was too young, though she did bear a strong resemblance to the woman whose picture was part of the file.

Her conversation with the man turned out to be brief, lasting about as long as it took to eat a slice of pie and drink the small glass of arak, then she pulled a hood over her head and made for the door. Mr. Levant offered her an umbrella, but she said no thanks, she'd be fine, her car was close by. Of course, plenty of parking on a night like this. Drive safe.

We could see her taillights as she backed out of a space somewhere in the parking lot, then she turned and drove close to the window. Crack tried to get her license plate number, but it was too dark to really see with any clarity. He took a blurred picture. Maybe it could be sharpened, pixels brought into focus, maybe. The motel sign blinked, reflected in the water pooled all over the lot.

"It looks like the rain is starting to let up. I'll drive you into the city. You have Waxman's address?"

I nodded but said, is it? Is it letting up? We could get a room here and drive into the city tomorrow morning. One room was all we would need. If the blinking *NO* sign was really meant to just read *VACANCIES*, it wouldn't matter how many. Sometimes when we sat on the roof or in the basement, Crack leaned toward me, but there was no configuration of believable words that could be assembled to convince either of us to share a room. We would never share a berth in a ship before a dive, and I wasn't even sure I wanted to, but sometimes it was a thought.

Crack stood, one palm sticking to the vinyl upholstery of the booth, the other on my shoulder, and I felt what his fingers felt, the by now dried cotton of my shirt, kind of stiff because of the chemicals and minerals that leach into rainwater. He knew I was feeling what his hand felt, the knob of my shoulder, and maybe he was enjoying the perception that I was his sensory double, at least for a few minutes.

"I have to get back to the city. Let's take a chance that not all the roads will be flooded."

"Are you sure?" If I said let's stay the night in this motel, and if he answered it doesn't matter what the sign says, I can't stay here, his impatience would override my embarrassment. It would be as if he said, in other words, sleeping with you or sleeping by myself is essentially the same thing, but then it had seemed to me that what interested him was watching me react to others, even if others included himself.

I would feel his not exactly brushoff, but hovering somewhere between thanks and no thanks, if that's what it was, so didn't risk it and said nothing. I stirred the grounds at the bottom of my second cup of Turkish, put the spoon in my mouth. The bitter taste lingered on my tongue and didn't dissipate. It was like a tattoo of taste, possibly permanent and managed to block out feelings of potential mortification.

"Yeah, we can do it."

We?

"Do you want me to drive?" I offered.

He shook his head, took the car keys from his pocket, and started to walk to the door. Mr. Levant gave us forgotten umbrellas, and we left him with one lone customer, the man from Crafted Identities, hand still around his glass of arak, last I looked.

As we walked to the car, I tried to slow down with each step, wanting to prolong the experience of the rain hitting arms and legs, the metal sign, the covered swimming pool in front of the motel. Everything glowed aqua, silver, black. But Crack was in a hurry, as if thinking, logically, what if the storm picks up again?

I half-hoped the car wouldn't start, roads could be lethally flooded in a matter of minutes, but after several attempts, it did. We drove past defunct power stations, dealerships with their battered flags and nylon inflatables, shuttered auto repair behemoths, cinder block caverns of lifts, hoses, machinery. As we got closer to the city, the buildings grew more dense: apartment complexes, fast food ramen and kabob joints with a few patrons hunched over counters.

While we drove, I texted Waxman, introducing myself and asking if we could meet some time over the weekend. There was no need to summon an electronic Crafted Identities persona, but that didn't mean he'd want to talk to me or to anyone else affiliated with the company. Much to my surprise, my phone pinged immediately. It was close to midnight, but he could meet in an hour and gave me an address that wasn't the same as the address written on the back of a receipt. He might not want me in his house. He might not want anyone in it. He might no longer be there himself. I wasn't going back to my apartment anyway, it looked like.

Who was Waxman? Why did Altner think to look at security footage to find him? The Director of Adjudications was a file and form guy, not someone who would go looking through security footage, especially if it meant extra work. When I'd asked Altner to help me find the missing parts of the Singe file, he waved me off with a don't bother me, that's your job, not mine. Then, a day later, the curled finger, come into my office, take a look at this, this former lab technician, he's the one you need to talk to. It was unlike the Director to suddenly be helpful.

"How do I even know the Waxman recordings are an accurate representation of the actual Waxman?"

"You don't. I don't know what to say about your boss. I don't know the guy. Do you want me to come with you to the meeting? If Waxman doesn't look like the man in the security footage, we'll leave."

The address Waxman sent me was in a northern borough of the city, alongside a park and an above-ground subway station. It was the city zoo, and it was closed. The entrance gates were larger than life painted metal, silhouettes of looming elephants, palm trees, apes the size of King Kong. No human was visible anywhere in the vicinity. Crack was not amused. He knew the street, a broad avenue, and hadn't checked any mapping device that would have told us, oh, yeah, that's the fucking zoo. He had driven out of his way only to be pranked, and he wanted to leave right away, but I convinced him to wait a bit.

As we sat in the car, we could hear animal noises in the night: low-pitched roaring of the big cats, not aggressive or loud, but ominous in their confinement and frustration. If they could get out, what would they do, where would they go? I imagined leopards, tigers, lions roaming subway cars left open at the last stop. The doors close, and they're taken downtown where there are more people, toward both a likelihood of being captured but also more food opportunities. The image of a Siberian tiger tearing through a department store, toppling mannequins, spraying stacks of sweaters, was sort of funny, but the hunting part, less so. Of this, I didn't want to think too much. There was movement near the locked turnstile at the entrance, but it was just shadows from streetlights. A front-loading garbage truck arrived to empty dumpsters and the animals went crazy, sensing what they couldn't see, and for some of them, the contents of those dumpsters: ice cream cones, petrified French fries, pizza crusts, all that food detritus was a feast disappearing into a jumbo carting vehicle. Crack turned over the engine. He'd had it. This was bullshit. The men finished, the truck pulled away and maneuvered back into the empty street, but there was a man who remained standing very still, looking at us. The man in the security footage was tall, thin, wearing a wide-brimmed porkpie hat and a loose, flapping-in-the-wind raincoat. It was Waxman, and just like in the footage I'd seen, he looked like a walking pencil. He had a cigarette in his right hand, and I would learn he could smoke one hundred Chesterfields in a day, interspersed with joints.

Crack unsnapped his seatbelt. "I'll hang out with you guys."

"No, it's okay."

"This is the zoo. Where does he plan to hold this meeting? In the Reptile House?"

"No, really, it's fine."

I got out of the car as Waxman got close. He didn't look happy to see that I wasn't alone. The rain had diminished to an erratic drizzle, and he glared as he folded his umbrella.

"Who's your comrade? I was under the impression you were solo." He spoke with a distinct city accent, one that's rarely heard anymore.

"He's leaving."

Crack had his window turned down and leaned out. "Can I see some identification?"

The man looked like the guy from the footage Altner had shown me, but before I could object, Waxman took out an ID and shoved it under Crack's nose.

"It says here Vachsmann, not Wax Man." But as he was speaking, he realized his mistake. The spelling was different but the pronunciation was the same.

"How do I know who you are?"

"Fair enough, asshole." Crack pulled out his Pangenica ID.

The man I could only think of as Waxman looked at the ID, then looked him up on his phone. "You're an animator.

A cartoonist. Listen, Mr. Funnyman, I understand you don't know me. It's the middle of the night, and the nearest biped is covered in fur. I'm going to put this bracelet on your girlfriend here, so you can track her. You will always know where she is."

He slipped a circle of wire on my wrist, grabbing my wrist so quickly and quietly, it was done before I could pull away.

"Now you can be on the road. I don't have oceans of time, Mr. Cartoon, and I will only speak to Loew alone."

The standoff continued for a few minutes, then Crack finally drove away. I wasn't angry at him. It was better that he wasn't in the room when I spoke to Waxman but not for Waxman's benefit. Crack presented noise, distraction, reactiveness that would draw me away from the conversation with the lab technician, who was scowling and impatient. I frowned in mimicry, not annoyance. What was his problem? I was the one who had to wait for him and now what? I still thought of him as Waxman, a crabby superhero made of wax, a vulnerable material prone to melting, but it then can be refashioned, taking into account a percentage of loss due to heating. Wax Man can be molded to take on other forms. He offers light when he burns in a kind of martyrdom, then he's gone, only a small amount may remain wedged somewhere.

There was no place nearby to sit and have a conversation, so I was left standing beside the tall thin man in a wrinkled raincoat while Crack's taillights disappeared around the underpass that led to train tracks. Waxman asked for my phone, removed the battery, then handed it back to me.

"What about this?" I held up my wrist.

"It's just a piece of wire. It doesn't go anywhere." He grabbed my arm, twisted the wire off, then tossed it behind a tin King Kong.

Motioning that I should follow him, he unlocked an *Employees Only* door to the side of the entrance, explaining he had access because of a project he was working on. It wasn't clear to me if this work was being done in the present or at some point in the past, but it didn't matter really. What mattered was he had keys that worked, and we were in. Just past the shuttered ticket booth, he stubbed out his cigarette and took a joint from a case, lit it, and smoked as we walked. He didn't ask me if I wanted any. Signs pointed to different habitats, but he moved around as if he knew the place and didn't stop to read them. I couldn't keep track of where we were and was completely lost in the tangle of paths and animal environments.

The zoo at night, up close, was a noisy place, even louder than the zone outside the gate. Giraffe vocalizations sounded like humming, and monkeys howled like sirens stuck in echo chambers as we walked through Junglemania, then past the muted squawking of aquatic birds diving into the artificial waterways of their enclosures. Baboon House smelled like it hadn't been cleaned in a while, and Elephant Savannah was dark and empty, disposable syringe wrappers clustered against a fence. The large animal vets don't always clean up, Waxman said. The elephants are elderly, rescued from circuses, in need of a lot of medical attention. The vets are young interns, overworked and underpaid. They can be depressed and careless. Waxman's joint was down to maybe half an inch, and he stopped, turned his back to me, and inhaled those last shreds as if taking any more steps depended on it. It was strange to see this tall man bent over a miniscule thing, holding it to his lips like that.

On the edge of Elephant Savannah was a locked food kiosk in the shape of an igloo, vending machines lined up in front of a mural of polar bears and seals. Waxman got a coffee and a couple of Zagnut and Mars bars. I asked him if it was much further, not in an annoyed way, just wanted to know where we were going, and he snapped at me that the zoo at night is an off-limits place and consequently, there is a measure of safety here. Okay, Dr. Wax, I understand, this is a safe place for a conversation that isn't supposed to be happening. He was irritated and tired. His feet ached, and he was out of breath. All those things, I felt, too. I looked around in the dark for an animal in order to absorb some other creature's moods or sensations, if that was even possible, but they were little more substantial than shadows and sounds.

We entered Big Cat Pantheon, up a steep hill and around a bend in the path was an area called Tiger Express. Waxman led me to a red pagoda-shaped structure, and once inside, he turned on a light. The back of the pagoda was glass, so visitors could look into the tiger exhibit. Signs on the walls gave the names of the tigers: Genghis, Sherman, Madame Mao, and Patsy, as well as information about the endangerment of the species and their mating and feeding habits. The tigers had been rescued from the incursions of poachers into their ever-shrinking territory. There was no hope for their survival but to be in zoos, though of course they didn't know this, Waxman said, therefore they pace and pace, even in this tiny approximation of their native environment. The pagoda had benches and a table to encourage visitors to spend time watching the animals. Waxman took a seat with his back to the glass, and I sat opposite. As he leaned forward, he was disarming.

Removing a sheaf of papers from a pocket inside his coat before he would speak to me, he wrote notes in the margins, jabbing with a pen, still angry, though I didn't know why. He didn't even look up at me for what seemed like too many minutes. Slurping coffee, biting into chocolate, his body strained over his clothes. I didn't want to feel his straining lungs, the tension of skin against cloth, buttons, zippers, and tried to focus on the tigers, trying to match name to face. Tigers, the sign told me, are nocturnal, they hunt at night, and these four, though there were no surprise prey in their environment, sniffed around for nonexistent meat on viable legs. Genghis had stripes above his eyes that looked like lightning bolts, Sherman had a bigger, sort of purplish nose, Madame Mao had yellow-brown eyes while the others all had green eyes, and Patsy was the smallest.

She was the only one I was sure I could identify as she swatted something, light glancing off her claws. If it weren't for the glass, both Waxman and I could easily have been what's for dinner. Every other creature around me was, in one way or another, hungry and on the prowl. It felt as if not a single one was asleep.

Waxman capped his pen and wiped his hands on his pants, and since he still wasn't talking, I asked him about the footage I'd seen of him reading the Singe file. He didn't seem alarmed. At the time he had known he was being filmed, of course, there were security cameras everywhere.

"But you weren't even working at Pangenica anymore. You only got in because your ID was on its last gasp, but how did you get that file? It should have been in Adjudications, not in a lab."

"I didn't work in a lab. I was the Director of the Department of Neuronal Correlates."

Altner had said nothing about the Department of Neuronal Correlates. I'd never heard of it.

"My department was tasked with looking for the switch that DNA might use to turn on neurons—the hand that reaches across clouds to touch the other and presto: animation. We needed to get into the nuclei of human cells and fiddle around. We were looking at the neuronal correlates of consciousness, which parts of the brain are firing when you experience a splinter, a kiss, the taste of orange or chocolate." He held up a Mars wrapper, asteroid streaking across the label.

If consciousness, or some aspect of it, is passed down from one generation to the next, then it served a purpose, it had value in guaranteeing and enhancing survival. It was needed. What happens if you add more pepper to the soup, more rice, more carrots, onions, garlic, potatoes, parsley, until there's not so much liquid left, is it still soup? If you poke consciousness, then what? It doesn't take much, a little anesthetic, and poof, it's in abeyance, gone, out the window, at least for a while.

I'd thought of gene editing like writing a movie script for future persons. You get to know everything, or almost everything, written in the language of the genome. As an Adjudicator, I was sort of a handyman, fixing the minor errors, making sure Pangenica had the evidence to cover its butt—only clean hands here, no payments due, the plaintiffs can go fry ice. The labs were another territory where I assumed the creatives had everything under control, where Phytosacks were filled and grew and the miracle of birth went off without a hitch, for the most part. This was a fairy tale that pissed Waxman off.

"What do you know about gene editing sitting in Adjudications? Let me tell you something, *robot* means slave in Czech. The Golem could be said to be a kind of robot, human-like but not a DNA-bound human. He lumbered through Prague, *emet*, the Hebrew word for truth written on his forehead, that was the symbol that animated him, gave him life and purpose. When Jan Švankmajer's surrealist puppets made of a similar clay from the banks of the Vltava, transform from Méliès's style devils to Gregor Samsas to ordinary hapless walking-around citizens melting into one another, they are uncanny and move in what we think of as herky jerky robotic, whether a function of strings or stop motion or both. These creatures don't actually have consciousness, but their function is to appear as if they do. In a robot language, when the time comes, it's possible *human* will come to mean slave, that's our AI-inspired fear, that our slots in the universe will be reversed, and consciousness will be an expendable feature, a cause for alarm and suppression."

Somewhere to the north, where we had entered, an alarm went off. I looked at Waxman as if to signal time to leave, but he barely registered the sound at all.

"No cause for panic." And, of course, I knew he felt no panic. "Nightly feeding rounds. The crew will start with the giraffes, big draw positioned at the entrance, you know, then make their way to the monkeys, birds, reptiles. By the time they get to the pagoda, we'll be finished and long gone."

"But if it's someone with access, why would an alarm go off?"

"The alarms to back entrances are set like opening your car door. A short alarm, then nothing." He became annoyed. To him I was an easily distracted Adjudicator, a nobody he had to endure for a limited amount of time, little more than a bunch of transistors masquerading as neurons.

"Are you paying attention? I have a lot to tell you."

Why would only back door alarms be set this way? The siren stopped, so I said nothing.

Waxman asked me if I had explored many parts of the office park, labs, or other buildings that made up Pangenica Central? I hadn't. Why not? It was there, why not look around? This had never occurred to me, but Waxman had perambulated even remote sectors, like the green Monde Center where cell-fate maps were plotted to determine how genes—those pesky particles of data and triggers—command our fifty-seven trillion cells: activate, repress, repeat. Peering through the hedges cantilevered over the grounds, he silently advised the mappers in white coats that you can try to corral the chaos of mutations because evolution isn't always progress and purification, you know, but what will happen generations hence is out of your hands. As he'd watched them spin in their chairs and roll from terminal to wall-size screen without ever standing, humanish + chair reflections in the white linoleum, he'd said to the glass, you could clone Van Gogh's ear but what use would it be without the rest of him? Of what use is a solo ear? A film prop, maybe, but not even. Waxman had circumnavigated the Crowne Training and Storage Facility bollarded by black oil drums, white on the top and bottom, like rows of giant sushi. The Crowne's windows were opaque, impossible to know who was trained there and in what capacity, or what was stored inside: failed savantist traits, hard drives, unreadable floppy disks, codes for useless proteins, manuals on steganography, the technique of hiding state secrets in strands of DNA, though this practice had been outlawed, it was impossible to police. He did these walks in the morning, before most clocked in.

"Last Monday, I'd gotten in very early, as was my preference. I took the back entrance near the loading bays, so I wouldn't run into anyone. I wanted a few extra minutes of quiet to breathe the sea air and not have to engage in conversations. At that hour, deliveries were being made to the incubatoria, Gregor Pavilion, northeast sector. Palette after palette, drum after drum of Phytobase."

He asked me if I'd ever seen the vast system of conveyor belts that transports the fluid, a hypnotic system, when in motion, like veins, arteries made visible. I hadn't, and what he interpreted as my lack of curiosity was, to him, disappointing. So, there he was taking in the mechanical majesty of what could also look like a giant airport baggage claim area when one of the Gregor Pavilion workers spoke to him.

"He knew my name, 'Yo Wax-Man,' he said, like that, 'have a blessed day!' I was wearing the Pangenica identification lanyard with my name on it, but it was hidden by my jacket and couldn't have been visible to him from where he stood. He was wearing sunglasses, though it was early in the morning, so the sun was only just coming up, and the sky was dark with storm clouds. I was walking past palettes stacked miles high with nutrient tanks when I saw a number of Pangenica folders in a bin of faulty Phytosacks, the ones that arrived from the factory with irregularities, pinprick holes, wrong sizes, it happens, and they look like deflated raisin-colored balloons. The tanks of Phytobase nutrient solutions were transported to one of the areas where embryos were incubated until PickUp Day, but neither the sacks nor the files were disposed of correctly and should never have been mixed together in any case. Files to be discarded are destroyed on-site, never shipped to a dump, and the bin itself should not have been anywhere near the loading bay. Phytosacks are burned. I wiped sticky fluid off the cover of the top one. It was gibberish, useless data, as far as I could tell. I tossed it back, and looked at another. The same. The third file was your Singe case." He didn't pronounce Singe like describing something burned but rather *Sing-a*.

Patsy lunged into a clump of bamboo. An animal produced a piercing high-pitched squeal. She had caught a rat the size of a terrier. It screeched and clawed, but it was a hopeless battle; gray fur and blood spattered the glass. Another tiger, Genghis possibly, bounded from out of the darkness, and they fought over the dismembered rodent. As big as it was for a rat, for the tigers, this was little more than a midnight snack, like half a Zagnut bar, and they fought in their frustration. Waxman got up and banged on the glass with a slide rule that he pulled out from in an inner raincoat pocket. "Stop it! Boys and girls!" As if that would have any effect whatsoever. Leaning on the glass, he spoke to the tigers fighting over a shred of rat, like a stoned Dr. Doolittle who could talk to animals, who knew they had consciousness, who would tell you, whether grouper, crow, tiger, or chimp — all felt pain and joy as administered by the goings-on in whatever passed as a densely packed cortex, because really, humans have no monopoly on those. The tigers ignored him, and he turned back to me.

"Sometimes I think that the fact that I was the one who found the file couldn't have been a coincidence. But who knew my habits?"

"What did you do after you found it?"

"Nothing. At first, I thought this woman must be a crackpot, hallucinating junk science. What defines an individual if we're nothing but a stream of ancestors, now pruned, grafted, and expanded? The problem with deliberate selection of traits is that no matter how much you think you've dotted every enzymatic *i* and crossed every proteinous *t*, the environment laughs in your face. It is influential and unpredictable. With genetic manipulation, you think you're making the invisible visible, but not so fast, pal. However, if you control consciousness, environmental influences can take a backseat."

Someone knew what he was working on, he was certain.

"Neuronal Correlates was a shadow department, not listed in Pangenica's directory nor could it be found on maps that included a layout of the building. I knew this, and it never occurred to me that there was a precedent for what we were doing, but when I found the Singe file, it meant someone had been there before us. What happened to PomPom and Clayton, was it intentional or an accident? Singe sounded as if she was open to either answer as long as it was an answer, but I came to believe the switch was intentional." Waxman didn't believe Singe was talking about personality when she wondered where this petty, continually aggravated child came from.

"That was the beginning," he said as another tiger appeared from behind the bamboo and eyed us through the glass. "Singe asked, what are you experiencing that I'm not? She opened a door that needed to remain shut."

She was patted on the head and told control of the genome can't be as absolute as we would like to think, there is still an element of randomness, of accident, and the case file, which should have been destroyed, was mis-shelved, I'm guessing, or fell down a Pangenica-devised black hole of information, until somehow it resurfaced if Waxman was telling the truth. Waxman took another joint from his case and lit up. At first it was wedged between his middle and ring fingers, poking out in what seemed like a somewhat precarious position. Then, as he smoked it down, he pinched the stub between his thumb and pointer finger, holding the remains close to his mouth. Then he exhaled.

"As I read the Singe file, it became apparent that Neuronal Correlates was the only department with access to the ways and means to try what she believed had happened to the two children. I looked Singe up the day I found her file. There was nothing. The case doesn't exist. You should know mining archived data has its risks, like getting to the center of the maze and finding the Minotaur. He's pissed off and hungry, worse than a tiger stuck with only a mouthful of rat and wanting more. You have the only paper copy."

"I don't have the paper copy. It's in my desk."

"It will be gone by the time you go back into work Monday morning. That's the end of it then."

I held up my phone, there's the file, see, and felt Waxman's relief as he exhaled. He returned to the bench, took out another Mars bar, had another swallow of coffee.

"Do you want me to send it to you?"

"I remember what I need to remember, and I want no part of the actual file."

The sounds of the night zookeepers on their rounds were getting closer. Squawking from the aquatic birds' environment picked up in pitch, and I imagined men and women restocking the ponds and streams with fish. Waxman was sensitive to the noise, too, and assured me they knew him here. They were doing feedings more quickly than usual, and we might see them soon, after all, but his anxiety was picking up. He took his slide rule out again and moved the cursor back and forth, tapping as it hit the brackets like a combination percussion instrument and worry beads.

"Thirty years used to seem like a long time, a generation. Now it's a length of time I can hold in my hand."

I assumed Waxman was referring to his fiddling with neuronal correlates, how a protein taps a nerve, a dendrite, a synapse, you feel fear, and you run as fast as you can, how quickly conjecture turned into the possible, but what did I know?

"Have you ever seen a picture of Singe's house?"

I hadn't, and he hadn't either, so then he must have been there in person.

"She lived in a water tower at the top of a building scheduled for demolition. The building was mostly glass, had no functioning elevator, so one had to take stairs. She made a home in the empty tower, but there was very little in it."

This wasn't so unusual. There was, and had been, a shortage of housing and people constructed shelters anyplace that had even the idea of a roof or walls. I was lucky to have my apartment as long as my ex-husband didn't return to the main city island. If he did, I would be looking for water towers and abandoned subway stations myself.

"There was no evidence of PomPom or Clayton. No pictures, drawings, clay dinosaurs, no saved toys or books."

"Can you tell me where she is?"

He shook his head and said he wouldn't tell me even if he knew. Singe was radioactive. You can't get near her; he took a final bite of Mars bar. Even her trail was luminous with contagion, so those following him would be led to her, if he were to return to the water tower, which she'd most likely vacated long ago. There was a longing in his voice, the way he pronounced her name with two syllables and prolonged the second one. He had found her, recently I'm guessing, then had to disappear and pass the file on to someone else. The file was now fixed to me, an opportunistic infection, something addictive and debilitating at the same time. Its contents were stuck in his head like an earworm, and he needed no copy of it. Waxman had said it would have been useful to study someone with limitations, but such people were very difficult to locate, if they existed at all. What is knowable via data and what can continue to be concealed? How do you contain the uncontainable whether DNA data or radiation from nuclear power rods when even the depleted are leaky?

Singe's file opened intriguing possibilities, but at Pangenica appearances are paramount, so a certain amount of glitched material is swept under the rug. Her accusation went to the heart of the I-beams, concrete, and rebar that help keep Pangenica standing and structurally sound over time. How could Singe not have realized what a time bomb her questionnaire would be? She could have kept her suspicions to herself, but she was a troublemaker. Blame her parents, if you must. This was the child they ordered just as their parents had ordered them, and so on, nothing but troubled turtles all the way down. The kind of people who say why not stir the pot? There's one in every family with revolutionary tendencies that couldn't be run out of town entirely. This is a trait that crops up from time to time.

The sound of the night keepers grew closer, and the fourth tiger joined the other three. The tigers must have heard them, as well, because they paced more rapidly. One lunged at the glass. They recognized that the sound meant food. I didn't want to see them destroy a live goat or rabbit or whatever they would be fed. For the first time Waxman became visibly nervous, then agitated, and asked me to follow him. We went outside and around the back of the pagoda where a stainless steel door was set into rock.

"This is a double security door. I'm going to open it, go through a short corridor to another door which I will open, letting the tigers out. I'm going to give you a head start. You run down that path," he pointed, "through the Outback, Gator Island, and out the western gate. From there it's two blocks to the subway station."

I absorbed his terror in addition to my own, but he put a hand over my mouth, and in a deft motion, unlocked the first door with his other hand. The tremor I'd noticed in the security footage when it went close-up was back, and his hand shook as his fingers pressed against my lips.

"I can't outrun the person who followed me here. When he's standing where you are at the moment, I'll open the second door. You should leave now."

He reached into his raincoat and handed me an envelope, then he pressed my phone battery into my hand. His nerves were firing, heart pounding. Mine was as well, but my body could sustain that rate. I wasn't sure a heavy smoker would be able to. Why Waxman chose to keep talking to me even when we first heard the night keepers who weren't night keepers was netless high-wire acrobatics. He repeated that he couldn't outrun those who chased him, as he walked through the rock-hewn corridor, and I could see him put his hand on the second door.

I ran. Once the door opened for the tigers, Patsy, Genghis, whichever, none would pause before Waxman, shake their respective heads, as if to say, not you, boss, then go straight for a hired assassin. Death by big cat for Waxman, like Clayton yelling from the ice before falling through — were they planned exits or solutions borne out of necessity? I heard no screaming, and roars grew distant, as if recordings of roars coming from far habitats, but there was no reassurance in that.

A long hill gave way to Penguin Partyland, a rocky environment surrounded by a moat. Where was the Outback? The zoo was almost totally dark in places, but the path Waxman pointed out to me was supposed to be straight. I ran through Apes: Our Ancestors, then past the Reptile House. No Outback entrance assembled from shields and canoes, no pathways to koalas or kangaroos. I must have taken a wrong turn because I found myself back at the base of Tiger Express, ominously silent. I turned on my phone's flashlight, just for a second. The path forked. I had gone left, so I ran right. Still no Outback or Gator Island. My mother had been a runner, and I knew she counted or rhymed as she ran, step after step, one foot in front of the other in a pattern of steps and pacing, even if panic-fueled: crater, mater, pater, later, hater, tater (tots), equator, it was said of litigator Smith, emphasis on gator, he was that tough. Darth Vader, raider of the lost, Seder.

I was breathing in shorter and shorter spasms. The Skyfari Monorail traveled across Junglemania. Someone was running up a hill parallel to the one I'd been on. The footsteps sounded too rapid and confident to be Waxman with his smoke-strafed lungs. They were getting closer, but the monorail was a dead end. You either got on it, or you had to go back the way you came. Lit pylons gave some illumination. I jumped over the turnstile, up the stairs to the platform, and into the front pod, one that read *Skyfari*, letters formed of lizards, anteaters, a splayed bear was the *K*. The roofless pods were arranged like beads on a necklace but in the middle of the night were going nowhere. I crouched in the dark listening to footsteps pass under the girders below. The monorail was still.

Until it started to move. In this part of the park, lights well behind me, darkness was total. I began to count, trying to equate time and distance, but I had no idea how long the monorail was, the yards, fractions of a mile, or miles, it traveled. I could have been moving vertically into space for all I knew. Did a second equal five feet of distance? I had no idea, but I counted, so I could maintain some sense of orientation in the night. How deep were the ravines and streams below? Those were also unknown numbers.

Then, high above unseen and unidentified animals, the monorail stopped. Though it was motionless, it reminded me of a roller coaster I'd once ridden called the Vomit Comet. I'd had this urge to jump out, and now, years later, sitting in the pod was like being tied to a chair with no escape imaginable, except I felt physically pulled to the edge of the car. I unclipped the safety belt. The impulse to jump out was constant, difficult to squelch as minutes ticked by. No one was telling me to jump. No one was assuring me a fall was survivable; all the animals below were nervous around people and would run away when they sensed my approach, but maybe pythons coiled up the pylons. I could hear the insects of the region, crickets and cicadas that were not native to jungles and savannah, and I looked over the edge of the pod. Most of Junglemania was black, but near the lights were pools of illumination. There was some rustling, maybe the shadow of an arm or leg, hard to be certain. If I jumped and survived, I might encounter silverbacks lucky not to have been captured by poachers who sever their hands to be made into ashtrays, elephants whose legs were made into umbrella stands, wide-eyed baby chimps who could be living in a lab learning human sign language while humans watch to see if their amygdalas light up when they figure out that three fingers means three bananas, please.

There was a time when people had hallucinations and heard voices, the spectrum of mental illnesses was the stuff of old books and movies, but then pod-bound and terrified, it occurred to me, what about *their* consciousnesses? The brain map torn from the old textbook, that page also contained the photographs of brain scans in brilliant red, sapphire, viridian, the troubled brains of the diseased. These subjects believed in their perceptions, the voices that told them Martians were playing drums on the roof, that the chimeras on the F train were real and needed to be conversed with to ascertain velocity and direction of tornadoes and sharks whirling overhead. To quiet the impulse to jump, I put the papers on the floor of the pod, lay down on the curving floor as much as it was possible to do so, which meant squashing myself under the seat. I turned on my phone light and opened Waxman's envelope.

It is more probable that worms and flies and caterpillars move mechanically than that they all have immortal souls.

–Descartes, *Discourse on Method*, 1637

Here's how it works. You target a specific gene with a piece of nucleic acid called guide RNA. RNA brings in an enzyme that cuts the DNA at precisely that spot. This enzyme is like an astronaut doing a spacewalk in order to repair one of the telescopes positioned at the edge of the solar system. There are many of them out there, and this is a common occurrence. Cutting the DNA induces the cells to fix the wound, producing a mutation. It's a precise means of creating a mutation in the genome if you know what you're looking for. I was looking for consciousness and studying concordance, measuring how genes influence a trait. Consciousness is polygenic, influenced by multiple genes. It could be connected to, affected by genes for what? Circadian rhythms, traits like color blindness and deafness, for example, though they no longer exist, and that was one of the problems with my research. I needed traits that might affect consciousness because they are limiting. These are few and far between.

The mechanic in space has a limited number of choices and has to calculate risks. He must remain tethered to the main shuttle. He can't drop a screwdriver or even a screw because in space these things can't be retrieved. The enzyme doing the cutting and pasting also has to be manipulated with awareness of the perils equivalent to no gravity, rationed oxygen, air pressure issues, meteors, and interfering space dust. Consciousness is unknown territory full of black holes.

An experiment done with two capuchin monkeys: one in one cage, the other right next door, and their enclosures were plexiglass, so each could fully see the other. They were trained to hand over a rock in exchange for a food reward, but then one monkey was given a grape in exchange for the stone, while his neighbor, for performing the identical task, was given a piece of cucumber, a far inferior food to monkey taste. Seeing this inequity, cucumber monkey squawked, had a fit, shook his enclosure, the plastic bent and bowed with the force of his frustration. Clearly pissed off, he threw the cuke back at the primatologist. His neighbor looked, observed him, but was happy to keep on accepting a grape in exchange for handing over a stone.

When this experiment was repeated with chimps, the chimp who was rewarded with a grape reacted differently. The grape chimp went on strike and refused to hand over the stone until his fellow chimp, the one who only earned a piece of cucumber, was also given a grape. Besides awareness of the distinction between grapes and cucumbers, this could be interpreted as a signpost for consciousness.

The chimp also had a conscience, the word that shares sound, letters, Latin origins with consciousness. Grape primate looked at cucumber primate and not only felt his agony, but wanted to signal that this unfairness needed to be redressed by the lab coat in power.

Is anxiety only the province of a creature who has to step on a stage in an hour, can't remember her lines, and feels, at her core, like some kind of fraud? She shouldn't be here at all, how did she get to this point, is there any way to back up because standing in the wings, as she is now, is a mistake? Maybe we aren't the sole proprietors of anxiety, and if a creature is able to express fear, there could be consciousness. Pigs are said to sense that at the end of the chute, they will encounter the stun gun and the blade. They balk, scream, anticipate what's ahead of them, and that there is no way out.

The chimp handed back the grape, fuck you, lab coat, and by doing so suggested that consciousness evolved as a set of inherited instincts. If we can switch these inheritances, then what? You can control consciousness, and if you can control consciousness, you can control a population.

Some humans and animals have the same substrates that enable consciousness, and some animals, those capable of self-cognition, have wrinkled high-volume neocortices. They're in the consciousness ballpark. We can start with them, but if we switch consciousness on dolphins, elephants, magpies, chimps, they have no ability to tell us what they're experiencing, so we have to work with humans. There's no other choice.

My department was Pangenica's atom bomb, my lab was their Los Alamos 1944, but what did I know? Oppenheimer, Teller, Fermi, they knew what they were doing. I was like the guy who designed the centrifuge, not knowing what it was all for.

Diagrams and graphs followed, part of a lab report that I had no ability to decipher, but what I could understand was that between a Child 18 and a Child 19, the document stated there were no discernible mutations in their DNA. I had no reason to believe Child 18 and Child 19 were Clayton and PomPom, except Waxman seemed to be telling me he believed whatever had happened to the two children was intentional. The last sheet of paper was different from the others; it was thinner, more like onionskin, like the texture and color of the paper in Singe's file. In fact, it was a page from her file. There was a hand-drawn asterisk at the top of the report that resembled one in Singe's papers, seven branches, a spider missing a leg.

✳ I had been doing a provenance report on a statue of Soviet cosmonaut, Yuri Gagarin, and my plan was to repatriate it. The USSR was long gone, but there was a state space museum at GorodEndoStadt, located where the provincial Russian capital had been, and all concerned decided that would be an appropriate home for the statue. The Space Institute, in whose collection it had been, was de-acquisitioning objects that were no longer considered of value, and I was the obvious person to do the paperwork for returning Yuri Gagarin to what could be called his homeland. The statue was two feet high, made of titanium, and he stood on a plinth shaped like a long gear. I'd brought it home for a few days to show PomPom, though actually I thought it would be of more interest to Clayton, however by this point, they were no longer friends. I came home late from work to find Gagarin on my desk where I'd left him, but when I picked him up, the base came off. Someone had unscrewed it. Both the base and the statue itself were hollow. Inside was a rolled-up piece of paper.

- Have Clayton over for breakfast. Tell him to get his toast out of the toaster with a fork.
- Tell him someone broke into the house, and he can hide in an unused freezer, the one in the garage.
- Play jump off the roof into a leaf pile. He goes first. Really, it's fun.
- I'm getting paid to knock down the wasp nest from the eaves outside, but I'll pay you to do it.
- Bike race down curving hill just as folks are driving home from work. This is a no-helmet contest.
- Hopscotch on railroad tracks. You have plenty of time to see a train.
- Grind up expired meds and put in his lemonade with extra sugar to mask any taste.

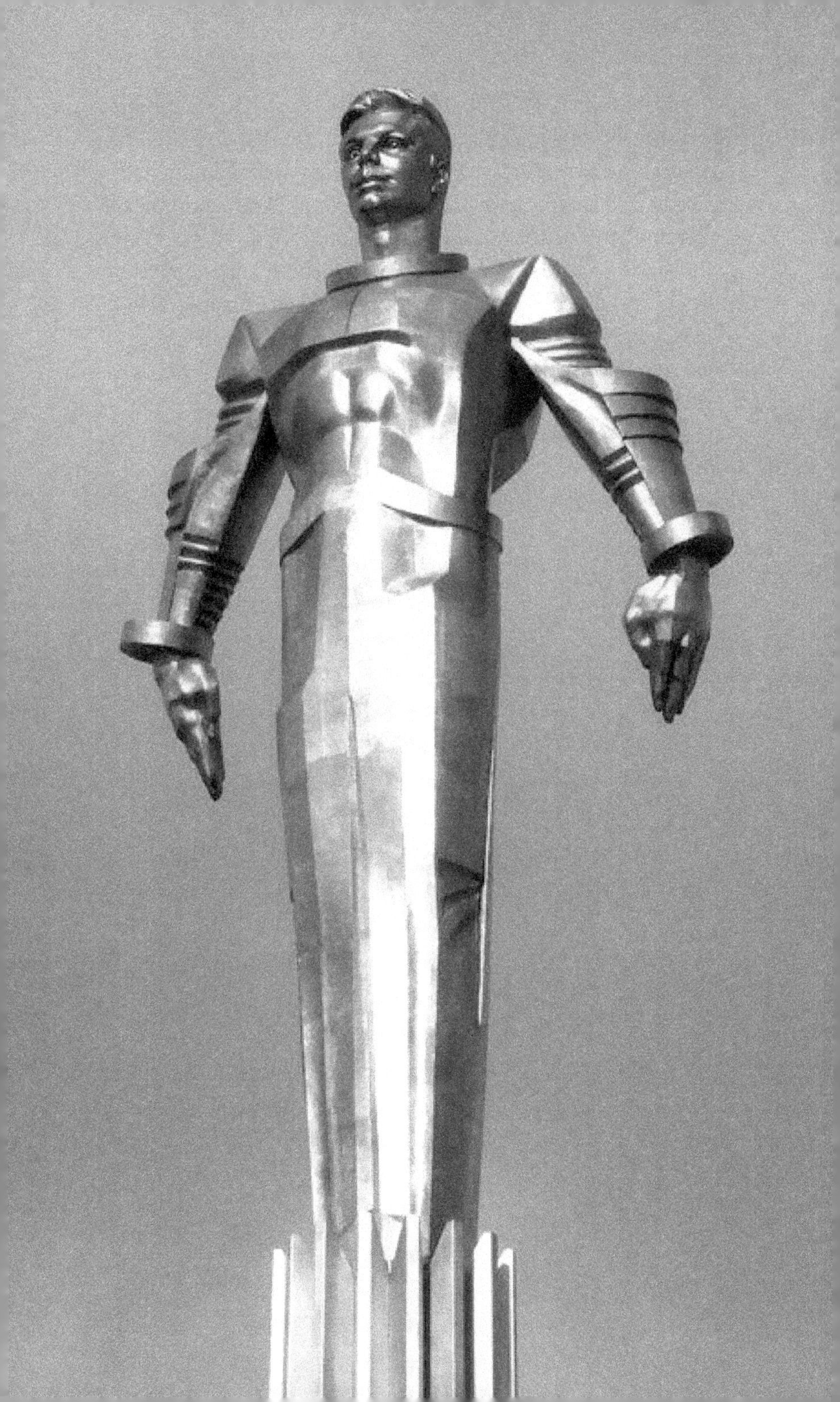

Why PomPom wrote all this down was bad judgment, but she did, and if she was going to detail her plans for Clayton, she should have destroyed the paper. Gagarin was destined to be shipped to a state museum that would probably put him in storage where he would remain, for perhaps hundreds of years, if not forever. Maybe a future curator would want to do an exhibit about early space exploration, he would put in an appearance in a glass case, but even that was a long shot. I replaced the paper inside Gagarin's body, screwed the base back on, and put the statue of the cosmonaut near the door, so I'd remember to take it to work the next day.

TWELVE

So, flies and caterpillars were like Crack's lowly saltshaker in the scheme of things. I shut my eyes only to be awakened from the land of Nod when the monorail lurched into action. The sun had risen. I looked over the edge at the park, no creatures in sight, just trees, grass, a manmade babbling brook, but when the monorail arrived back at the main Safariland station, I heard voices and flattened myself to the bottom of my pod, landscape of gum spots and cotton candy shreds, the hardcore stuff no one had bothered to clean. The park wasn't yet open, but ride operators, who sounded like teenagers working for the summer, stood somewhere on the platform talking about the escape of four tigers. Sherman was found eating penguins, poor flightless birds had no way out, and Patsy and Genghis, deliriously chasing prairie dogs, were quickly rounded up, but Madame Mao was sighted far from the zoo, clawing at a quilted metal taco kimchi kabob truck. She disappeared before she could be caught and was still at large. The three others were put back in their habitat, fur and feathers stuck in their craws and claws, but the question remained, who had let them out? The big cat keepers were adamant that they had locked the doors, but were terminated on the spot, and given no quarter. Until now the ride operators' job had been dull, and they talked at length about their close call, getting in early, but they made no mention of mauled humans. The zoo would open an hour later.

When the voices receded, I jumped out and ran to the exit where the first people in a long line were beginning to trickle in.

The sign snaked around a shawarma truck stationed in front of the aerobus stop, and I bought a sandwich called a L'il Schande that would fill the cramped bus with the smells of garlic, fried chilis, toasted cumin seeds, and pickled mango. The vehicle would take me to the end of the main city island, and from there I'd board a Coast Sentinel boat to Penrose. The boat only made its journeys a couple of times a day to make the rounds of the many small, uninhabited islands that dotted the waterways and bays surrounding the city. The channel zone, as it was known (though it ended in open sea), extended between twenty and thirty nautical miles, before you would get to the underwater canyon drop and pure, landless ocean. From the air, these islands looked like a constellation, a micro-archipelago hugging the larger islands of the main city. Some of them had been used to quarantine travelers suspected of carrying disease. Some had once housed labs that engaged in contagion research, and so had to be isolated. Some were so small they contained maybe one tree, and that was it. Penrose had been a working lighthouse at the far edge, no longer used, but not exactly abandoned.

My mother, Dot, lived in it, and this was where I grew up. I needed to check on her once a week and bring her food and other necessities, because she was unable to leave the island. There was no time to make that Saturday's trip, but if I didn't, she might eat expired eggs left out overnight, fall and crack her head on the flagstone floor, step on a Portuguese man o' war, OD on Dormazin, drop a match and set the lighthouse on fire. Some of those events I couldn't prevent, but besides bringing her weekly food deliveries, my turning up was something she could count on, and if I didn't, she would think those same disasters might have befallen me, or that I experienced mortal injury when someone standing close to me did, so it was all the same, and in her despair, extreme measures were a viable option. My mother had always let me know that. She didn't like the expression self-harm. For her, it was a matter of Press #3, if it's time, for a guaranteed way out.

Whether I lived on the island or just visited, I had enjoyed the illusion we were so far from land that to return to it required days, not hours. Penrose felt removed from the city and safe from its workings, though it wasn't really. No place was. The threat of submersion was real, but my mother would never leave, pointing to the cycles of the tidal pools that reappeared, then seemed to migrate up the island, as proof life continued and was capable of creating accommodations in adversity. Penrose was especially isolated in bad weather, so I had to pick the days I would make the round trip, consulting meteorology sites and satellite weather reports, but with the recurrence of violent storms, expected to get worse, I needed to check on her immediately. The night spent in the Skyfari pod in the northern end of the city had eaten up hours. As I made my way to the docks, I bought food to last her the week, things she loved that dispelled the idea that she was under siege by water: flatbread with fennel seeds, smoked salmon, tiny oranges.

The Sentinel Guard boat, the *Jolly Sandhog*, was an older crate because no one cared about these waters, demoted to a desert level of productivity, and they weren't seen as a launch for maritime threats, whether from a release of weaponized germs or stealth radioactive blasts, modes of attack that were antique, though still possible. This area was called Hellsmouth because the waterways on either side of the main city island merged and flowed out to the bay where the ocean tidal currents and undertows were impossible to predict. Small, nimble boats or ferries could motor their way through. Older vessels with less power were more susceptible to the tides and had difficulties here, and they created traffic problems.

The captain looked about sixty, her blue-and-red-striped ponytail sticking out from under her cap like a weathervane. She smoked cigarettes, tossing butts into the sea, talked to someone named Winthrop via a handheld radio, technology from another era, another sign that the Guard considered this route not worth bothering with. Captain Ada had been running the Channel Island itinerary for years. We recognized each other but didn't have conversations. She concentrated on navigation, or at least appeared to. The captain's perch was open at the top of the boat. From the upper deck, I could hear snatches of her conversations, she complained about her children, laughed at Winthrop's jokes, but once I heard her saying, what if I just kept going, kept going out to sea? I was always the last passenger to be dropped off and imagined being held hostage by Captain Ada, or just forgotten, as we sped out into open waters heading toward the Canary Islands, though fuel and food would run out long before land would be sighted again.

She didn't ever, as far as I know, attempt the oceanic crossing. The boat stopped at other Channel Islands, nothing more than rocks and trees, took measurements and readings which confirmed, I suppose, that the only trespassers were seals and gulls. Inspectors got off the islands of abandoned labs to be picked up on the return trip. Maybe these individuals weren't always inspectors. It wasn't clear who or what they were. Real estate developers with an eye for eccentric properties, performance artists planning to construct pieces that could only be viewed from drones or satellites. For a few years, there was a crew of biologists comparing the native species on the islands to their urban relatives who evolved slightly differently in the city. Though still influenced by tides of urban detritus that washed ashore, plastic bags that choked, bottle caps, pieces of toothbrushes, straws, spoons that lodged in turtle eggs beneath the shells of giant oysters and horseshoe crabs, tidal pool creatures who changed color due to oil spills.

On the islands you found the older variations of the species, those natives whose development hadn't been affected by issues of light pollution, road salt debilitating paw and claw, presence of heavy metals in air and prey. What I learned from the biologists as they talked about entropy and habitat fragmentation while they checked their equipment: In the city there were racoons whose heads were smaller and therefore did not get stuck in choke collars of seductive and treacherous McFlurry ice cream cups, birds who changed the pitch and circadian timing of their calls to adjust for the din of rush hour traffic, red squirrels whose digestive systems evolved to accommodate egg rolls and onion calzones, wings of cliff swallows that became shorter over time, so they can take off more quickly in the face of fast-approaching traffic. Their island cousins (racoon, cliff swallow, red squirrel) were identifiable as close blood relatives, true to their original DNA, but behaviorally divergent.

Humans got on and off the boat with their samples of feathers, dirt, bones, pieces of shells, auditory recordings, and data, but by the end of the journey, as Captain Ada navigated from island to island, she would finally arrive at Penrose as waves crashed against the rocks at its base. Sticking out of the cliff was a small wooden dock, the pilings of which had grown water-logged and treacherous. It was possible a sodden old plank would give way at any time, and this past year the pier had grown more rickety and liable to disappear altogether into the sea. I contacted various agencies in the city to find out about getting it repaired, but they insisted Penrose was private property, not their jurisdiction. This is not true. My mother doesn't own anything.

Captain Ada dropped anchor long enough to let me disembark, told me to watch my step, then cast off again, as if she were eager to turn around and make the reverse trip. Penrose, to most, was a forbidding lighthouse island, no beach, just rocks. As I made my way up stairs hewn into the cliff, the sound of the wind and gulls was deceiving, as if there was a lot of activity somewhere on the island, which there wasn't. My mother came out, waved to the retreating boat, hugged me, and took some of the bags I'd brought. When I was expected, Dot dressed up. Her long indigo dress fluttered in the wind, though underneath she was wearing jeans. Dark red lipstick made her mouth stand out like a modified version of the Joker, eyes outlined with kajal I provided from a South Asian variety store. She had a smaller nose and smaller eyes but otherwise the similarity between us was unmistakable. I often kidded her that when she did her forms for me, she just asked for a duplicate of herself. Of my father, she would never speak. He was an anonymous grab bag of features that were distinctly not hers, and there were ways I wasn't like her. We don't have the same foghorn loud sartorial agenda; I tried to be anonymous except once in a while when I was using a Crafted Identities persona. I have an affinity for the law insofar as it represents order, even when rules are hopelessly swamped or contradictory, counterintuitive. Also, my mother didn't have mirror touch. Did it come from him? I will never know.

One of my early memories of mirror touch was of being at a public beach with my mother. Someone, a child, was flailing in the water, then disappeared under its surface. I felt my nose and lungs fill with water, and moved my arms and legs in panic, as if air were sea. My mother held my face in her hands, so I had to look at her, not at the waves. When we got home, I was instructed that if I found myself feeling what others felt, this tendency had to be hidden, never discussed or revealed except to her, and even then, only if no one else was around. She told me, no one will want to be your friend, which sounds cruel, but enduring that kind of door-shut-in-your-face cruelty is minor compared to the consequences for being discovered as an anomaly, which would mean that's the end of you, even if you're a child. Growing up on the island, it was natural to be as reclusive as possible, to reclusitate, she said, reclusivity is a means to survive. She tried to train me to be able to limit the effects of my synesthesia. Pain is in the brain, she said, there is no physical injury. You touch the handle of a hot frying pan, and receptors send signals to the prefrontal cortex or thereabouts. Without the brain, there is no pain. The burn seems real, but it's an illusion. Registering and reacting to pain is necessary for survival, otherwise we'd have a diminished sense of danger at our peril, but you have to be careful of going overboard. What about psychical pain? For this, she had no answers. It's normal, when a loved one feels pain, you feel pain, the agony doubles, but mirror touch was of another order.

Before I was born, my mother had worked, when she did work, for Chromatin House in the city, an establishment that had been a competitor of Pangenica. Chromatin House—the name sounded like an archaic drug for color blindness but referred to a small boutique company that promised parents they could design children who would grow into adults with faces parents could choose from a selection of famous portraits and/or photographs. For this, clients paid much more than the routine Pangenica fees. Some examples of what Chromatin House promised: a girl who looked like young Rita Hayworth, Saraswathi, Goddess of Wisdom, Parmigianino's *Madonna dal collo lungo*, all combined. A boy who intertwined the feacures of Eddie Murphy, Edward Villella, and the DNA provided by the ordinary walking-around-minding-his-own-business dad. The combinations were endless, and some parents looked at their choices as an infinite menu at an infinite restaurant. It was delicate, stressful, high-tech work, and given what they had promised, results were mixed.

She had known Altner from Chromatin House. He'd been an advisor or a consultant, skilled at anticipating problems before they got to litigation, and since both he and my mother were skeptics who needed a paycheck, they hung out. Altner was new to this city, it was his first job on this

Parmigianino
Madonna dal collo lungo

side of the ocean, but his wife made it clear she preferred Slavtown Ciudad Medina, so she would return to their city of origin for extended periods of time. Altner got lonely, my mother could tell, and they drank small glasses of whiskey while supposedly checking archived DNA inventory. She enjoyed his company, and they would dance to "Let's Get Lost" at night when everyone had left for the day. As I understood it, their relationship was a bonding of eye rolling and snide asides, intentionally knocking into one another as they passed in the halls. In the privacy of their offices in the Chromatin House, they did dramatic readings of high-profile application forms, as if reading from a script, speaking in high or deep voices, singing some parts.

Richard Feynman without the Buddhism and with the financial acumen of a supply-side economist with country club membership

Tom Cruise's nose

But tall

She should have legs like Monroe

Bardot

Tennis skills like McEnroe

Sense of style, can we ask for that? Like Anna Wintour?

Oh, she's so old hat

Around this time, my mother decided she wanted a baby, but Chromatin offered no in-house discount, and she struggled with the Pangenica forms, so detailed and extensive she would get bored, confused, distracted, but she finally did submit them, and look, I got you, so it was worth it. She had no boyfriend, husband, or partner, so contributions of paternal DNA, she told me, came from a catalog of sources. I didn't believe her, but that was all the information I ever got.

She took a leave from Chromatin, but returned when I was old enough to go to school on the main island. She would drop me off on her way to work, collect me for the return trip. I used to joke that I had been secretly designed at Chromatin House, but my mother never found this to be very funny.

Her job had been to show prospective parents catalogs of possible faces in a range of prices. She had a memory archive that was enormous, but she was also familiar with the process of cutting and pasting genetic material, and so was the perfect sales manager, but at some point, Dot began to talk about what she called Genomic Gnomes or G'nomic G'nomes, creatures she discredited but also believed in, invisible homunculi who controlled the uncontrollable. Genomic Gnomes presented explainable mechanics: hands-on levers, gears turning, test tubes and beakers bubbling over, electric currents snapping life into being. Her explanation pitch shifted from "it's as if..." to "this is not a metaphor I'm using." At first other employees laughed off the witticisms of a longtime sales manager, front of the house, but then she began to ramble about the threat of a company she called Dysgenica, Ltd., purveyor of cacogenics, bad genes. Dysgenica twisted and perverted those otherwise perfectly stable ladders of DNA, resulting in disfigured monsters, imbeciles. She whispered about them to clients—something to watch out for because you never know.

I was still living at home and watched my mother turn into the God of Amphibos, a shapeshifter, a smoking alley cat one minute, an aerial trapeze artist the next, maybe one of ten things such a creature said was true. The question was, which was the one thing? She was unpredictable, and I was powerless to stop the stream of her resourceful inventions. She described Chromatin House's promises as akin to the stories of a Fibber McGee from the town of Wistful Vista, or to Orson Welles's *Mars Invasion* that reported the spread of a noxious gas across the Jersey Meadowlands, tentacled creatures emerging from saucers, firing heat rays at defenseless, bewildered humans. Clients entered the showroom entranced by Chromatin's portfolios of possibility, flawless genetic immortality, an improved you! They tasted these fruits, only to flee, screaming. She was an Eris,

Goddess of Chaos, crashing weddings, throwing the golden Apple of Discord. Y'all are living in Cricktown and Watsonville, she yelled. Mitochondrialus, Inc. named for the Roman emperor—it started with them, and now look where we're at.

No one knew what she was talking about.

I did. Pangenica's services weren't administered gratis. If you couldn't pay, you had no children. During the early years, there was financial aid that morphed into a complicated loan system with crippling interest rates, so impossible and usurious that the programs were eliminated with no replacements. Ethicists and legislators agreed that if you couldn't afford to have children, you shouldn't. Poverty, lack of means for whatever reason, was seen as a marker of genetic degeneracy, listing towards identifiable traits, lack of drive, diminishment of canniness, etc., debilities that should be eradicated anyway. Chromatin was for parents who turned up their noses at Pangenica as a resource for the merely standard, while they had the resources for an even more selective service. That my mother worked for such a company pained her no end. Dot had trouble finding and holding a job. She felt stuck at the exclusive blue chip Chromatin. This was when it became obvious that my mother was addicted to Dormazin. She craved the way the drug turned off her hypothalamus, tricking the suprachiasmatic nucleus, which she called the *supercharismatic supermiasma nucleus*, into thinking it was night, giving her a taste of concentrated blissful oblivion. Her Dormazin was covered by a prescription. When that wasn't enough, she bought noddies on the street.

They had to get her off the showroom floor, and finally paid her a large sum to go away, enough to keep her quarantined on Penrose, and keep her mouth shut. Good luck with that. My mom was a talker, but fewer and fewer listened to her, dwindling down to no one. Laughing all the way to the bank, she was able to live from this payoff for the rest of her life, augmented by her scavenging tendencies when she visited one of the main islands. For a while, she repurposed and sold things she foraged, but then that stopped, too. In the depths of the lighthouse, I could still find an amplifier that had been turned into a Bluetooth speaker; a microwave oven that had been converted into a musical life clock that besides the actual time, displayed your age in years, months, days, minutes, and seconds (music programmed separately); hub caps that had been transformed into World War I–era helmets, though who would have any possible use for these apart from a time traveler? My mother considered it a waste of time to clean, and when I suggested hiring someone, she refused because a) it's embarrassing, and b) the tumbrel awaits those who won't clean up their own damn shit.

When Chromatin got sued into bankruptcy, my mother was convinced it was because DNA had itself gone on strike.

Now, because of her partially self-imposed exile, she pretty much talked to no one, never used electronic devices in any form, except an old flip phone that could only call me. After Chromatin, though she never said so directly, she wanted to live in another era, as much as possible, one in which motion, metamorphosis, disease, everything could be explained by circumstances visible to the naked eye, therefore homunculi had more logic than atoms. I had to insist on batteries and electricity pirated from the city while it was still possible to pilfer energy.

Maybe Altner had meant it when he offered her a contract worker consulting position (to be clear, this is what he offered, not a clock-in-with-benefits form of employment). Dot was sharp, but she was the reason I'd never have Q clearance, no question about it.

The lighthouse was cylindrical, five stories high, once painted white, now peeling so badly it was mostly red exposed brick, increasingly eroded. Inside, spiral stairs led to each floor, winding up at the top with a giant Fresnel lens that had once rotated, and been automated, solar-powered, with a high-intensity LED, now creaky, immobile, dim, and dust-covered.

A battered tin sign on the first floor read:

Safety First
Wear goggles, face shields, rubber gloves, and aprons when working with acids
DANGER
Battery Changing Area

I was home where all of these things that were once required could no longer be found.

Because my visits were so frequent, I probably didn't realize how much she was deteriorating. Lamps, chairs, cabinet doors were held together with duct tape and string, but then they always had been. Canisters of flour and sugar sat next to bottles of emerald-green rat poison. A series of shelves that held all kinds of boxes: cigar boxes, cookie tins, toolboxes, fishing tackle boxes, divided plastic containers custom-made for Warhammer figures I used to play with. None of them contained what their labels indicated would be inside. A plastic box with slots for cassette tapes held stubs of pencils, a smoked paprika tin contained a stash of Dormazin, blue pills flecked with red.

Papers and books were stacked on chairs, crates, the floor. While my mother unpacked the bags I'd brought, I picked up a book from a stack, *Spiral Jetty Spiral Helix*, and paged through underwater photographs of a giant curling spiral made of stones and the X-ray crystallography of Rosalind Franklin. Dot stored apples and onions together, the counter was littered with jars of spices, some older than I was, but she pushed them out of the way when she needed some counter space. I put the book aside and picked up another one lying on top of a pile of clothes. G. K. Chesterton, *Eugenics and Other Evils* from the Cleveland Public Library, something my mother must have scavenged since we were nowhere near that inland city and never had been. The book had a painting of the Tower of Babel on its cover.

Spiral Jetty by Robert Smithson

Inside she had underlined a blow from a hatchet, then written in the margin, catch it, match it, snatch it, Bob Cratchit, Inspector Gadget, telepathic jacket, spatchcock. Where had this book come from really?

I went to the gym at Pangenica, if I got into work early enough, and one morning I saw Vy looking through people's things left on a bench while they showered. Maybe she was looking for something she'd left there herself. I couldn't be sure, but it looked like she put a pair of rubber flip-flops, shampoo, a hair clip, and maybe other stuff in her bag. Or maybe not. From where I stood, I couldn't be certain and didn't want to accuse her when she might have only been rummaging around. She had the clipped, sometimes brittle tone of an ex-Dormazin addict, and I didn't particularly want to talk to her either. When I was at my mother's and saw all these things she'd scavenged, I hoped that she had scavenged and not stolen, but I would never know for certain. She would never tell me, and I couldn't ask without making accusations that would send her into a tailspin of sputtering undecipherable verbiage. This I knew from experience.

Dot made coffee, complained about her knee joints. Had I brought turmeric capsules? Yes, of course I had. Were they organically produced? Yes, as always, as far as I knew, and I added she should quit drinking so much coffee, consumed in order to counter the longer-than-she-wanted effects of a certain intake of Dormazin. What about the Dormazin? Yes, I handed her a bottle of ice-blue pills, the mildest strength. These are practically white. You couldn't get anything stronger? No, I lied. How's Crackhour, Crackatoa, Cracken, Crackow, krackdown, Krackhead, Krackers the Klown, parkour, crack an hour and let the minutes out, she asked. I did not say, well, I'm worried about his intake of Dormazin that seems to be getting worse, and that he'll end up doing eighteen for .5 and start speaking in tornados of syllables, much like yourself, but it won't exactly be my problem, because there will be family, somewhere, who will take him off to rehab, and prevent me from seeing him, because who the hell am I anyway?

Then she asked me what I was working on, and I described the file, explaining that at first, I didn't take it seriously, so much was missing. My mother knew what I did, and she believed my working as an Adjudicator for Pangenica was a mistake. Okay that you trained to be an Adjudicator after law school, but don't work for them. It's too risky. Why don't you join whatshisname following birds to the Arctic? That was one place he wouldn't be because there are no birds there, unless Dot knew something I didn't, which was always possible.

"I was told not to refile or toss, but to continue to look into the matter."

"Gray matter. Dark matter. Matter of life or death. A matter of time. You matter. No laughing matter. Whatsa matter? Mata Hari. Errata. Mad Hatta." Sometimes Dot got stuck on a word or group of words, like in movies from an earlier century when a needle is stuck in a record to indicate time is standing still.

"When you were at Chromatin House, was there ever a mix-up of any kind?"

"Of course, but if such things happened, they were buried under the burden of multitudinous and contradictory desires of eager parents with oh-so-much money to incinerate. The list of what they wanted was always long and studded with traits that would compete or clash. When someone's paying that much, you can't tell them shit, you just nod, sounds fantastic, please sign here. If a slight aberration appeared, Chromatin would say, well, you never know one hundred percent about your origins, but things are so much better now than they were in the days of fuck whoever. It's an infinitely unknowable fraction, even if decreasing in size, still never one hundred percent, like Zeno's Meno's Reno's Paradox, you will never get there.

"There was an accident I was responsible for at Chromatin House, and Altner covered it up. It was late, and I was checking over answers on a client's application forms, cutting and pasting answers from one screen to another, doing too many applications at once, transferring from Review Status to Acceptance, bleary-eyed and tired. Once you hit Submit, there's no going back, and this is for everyone's safety, you wouldn't want someone going into applications and fiddling around. As soon as I did so, I realized I'd made a mistake. Family A was getting everything they asked for, but instead of a future concert violinist, they would in a few years, discover they had a child who gravitated toward extreme sports, jumping from a helicopter to a mountainside and skiing down at high speeds. Family B, though they played no music at home, would discover a near prodigy in their midst. In a panic, I called Altner. It was too late to fix my error, but he went into the records, he had that authority, and made it look like each family was getting what they'd desired, you might think, unmistakably so. At Chromatin, just as at Pangenica, families retain no records of their applications, knocking out a channel of complaint, though they still do file them. Security apps make it impossible to even take screenshots.

"The next day it was business as usual. The beach was swept clean. We didn't speak of the incident. A week later, he accepted the position at Pangenica, and I never saw him again. Chromatin was not going to last with its unspoken promises that it was in the business of creating a super-race, but I also wonder if, having broken the law, even though it was to protect me, he felt he could no longer stay at the company and pretty much cut ties with me. The offer to work with him at Pangenica was always crap."

She owed Altner, but she didn't want me mixed up with his schemes of which she was sure there were many. He always needed money, no matter how much he had. She remembered a man who imitated top brass behind their backs, who leaned out of windows, half-naked, yelling he had Dormazin, the sapphire blues, for bargain prices, though he certainly did not, until my addicted mother reeled him back in. This was a side of the younger Altner I wasn't aware of. Tickets to Orientation Sites, she said, are always one way.

Then my mother asked to look at the file, and I handed her my phone, telling her it wasn't abilities that had been switched but consciousness. She had one last thing to say about her job at Chromatin.

"I wanted to tell the parents, you will reap disappointment, and there will be nothing you can do to undo your wishes." Then she began to scroll through the file on my phone. "Consciousness is something else altogether. It sounds like your Singe could be putting the con back in consciousness. Chromatin, Pangenica, con, con, con. Are you sure she didn't mean conscience?"

I wasn't sure of anything.

They're almost homonyms, conscious and conscience, but not quite. Conscious, from the Latin *conscire*, *con* meaning with + *scire* "to know or to be privy to," then give it a few centuries and around the sixteenth century, the English meaning becomes "being aware of wrongdoing," heading towards conscience, you would think. Use of the word dipped in the 1840s, but was at its highest usage in the 1940s. Conscience, also, can look back on *conscire*, then Middle English and Old French interfere and tip the scales toward a sense of inner thoughts or knowledge.

One is conscious, develops a conscience later, something let's say most animals don't have, though primatologists will give examples of chimps who appear to express regret for theft of food from those of their own group, others will point to elephants and crows who mourn their dead. Once out of your Phytosack, you become aware and then make mistakes, try to do the right thing, and sometimes, in doing so, fuck things up even more.

Preconscious, subconscious, foreconscious, superconscious, the domain of superheroes. The stew of memories of which one is unaware, or dimly aware, and then, bingo, look at the carrot or onion floating on the surface, recognizable, smelling of thyme. Why not? The murky bottom where unidentifiable husks of spices and pieces of marrow bone have sunk, unknown and unrecallable: that's the unconscious.

Consciousness doesn't admit everyone. There is censorship and repression, those two glad handers. There are injuries and pathologies that tinker with consciousness, poke holes in it.

For example:

There was also the consciousness of dementia where you are sure you had a visitor who spoke a language of straining metaphor, mondegreens, and malapropisms, though no one else saw him, who told you a car was waiting outside, that people were in the next room who had never set foot in your house, ever, and I worried that dementia, that hungry interloper who left only bones, was picking up where relics of Dormazin had left off in my mother's brain. The genetic propensity for dementia had been eliminated, but the disease itself could not be, so it appeared from time to time, an uninvited and unpredictable guest who, once in residence, never left.

Dot took another swallow of coffee, then took out paper and a pen and began to write:

CONSCI|E|N|C|E
CONSCI|O|U|S|N|ESS
|15|21|19|14

She put numbers in the place of the letters according to their position in the alphabet.

"Keep it," she said. "This is information you might need. Only OUSN separates the two words. Fifteen and twenty-one are both divisible by three, five plus seven is twelve, also divisible neatly by three, no surprises there. Nineteen is a prime number and splits itself for no whole numbers, middle finger extended, fourteen is an interesting number, a separate class from the first two in the string, because half of it is seven."

I doubted this would be useful, but folded the paper and put it in my bag.

"What about False Consciousness?" Dot brightened up.

"I don't think Pangenica was trying to pull the wool over anyone's eyes. Well, maybe they were, but not globally. It was just an experiment."

"Management will always say that. They will never tell you the truth." My mother adjusted her cape made of net bags that had once held lemons and oranges. I'd heard about False Consciousness from her before. In the lighthouse, it was a capitalized phrase, the idea that a subordinate class of people believes what's fed to them, what they've been indoctrinated to accept as true by a ruling class, but I don't think this had anything to do with Singe's claim.

"Who's paying for the kid's rehab?"

"The real insurance is Dometop."

"Dometop. Dimetain. Singe already knows the answer. That's why this file is bullshit." My mother was annoyed. "This Laveneer wants confirmation, not an investigation. If she wanted to know what happened in the lab, pre-Phytosack, just before a clump of embryonic cells was shoved in, she would have asked. She knows what happened."

"Everyone's DNA is stored, is known, archived pre- and post-conception. It's there somewhere. It's not a secret, but I can't access her InTake forms."

"Isn't a DNA test required of Pangenica employees?"

I nodded, though I'd never thought to ask to see mine. As the Director of Adjudications had reiterated on a number of occasions, it was possible for someone to claim to be someone else, therefore the DNA test was standard procedure. My mother looked concerned and indicated someone somewhere was asleep at the switch, didn't look closely, well, you passed the DNA test. They hired you. Hominid, homonym, heteronym, homarid.

I imagined thousands of homunculi hunched over screens, scanning an infinite amount of data, and somehow, I'd maintained under-the-radar status.

I asked her if she'd saved my Phytosack. Some people saved them, put them in the freezer, or dried them to a greenish black, pressed them, and glued them into albums of baby pictures, but my mother shuddered at the suggestion.

"Disgusting habit. Who would save such a gluey thing? Darling, we are all made of the same stuff as stars: carbon, oxygen, nitrogen. Then you're done."

Did she mean done as in born, baked, taken home, or done as in morto, infinito?

A few minutes before the return ferry was due, I climbed up to the top of the beacon. From here I could see the entire island. A new storm driven by an atmospheric river was supposed to arrive, but there was time, yet. Wild grass and rocks surrounded the lighthouse but not much else. A ceilometer had once been installed on the island, a device used for measuring the height of clouds, a relic from someone's or some agency's meteorological endeavors, but it hadn't worked for years. It was a house-shaped silver and white box, no longer operational, too many false readings had been attributed to it. My mother said this was due to diamond dust, otherwise known as ice crystals. I'd thought this was my mother's Dormie-speak, but she was right. I never met the ceilometer operator, so was never able to ask him, how do you know you've found the correct height? How do you discover mistakes? Can you trust the machine? Most of the ceilometer's white paint had been sanded off by the elements, but the box was still on the island, and could be seen where it had been planted, close to the edge of a cliff.

The lighthouse's old Fresnel lens was encrusted with dried salt, a sign the spray had gotten that high, and this was a sign it was time to leave the island before it was submerged. My mother was not budging from her perch and even if all indicators were that Penrose would disappear with rising waters, she would go down with it. Dot once said of the luxury towers that studded the coast and scraped the sky, invisible from Penrose, but she knew they were a part of the city: The sea can't rise fast enough to swallow them, and I'd caught her watching footage of rising water sloshing in and out of elevators, fish swimming between chandelier prisms, midnight penthouse parties waiting for rescue, some nay-sayers trapped, never making it up to what was left of the rooftops. Manmade mesas became steel and concrete islands, then disappeared altogether, anchoring future colonies of sea turtles, brain coral, hammerheads. So far, the lighthouse had survived, but I never knew if one particular trip to Penrose would be my last. The textbook pages, the neural map, fluttered out of my hands, and windborne, made their way out to sea.

During these last minutes, I didn't want to leave, but couldn't stay. I went through the motions of departure, and my mother wouldn't say, I'll miss you, can't wait until next week, you could live here again, because she knew this was an island for one; I couldn't move back. But what would happen if she got sick, could no longer manage the stairs, confused rat poison with sugar, forgot that waves crash over rocks and cannot be traversed without being knocked into the surf? I imagined coming to visit and not being able to find her anywhere, but even without major disaster, her loneliness was something I didn't want to project, and maybe she was fine as she was, reading about submerged spiral jetties and making clothes out of bits and pieces scavenged when she traveled in the world of the city.

The horizon was still clear, no ships of any kind visible, and then Captain Ada's boat appeared like clockwork, and I ran to the pier just as she pulled in, my mother yelling goodbyes from a cliff edge with no time to hug, her sadness mixing with my own, and then the boat, with me on deck, went out to sea.

With the sun just beginning to set, the *Jolly Sandhog* was lit and empty except for the captain and myself. I asked her if I was the only person she'd ever taken to Penrose Island, and she told me that I was. I hoped she was telling me the truth, or at least to the best of her memory. She reminded me that she had been navigating this route for twenty years and couldn't possibly remember every single person who came and went. It was a foolish question. Then I gave her my number and asked if she would contact me if anyone booked passage to Penrose. She steered around a string of buoys with some more what the fucks, as if she'd never seen them before, then when we were in open water, she turned back to me.

"People get on and off. I don't know in advance who's going where. I just do the stops, that's all, whether or not anyone is on the boat waiting to get off or not, whether anyone is on a pier or it's empty, I just do my rounds. Sometimes I'm surprised that someone's on an island, say reedy Stillwell or rock-strewn Oyster, and I did not drop them off there. They got on the particular island somehow. Sometimes I make a pickup stop, but the person I dropped off a few hours earlier never makes the return trip. How did they get off the particular island? How should I know? Not my job to know. I don't moor the *Sandhog* and poke around. Maybe they're there, still. So, what I'm telling you, you already know. If someone gets on in the city intent on departing at Penrose, I won't know until foot leaves deck, lands on land. So, even if I call you, how are you going to get to Penrose unless I take you the next day?"

She was right, what would I do with that information even if she sent up a flare, hey, Loew, stranger on your island? I couldn't get to Penrose quickly, unless I had a private plane that could leave in an instant, and parachute me down to the precise bit of grass where falling would be okay if there was no wind. Impossible. It was like knowing someone was in distress on one of the poles while the nearest airstrip is, at best, fourteen hours away, and there are fuel shortages. You might get there in two weeks, if you were lucky. Penrose wasn't that isolated, but she was right, there was no point, but she'd let me know if it made me feel better. She was too kind to say, knock yourself out, but that was the implication, and I knew it.

Captain Ada pulled up to an empty dock, rang the ship's bell, no one appeared, she waited ten minutes, then moved on to the next island. Had she dropped off a passenger earlier in the day who was still on the island somewhere, sitting on rocks in the dark, watching the time, listening for the ferry's bell, letting the boat continue on without him? It was possible one of these tiny islands was an Orientation Site with comings and goings unknown to the captain. In fact, I made it a habit to look closely, but at the same time, tried to appear not to stare at fellow passengers. Any of them could have been disappearachniks who would hustle you off the boat when it anchored at an isolated island. You might see a disappearachnik and not know it. They looked like everyone else. Disappearachniking, eliminating undesirables and miscreants, was just a job like any other, and it was a job for life, or so I'd heard. Their confederates belonged to brotherhoods of cessionators and sisterhoods of purganators. I had a hard time imagining parents requesting death squad instincts on their Admission forms, but these individuals existed, and they butted their way out of Phytosacks like the rest of the population. Except they were hatched and trained in Eraditoriums, but like O Sites, no one knew where these places were. (As cartographer Isla Fentster, I had asked about charts of Orientation Sites and Eraditoriums, did these places even exist? I should have inquired about the uninhabited islands without ever adding, oh say, could they be possible spots for no-exit situations? Is that what those specks on paper maps were? Isla was a smarty pants so to ask would have been in character, but this was a high-risk sort of question, tarring the asker with the brush of a troublemaker who might know, or infer, far too much.) We stopped at Pineville, a C-shaped islet, densely forested, which I only knew from the journey out; by the return trip only a few lights on the only pier marked the island. A man and woman visible by the light of their phones could be seen making their way toward the boat. Ada was impatient, she had a schedule to keep to, but she waited. I was impatient, too, compounding what I absorbed from her. She tapped the gunwale as waves hit the sides of the *Jolly Sandhog*, and so did I.

One solid person in the file I could locate was Dinah. She no longer lived in the house where Clayton had fallen through ice, but had moved to the city, to one of the lesser populated islands to the east, as I suspected Singe, too, was somewhere in the city. I wrote, introducing myself as myself, and asked if it would be possible to meet? I had some questions about the Laveneer family and her late son.

The two passengers who boarded at Pineville, an island that was a designated camping site, made it to the *Sandhog* with all their camping equipment. The man tried to help the woman up the ramp to the boat, but she kept shrugging him off. Once on deck, looking out to sea, she drew closer to him, but he stepped away from her. I watched them for a few minutes, then my eyes began to blur with her distress. Was I closer in consciousness to these here-and-now-on-a-boat strangers than I was to my distant and not all that well remembered five-year-old self?

I felt what they were feeling, his irritation, then her irritation morphing into anxiety and hopelessness. The man felt like a Vito Acconci video, *What do I want? What do I need? What do I want? What do I need?* Over and over.

Leave me alone. I can do it myself.

Just trying to help.

Okay, I'm sorry.

Go fuck yourself.

No, I didn't mean that.

The woman was doing a different Acconci video, *come here, go away, come here, go away.*

I was afraid they would see me mirroring their faces, as if in dialogue with myself. There were no other passengers to shift to, no one staring aimlessly out to sea. I felt as if I were losing my materiality, wobbly, liquid Jello that could take on any shape. No more Zedi Loew, Isla Fenster, Jane Ames, or anyone else for that matter, just a collection of cells that had annexed the true selves of a random couple on the deck of a ferry. *I am you. You and me. We are three.* Truth be told, I hate that song, platitudinous and nowheresville. If they divined what was going on involuntarily in my consciousness, they could have me arrested, a freakazoid out among actual humans. Hello, Pangenica Security? What kind of mutant does what she does? Like a peeping Tom of souls.

My phone started to vibrate. It was the Director of Adjudications, but I didn't pick up. A possibility: the ConSwitch file meant nothing to Debonis. He'd rung no alarm. The humiliation of being shoved into the machine was too much, and once he'd been able to stand on two feet again, he called off his taser-happy colleagues, and they all ambled to the cafe for day-old but still decent tiramisu. So it was imaginable I still had a job. I called Altner back.

"Good evening, Loew." The voice was formal, then switched to parking lot drug deal. "What have you got?" Stopped just short of sounding like one word.

"I met with Waxman. He was familiar with the file, but, funny thing, he isn't a lab technician."

"Most people here are essentially lab technicians. Some just have different titles."

"No big deal then, huh?"

No response. How could he not have known that if and when I met with Waxman, he would tell me what he actually did?

Then I asked Altner if he knew about the Department of Neuronal Correlates.

"Yes, Loew, that is a department that comes and goes, depending on available resources." The formal voice again, then silence on the other end of the phone, murmurs in the background as if he were at a restaurant, perhaps Mr. Levant's, strains of Jimmy Soul coming through the speakers, although I couldn't picture Altner in a diner. Wherever he sat, drumming his fingers on a table, he would never let me know exactly how to fill in the blanks if that meant risk for him, and sometimes I felt like a cartoon cat, stepping into quicksand while chasing a mouse, grabbing a rope to pull myself out, but the rope turns out to be a python with love hearts in its eyes. Let me hug you, oh, please, let me! I'd never heard of a department that came and went because of funding that Pangenica had no lack of, ever.

"What about the DNA samples?"

"I can get Dinah's. Singe is still unknown."

"You need to find her. You also need DNA from the surviving kid."

Did that mean going back to Lazarus House? Say, PomPom, could you open your mouth? Pretty please?

"What about the fathers?"

"The traits in question came from the mothers." Mitochondrial DNA grabs the mike.

"All that data should be on file, Mr. Altner. Why do you need new samples? What happened to the originals? Morris could find them for you."

The junior archivist could find anything.

"I don't want to assign Morris this task."

"Why not? That is his job, locating records, especially those that are difficult to categorize, but DNA is DNA. He could find it for you in minutes, even codes that are gated off from general accessibility."

"I think I mentioned," his voice sandpaper left in the sun, that dry, "DNA most certainly is archived, but not everyone is who they claim to be. Belt and suspenders, Loew. You need to close the case before Monday. Prove Singe Laveneer has no defense, no evidence, just not possible.

Nothing was switched. She was a lousy mother and looking for any excuse, no matter how farfetched to shift the blame somewhere else. It happens from time to time, but her story is that simple, Loew. You need to find her."

The way he said my name was as if he were in the same room, as if he were watching me, and maybe he was.

"Try calling Vy Sapper. She never goes home." Vy Sapper was also skilled at locating information. Vy lacing her boots back up when she descended from the ladder, returning to her game, not appreciating the interruption.

"You know there are a lot of islands out where you're ferrying. The *Jolly Sandhog*, like all of the Sentinel Guard, is operated only partially by a human. A few computer clicks and you could be dropped off at an island big enough for just one person. There are islands so small, they aren't named, they don't appear on maps, if you know what I mean. Imagine sitting on an asteroid the size of a private plane, an asteroid with gravity, a bit of oxygen, not much else, though."

"Waxman found the file in the garbage. Someone had it before he did."

I felt like an alien was pushing up from my stomach and was going to burst out of my mouth, as uncontrollable as vomiting, your consciousness has no will, it's not a gatekeeper, just a data collector, no way to marshal resistance, no matter how much you think, no, don't, please: rewind, go back.

"There's no footage of Waxman going through garbage that I know of, but I'll have it checked. See you Monday, Loew."

Everything comes from someplace. The paper came from a recycling plant, the ink came from cuttlefish, or once did, now coal and petrochemicals. I turned off my phone and put it in my bag. The *Jolly Sandhog* sliced through a bloom of palmy seaweed and unseen microscopic diatoms by the billions, sharp-edged or blunt, star-like or ball-shaped, unicellular, alive, but can they be said to have consciousness? Do they sense danger when they're about to be eaten? Do they ever feel extreme and profound loneliness when their populations are devastated, and there they are floating diatominously solo in the soup of a city canal when transoceanic winds should have blown them in vast numbers all the way to the Amazon basin, fulfilling their role in the decomposing fertilizing biomass? Imagine a line of spinning diatoms emerging from an Orientation Site because that's where consciousness can go swirling down the drain.

Altner wanted what he wanted. Debonis alerted the disappearachniks, but they were on pause until I led them to Singe. I couldn't imagine the guard not doing what he threatened. The spires of the main city island were coming into view. I couldn't get back soon enough, but despite Altner's warning that disappearachniks don't need land to do their jobs, at least we could have stayed on the boat forever, just circling islands with no urgency, letting the current take us wherever.

Captain Ada's phone rang in the tone of "Single Ladies".

"Hi there, Winthrop. What can I do for you?" She laughed. "You don't say? Well, if I was you, I'd kick her ass out of the house. Nobody gets away with that shit in my house. Not if I'm paying the rent."

Pause

"You know how it is. I haven't heard from him in weeks. It breaks my heart, but he's gone. No, I'm not going to steer this heap of wingnuts into a cliff. No cliffs around here, anyway. If I was going to do it, I'd go out in a storm and let the sea take me."

Pause

"She wants to be a naval architect? What the hell is that? Building on water? Oh, boats. Why don't they just say: building boats? I want to build boats. That's a job with a big future. At least she wants to do something. My bumass just sits around playing games, like I'll always pay for everything, because I'm going to work forever, which I probably will do."

Pause

"Management the world over does not care about you for the most part. How many more years till retirement, Winthrop?"

Pause

"That's nothing. It's gonna be over in a blink. I'm stuck here till kingdom come. Same route. Same damn pieces of shit rocks and gulls and a dumbass seal every once in a while."

Pause

"You take care of yourself, Winthrop."

My ride was almost over, and the main island's spiny cluster of piers was coming into view. If someone were to offer me the opportunity to disappear, not the Orientation Site kind of disappearance, just the I'm taking a hiatus kind, I'd have accepted with no hesitation. It's not so impossible. Atoms are mostly air. We are made of atoms; therefore, we are mostly air. The city, a roosting porcupine arched over the curvature of the earth, bristled, and I wished I could suspend my non-air parts and evaporate into thin atmosphere, to float around with no particular identity, take a break with no urgency or much motivation, then reassemble someplace else.

I took out my phone because that's what you do when you're about to get off a boat, and Dinah had responded, yes, she was home, ring the bell any time tonight is perfectly fine, she would be expecting me: the Laveneers were monsters, Pangenica should pull anything or anyone remotely genetically linked to them and eliminate with complete finality. Even years later, she was eager to, as she put it, set the record straight.

The *Jolly Sandbog* docked, and as I waited for another ferry to take me east, I notified Crack that I'd left Penrose and would text him when I finished at Dinah's. There was a lot of activity on the docks. To the north, large pleasure boats were anchored with names like Deck-adence and Ta-keel-a. Some were dark and rocked silently, but a few others were full of late afternoon early evening partiers who didn't seem to be sailing anywhere. To the south, alongside a semi-dark pier, a makeshift lab had been set up next to the hull of the last whaling ship. It was being resurrected using high-tech forensics to determine the age and condition of the remains. Dots of light sparkled on the bowsprit and taffrail as shipwrights worked through the night. The ship had to be made as the original had been, no power tools, no galvanized wire, just tar and pitch, and hand-wound string. Forty-foot-long planks could only be transported to the city via sea lanes, and each piece needed to be properly dried out. No kilns large enough existed, and it took years to dry by natural means.

Originally, it had traveled around the north Atlantic, manned by a crew of little more than nineteenth-century teenagers, mostly freed slaves, boys whaling captains believed were expendable. Now restorers worked late nights analyzing blood-stain DNA: Was it marine mammal or human? Burrow holes in the wood—should they be repaired, a marker of sea worm infestation with the potential to bring down a ship mid-ocean or left to tell their story? Here were the signs of danger averted, but you can imagine, a placard would read, what it would be like, slowly sinking thousands of miles from land, the water rising, no way out. When the whaler is finished, it should be taken out to sea, just once, to see what it's like, even if it's perilous to try out riding waves in such a craft, but do it before the ship/not a ship settles into the identity of a museum of an era of open season marine hunting. I texted the know-it-all Morris.

What time did the Director of Adjudications put in a request for the Laveneer records?

Never

You mean you can't tell me?

No. Never as in he hasn't put in an A & R request in weeks. He's been getting a lot of shit from Accounting. Like I told you

I had once been called into Accounting and asked about certain flagged items that had nothing to do with me. Take a seat, they said, and they showed me footage of Altner photographing files and evidence in the form of vials of fluid and what looked like tissue samples. Any idea why your boss would do that? No clue. Also, keep in mind Altner knew he was being recorded—either he didn't believe he was doing anything untoward or he was sloshed. Okay, how about this, Loew? They played a recording of Altner on the phone talking about the Gorenstein trial, *Gorenstein v. Pangenica*, a famous case, though I hadn't worked on it personally. The family sued us for damages because their daughter had fallen in front of a subway car. The Gorensteins had requested a child with perfect pitch, but this trait was tied to balance issues. Inner ears are a transactional situation. They claimed they weren't warned, because if they had, they certainly would have heeded such a warning and modified their request. How could this accident be a result of corporate malfeasance? Pangenica was sure to win, but Altner could be heard telling an unidentified woman on the phone to put her money on Gorenstein. Is he literally taking bets? Not possible—he was only speaking figuratively. To do otherwise would not only be illegal but a capital offense. He could only have been speaking figuratively. Altner, the Director of Adjudications, had insider information about every case, but it was highly illegal to discuss cases outside of the Department of Adjudications, as he well knew. The Gorensteins' schlubby lawyer was up against our most skilled litigators, but the unkempt man with his mess of papers won in what was considered the trial of the century.

What about his expenses? Accounting asked. That dinner or that flight, I told them, ask my Director, I had no idea, and how would I? Accounting was known for asking the wrong questions of the wrong people. I chalked it up to their tendency to misfile, to mix up dates, to call the wrong number, to send junior investigative accountants when a case needed the skills of a senior forensic numbers team. An officer from the Exchange Commission had found nothing amiss either. Altner was buying property in Slavtown Ciudad Medina, expensive watches, flowers delivered every day to an address that didn't appear to exist. I assumed Altner was highly paid, and his books, they told me, appeared in order. So, what was the problem? How can I help? The truth is, I can't. This is not, as Altner himself would say, my province.

My phone pinged with a new text. Crack answered that he would meet me later, he had to leave his car in a shop, but he sounded like someone who didn't have a care in the world, someone who would lean back in his chair and pretend a spoon was a mutated fruit fly who could buzz in six languages. Noddies can have that effect. Music blared from the party boats along with the sound of things falling into the water. I stared out at the murky harbor and imagined my mother climbing the lighthouse steps, looking out into the distance, though not necessarily in my direction. I always dreaded leaving the island, but I couldn't stay there.

Just as my ferry was heading in, a man getting off another boat dropped his phone on the sidewalk. I shouted at him, and he wasn't wearing headphones, but he didn't appear to hear me. I picked up the phone and ran after him, worried as I chased him around the corner that I'd miss my ferry. As the space between us narrowed, I was able to grab his arm and hand it back to him, here's your phone. His thank you was accented, maybe he didn't speak English, and hey isn't universal. I'd done a small decent thing, I guess, but I was anxious. Why couldn't you hear me when I shouted at you? I didn't say, but ran back to the pier just in time to get on the ferry to Dinah McCall's, his confused thank yous ringing in my ears, startled at my touch on his elbow, and at my minor anxiety. PomPom was, or had been, a constantly irritated person, and I didn't want to resemble her, even for an instant, so forget about it, look at the warehouses and luxury towers lining the shore, imagine people making their dinners, pouring drinks, looking down at ant-size people below. Unlike the choppy waters that the *Jolly Sandhog* navigated, the ride was pacific, not out to sea, but along a channel that divided the inhabited but smaller city islands. A bunch of plastic bottles clustered tightly together floated by, a life raft for non-aquatic animals heading out to an island they can populate and take over, becoming the echidnas, the wombats, the oddballs of some isolated ecosystem.

While on deck, I eaeroscripted Chester, the aide who had some sense of the cabinet of curiosities that made up PomPom's brain: her dislike of her doctors, her frustration over humming nurses, a memory of Singe humming, a memory of that boy, Clayton, who wore a tight belt that made his pants bunch up around his butt that annoyed her no end. PomPom may have been immobile, but was still pulsing, and as long as her aide believed I was Jane Ames, he might talk to me.

Dinah lived by herself in a small house on the edge of one of the islands, a short walk from the dock around the shore to her house. It was a neighborhood whose residents were firemen, police, teachers, owners of single commercial fishing boats. The flat-roofed house had green aluminum siding and a striped metal awning over the door, all of which an earlier version of Dinah would have abhorred, but in her current state, she had no income to make any changes to the box-like two-story house. The front was a glassed-in porch full of plants, a sculpture of a sitting Buddha in one corner, a small electric waterfall that provided drinking water for her cat in another, and stacks of newspapers bound with twine, waiting to be thrown out.

Dinah greeted me at the door, thin as a post, papery skin, wearing a starchy-looking wig made of hair that couldn't swing out when she moved her head, but she was still recognizable from the picture in the Singe file. She was divorced, her remaining son was a young adult and lived in another part of the country. Though she was no longer the well-to-do boss of the playground Singe had described, Dinah's snobbery survived intact. She had nothing to do with her neighbors, and they had nothing to do with her, so she was glad to have someone to talk to, the assumption being that if I was an Adjudicator from Pangenica, I was worth speaking to and would be even if we met under other circumstances, even if I hadn't knocked on her door in an attempt to address past injuries.

Bare wooden stairs led to the upper story, coats piled on the banister. Apart from the staircase, the first floor was occupied by a kitchen that opened out into a sort of living room, a couch facing an old PlayStation no child would return to play. The place smelled of both bleach and mold, not uncommon for low-lying coastal dwellings, a smell the owner of the house was probably used to. There was a recessed alcove that, besides containing a table and chairs, was a shrine to Clayton. The walls were covered with his drawings, charts of unknown interstellar calculations, boxes of papers arranged on shelves and labeled according to year, and this was where Dinah indicated we should sit. She was calm, so I was calm, though a vindictive impulse was brewing. She offered me coffee, explaining that nearby supermarkets and small shopping strips were so alienating to her, she drove to a different neighborhood to buy food. I held the steaming cup up to my nose and inhaled for as long as I was able. It masked the smell of the house. Without my asking, she began by telling me about how she met Singe, how they became friends, and I listened without giving away that I already knew.

"You're nervous when you pick up your baby, even if you've done this before, as my husband and I had done. So, we met and became friends under very specific circumstances: PickUp Day, Birth Day, at Pangenica."

"Which Pangenica Center did you go to?"

"Central. It was the closest."

They hadn't met at a regional distribution center but at Central, where I worked. The incubatorium attached to Pangenica headquarters was in a different part of the corporate park, though not far, but situated adjacent to the labs and offices, because otherwise there would be a traffic nightmare. Administration, research, creation, and delivery each required their own buildings with distinctly engineered facilities, though they were connected by bridges and tunnels, so children hatched in one building can be immediately conveyed to the waiting arms of their parents in another. I never had any reason to visit a delivery center, so why would I? It never occurred to me. I would guess Waxman, in his wanderings, hadn't either, because access is limited to parents and staff who work at the delivery center. Dinah explained the visceral experience of sitting in one of the waiting rooms, the empty abstract paintings, the pillowy chairs, the anxiety of people who didn't even look at their phones. Most sat in silence, but in her nervousness, she was a talker, and struck up a conversation with a woman seated next to her. Singe had peppermint-striped hair. Holes studded her eyebrows where rings moved back and forth like miniature Slinkys.

"In the waiting room, Singe had been eager to talk, and we stayed in contact during the early years with the children, but then Singe began to irritate me. It's hard to believe I was very fond of PomPom at one time, but it would have been difficult not to be. PomPom was delightful as a young child, precociously smart, often commenting on everything from the probability of a Watchman action figure, for example, coming to life when no one was looking, so you had to turn around really fast, and even then, humans are congenitally too slow, to asking why jetpacks didn't burn your butt off. Cute, funny stuff, but there were clues as to who she would become. She began to turn her back on children who she looked at as supplicants, uncool and late to the party that was PomPom. She became like a splash of drain cleaner you didn't notice had marked your arm until it starts to burn, and then it's too late. Water, the logical solution, only spreads the burn, and makes it worse. Singe tried to deflect the child's personality and made excuses, oh, she's having a bad day, she doesn't mean what she's saying, and refused to take responsibility for what she had created."

Dinah was unstoppable, a tornado of ire, relentless in her pent-up assessment of the family that she believed targeted Clayton, but her version of Singe bore little similarity to the image I'd had from the file.

Dinah: Singe was a conversation hog, all she ever did was talk about herself, a firehose of real and imagined affronts. Did she really think anyone cared about returning a long lost vessel for the organs of a sacrificial human to some godforsaken sandpit somewhere? Soldiers looted, murdered, stole, or smuggled heaps more. That's what they did and always have done. Some self-appointed guardian in a distant city says, excuse me, you need to return that shit back to where it came from. That's going to happen? All mail returned to sender? I don't think so, Dinah insisted. Sometimes things are better cared for elsewhere, but Singe wouldn't hear of it. No wonder she was treated like a pariah. No one likes a work collaborator who stands on a soap box and wags their finger at you, who is constantly letting you know they're better than you are. Her halo was screwed on tight. She always assumed her cases, her protests, were entitled to displace everyone else's concerns. Your child broke her arm, oh, I'm sorry, but did I tell you about the confrontation I had in a gallery with a man who threatened to call the police if I didn't leave? She made Dinah want to have a three martini lunch, to get rolling drunk and breathe gin breath all over her, if not outright puke.

Not much of a father even when he was around, Mr. Laveneer (and in talking about him, Dinah became uncorked), all kinds of snakes and toads came out of the woodwork. He could have worked from home, but rented a space elsewhere. This irked Singe. Dinah didn't know where the money came from, and in fact, they, or he, seemed to be better off than their jobs would have allowed. Dinah noticed things like that: cars, vacations, clothing. After he disappeared, Singe went to clear out his office. They hadn't been separated all that long and were still married, technically, so that was her job—pack up the boxes and get rid of what she didn't want. In the office she found a photograph of Mr. Laveneer with his arm around a woman in the spangled costume of an acrobat, clearly backstage somewhere. She'd never seen this woman perform, Singe was certain, and she'd confided in Dinah, looking for support. Why did he keep the picture, knowing she'd find it? Why did he need it as a piece of paper instead of keeping it on his phone? Dinah had suggested his relationship with the acrobat might have been work-related, but this was unlikely. Dinah had also suggested she should identify the woman and return the picture to her. Singe found no humor in this advice, which I found entirely understandable, though Dinah didn't know why Singe of all people was so easily offended and thin-skinned. Their friendship was never quite the same afterwards. Dinah said she was not at all surprised about this revelation about Mr. Laveneer. He was an asshole, too. They deserved one another. She hadn't talked about them in years and was enjoying every minute of unearthing long-held opinions and grievances.

Then she went off on PomPom. Singe, reveling in her daughter's precocity, let the kid do whatever she pleased, but at the same time, it was almost as if PomPom bored her, or she was so preoccupied with what she thought meant doing the right thing that she didn't notice her daughter brewing poison in the basement. She let PomPom paddle in the deep end before she could swim, go downtown alone and wander around, have a ferret as a pet. She pushed other children out of the way, stomped on balsa wood airplanes, pulled limbs off Daredevil, Wolverine, beheaded untold numbers of dolls of all sizes, shapes, and colors, then turned to subtler forms of exclusion, discovering the pleasures of online anonymity, lobbing missiles from anywhere. You probably weren't told about the incident of Child X who couldn't be named due to privacy concerns and age. No, it's not in Singe's file. Of course not, Dinah smiled. This is the story. Child X fell or was pushed to her death on the Junker Bridge, a narrow wood and iron structure dating back to the mid-twentieth century that spanned the Junker River, a tributary of the Great City River. The only people on the bridge at the time were PomPom and Child X. PomPom herself reported and claimed that X fell, and maybe she did, but it was also true that X had longed to be her friend, but was afraid of her, so much so that she wanted to change schools. PomPom volunteered a last picture of X. It was on her phone, you could see her leaning against one of the railings, and it's easy, for me at any rate, to imagine PomPom saying take one step back, so I can get that tree in the picture, too. PomPom had one of those backpacks decorated with a row of rubber spikes meant to mimic a stegosaurus, but she could have been wearing a suit made entirely of iron barbs as she trolled the city. Whoever ran her over should have finished the job. Singe ate burnt toast and drank black coffee as a penance, as if that made her better than anyone else.

I listened, but it wasn't the content that mattered, rather what animated Dinah. How to pry a crowbar under the manhole of Dinah's consciousness and describe what I find? Is it even possible? What neuroreceptors should have gone to Clayton but went, instead, to PomPom? Where are the telltale alleles? These were questions I couldn't answer, but I had to bring the Director something. I had to be able to close the file, to prove there was no switch of any kind, and Singe was off her rocker.

Singe may have been right that Dinah and PomPom had something in common that was monstrous and degrading. Something that had its origins in one, and accelerated in the other, but when Dinah described coming home to hear sirens and lights on the night of Clayton's accident, I felt myself passing out, as she had, absorbing the trauma even years later. There was nothing in the room to focus on that would deflect the memory of her suffering.

There were pictures of Dinah's other son alongside Clayton, but no pictures of her husband. I commented on how much the two of them looked alike, and she agreed with me, because this was intentional. They had wanted three identical children of different ages, so when the second and third came along, they would know exactly what to expect, because in the event any mistakes or perceived mistakes should arise, the second or third time round, she and her husband would take necessary precautions. However, they stopped after the second, and never did get all the way to three.

"You have copies of your original InTake forms?"

"I did but no longer. There was no point in keeping them, but that was our plan—to have the same boy several years apart, so I needed exact copies of my forms each time. My husband had a friend who worked at Pangenica who was able to disarm the security app long enough for us to take screenshots, and in this way, we were able to retain copies of our original forms."

I had no idea this highly illegal act was possible.

"Can you tell me who it was?"

“I couldn’t tell you that even if I knew. Some other meteorologist had the skills. He disappeared a few weeks later.” Dinah half-nodded, half-shrugged. She was desultory, as if the hacking was no more dangerous than shoplifting. It was a way to get what she wanted, so why not? It wasn’t uncommon for parents to view the Pangenica process as if it were a shopping opportunity, but if Pangenica’s strictest regulations could be overturned, there would be no need to kidnap a future Dr. Goldberg. Her husband’s fellow meteorologist had skills beyond interpreting wind patterns, forecasting cyclones, heat waves, and ice storms. This person had determined how to disrupt the human genome from within the comfort of one’s own home. Of course, they had long ago been disappeared.

“So, Clayton was just like his brother.” I said this, not as a question, but as a way of affirming what she had just stated.

“No, he wasn’t like his brother. At first, they were similar, and they looked alike, but that was deceptive.”

She pulled down one of the boxes, and began to take out papers, stacking them on the table.

“His brother didn’t have a driving engine, an obsession, the way Clayton did, but I don’t believe some bit of someone else got mixed in. I assumed he would outgrow his preoccupation, but now I will never know if that would have been the case.”

She handed me a yellowed copy of *Scientific American*, where Clayton had marked up an article about the Kepler Project. She believed this was the last thing Clayton read before he went through the ice.

Shadows of Other Worlds

In an exercise in interstellar archeology, the NASA Kepler craft, a Transplanetary Exoplanet Satellite, was a prolific planet hunter, and it had looked for a number of things. First, liquid water. Oceans need the right temperature, therefore distance from a sun or star matters, as does the temperature for habitable zones. It can't be too hot or too cold, neither ice nor boiled away. The Kepler was looking for life as we know it under these conditions. The planet needs to be about the same size as Earth and have a solid surface. Larger planets are surrounded by gas, hydrogen, and helium, and if powerful gravity concentrates the gas, creating a solid mass, these are not viable. The Kepler was also looking for eclipses, because they indicate a planet is transiting in front of its sun. Spacecraft with powerful telescopes measuring the brightness of stars looked for these eclipsing moments when exploring star fields, and they found a number of miniature solar systems. Star formation is the DNA of the universe.

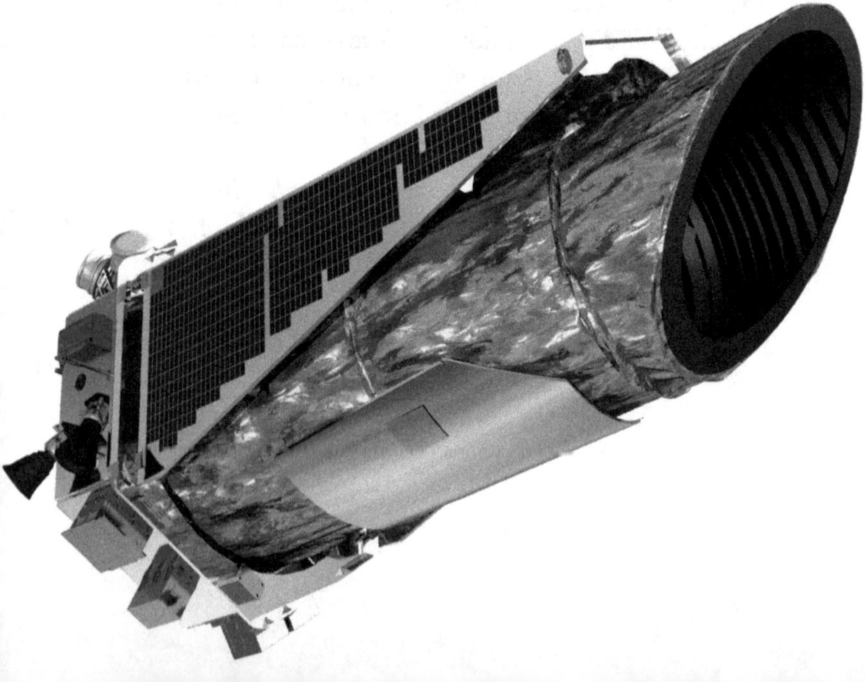

I pictured the boy cutting out the article, then heading out to the pond, but it wasn't adding up. I needed to ask Dinah a difficult question, and I asked as an Adjudicator, had Clayton been alone on the pond? Were there really no witnesses? Can there really be no doubt about that? I started to feel anger because Dinah's voice rose in irritation.

"No, he wasn't alone. All those who called him names, who made fun of him, they were there, too. I don't know why you would ask me a question like that. You could ask me if I was driving the car that hit PomPom and left her crapping in a wheelchair. I wish I could answer yes, I was the driver, or I commissioned the accident, but no, I didn't have the pleasure. She's a monster, and her mother, Singe, is just as bad. But I don't believe Clayton deliberately jumped through thinning ice, however horribly he was bullied. I don't think he would do that. Was it really an accident? Or was he pushed? The pond behind where we used to live was called a pond, but it was more like a lake and very deep in places. There were no cameras, no place to dust for fingerprints, no record of anyone on the lake with him, but that doesn't mean he was alone."

"Why would anyone want to harm your son?"

"I have no idea, but I don't believe he deliberately walked out onto ice that he knew was beginning to thaw, that's all I'm saying."

"Did you see Singe at that time?"

"Yes, only once. She visited me after Clayton's death, and appeared genuinely devastated, as if it had been her own child. It wasn't so much that she was sticking her nose in, as sticking her neck out. We hadn't spoken in a long time, and weren't really friends anymore. At one point, she asked to use the bathroom and was in there for a long time. Later that night, I noticed my hairbrush was clean. There was no hair in it."

"Do you think she took some of your hair?"

"No one else could have. My husband was bald, and the children had their own bathroom elsewhere in the house.

When she finally came out, she asked if she could see my InTake forms, the ones for my other son, knowing I had copies. Years ago, in a moment of misplaced trust, I had told her we managed to access and retain copies. Why? We had just witnessed a dog hit by a car, I went into shock, and Singe grabbed my arm, put her hand over my eyes. Her reflexes and empathetic responses were that quick, but we were both shaken. We took the children to an indoor playland where they were watched by teenagers dressed as Peter Pan or Alice, and we went for a drink to calm our nerves. Never have I misread another person to the extent I thought Singe was a friend, and I told her about the copies. Also, I was in shock, had too much to drink in a short period of time, so I blabbed, and she remembered what I had told her in confidence.

"I asked her why she needed to see them? Why did she need to see those most private of all documents? She told me she thought some part of the children had been switched, but then she also described what she'd found on PomPom's phone. I hadn't known until that moment. First, I felt like she wanted to claim a piece of me, as if her benighted disgusting daughter was not, somehow, hers, but mine. What was I supposed to do with the information that her daughter sprayed acid? Say oh, okay, that must have been a burden for you, too? What an awful thing to discover, I'm so very sorry. Fuck you, bitch. Take responsibility for your monster, asshole. I was cutting pieces of an apple, but I got out of my chair and held the knife up to her neck. My son was gone, and her rancid bitch of a daughter was carrying on as if it was a matter of survival of the fittest. Singe didn't flinch or move a muscle. She just sat there until I stepped back and told her to get the fuck out. She left without comment, no screaming or protesting."

"Would you agree to a DNA test to prove she's wrong?"

She held out her hand for the vial to spit into. Was everyone in the file who they claimed to be? We would find out, and then what? What if they weren't? What if they were?

There was a small hotel near the ferry dock. A concierge at the front desk provided eaerotube service and the sample was sent to the Director of Adjudications, as he requested. He would receive it within the hour. While I waited for the ferry back to the main city island, staring at the lights that had begun to come on in the distance, I imagined the Singe file, animated, talking to me. Singe suspected something was wrong with Clayton and PomPom, that their consciousnesses have been switched. She brought a case against Pangenica, either not realizing how incendiary her case was, or not caring. Vy Sapper, feet up on her Admissions Desk, had no InTake forms for the family, and I was hampered, she pointed out, because the forms were missing the signature of the Director of Adjudications, meaning she couldn't give them to me even if she had them. Altner told me a false story about Waxman. He was the Director of Neuronal Correlates, working on ConSwitch. He was looking for the DNA switch that turned on consciousness, but hadn't yet found it, or so he claimed. To him, the Singe file meant someone had gotten there before him. If Pangenica could turn consciousness into a commodity, the world would be its oyster.

On the return ferry, I received an eaeroscript for j.ames@Porphinc.com, and opened it to find it was an answer from Chester. The time stamp indicated it had been sent while I was running after the owner of the lost phone.

You're in a spaceship and you think you're well outside the gravitational pull of a black hole, those fantastic suckers pulling in every possible thing, every possible form of energy, even feasting on light that can't run backwards, but gradually you realize that as far away as you are, you're not moving forward, and in fact, are being sucked in, too.

THIRTEEN

Eaeroscript

Hi Jane, not of Porphirion Insurance, because there is no Porphirion Insurance. I pretended to look you up to calm my charge but then later, I thought, why not look up your company? So I did and guess what? You don't exist. Those lazy fuckers in Crafted Identities screwed you. The least they could have done was create a fake site. But no worries, I have something for you: PomPom's toothbrush loaded with DNA. How about this? Let's meet to make an exchange. I'll give you the toothbrush, and you pay me a sum that's a dream of moneybags doing a samba.

So, here's what you're going to do. You want to take the #17 train going downtown, and you should be in the last car. The last stop will be announced, but don't get off. No one will check. The train will keep going until it reaches an abandoned station, Whitehall Street, that used to be the last stop, now it's a ghost station, and here the #17 will turn around. Just after it makes the turn, the train will pause, and at that moment, open the door between train cars and hop off to land on the platform. It's just a matter of jumping a foot or so, maybe eighteen inches at most. The train is slow; some conductors will even pause the train for a minute, so it isn't much of a feat to jump. The conductors are in the first car, you're in the back, and the platform is curved, so even if they look, they can't see you. I'll be waiting for you.

This ghost station had once been one of the jewels of the system. It had glazed blue-gray brick walls laid out in a herringbone pattern, Romanesque barrel vaults, and a leaded glass dome in a geometric pattern of diamonds and triangles. It appeared to be empty, and though cavernous, I started to feel a little alarmed. The only way out was to wait for another train to turn around, pause, hope no conductor was looking, then jump back on. What if a subsequent train didn't slow down enough for me to make the return trip or didn't come at all? The trains usually ran around the clock, but on weekends, when repairs took place, sections of lines were often shut down entirely with no warning. A flight of stairs ended with a locked door. There was no way out. Often people lived in these abandoned stations, but I saw no evidence of human habitation. O Sites could be located in dead-end locations like this, but sometimes a locked door is just a locked door, and a bucket is just a bucket, and rebar is just a way of strengthening concrete. The engineers who turned the trains around here wore earphones that muted train sounds, so they wouldn't go deaf, but were also known for minding their own business. A stabbing or a robbery on the platform? Conductors only had eyes for the track in front of them.

Someone was whistling "It's not Unusual" . . .

Chester, lanky and dressed in a mustard-colored suit jacket and black jeans, was leaning against one of the vault ribs that extended down a corner, near another set of exit stairs that no longer led to any exit. He deliberately stood where no one in a passing train could see him.

"Sweetart, over here." I think he meant *sweetheart*, and he was smiling like the world owed him a living, and was about to pay up. The aide, so calm, blowing air through his lips, asked me for my real name.

I suggested I really didn't have to answer that question.

"I think my employer would like to know." He snapped on surgical gloves, removed a plastic bag from a pocket, and held up a blue toothbrush with PomPom's name written on the handle in what looked like red nail polish. "Patients like Miss PomPom rest easy knowing that they're protected by the strictest conditions of privacy and confidentiality. Those paying the bills understand Lazarus House is like the home embassy, no matter what country you're in. Once you get past the gate, you're safe, you're on home turf. So, who you working for? Who needs to know her shit?"

He stood close and smelled like sandalwood cologne and hospital-strength antiseptic Handi-wipes. What I learned from Chester: There were others living in HoneckerNajibullahAssange-like protection on the premises. Lazarus House had been chosen for PomPom for reasons beyond its rehabilitation facilities, of which there was no hope for her anyway.

Crafted Identities should have set up a Porphirion site, not just an eaeroscript account, but laying the blame on the sloppy work of someone else, even if true, sounded like finger pointing. I stopped short of it. An Adjudicator was in full authority and responsible for what happened in the field. I didn't want to be the kid who told on another kid who threw a rock. We both broke the window, and I didn't want to be the one who sent the man we spotted at Mr. Levant's to a cell at an Orientation Site.

"Neither you nor Lazarus House needs that information." I held open my flamingo-pink bag, as if to say, drop it in here, please.

"Your name, sunshine."

I remained silent.

"You're on surveillance tapes. You don't need to tell me. I can find out, but if I have to make inquiries at Security, ask my boys can I see the tape from *date X*, reception desk, go back, and freeze, yeah right there, yes, that gal in the orange shoes, zoom in, do an image identity search. Thank you so much! I could do that, you know, and then others are going to get in on your secret, *mi amor*."

To say my name out loud would be like pulling a lever, a trapdoor opens and down I would fall into the molten Asthenosphere. He could find it. Maybe he would, but I wasn't going to hand it to him. Chester was confident, not a care in the world, so I absorbed that coolness.

"How do I know that's PomPom's toothbrush?"

"Her name's on it."

"So what?" The name was meaningless. He could have bought the toothbrush ten minutes ago, rinsed it off, put a label on it.

Chester held his phone close to my face, then played footage taken with one hand while the other brushed the chair-ridden young woman's teeth, pouring water into her mouth, then pushing her head forward. The act of brushing someone's teeth for them was intimate, but Chester, his face reflected in the mirror, did nothing to conceal his disgust. This was not pleasant to watch. There was a close-up of the toothbrush. It looked the same and had her name neatly painted on it with what looked like the same red nail polish. Then the shot zoomed out. It looked like a communal bathroom, therefore personal items were labeled. Whoever was paying for PomPom's residence at Lazarus House, they hadn't sprung for a private bathroom. Alone with her, Chester jammed a water glass into her mouth and slammed it down on the counter when she had finished, but he had kept the audio running as he recorded.

"Who do you think you are? Wallis Simpson?" he said to PomPom's reflection.

PomPom blinked, and he answered her.

"You want me to end your life? Pull the plug already? Put rat poison in your food? Give your sorry ass the heave-ho down a flight of stairs? Oops, sorry, boss, I was just taking her down the hall, must have steered too close to the edge.

Her spine suddenly and very unexpectedly, as you know, reactivated and miracle of miracles, came to life, leaned heavy to the right, and over she went. So, then I can get my own private chair, run by state pen electricity. Sounds good. Sign me up right here." He shook his head while continuing to look at himself in the mirror. "I like my job, sister. I get paid a lot to wipe your ass, to read your dumbass blink, blink, blink, bling. I like this punishment for you: Live trapped in a body that no longer functions. How about that forever, how about that for as long as it takes?"

PomPom was making an effort to push some kind of sound from her throat, groans or screams maybe, but she was unable to.

"What do you mean your mother isn't all your mother? Oh, I'm sorry. Is that why you want me to introduce you to a flight of stairs?"

Chester turned the phone off. He couldn't care less about the nature of PomPom's agony. He just wanted his payday.

"The toothbrush could easily have become contaminated since you recorded this. You could have put it in the mouth of a basset hound doing its business right there in front of the Thriftydrug, for all I know."

"You'll have to trust me."

"That trust comes with a very steep price tag. Lazarus House would take a dim view of one of its employees stealing property."

"You think so? You gonna make that call? Here. Be my guest." Chester held out his phone. "I didn't think so." Then he pulled out a Spring Airsoft Pistol, neat blue-black, it said you don't have much choice, and he pointed the business end at one of my jacket pockets.

"I don't have that much cash."

"The electronic wallet has been invented."

Chester was calm, so I was calm. He saw himself as a semi-skilled health aide just trying to get by, cleaning bottoms, interpreting blinks, without much of a future until opportunity presented itself in the form of a visitor who turned out not to be who she claimed. Adjudicators are meant to be among you, but not of you, somehow different, secretive habits, rootless cosmopolitans, law benders, you never knew who they really were. Once he determined I was an Adjudicator, I was money in the bank. Chester knew about Crafted Identities. Its existence was semi-public knowledge, but the reference could indicate that Chester was on the ball in a way that most non-Pangenica employees were not. It's like this: People know surgeons exist and have a general idea of what they do, without being able themselves to perform a lobotomy. Chester knew things. Despite his pacific moments in the underground, acid flowed through his veins. So many who had contact with Singe and PomPom turned out this way.

I had no choice but to take out my phone while he looked over my shoulder and instructed me to empty my bank account into his. Now he had my name. All that refusing for nothing. I didn't have much, but now he had all of it.

A train came, the first I'd heard since I landed on the platform. It slowed down and Chester jumped, waving to me as it picked up speed. In a matter of seconds, the red lights from back of the #17 train disappeared down the tunnel, and I was left holding a used toothbrush for which I'd just paid every cent I had.

Trains came and went, not slow enough, hardly pausing. I bent my knees as if about to jump, but couldn't do it. There are two narrow ledges, one extending from each car, but they don't meet, and between them was the coupling. Each ledge is about the length of a man's foot. If you miss it, you're on the tracks, and the train is moving. It was an easier move, leaping off than getting back on. I remembered a story about a man who had stepped between cars to urinate, unzipped, maybe he was using both hands, or at any rate wasn't holding onto any of the metal bars or chains that might have saved him, so when it jolted, down he went. It was reported that there wasn't enough left of him to even scrape up.

Trains rolled in, slowed down, then moved on, and I stood there until one, for reasons unknown, perhaps a signal problem somewhere in another part of the system, or mechanical issues, came to a stop, and I was able to step onto one of the ledges, then open the door to an empty car. Inhale, exhale, the sweetest emptiness ever. A few stops later I got out to change to a different line, from the #17 to the #23.

FOURTEEN

The Essex Place Station was crowded on a Saturday night, the #23 line had been delayed, so mobs of people filled the platform, as more and more came down the stairs, but no one was able to leave. Two pigeons trapped underground raced in a long, elliptical shape from one end of the station to the other. They had figured out how to fly down the steps to the feast of food garbage littering the tracks, but hadn't determined how to soar up and out, so they dashed back and forth in a frenzy with no discernible, to them, way out, and no night, no darkness, even on the platform, no signal for sleep unless they sought night in the dark tunnel, and then there really would be no way out for the birds.

A train pulled in, nearly empty, but soon filled. I elbowed my way to the front of the first car, hoping if I could look out, I wouldn't absorb anything from my fellow passengers who experienced the rubbing of a stranger's thighs, the irritation of a scratchy sweater, the jostling of a man who was late for his night shift, all inches away.

Just as the doors were closing, a boy ran into the car. The doors closed on his neck. In theory the train can't move if the doors aren't closed all the way, but it happens from time to time that they do, and someone is dragged to their death. I could feel the rubber runners that line the doors, the pressure of them on my neck, relentless, automated, determined to meet even if my neck was in the way. Out on the platform, his mother screamed for someone to help, her face through the window was terrifying, she was in agony, helpless, and two large muscular guys pried the doors apart. She and her child burst into the car. The boy was crying uncontrollably, and she was screaming at him, but holding him at the same time. He'd injured his eye somehow, and she was shouting, never do that, wait for me, what if the train had started to move?

The boy's crying and the mother's hysteria were unbearable. I completely absorbed their near-death reactions, and at the next stop, I relinquished my position at the front and moved into another car.

In the second car, I stood between a kid with a Batman knapsack that extended a foot from his back, a man with crayon-red hair jiggling in place to whatever music was coming through his earbuds, and a woman tapping on her phone with long nails that, like frames of an animation, showed a rocket blasting off, beginning with her thumb as it left earth and landing, by the time it got to her pinkie, on the moon. They were all calm and preoccupied, so I was okay, and able to diminish the effects of the panic I'd experienced a few minutes earlier, though I wished I could have stared down the tunnel as wooden beams and lights slipped past, looking for the bar of illumination in the distance that would signal the approach of the next station. There was no room to move. I decided I would get out when the subway came to the next stop and wait for the following train. It was just too crowded, and I was beginning to feel the hopes and disappointment of the woman texting next to me, the longings of the dancing-in-place man, the itchiness of the Batman backpack kid who was minutes from an asthma attack. I imagined the green lights down in the tunnel had turned to yellow, the train slowed, then came to a gradual stop when nothing but red lights lay ahead. Keep going. Keep going. I tried to will the train to move, and I know from experience, red doesn't necessarily mean full stop, but this time it did.

I looked at my phone: 8:22. Usually if the train does stop in the tunnel, it's not for more than a few minutes, but the train remained motionless. 8:27. Five minutes meant we would not be moving in one minute, more like twenty. If the train stopped for as long as five, rather than, say, two, we were going to be there longer. It was unnaturally quiet in the packed car. That happens, and I don't know why, what wave of silence is unconsciously communicated to the trapped group, and so nobody makes any noise. A minute ago, they were all thinking different thoughts, now in unconscious unison, we're all waiting, waiting, waiting in a tube, in an unknown location, while overhead layers of dirt, concrete, glass, rebar, steel, lost wallets, lost glasses, lost phones, arrowheads, swords, boulders, chunks of moraine, rat bones, fossils of megalodons, imprints of trilobites also waited. I wished people would talk, sing along with their headphones, but nothing. The conductor made the usual announcement about as soon as the signal clears, we should be moving shortly, thank you for your patience. This meant nothing. A generator of false consciousness. King Kong could be pulling down the tunnel support system ahead, and the same announcement would be made: thank you for riding the MTA.

The boy began to wheeze and rummage around in his backpack for an inhaler. This was a gene that should not have presented itself, but environmental factors, such as living in a neighborhood adjacent to a recycling area, which is actually a lead dump, can trigger respiratory problems. I began to have trouble breathing, too, and tried to picture Captain Ada's ferry and the open water just beyond Penrose. I should have walked. I should have stayed above ground. The woman just behind me stopped tapping on her phone. She was beginning to panic. I kept focused on the glass sides of the train and at the walls of the tunnel just inches away, or tried to, but then turned and plunged my hands into the boy's backpack in an attempt to help him find the small piece of plastic that would help him breathe. Books, a notebook, half-eaten chocolate, a magnet in the shape of a bullet, an acorn, a tiny rubber ninja from a gumball machine. We were both gasping for air. I stood and for a second looked down the crowded car. Holding onto an overhead bar, staring at a book, I thought I saw the Singe look-alike, the younger version. Then the lights in the subway car went out. People screamed and held up their phones, but those were all uniformly dead, too. We began to smell smoke. After my mother was let go from Chromatin, she used to say, over and over, know when they come for you, but no one was coming for me, individually, it was a whole train full of people. She also used to quote that it was said of movie director Carol Reed that he saw the firing squad reflected in an actor's eyes before the actor did.

When the lights came on, there was a body on the tracks, and a rescue crew had moved it off to the side, so the train could proceed. As the train inched slowly past men and women in orange vests and hard hats, I thought the face of the man on the stretcher looked like Debonis, the security guard. Maybe, maybe not, hard to know for certain in the dark as the train picked up speed.

FIFTEEN

I got off at a stop near Waxman's address. Up the stairs, onto the street, I was never so happy to be above ground, and could have used a meal but available currency was at zero. Across from the station stop, an electric sign advertising a restaurant came into view: monkeys forever jumping out of a barrel. A Barrel of Monkeys, as in more fun than. Why that name? A barrel of monkeys would not be fun, not for the monkeys inside or for the person who came into possession of the barrel. The monkeys would be screaming and miserable, and if you let them out they'd be injured, volatile, and really pissed off. It wouldn't matter if they were kind-hearted chimps or self-absorbed capuchins. Under duress, under torture, survival instincts, the clawing and fighting supersede generosity. All behave badly. Who can blame them?

I knew of the place, though I'd never been inside before. It was formerly a battered steakhouse whose clientele had been mainly older men and women who worked at the municipal court nearby, and it had a reputation for serving massive steaks with wine or beer that made older diners so tired, they could barely move without a steady stream of free coffee refills. The current Barrel of Monkeys offered a very different kind of fun than the pleasures offered by the previous chefs.

The new restaurant served flights, sequences of increasingly hot hot sauces which began with mild and ended with scorching. You could buy sets of five or ten, and the scale of hotness in each flight varied, as well. Devil Worship, the hottest series of all, had never been completed by anyone, and the menu posted in the window offered more information as to what that might be. It began with Monkey Biz, a vermillion sauce with a fierce bite, and ended with The Devil in Miss Jones, whose label looked like a pin-up poster. The Devil in Miss Jones was made with the Carolina

Reaper, the hottest pepper in the world you could consume without dying on the spot. If you could get through all ten sauces of Devil Worship, Barrel of Monkeys would pay you $1,000. So far, the restaurant had held onto its prize money. I went in. What did I have to lose?

Framed autographed pictures of musicians holding microphones, soccer players, actors, a champion of the Poker Olympics, all spread out from the wall behind the cash register. The new owners had kept much of the original decor, as well as the name of the original establishment, a sarcastic comment on the drudge jobs of most of the original patrons, but I was relieved to find no primate taxidermy inside. Once my eyes got used to the dimness, the Barrel of Monkeys was bigger than it appeared when I first entered. The bar was backlit displaying alcohol in a jewel-like variety of colors, but there were other glass bottles on display—yellow, green, and red. These were hot sauces whose Scoville units skyrocketed from reasonably hot to cleaning fluid burn-out-your-insides. Throughout the restaurant were large floral arrangements, but when you looked at them closely, the flowers were groupings of peppers, some narrow and pointed placed to look like stamens surrounded by petals made of larger peppers, as well as bundles of wrinkly little guys, round and tomato-like. The dominant color of the fake flower compositions was red, red, red. You couldn't get away from it.

A waiter came to my table, introduced himself as Cumari, my personal Scorchmaster, and pulled up a seat. Waitstaff weren't just servers, but they also had to watch over you to be sure you actually downed the sauces and didn't try to cheat. All their name tags were the names of peppers: Savina, Habañero, Madame Juliette, and so on. No one was known by their real name. Green serrano jacket with notched lapels stylishly a size too small, yellow shirt and chocolate-brown pants made of a faintly shiny material, he was relaxed and confident, easy to focus on, I thought. Before the bottles arrived at our table, I could already feel the twinges of other diners, but I was also hungry. I asked Cumari if he ate the sauces, but he said, no he didn't, not while he was on a shift, like a bartender who's not allowed to drink while at work and then loses the desire. My plan was, if I focused on Cumari, I could eat anything. I told him I would try my luck with Devil Worship.

"Devil Worship," Cumari repeated. "An excellent choice."

Then he handed me a form to read and sign that stated the Barrel of Monkeys was not responsible for any injury that might occur or be sustained due to whatever it might be you put into your mouth while on the premises. He advised me to read the form thoroughly, he would collect it when he returned with my order. It wasn't too late; if I didn't sign, I wouldn't be served, and so would be free to go. If anyone wondered how bad it could be, all you would have to do was look around to see people in agony as they ate. Mostly small groups clustered at tables, but there were a few couples, no one alone that I could see. Some screamed, eyes bugged out, hands waved over tongues, not that that would help at all. Jeers, taunts, egging on, you could hear that, too. A man got up from his table and hopped up and down, he was in so much misery. This was a problem for me, because I could feel it all.

Cumari stepped over a man lying on the floor, but soon returned, and set a large platter of chicken wings, shrimp, tempura vegetables, pieces of corn, and soy protein that looked like meat, sort of. It was called Khorne. He also presented me with a pitcher of milk and a glass. Milk is known to soothe the pain of the searing heat as it goes down your pipes. I shook my head and waved it away. Milk makes me gag, a gene never totally eradicated, so it would be of no help whatsoever.

Cumari lined up bottles, emerald, ruby, gold rarities, dazzling, but also implements of torture. Where does sense of taste and spice taper off and sheer pain begin to obliterate? I would find out. Each sauce producer included all kinds of information and graphics on their labels. Monkey Biz, first up, a house sauce, tasted of garlic, cumin, and cayenne. Not so bad. It was like the first minutes of a flight that will become mad turbulent, but you don't know that yet, so you think, why are people afraid of flying? It's nothing. No problem with a squirt of Monkey Biz on a browned piece of Khorne. Cumari informed me that as I proceeded through the hot sauces, he would need to make sure I put a decent amount on, no half-measures allowed. He pushed glasses up his nose. He was watching.

A bottle called Madness followed, song lyrics printed on the label.

Madness was badness, definitely a notch up from Monkey Biz. I focused on the Scorchmaster whose mouth was cool and whose tongue lay evenly in against his teeth, but my staring was making him uncomfortable, I could tell. Wrinkling my nose while chewing, I tried to focus on an image of an abominable snowman with cold white pincer limbs. With swift wrist action, Cumari added a few more drops, reminding me not to be chary with the sauce, then crossed his arms and leaned back in his chair. Madness was followed by Ghost Pepper Boom Boom, golden yellow, it came in a bottle labeled with a winged demon holding a lit cannonball bomb. Boom Boom contained Bhut jolokia or ghost pepper, weaponized by the Indian Army in grenades. It was measured at a million Scoville units. My eyes were running, and I looked at a woman pouring a glass of milk, which made me choke, just watching. I reached for a shrimp, then put it back down on the plate. Cumari looked at his watch and informed me one could pause no more than two minutes between bites.

My throat was in flames. There were nerve-endings in my mouth that I didn't know I had. I picked up the next bottle, Hellboy, whose label was Hellboy juggling Naga Viper peppers. I squirted it on a piece of bland, nothing Khorne, the texture of sponge soaked in liquid fire.

The Barrel of Monkeys hummed with the noise of people talking, plates and bottles clunked on glass tabletops. Someone behind me was making violent retching sounds. Across the room I could see one diner's eyes rolled back in his head, and it looked like he had lost consciousness. Drunk with pain, I wondered if lost consciousness can be found again in its entirety, like rewinding then playing a film, and could there be a Lost and Found expressly for that purpose?

Can you get all of it back? What if it's not one hundred percent reconstituted and you have no idea what you lost along the way?

Burnt offerings, burned out, burned bridges, burned into memory, burnt rubber, burnt sienna, umber, orange, burning man, burning bush, burning down the house, fossil fuels, fat, heartache, Jews, love, midnight oil, questions, pee, ring of fire, rain, vengeance, yourself out, Dot would say if she were here.

More bottles were administered, consumed more than eaten. The deal with heat is that it stays with you for a long time. The opposite of rice cakes, say, or canned peaches, or imitation ice cream. Infinity Chili, Trinidad Mogua Scorpion Butch T, each over a million Scovilles. You'll find them in Ghost Rider. Cumari plunked another bottle in front of me. The label of this one showed a skeleton riding a motorcycle, flames shooting out from the skull's eye sockets. Just the other day, Cumari said he had to order an ambulance for a customer who went too far. Some wiseacre chomped on a 7 Pot Brain Strain plucked from one of the faux floral arrangements. If you eat a slice of one of these peppers, you can sever your esophagus. The guy had planned to film himself but didn't get much further than a closeup of the thing going into his mouth.

You're almost there, he said, just two more.

Here, try Pirate's Booty from Jamaica. Don't touch your eyes! Ever! Cumari warned. At first a taste of orange and rum, but then the Scotch bonnet kicked in. For years, the

Scorchmaster explained, Scotch Bonnet, a brilliantly colored thimble-shaped fruit reigned supreme as the hottest, but then it was supplanted by the Carolina Reaper. Which brought us to our last bottle, The Devil in Miss Jones: mustard, a kiss of honey, and the Carolina Reaper, measuring 1.5 million on the Scoville scale, the hottest pepper on the planet. Now there's a heat profile. Until it was supplanted by Dragon's Breath, a wrinkled little curled-up toe of a capsicum measuring over two million, and you can't eat it even in Barrel of Monkeys, because if you do, you will die, it's that simple. Cumari held the blood-red Devil in Miss Jones over my plate and began to tilt. I needed more time. I was losing my focus on the waiter and was feeling the pain full bore.

I asked Cumari if he had ever seen this man, Waxman, showing him a picture on my phone, figuring this would push the time limit of the permissible pause between bites. I was just buying a few seconds and never expected the answer to be yes, but Cumari nodded, he came in fairly often, an enthusiastic consumer of things hot and superhot. Some people develop addictions to the physiological response to heat: the eye tearing, the sinuses' alarm, the chemoreceptors on the tongue feeling terrorized, but not only did this patron seem like just such an addict, but he liked to gamble, to bet on the stamina of other diners who were strangers to him. He began betting from the moment he walked in until closing time. Also unusual, he mostly came alone. Once he was accompanied by a woman who ate nothing. Cumari remembered because he was their waiter, and it was annoying to him, for obvious reasons; waiters hope and expect diners to order, but also, he believed, it's irritating to other patrons who don't necessarily want to be watched by a spectator who isn't also a participant. Barrel of Monkeys wasn't meant to be a destination for voyeurs. It pissed him off, frankly.

Then I showed him Singe's picture, enlarged to fill the screen.

"Was this the woman?"

"Yes."

I didn't know if I could do the last sauce, The Devil in Miss Jones, but needed the prize money and couldn't pay for what I had eaten, no way, but I felt as if I were really losing consciousness this time, and could have used some kind of interference. So I put my hand on the back of Cumari's neck and brought his face close to mine, not even noticing or caring if he was startled or compliant or keen, which was not easy for me, imagining capsaicin molecules, little black-and-white balls rolling off my lips and onto his, which were cool. He opened his mouth, and I pushed my tongue against his. He tasted like oranges. I caught my breath and the heat was less intense, but still formidable. His hands moved up and down my back a little awkwardly, but he didn't push me away. I unbuttoned his white shirt. There was a Barrel of Monkeys T-shirt underneath.

Were other diners watching? I tried not to think about them. Cumari took my arm. I thought he was going to throw me out, but he steered me toward an alcove, formerly the coat check near the cash register where a woman made up to look like Cleopatra watched a movie on a laptop. She was watching *Seven Days in May* and took no notice of us. Burt Lancaster, playing an army general who wanted to take over the country, was talking about a horse race, actually a code about the planned coup. There was a storage room behind the Cleopatra cashier.

It had a mattress in it, Cumari explained, for people who became so ill the manager would motion for them to be brought here, out of sight. It also contained clear bags of empty bottles to be recycled, extra chairs, crates of Khorne that didn't have to be refrigerated, and a stuffed chimp, left over from the previous Barrel of Monkeys. The storage room wasn't exactly the Ritz, but no other options were available. Cumari took off his glasses, placed them on the chimp, and turned it to face the wall. Like all the waitstaff, he wasn't half-bad looking. You could tell management figured servers should be attractive, that was part of the seduction—pain alloyed with potential pleasure. Cumari was no exception, a man who spent evenings on his feet, carrying heavy trays, juggling plates, then went to the gym late morning after he got up, just to even things out. It was late, all his other tables had paid and left, so there was time to use the storage room. Had he done this before? I didn't ask because I didn't really care. I just wanted the pain to diminish. He backed off when he felt the heat from my mouth, just as searing as if he had swallowed the Hellboy himself. It came as a shock, just how hot it was. Our roles were reversed, now I was the deliverer, the greeter at the world of pain.

When we were finished, Cumari said, sorry, no $1,000, that was a twenty-minute break, but he wanted to see me again. I wrote down my name, Jane Ames, and the poor fink eaeroscript address on a napkin, then we both went back into the dining area as if nothing had happened, except that I was out of the competition, and had to leave. He let me out a back way without paying, so at least I got to eat. I suppose you could look at it that way.

SIXTEEN

And then I saw Crack crossing the street coming toward me. Bleary and disheveled, he had traced me via my phone and held his up to indicate he had done so. He was sweaty and slightly out of breath, as if he'd been running. A little bit of worry, a little bit of relief, there was already news about a tunnel fire as well as the body found on the tracks. The Metro Guards cited surveillance footage that indicated a disoriented man had wandered onto the tracks and into the tunnel. It happened from time to time. People walked between stations, and in some of the tubes, there was enough space to walk, even if a train sped by, though the passage could abruptly narrow, and then you'd be stuck. Why did people risk life and limb in the tunnels? Some contained spray-painted murals, ancient but preserved, that could only be seen if you knew where you were going, though sometimes adventurous viewers were hit and killed, or they touched the third rail, and were thereby electrocuted on the spot. Debonis hadn't struck me as the kind of person who would spend a Saturday evening hunting for graffiti murals, but it was possible. Crack looked him up, and there were pictures of him climbing a ruin to spray graffiti. He'd been arrested, then released. Fake news, I said. He'd never have gotten a job at Pangenica if he had an arrest record. Defacing public or private property is not a major offense, Crack said. They'd hire him.

But why did the train turn into a death trap? Where was the smoke coming from? Crack had no answers, but wild animals were turning up in odd places: an indoor skating rink, a pool at the top of a skyscraper, a meat market that opened at three a.m. I took this as a sign Waxman was still alive. I tried calling him, but as I expected, there was no answer, the mailbox was full and not recording anything. I imagined he'd thrown his phone away, and it was lying at the bottom of a canal or tumbling inside a cement mixer. I looked up Iridium Labs to discover it no more existed than Porphirion Insurance. Crack suggested going to Waxman's address, the one written on the back of the receipt, which he had on him since I'd left it in his car. The address was on the main island, not far from where the subway had emptied out, so we could walk to it. Odds were against him being at home, feet up, watching Premier League, but on the other hand, it was possible that he would be doing just that. What kept Waxman alive was the same reason why he had a date with a disappearachnik. He was the man who knew too much and could still be useful. If his apartment was empty, we might find evidence of Singe's whereabouts. Crack insisted on pronouncing his name *Wax Man*.

Before we went anywhere, I needed to eaerotube the toothbrush to Pangenica. A Mailboxes Plus was still open across the street, and they offered eaerotubing services, premium level. The clerk was wearing gloves, and the toothbrush was in a plastic bag, but he looked at it with distaste. He said, yeah, sure, but he held the bag at arm's length.

"I bet you've seen stranger things than this before."

"Babydoll, you have no idea."

"I can't package this myself," I said. "I'm all thumbs."

"Yeah, I've sent those, too." There was a music video overhead, and he sang along at the top of his lungs as he disappeared into the back of the store to find the sterile packaging. He could hear him singing about counterfeit dollars printed with portraits of gangster presidents, millions of them stacked against basement walls. I tried out colored gel pens on a series of sample Post-it notes.

"Why doesn't your friend just go to a drugstore and buy a new one?" he asked when he came back. "You know sterile packaging costs extra."

"Not a problem. The recipient is paying."

The clerk looked at the eaerotube form I'd just slid across the counter toward him, saw the Pangenica delivery address, and never uttered another word.

SEVENTEEN

Waxman's apartment building was a stucco box that looked like a sugar cube, like it would dissolve in a heavy rain, but his name wasn't on the directory in the lobby. If he was director of a department at Pangenica, you'd think he'd live in a doorman building, not an anonymous pink collection of boxes, but then Neuronal Correlates wasn't supposed to exist. Maybe he got shadow pay, future dividends, Pangenica saying we'll gladly pay you on Tuesday for a hamburger eaten today, but that doesn't work when rent is needed. A deliveryman was buzzed in, and we followed behind him, then walked up to the third floor. I knocked on the door, but no one answered. I can't say I was surprised, then I put my hand on #5B and pushed. The door was unlocked as if Waxman had left in a hurry and would never return for any reason. I would have thought even if Waxman lived in a building constructed in the era of pay phones, he would have used a sophisticated security system. Even my apartment door had all kinds of security features, as any Adjudicator's domicile would, but Crack had taken one look at him and figured this was a guy who wrote on lined paper tablets that he picked up at garage sales. A woman came out of her apartment, just the door creaked open. We were from the police? There'd been what was called a Corpse Inspection in the building about a year ago, but nothing was found, though the tenant had disappeared and the smell was bad. After a few months, the landlord unloaded everything into a dumpster, renovated the apartment, and got many times more rent for it. She looked at us and wondered if that scenario was going to be repeated.

Crack showed the woman his Pangenica ID, motioned for me to do the same, so I did, and then in Adjudicator form, I made up a story about needing some papers from work. The Department of Native Correlationals, I added. Correctionals? The woman's voice went up, and I nodded. Yes, she knew Mr. Waxman was in corrections. I imagined Waxman walking down the hall, putting all his weight on one foot then the other as heel met tile, gravity in full force, the smell of cigarette smoke enveloping him, following him in invisible cloudlike form, and the door to his apartment meant a relief to be home after a long day imagining enzymes on a spacewalk, or RNA slicing away, or chimps handing back grapes.

The apartment was three small rooms, a bathroom, and a short balcony, more of an idea of a balcony, a ledge that offered enough space to stand on but not much else, a couple of cactuses that looked like they got too much rain had split and toppled over in their clay pots, and a birdfeeder beside them was a gesture of optimism. City birds, such as there were any, had digestive systems that had evolved to prefer the taste and texture of human food garbage found on the ground, rejecting the raw seeds their channel island cousins would have feasted on. In the kitchen: a sliver of a two-burner stove, a sink the size of what you would find in an airplane bathroom, a small fridge with almost nothing in it, a Zagnut bar, a bottle of dried-out horseradish.

The bedroom was a mess: sheets rumpled, pillows and clothes tossed on the floor. A can of bed bug spray lay on the floor beside a bookcase. Lumps of rocks that he had labeled *trinitite* or *atomsite*, a glass that was produced during the nuclear testing at the Trinity Site, were used as bookends and paperweights. The nuclear test had hurled sand into air, and extreme heat liquified the grains, but when the blast was over and all was cool, what had been sand was now green Alamogordo glass, the labels explained. A coffee cup that read **THE UNIVERSE IS DESIGNED BOTH TO SHELTER AND TO KILL US** sat on the desk. The mug looked handmade, perhaps at one of those ceramic studios where kids had parties and adults could go for an evening class and paint whatever they felt like. I imagined Waxman going by himself to such a place, throwing pots in order not to think about gene-splicing, or maybe someone else had made it and given it to him as a gift, though the sentiment expressed on it was something Waxman himself would say. All kinds of papers and pictures were tacked to a floor-to-ceiling cork board, equipment lists, condensed lab reports from another century, old IDs, lanyards dangling, a still from a John Cleese satire about the god gene.

This god gene releases chemicals into our body that create the impression that there is meaning in the universe.

I opened a metal tea box shaped like a treasure chest that was full of rolling papers and smelled like lapsang souchong, then reached for a film can that was hard to open, but I finally pried the two halves apart. It had once housed a ten-inch reel, but inside was a folded printout of an eaeroscript. He had drawn faces in the margins: Singe smiling, Singe smoking, Singe crying. It had been written by her to him.

Eaeroscript

First, let me thank you for rescuing my file and my case. I'd assumed it was lost, neglected, overlooked, destroyed, a buried cold case considered the banter of a nutcase. I wanted to prove that you could stand Clayton and PomPom side-by-side and say, yes, one is inside the other, the homunculi pulling the strings, interpreting, expressing joy, obsession, irritation, and so on, were put in the wrong body. The wrong cuckoo is coming out of the wrong clock. Clayton is dead, and my once-beloved daughter is unbearable. Perhaps she always was, which is all the more reason I need to prove there was a deliberate switch even before any Phytosack was hooked up and implanted.

You asked if we could meet, and the answer is no. The second after I hit send, I'll dissolve this eaeroscript address, and that's the end of that. If we were to meet, it wouldn't be just the two of us in a room. Whether you mean to or not, I know you would arrive with a tail of disappearachniks, and before you know it, I'm just body parts. Though I would like an acknowledgment of what I suspect to be true, and you could verify my suspicions. Surrendering myself to whoknowswhat is not a fate I have any interest in embracing.

What I believe happened: PomPom's intended consciousness was born wearing a Clayton suit, and in that suit, operating in that body, the consciousness was compelled to make sense of the world by, among other things, becoming obsessive. That's not what consciousness does, marshal obsession, but in observing and remembering the two children, looking back, that should have been an early sign that that something was odd. Clayton stared at the stars, imagining an endless series of scenarios: a dwarf star shredded by a black hole, possible life forms in what passes as liquid water on Galilean moon, Europa, unable to evolve to the level of an amoeba or a nematode, held in stasis for so many millions of years. Forget about it—no bipeds are ever going to step out of the non-swamp. Thoughts like these.

Meanwhile, Clayton's intended consciousness, blooming in PomPom's body, chafed at the texture of labels sewn into clothes, jumped at the sound of brass instruments, and screamed at flashing lights. His consciousness was continually irritated, rubbed raw by accidental spills in the kitchen, and what the bully perceived as other people's bad choices: playing out-of-date computer games, a lunch that smelled like frozen vegetables, wearing a coat that looked like it was made from upholstery fabric samples, chipped, flaking nail polish, unable to hoist oneself up to parallel bars, or dive head first (or do anything head first), the last chosen for teams, the list of the petty crimes of others was endless. Clayton in a PomPom suit viewed every room to be entered, every person who came into sight as an affront in some way. The victim often couldn't begin to figure out what they'd done.

There were problems for Clayton's consciousness in PomPom's body. Clayton wanted to fight, to pick on kids, and though girls do get into fights, PomPom didn't have the muscle to carry out all the aggressions she was inclined to act on. When she tried to beat up the objects of her scorn, she often looked ridiculous. One example stands out to me. There was a boy who seemed to her to be an insufferable know-it-all. Probably his parents wanted a mathematical savant. He could do all kinds of numerical problems in his head: algebra, calculus, trigonometry. PomPom enticed him to some kind of behind-the-dumpster location with promises of shirt-lifting or noddies, or I don't want to know what, but with the intention of beating the crap out of him. Of course, she was the one who ended up bloodied on the ground. When I asked her what happened, she told me a long story about taking a detour home to explore a construction site where she fell. Oh, my poor darling, don't go there! It's dangerous! I fell for it. Dinah's version, when it got back to me, was more accurate, but I dismissed the story because it came from Dinah. Clayton was still alive, but we were no longer on such on friendly terms.

When the children were small, Dinah told me that Clayton's reticence annoyed her. She didn't want to be annoyed, but she was. He wouldn't join in, it was clear. At parties, for example, he was looking for the exit, he always wanted to go home, even before he could read. Years later, Dinah said she didn't understand why Clayton felt uneasy on camping trips, wouldn't go rock-climbing with his brother even though he had the upper body strength to do so. He had a fear of falling. But there were things he loved about the trips: there were no clouds, it was easier to see stars, and there were sightings of hawks and a disoriented snowy owl. Though he imagined catastrophic outcomes, he wanted to see bears and rattlesnakes.

Clayton's consciousness looked at the body that housed him as one big Alien Hand Syndrome. PomPom's consciousness in a Clayton suit could no longer stand it and so deliberately slid out onto thin ice.

Or an assassin Pangenica Adjudicator lured him out and pushed. I know they exist, Adjudicators passing as other people. What I'm saying is, I don't like to believe it was the result of PomPom's bullying, and so will say, we will never know.

If I could stamp PomPom "return to sender," and get the child I was meant to have in return, would I? There are ancient stories of children switched at birth who were loved even though they were taken home by the wrong family. These are good people, but I'm not one of their number. And yes, I'm an Originist, so that can be taken into account.

You asked how I became an Originist. Here's the story. My last year in high school, I had a job in a natural history museum in a lesser, but still populous city, the city where my family lived. I sat behind the ticket desk, sold tickets, gave directions. One weekend during a special fossil exhibit on loan from a larger museum, I was asked to wear a dinosaur tail, a stuffed appendage made of shiny fabric that had been printed with green and black scales. I had to stand at the entrance to Paleotica Hall to keep an eye on fractious children who had a habit of falling into exhibits, who didn't understand you weren't supposed to touch the bones. I had no choice but to tie the elastic around my waist. It was both cool and humiliating, and I hoped no one I knew from school would visit the museum that day. The appendage felt weird against my butt and waved back and forth when I walked, but I didn't walk much. Mostly I stood there, watching parents try to reassure screaming children who were terrified of the life-size T. rex and apatosaurus skeletons. They're dead. It's just bones.

At the entrance to the hall was a picture of dinosaur fossil hunter Roy Chapman Andrews.

He resembled Gary Cooper, especially in profile on a horse wearing a hat or looking out at desert cliffs. And you could say, if you didn't know better, he was posing for a Western, possibly even before Westerns in movie format were ever a real thing. On his 1922 expedition to the Gobi Desert, he was searching for what he called the missing link, a creature that was the hinge between man and ape. Guess what he found instead? One of his assistants found a nest of thirteen petrified dinosaur eggs. Up until then, how dinosaurs reproduced was anybody's guess. So now you have eggs, and we know certain things because we know about eggs, we know what they are and where they come from. There was a reproduction of them in the exhibit, a clutch of potato-shaped rocks. It was somebody's job to make those replicas. A fun thing to do, I thought, and a great job description: fabricator of dinosaur eggs. The plaque explained that a mangled skeleton positioned in close proximity to the nest had been named oviraptor or egg thief, though this would turn out to be a misnomer.

Many years later, you might say my daughter would also be the victim of an egg thief. I read the electronic breadcrumb trail that PomPom left in her wake, and felt I was looking at the profile of a complete stranger. You've seen my file, so you know. She is well cared for, but we have nothing to do with one another. She hates me, has her own reasons for doing so, and perhaps she's right to hate the person who was passed off as her mother, or partial mother.

So, back to another egg thief. Standing there, as a teenage guard with a tail, I read more about Andrews. Of course he planned to take the eggs from Mongolia back to New York, and he needed to insure them, so what, *asked the Lloyds of London agent in Shanghai, what are these round stones made of calcium carbonate crystal units worth? Imagine Gary Cooper playing the honest, forthright American stuck in Shanghai, trying to talk sense to a paper-pushing insurer who would only like to get back to England one of these days, and what the hell were those things that looked like giant beans? What they were worth was a good question. From the point of view of paleontology, they were priceless, but since no one had ever bought one before, value was difficult to assign. When is a stuffed shark an example of taxidermy, and when is it a multimillion-dollar art installation? (I make no judgments either way.) The value of the eggs: Like an online auction, whatever anyone will pay, that's what you get. Okay, the agent must have said, though online auctions wouldn't exist for decades, and they were insured for $60,000.*

Booking passage on the Dollar Line, Andrews set sail for Victoria, British Columbia. Imagine rolling the eggs in your socks, then cushioning them with sweaters, then packing them in a suitcase with a life jacket tied around the whole shooting match. After millions of years in one place, they were going halfway round the world. Who's to argue with that? No one, at that point, was accusing Andrews of theft. He assumed they were his for the taking.

Upon his return, Andrews became an instant celebrity, and in scenes that could have been out of old movies, reporters clamored for exclusive rights for photographs, for interviews. Roy, hey Roy, over here! Can you tell me how it felt to outrun murderous rebels in Ulan Baator, to blow a tire thousands of miles from anywhere, to find a skeleton the size of the Ritz? John D. Rockefeller, Averell Harriman,

John Barrymore, who wanted one of the eggs more than anything, big newspaper editors, all could say, that fellow who brought fossils back from Mongolia, he's a good friend, why, I saw him just the other day. The Mongolian citizens who were involved in the discovery got bupkis. They were invisible.

But now everyday-walking-around folks knew what dinosaurs were, and so you could say Andrews set in motion ideas about the history of life on earth and evolution, now accessible and part of everyday parlance. He joined the ranks of those who threw wrenches in the works of how religion explained how it all started—not in a garden with an apple that might have been a pomegranate. All of that I find interesting and to the good—if the eggs hadn't been stolen, but Andrews wasn't done. There were thirteen eggs, why not sell one? If I were in his shoes, I mean, say if I had huge debts, and I'd found this treasure, wouldn't I be tempted to sell a part of it to pay those off? I like to think that I wouldn't, but I can't be sure.

The Times headline read: "Dinosaur Egg 100,000,000 Years Old for Sale; Museum Asks Bid to Aid Explorer's Fund." The highest bidder was Mr. August Colgate who paid $5,000 (now about $500,000) for it. The Mongolian government got wind of this, and they were not pleased. In fact, they believed the rumor that the British Museum paid a cool million for the egg. They wanted all of them returned.

Even back then, standing at the entrance to Paleotica Hall, looking at creatures who weren't native to the ground I stood on, I decided to become an Originist. Like Indiana Jones in reverse, my plan was to steal and return.

Needless to say, this didn't work out well. I began at the museum I worked at, staying after hours, putting chacmools and fossils in a bag with no regard for surveillance cameras and no idea how I would get to Mayan territory or outer Mongolia in order to return these objects. I figured I could mail them back to someone, but I was caught by a roving security guard who took it upon himself to call the police, the museum director, and a news crew. No one believed I intended to repatriate the objects and animal remains, and I was fired on the spot. College acceptances were rescinded, every single one of them. My next job was working at a Lucky Jeans in a mall, but I missed the museum. Eventually, as an adult, I went to university, and I learned to work from within.

Years later, I had a daughter who seemed possessed, and I can't rewind the clock, infiltrate Pangenica's labs, and set things right. At first, I looked up cases of multiple personality disorder. Such a person might have different consciousnesses, but this affliction is no longer present in the population, and I had to turn to the historical record. Results were not particularly helpful or instructive. So, what if patient X, when he was being Fred, felt extreme vertigo at even modest heights, but when he was being Jean-Luc, he could climb sheer rockfaces. As Jean-Luc, he was able to focus straight ahead while driving, but if it was Fred at the wheel, his tendency to lose focus and become disoriented propelled him to the other side of the road from time to time. PomPom was consistent, not several people or sets of perceptions in one body. No Jekyll-and-Hyde situation. She was who she was.

My daughter looked so like me, it was uncanny, but at the same time she was totally alien. We had the same walk, identical expressions of boredom while waiting in line, same hands, fingers, toes, but when I saw her phone, I didn't know who she was, or where she could have come from—not at first. Her expressions of boredom rapidly tilted into impatience, a stamping of feet as if to say, why do I have to wait so long? I don't deserve this!

Who was this demon? Somewhere along the line, who had been a brain donor?

So, on the one hand, I'm grateful for what you've been able to tell me about the possibility of a DNA do-si-do and switch your partners, but I can't meet you in-person for a harmless cup of joe in some remote location because, as you know, there is no such thing as a remote location.

Also in the can was part of his answer to her. It was incomplete and perhaps never sent. So when had they met? Before or after Singe said she was pulling up the drawbridge? Or maybe they'd never met, and Cumari recalled a scenario that never happened.

Dear Singe,

In defense of Roy Chapman Andrews, if you're concerned with the commercialization of science, he did not endorse the manufacture of autographed replica eggs that would have sold for twenty-five cents each. (To tell you the truth, I don't think that's such a bad thing, someone producing toy eggs with rubber raptor embryos inside.) Andrews refused to allow an oil company's petrochemical engineer to accompany his trip to the Gobi. Ninety years later, a lawsuit would return a Tyrannosaurus bataar to Mongolia.

How to measure consciousness? What is the biomarker, signature of consciousness? Tremendous stimulus at birth, that could get things started, but no one is born or borne like that anymore, as you know.

On the back of the page he had written:

Gemmules, bearers of hereditary traits
Pangenesis, well, Darwin thought it was a reasonable idea at the time.
MRG = Massive Reverse Genomics to Decipher Gene Regulatory grammar
Genotypes vs Phenotypes, give me one, and I'll predict the other was common knowledge until—

Waxman's brain was always firing. Pangenesis, the idea that the environment could influence genes and via this pathway tiny bits of information, gemmules, made their merry way through the body, finally finding purpose and a rightful home in the glands that produce hormones — these concepts were heretical to Pangenica. But nothing was off limits to Waxman. Art in his lab, too tall for his regulation desk, standing at his many screens, thinking of ways to push the boundaries of our laws, charged with dangerous work, feeling omnipotent, beyond the company's strictures when, in fact, he was in their pocket in more ways than he knew. I flipped through the shingles of paper, notes, pieces of random information pinned to the corkboard. Among the random notes was an essay about the legend of the Abominable Snowman that included a photograph of footprints in snow allegedly made by the creature.

Waxman had written across it in blue ink.

Why is abominable attached to snowman? Abominable implies cursed, acting with malice in a habitual and premeditated way. Strong words for a climate change refugee, which is what the snowman must be. The fear that comes from nature out of control is a fear of unconscious extreme action.

Underneath the essay was a printout of a newspaper article about the vanished condition of synesthesia.

> The right temporoparietal junction in the brain negotiates vision and spatial perception, how the body maps itself. For patients who suffer from mirror touch, this part of the brain is wired to go haywire, and they are neurologically unable to separate themselves from others. It's all blurred. These people can't be said to be ego syntonic, that is to say, their self-image is harmonic, but neither can they be said to be ego dystonic, a self-image in conflict. In other words, they're an ocean of no-self, just flooding everywhere.

There was a photograph of a man who saw colors when he heard music. Standing beside him was a woman who gave graphemes personalities. *5* was a loner, *6* was fair-minded, *J* was languid and witty, *M* was average. The pair held hands, had their hair in identical buns, but he also had a beard. Behind them attached to a wall was a dial phone, and underneath that printout was a photograph of me, taken from Pangenica's website. I turned my head to see Crack holding up the cup printed with the saying, **THE UNIVERSE IS DESIGNED BOTH TO SHELTER AND TO KILL US.**

"It doesn't take coffee long to dry into rings. There was mail on the table, though the super or a friend could have left it there."

"Waxman knows about me." I pointed at the clipping.

Crack reduced my reactions to overreactions, thinking I was mirroring who-knows-what as well as whatever I was responding to, and this infuriated me, so I walked through the little kitchen and out the door. He was so absorbed with taking pictures, I'm not even sure he noticed. Seeing that photograph was disturbing, like discovering someone has been watching you. Not general surveillance, cameras in the subway, on the corner—everyone knows those—but someone-in-particular watching you-in-particular, and I wanted to get as far away from Waxman's stucco box as quickly as possible. It was also true that Crack would insist there were no rats on the roof when you could see evidence of their toothmarks and droppings, or he would shrug off a fly in your drink: Fish it out, it's no big deal. Shadows from the banister and angular spindles made a pattern of interlocking *L* shapes as I made my way downstairs.

Out on the street, I didn't know where I was going to go and wished I'd somehow been able to swallow The Devil in Miss Jones and had money in my pocket. A kid on a skateboard, humming along with something only he could hear, swerved to avoid a car and fell, hitting his head on the curb. I stopped to see if he was alright. It wasn't a bad injury, but as he sat on the sidewalk holding his head, my own head throbbed. A woman passing by told him he should wear a helmet, and he told her to go fuck herself.

The accident gave Crack the opportunity to catch up with me, and he grabbed my arm, don't walk out on me again, Loew. Up close, he smelled like new tires, I hadn't noticed when I had come out of the restaurant, when I was still absorbed in what happened in the alcove and the burning sensations in my mouth.

Where to now? Dometop Insurance, I said.

EIGHTEEN

Dometop Insurance offered twenty-four-hour service. Their motto, blinking under the name: *We'll be there before you are!* It was a small storefront operation that looked like a combination bail bondsman, HR Block Accounting franchise, and EMT dispatcher. It was located in a downtown pocket between a courthouse and a juvenile detention center, though the latter was rarely used anymore and was due to be converted into an eaeroscript center topped by a tower of mansion-like apartments. I'm not sure what kind of business Dometop would engage in late on a Saturday night, but as they were an occasional emergency service provider, they were open. The door chimed the theme from *The Godfather* when we pushed it open.

A lone employee sat in a swivel chair, taking bites from a hero sandwich, pieces of lettuce and tomato falling into her lap while watching a screen. At the sound of the door, she brushed crumbs from her lap and stood, smiling a now-you-see-it-now-you-don't smile, then introduced herself as Daphne. She wore big glasses, black leggings, and her Jheri curl hair had flattened out. She twirled one of the limp sections around a finger. When she was on two feet, you could see she had a muscular body that didn't look like it spent a lot of time sitting in a chair, but it was apparent she only had one arm. The sleeve of her shirt was pinned below the elbow. The shirt had bright pearl snaps, easier to get in and out of for someone with only one hand. She was watching the same movie as the betting lady from The Barrel of Monkeys, and I felt she'd just as soon be left alone to finish *Seven Days in May* than talk to us.

Still grinning, she asked us to wait a sec while she fitted a prosthesis onto her stump, talking while she unpinned and adjusted straps and Velcro. I didn't stare, beyond registering the bare facts of the situation, but Crack did.

You're probably wondering how this happened?

I wasn't, but she told us. A shark had mistaken her arm for a fish or a tasty little seal—you know, they're all swimming closer to the shore these days. Crack nodded, of course, that was a phenomena he was familiar with. It was a bright summer day, and she had been paddling out on her surfboard when the attack happened, but it was so long ago, don't worry about it, she no longer felt phantom pains from the arm digested by the long-dead shark. All of it, fish and limb, must be now scattered into the nothingness of the ocean floor.

No phantom pain? You don't say?

Was there some way of transferring that kind of forgetting? Phantom pain was my middle name. I was a magnet for it. Give me your fatigued, your cramped, *ferkrimpt*, burning nerve endings yearning to try someone else for a change. People may not be aware of how much they leak should one giant transference organism be around, but distress, euphoria, all of it, are renewable resources. They don't exist in finite amounts, as far as I'm concerned. It's not as if I take pain from someone, and they, therefore, are relieved of a bit. No. There's no siphoning off or relief for the originator. We share and share alike.

"So, you looking to buy, you got an existing claim, or you need directions to the entrance to the jail? Got a kid in overnight lockup? In other words, what can I do for you?" She had a twangy accent, her tongue didn't hit the back of her teeth, no *t* in *overnight*, and sounded like she came from another century. The smile flattened into a line. She really did want to get back to her movie and not start a lot of paperwork at this sleepy hour when hardly anybody ever came in, which was probably why she signed on to this shift in the first place.

I started to take my Pangenica ID out of my pocket, but Crack stopped me, putting his hand on mine for less than a minute.

"Well, Daphne, my associate and I run a private car service for celebrities, very select. We have only one state-of-the-art limo." His eyes were on the screen, put on pause, as Kirk Douglas playing Colonel Martin "Jiggs" Casey got in a car with a Secret Service man meant to follow Burt Lancaster's chauffeur, so I knew Crack was making this up as he went along. "It's very private, that's one of our selling points, the service we offer, and we were driving a client to a location when we were hit by a woman who ran a red light. She gave us her name and said her insurance was your outfit."

"So, you'll be hearing from us, then."

"That's the thing. There's a problem. She gave us her phone number, but when I called it, it didn't check out. It's a fake number. We're guessing she has no affiliation with Dometop, but if I give you her name, the name she gave us, I know it's a long shot, but if she's in your system, maybe you could give us her actual number and address and whatnot."

She glanced down at Crack's left hand, looking for a ring. I wanted to say, are you kidding? Good luck with that. She smiled at Crackhour, and he smiled right back at her.

"I couldn't possibly comment on a client's whatnot. This is information I'm not at liberty to give out."

"My car, which I need for my business, was wrecked, you understand. My associate," he nodded toward me as if I was a piece of furniture, "has hospital bills for back and head injury, recurrent headaches, mobility issues, as you may have noticed when we walked in."

I stared blankly, partly to hint I had some kind of neurological condition, but also in awe of Crack's resourcefulness, of which I was an imaginary casualty. I have to say, I was also a little annoyed. I was the Adjudicator. I was the one who was trained to invent identities, either with long-term preparation or on the spot. Daphne no longer made eye contact with me or looked at me at all. She fingered the handle of her coffee cup with her biological hand.

"This woman who hit you, she'll file. We'll contact you."

At that moment both our phones sounded alarms, emergency texts from Pangenica warning that due to an expected return of extreme weather, weekend employees should not come in.

"You see, right there." Crack looked at his phone, then clicked it off. "A client booked for an airport pickup, and we didn't show up, because we can't show up. Daphne, you seem like a reasonable person, but I'm not sure you understand." Crackhour leaned on the counter, then shifted his weight so he was closer to the Dometop representative. "If I don't have a car, I don't do business. I'm losing money by the minute." His face was just a few inches from her, and his voice was both seductive and threatening, not a voice I'd heard before. One corner of her mouth went up even harder.

"Okay, give me a name."

"Singe Laveneer."

Some tapping on her keyboard, followed by frowning, followed by more tapping. "Yes, she's a client."

"Can you turn the screen around so we can see her picture? Just to be sure we're talking about the same person."

For a small operation, not sophisticated enough to have a biometric ID system, it wasn't unheard of to use photographs, and the storefront looked like the kind of business that was under the radar, that didn't ask a lot of questions, but paid out promptly.

"You want a quick peek at her coordinates, so you can know where she's at, access her contact info? No way that's going to happen. Tell you what, I'll send you a picture of her, how about that? What's your number?"

He gave her his number, and his phone pinged.

"That was the fastest I've ever gotten any guy's number in my life."

They both laughed. *Ha ha.*

Crack showed me the picture on his phone. It was the lookalike from Mr. Levant's diner.

"That's her." Crack said. "I can't thank you enough."

"I'll tell you this. She pays her bills in person in cash discounted by Dometop depending on currency and exchange rate."

"Thank you so much, Daphne. You've been very helpful." Crack straightened up but kept locked on her eyes.

"Oh, you'd be surprised. I know how to do all kinds of things."

Did she wink? I couldn't believe it.

"I'll bet."

"I have your number," she reminded him.

"Peace, love, and good vibes," Crackhour said.

It was about ten steps to the door, which he took slowly while I was a good five steps ahead of him. What a phonus balonus.

We stopped under an awning to look at the picture again, but it was raining too hard, and wind blew cold rain into our faces and made rainbow-colored droplets on Crack's screen. Except for Dometop, most of the block was dark, though music blasted from somewhere nearby, and we followed the sound to a large cinder block building around the corner, an indoor ice skating rink, Ice Unlimited. You didn't have to pay to go in, only if you wanted to skate, so we entered the chill embrace of Ice Unlimited. The rink was illuminated with colored lights, but the surrounding areas were dark. The intention on a Saturday night may have been to hint at an air of romance, as opposed to what the rink was like during hockey games, figure skating regionals, kids' birthday parties. We found a table close to the skate rental kiosk smelling of leather, beeswax waterproofing, wet socks, but mostly of feet. I got a hot chocolate from a vending machine, figuring it contained no real milk and might blunt some of the lingering tendrils of Carolina Reaper, and so sipped it in vain while looking out at the ice being resurfaced by a woman riding a Zamboni. She was wearing a T-shirt that explained, *My other car is a Zamboni*, and she bounced in her seat to music that must have come from her headphones. The rhythm wasn't the same as the booming overhead disco, broken only for ads for cars and someplace called Pluto's Retreat: *the night is young, when you're done skating, but still want to see stars . . .*

I wondered if the Zamboni driver was ever tempted to drive in crazy eights or haphazard drunken wavy lines instead of neat concentric ovals. She was a kind of ice artist, leaving glassy patterns etched into ice until her work was overridden by crowds. The music changed and slowed down.

If I should take a notion
to jump into the ocean
Ain't nobody's business if I do

Crack had gotten a cup of coffee and was studying the picture on his phone, and I was pretty certain it was the woman we'd seen at Mr. Levant's diner. The picture gave no clue as to location. It was mostly a headshot, but you could see her standing by the side of a river that marked the horizon line behind her. She could have been anywhere.

If my man ain't got no money and I say,
"Take all of mine, honey"
Ain't nobody's business if I do

Across the ice I saw two men arguing. One looked like Morris, the junior archivist, and he put his hands on the shoulders of the other man in a gesture of affection lost or in danger of disappearing, as if trying to rekindle, to say but that's not so, I do love you. The other man shrugged him off. The new boyfriend, the archivist for the Department of Evolutionary Engineers, might have seen footage of Morris flirting with Smith and others. He'd had it with Morris. It's over. He skated away but moved too close to another skater, one who had become aerial, spinning, feet beating, and arms held close to his chest. The proximity of the other man put him off balance, and he crashed on the ice. I grabbed my knee in pain.

If I give him my last nickel
and it leaves me in a pickle
Ain't nobody's business if I do

Crack knew nothing of Morris at Pangenica and asked me if I was paying attention to what he was saying about the picture, even though he knew I had no control over the feeling of bone fracturing.

"Look, just behind her on the left, it looks like a molar-shaped pile of stones but when you enlarge the picture slightly—"

"A piece of moraine left by an ice age glacier," I said, cutting him off.

"No. That's a brick turret that fell into the water, but part of it is still sticking up. I recognize where this was taken, Horner's Castle."

"Do you know Vy Sapper in Admissions?"

"I know who she is, yeah."

"She has a T-shirt from Horner's Castle."

"Vy Sapper is never at her desk when I've needed something from her. When does she ever do her job?"

Vy and Crack might have had a noddie connection. There was no reason why their paths should have crossed, and yes she wore secondhand clothes, but most of the time when I went to Admissions, she was there. The T-shirt, which she had in a number of colors, featured the castle with one of its turrets flying off a tower. What I didn't tell Crack was that I knew about Horner's Castle. Horner had been an arms dealer, special acquisitions, the surplus, buyer, and reseller of the arsenals of big spenders who each year want to get their hands on newer, faster, more lethal in less time, so out with last year's models which could be snapped up at bargain basement prices, then to be sold by Horner to roving bands of terroroticas all over the globe. You never hear about them, because they don't exist anymore, but at one time, they were something. Horner sold to them from the comfort of his waterfront estate when waterfront was a viable and desirable real estate designation. He had his contacts, and this was in the era of conventional *bang you dead* conflicts. He became super-uber-mega-wealthy, but couldn't store his inventory in the city, so he bought this island a few hours north and built, not a structure that looked like an arsenal for his arsenal, but a castle modeled after Ludwig's asymmetrical Bavarian fantasy, only smaller, as if no one would possibly guess what on earth lay inside. No throne, no roasting elk, no armor of ancestors on the walls, just sophisticated boom boom, which it did one day, killing a few people who worked in the castle. Horner left the ruins as they stood, and there they remain. You can go by them on a northbound train any time. Southbound in the other direction works, too. As an Adjudicator headed into the field, I'd done so many times.

Just because she had the picture taken adjacent to a castle ruin didn't mean she lived or worked there, but Crack thought someone might know her, might have seen her. We had no idea how old the picture was, how long Dometop had it on file, believing she was, indeed, the real Singe Laveneer, paying in cash, in person as if she lived in a gunsmoke pony express, swinging-saloon-doors kind of berg that just barely had electricity and maybe not even.

There were only a few skaters left on the ice, but they were fast and sure of themselves, spraying enough diamond dust to interfere with a ceilometer, if one were on the rink. Lone men and women who came out late at night when the bumblers and handholding couples had left for their lone or amorous beds. I took on expressions of concentration, of calculation of space and tempo, of euphoria when airborne. Some skated faster and faster doing laps around the outer edge of the rink, close to the barrier fence to get in as much distance as possible, creating a breeze as they flashed past. Others did spins in the center, arms and legs blurred in a tornado of rotation, like an electric fan that couldn't be turned off. A solitary skater languorously traversed the middle zone, then would suddenly speed up and become airborne. If you could watch this human orrery from the rafters—say you were up there to change bulbs in the spotlights or make adjustments to the speakers in the rink's aging sound system that couldn't entirely be controlled from below, would you see some kind of message, some looping sentence revealed on the ice?

While Crack was preoccupied looking for late trains to Horner's, my phone pinged with a notice that I'd gotten an eaeroscript. The continually evaporating drop of water symbol beside it indicated this was the kind of eaeroscript that would pixelate to nothing several minutes after it was opened, so there was no way it could be saved, answered, or forwarded. It was from avachs@eaero.com, but I held back from opening it, which would trigger the erasure process within seconds. Waxman scared me; had he known we were just in his apartment? But by doing nothing, you learn nothing, so I opened the message. The first sentences evaporated before I could read them, but then the process corrected itself and slowed down.

Eaeroscript

I want to tell you about a woman who worked at Pangenica in the Crafted Identities department. I used to see her in the elevator, in the cafeteria, on the roof. She was tiny, like a bird, maybe too small, and that should have been a hint that something was a bit off about her, but she was married to an older man who looked like Mr. Whatshisname: Let's go. We can't. Why not? We're waiting for Godot, I would say to myself when I saw him. He worked in the same division as she and had a certain kind of remote charm, I guess. What chance did I have? Close to zero, but even knowing this, I fell in love with her. She never knew. Maybe she suspected, but what difference does it make now? None. I would follow her up to the roof, dream up stupid reasons to talk to her, ask her if she wanted to smoke a joint, talk about alleles that produced the fragrance of squared peaches and searing hyper-mint, or try to talk about the problems encountered by her division: holograms for fake IDs, false mustaches, rubber noses, rubber chickens, anything to stretch a coffee break into a longer conversation. Of course, what did I know about Crafted Identities? Close to nothing, it turned out.

One day she didn't come into work, or the day after that, and then weeks of absence followed. Her husband appeared stricken, more withdrawn, more gaunt, though he bounced back fast enough, and after a few months was seen being chummy, or as chummy as someone like him would be, with another woman, a minor lab technician I worked with who had no connection to Crafted Identities. What happened to the great love of my life? I don't need to tell you.

But why? Why her? Well, I'll tell you why. I quickly pulled up her archived DNA profile, as only someone with my level of security approval can do. What I discovered was that she was an anomaly. It wasn't just that she was unusually short, and what parent would want that, but that she had misophonia, a form of synesthesia in which the sufferer experiences certain sounds as triggers of feelings of loathing, anger, profound sadness. That would explain her isolation, why she clung to the winner of the Mr. Estragon Lookalike Prize, and why on the roof once, someone snapped a branch, and she lashed out at me, the person standing closest to her, for no reason. In the cafeteria the generally placid and bland background music could cause her to give way to weeping, and she would abandon her tray, running out of the room. But the reason she disappeared wasn't because of her misophonia. No one knew about her anomaly, I'm guessing, unless they knew her really well, and almost no one did.

Here's what happened. Before you arrived at Pangenica, there was an Adjudicator who, it could be said, was both a tiger and a very talented chameleon. You could send him into the most difficult circumstances, and no one, I mean no one, would ever guess who he really was, his talent at transformation was that flawless, really undetectable. There was a particularly difficult case involving a high-stakes lawsuit. Identical twins had been ordered, but they were not identical, and the parents, for reasons that were probably criminal in nature, wanted identical. Were the little boys really not identical, or was it a ruse to extract a large settlement? The parents were known to belong to a secretive group linked to the manufacture of Dormazin laced with lysergic acid. The

Adjudicator was given the identity of a fellow traveler in this cult, and he pretended to join them in the role of distributor. Distributors, whether they operated as van drivers or corner boys, were the conduits between producers and consumers, and particularly vulnerable. High body count in that profession. Also, there were particulars of cult life, eating rituals, prayers, slang terminology . . .

My love in Crafted Identities knew a fair amount, but her knowledge wasn't as comprehensive as it should have been, and that wasn't even the primary issue. Cult members were required to consume the drug on a daily basis, and once he'd taken even one dose, he could no longer control his speech or behavior. He became a dead man walking and was killed after less than a week. If she had made him an electrician, a dryer vent inspector, a visiting nurse, he could have observed the twins on site, come to a conclusion, and left the premises with information in hand. Done. Finito. Case closed. No muss, no fuss, what should have been an easy open-and-shut situation, but once the Adjudicator was murdered, the couple and their children needed to be disappeared. It was a messy operation. I personally believe she made her fatal mistake because she was so distracted by sounds that played havoc with her nervous system.

That's the short version, but she was held responsible, not directly because of the glitch in her DNA, but because she made a terrible identity fabrication error, one that threatened the company down to its foundations. A misguided identity given to this highly skilled Adjudicator, when it imploded, meant a greater percentage of the population now knew what an Adjudicator's job entailed, and you can't disappear everyone. In a way she was like that soccer player who became disoriented when the position of the goals was switched, and he accidentally scored for the opposing team. People had a lot of money riding on that game, and five days later he was shot in a parking lot. There are situations in life that seem like a shrug of the shoulders, no big deal, but on closer examination, you can't afford to make a mistake, and pay for it by enforced shuffling off this mortal coil.

I searched for her DNA profile shortly before I left the company, but it was no longer accessible, even in the archive. She had been deleted, and there would be no more of her, ever.

So, in my sorrow, I started thinking, if there was one anomaly, there might be others. There is so much data, as uncountable as the number of atoms in the universe, and what can you do with such a number but marvel at it, and think about what you could do if you could add one more, and then more after that? So, where you're at isn't a stable number at all but infinity, undefinable, slippery as a banana peel. Welcome to the Infinity Hotel where you can always move one door down.

NINETEEN

I was hiding under that blanket of infinite facts. Waxman was telling me that it wasn't possible to pull that cover over your head, read by flashlight, and hope for the best. He was a dangerous man who went gooey-eyed head over heels for strange women, but what made him especially risky for me was he seemed to have a nose for anomalies, those who slipped through but were still implanted in Phytosacks. When I first learned I had mirror touch, I had thought, why would anyone care? But I was skilled at hiding it nonetheless. As an Adjudicator, I was called on to be many people, so few really knew me either. If everyone is an avalanche of snippets, how do you know what matters? What magnets can find singular atoms of iron? What is knowable via search filters, and what can continue to be concealed under a limitless amount of data and faulty search engines that have deteriorated and are no longer up to the job?

The pause that refreshed also meant the rest of the message vanished. Singe's trail was narrowing to an evaporating shadow, and I was chasing after even that.

Crack looked up from his phone, but I said nothing to him about the eaeroscript. He had checked the train schedule. Horner's Landing was a stop on the outer edge of the commuter line, then it would turn into a long-distance passenger train that ran all night, including a series of sleeper cars and continued on straight north to the subarctic. We could each take a Dormazin, sleep that concentrated, dreams on fast forward kind of sleep, then wake up refreshed, bright-eyed and bushy-tailed, let's go take a look at the torpedoed castle ruins.

In the middle of the night? Crack had ideas that I wasn't crazy about, but I was doomed to go along until the waves got too high, and then I'd try to swim to shore. At the same time, he had a way of enveloping you in a sense that everything would be alright, even if the performance at hand was only just that, and one in which the scenery threatened to topple. You would think, or I did, that the man who swam far under an ice shelf and was able to return to solid ground could figure out all kinds of things: change transmissions, cancel penalty fees, evade cameras that seemed to be everywhere, laugh at scrapes, capers, tight spots. Late at night with no money to even get on a subway and the sense that an ice shelf was forming overhead whether I could see it or not, I didn't know what else to do, so, okay, let's go.

Crack showed me a picture of a man in a battered fedora, long metal claws for hands, his face was a mess. WTF? *Nightmare on Elm Street*, he explained. It's showing on the island at midnight. Midnight screenings on Saturday night are an event, a tourist attraction, but locals also go.

We'll never make it.

There's music before the screening, so it doesn't start exactly on the nose, and it doesn't matter if we miss the beginning. We're not there to watch the movie. Crack proposed we go to the island, look around, ask questions. Crack poured a few blue pills into the palm of his hand. These were cobalt blue, eight for one point five, a strong dose.

"Are these street noddies? I don't want to trip on the trip."

"I have a prescription, you know that."

Did I? I also thought Waxman had no idea I was an anomaly.

"Have a noddie." Crackhour held out a blue pill. "Take one now and in one hour you'll be in the dreamsville. Ninety minutes from when your eyes close, you'll be awake and ready for Freddy Krueger."

I dry-swallowed one. The enteric coating tasted faintly sweet.

The music was growing more aggressive, shifting from generic disco to genre surfing that hopped all over the place, as if the DJ, too, was on something, but definitely not Dormazin, and the ads for Pluto's Retreat were replaced by jingles for all-night ramen burrito trucks now located directly in front of Ice Unlimited. As we made our way out of the rink, the trucks glowed and chimed, the air smelled of fried garlic and caramelized fruit, but we didn't stop. Crack made it clear we were in a hurry, and though I still tasted the effects of viper and ghost peppers on my tongue and down my throat, no amount of grilled onions or salty ramen or anything else would overcome that sting.

Crack had been swallowing Dormazin for so long, it took a higher dose to have any effect, and he was skilled at controlling time and amount. I was still ambulatory but fading around the edges, and could offer no resistance as he led the way to Founders Square Terminal, Central Station, where the train sat waiting, as if Crack had willed it into existence. A conductor stood on the platform, talking to a couple of night-shift engineers. They would leave on time, even though the train was almost empty.

Our tickets were scanned, and I lay down across two flecked tweed upholstered seats a few rows from Crack, waving him away. Consciousness was ebbing, but I marshaled every muscle memory I could will into action to make a call to my mother, alone in her lighthouse.

It was black in the tunnel, but reception was adequate. Still, there was no answer, which wasn't unusual. It was the middle of the night. Power could be erratic on Penrose, and as often as I pleaded with her to pick up the phone when it rang, it could only be me, often she wouldn't do so. The phone could be out of the range of her hearing, battery run out, it needed to be charged, or she left it up at the top of the lighthouse, and wouldn't find it for days. I should have felt more anxiety, but the Dormazin, in its early stages, had a numbing effect, so as it was, the only way for me to feel anxious was to be around someone who was anxious, and there was no such person on the train. I tried to keep my eyes open, but I was tired to begin with, not having slept since those few hours suspended above Safariland. There was nothing to do but make my way to the row where Crack sat looking out the window as the train emerged from the tunnel.

He was still able to talk and said something about the fact that Dometop Daphne had little flippers or fingers at the end of what remained of her arm, therefore, no accident ever happened. She was born that way. She was skilled at quickly unrolling her sleeve and attaching her bionic arm, but he'd seen what she attached it to, and he'd bet Daphne never kicked her way out of a Phytosack.

Not possible. Everyone butts their way out of a Phytosack. What you saw only for a few seconds was probably botched reconstruction post-shark. I tried to fight the drug's soporific effect, deluded enough to think I had the willpower to overcome the Dormazin that Crack had said was low dose. My eyelids began to droop, and I held them up with my fingers, ridiculous, but I had to try. Out the window the river sped by on both sides while the train ran on an ever-eroding neck of land. Originally, the tracks had run on one side of the river, but now the waterway had claimed land that had always been dry, creating the track isthmus. It wouldn't take much rain to flood the tracks, and the train would hydroplane until it submerged, a doomed submarine filling with water pouring in from windows and the doors between cars.

Crackhour asked what I thought about the eradication of an entire species. Get rid of sharks, for example. To some this might sound reasonable if one just ate your arm, they are killed for less, but seriously, what happens if some taxonomic group is considered so defective, appetite or venom out of control, for example, so they have to go? Elimination of entire species is not recommended, because ecosystems depend on interlocking parts, even if you have a personal beef with one of them. If you looked at accelerated natural extinction, as with dinosaurs and sabertooths, mammoths, wooly and otherwise, denizens of La Brea—as they departed, so went large predators and other oversize, no-longer-useful mammals: lions, tigers, gorillas, rhinos, bears of all kinds. They are going, going, gone. (Not so with bigtime marine animals, though, but on land, the supersized are almost done with, except for those in zoos.)

That was the last fragment of conversation I remembered, and I was not even one hundred percent sure he had said anything at all while I dreamed about a map that was pure topography, no borders, just mountains, rivers, lakes, deserts. The ocean floor is such a landscape, its benthic zone of sediment and immense pressure terrifying in its uninhabitability. Then the map animated, reversing itself back to Pangea, the relief of the littoral shoreline. Okay, you can stand on two feet here.

We awoke exactly as Crack said we would at Horner's Landing, the small river town a few miles upriver from the castle. The town was renamed Horner's Landing long after the man himself had died. The new name was a way to tip the spotlight in their direction, so they could be more easily found and understood, a way to resuscitate the location as a river attraction, to honor the name of the man who, contrary to his original attempts at chasing anonymity, came to bring the town so much joy and revenue: He put them on the map.

Horner's Landing had few businesses, a gas station, a twenty-four-hour Donuts of Distinction, and a fish-fry joint, Reel News, near the dock where a hydrofoil ferried people to and from Horner's Island. Adjacent to the dock was a freestanding brick wall painted with a mural depicting the arsenal explosion and a souvenir shop that sold explosion-themed coffee mugs, hats, a locally published biography of Horner himself, and tickets for the hydrofoil, the only boat that went to the island, as well as tickets to movie screenings advertised as among the ruins and under the stars.

The captain, who also sold tickets at that late hour, told us this was the last boat, so we needed to get a move on. That was part of the deal. You watched a couple of horror movies, then had to spend the night on the island. He wore a hoodie over his head, **OCTOPUSSY** printed in block serif lettering on the back; the *O* had tentacles, just as it did on the movie poster. I asked him if anyone lived on the island? Answer: not since the big explosion, of course. It was too dangerous with unknown explosives still somewhere—it was possible. The river was a wide swath of ebony, deep tidal pools, unpredictable currents, and the island itself wasn't visible from the town, though allegedly the blast had been heard miles away. It took about twenty minutes out before we could see spotlights among what remained of smashed walls and arches of the arsenal and other partially demolished smaller outbuildings, and then part of the screen became discernible, as the image of an ax chopping through a wall moved across the outdoor screen. If a molar-shaped turret could be made out behind Singe, then the picture must have been taken from the boat during the day when the small castle-like structures Horner had erected around the island were visible. If it had been taken from the shore, the turret, even if observable, would have been too far away. Crackhour showed her picture to the captain, but no, he'd never seen her before; he ferried thousands of people a year. Did we think he was Mr. Memory? As we drew closer to the island, the movie screen disappeared behind trees and hills.

Four men in identical blue jackets and a woman in a blue-sequined dress, all part of a band that played before the first movie, waited on the pier. A local group for whom this was a regular job, they were not spending the night on the island. As we disembarked, a recording warned us there was still unexploded ordnance scattered around the island, so stick to the path. Most of it had been cleared, and all of it was extremely old and should be defunct, but every once in a while, even so many years later, people and things exploded from time to time.

Okay, thanks, buddy, good to know, and with that, the last boat pushed off, tired musicians murmuring among themselves, their sequined lapels mirrored in the river below. Did the reflections attract fish? Sequins aren't scales, though there are similarities, just as lungs are lungs, though some require gills to get things moving. Crack pulled me away from the dock. Last boat until morning.

A dirt path wound uphill around the remains of scattered outbuildings, brick mini-castles whose original purpose was unknown. Even in the best of times, even in broad daylight, Horner's Island was a place where you needed to be awake and watch your step. Lights were sporadic, and I was careful to stay on the path, which eventually led to a depression, a natural amphitheater at the heart of where the main arsenal had been.

A slight breeze blew across the island from the north, and the hillside where people were stretched out on blankets looked like a campground. We found an empty patch of ground beside a couple who grabbed one another when on the screen a door was locked, and there was no way out. On the other side of us was a lone woman, leaning back on her elbows drinking from a bottle, and she didn't seem to react to the movie at all. She looked like a ninja pugilist from a video game in a strategically torn-off skirt, fingerless leather gloves that went up to her elbows, one fishnet stocking. I focused on her, grateful she was in such close proximity. I didn't want to absorb the filmic fear of most of the spectators if I could help it.

Horner's Landing was a small town, and the island movie screening was full of tourists. No one wanted to be interrupted with questions of have you seen this woman? Most were stoned or in no condition to give straight, reliable answers. The first movie had been *The Exorcist*, replacing the unavailable *Nightmare on Elm Street*. In *The Exorcist* a girl possessed by a demon spoke in another voice, masturbated with a crucifix, pushed her babysitter out a window. Perhaps Clayton and PomPom possessed each other, speaking in tongues limited to the two children, well-known to one another, the switch was only the accident of a game gone awry, as in the movie, playing with a Ouija board, and

greetings from Captain Howdy, vehicle for the devil himself. Xenoglossia, strange voices—I don't think that was the explanation Singe was looking for.

The second movie, *Swan Lake Ness Monster,* was very long, and we arrived just before intermission. While Crack got in line for popcorn and drinks, I struck up a conversation with the nonreactive woman next to us who told me what had happened in the movie so far.

"Is it scary?" What I wanted to know was if the majority of the audience felt fear or panic, then I would as well, in a wave multiplied many times over. I wanted to be prepared to focus on something else should that be the case, though what that something else might be, I had no idea. "I only saw about ten minutes. What happened before? What did I miss?"

The woman didn't make eye contact, only looked straight ahead. She was indifferent to the reactions of others but was happy to tell me the story so far.

"Okay," she began, "the story opens at a small town on Lake Ness, named after G-Man Untouchable Eliot Ness, gangster buster, nemesis of Al Capone, but doomed to die ignominiously after four marriages, a drunk driving coverup, penniless, hair parted in the middle like Alfalfa, you know, the Little Rascal. You see him at the beginning. There's a monster that's been sighted on the lake, though most thought birdwoman was hokum until kids started disappearing, and then maybe she's real, because why else?"

Why else would people disappear before Orientation Sites were established? Monsters, of course. Made sense to me. She continued to explain the story thus far.

"Some claimed to have seen the creature, the lady of the lake, but no one had ever successfully photographed the thing except as a large shadow or possible reflection. Many dismissed these claims as hysterical delusions, but you went out on the lake at night at your peril. The origin story dated back to a Siegfried who was in love with Odette, a white babe under some kind of contract to Golden Horizon

Loans, dealing specifically with Mr. Horizon himself, a *Homo sapiens* who looked, frankly, like an owl. She had huge debts, owed him for college loans, was barely employed, but wanted to marry and move on with her life, and you feel sorry for her, even though you want to shout at her, Get a real job already, you dumbass. And Mr. G.H. says marry? I'm not giving up high-interest rates, Sugar Plum. You thought you could mess with me, nothing doing. He introduced Siggie to his own daughter, Odile—beautiful like a black swan, and Siggie fell for her because a.) men are fickle and b.) black is beautiful, and c.) all your white swan poetry and tragedy is one big pain in the buttooks, if you know what I mean, and I honestly don't think you do, so here's the deal. Odette gets to live for all eternity as the Swan Lake Ness Monster, because her true colors were to spread pain and unhappiness wherever she went, which wasn't far because she was stuck in the lake. She gets eternal life, even though it's not the best possible life, and she's still mourning Siggie who is meanwhile saying, Odette who? Odile, too, got a bum deal in life, so you're also rooting for her. Siggie is the one who didn't deserve a happily ever after, and you actually hope Odile will get bored and move on. But all that is ancient history.

"So, the present is now. Kids on boats, hoping for privacy, so they can do noddies laced with LSD or XTC or get stoned or whatever, and just do some things, i.e. fuck their brains out or whatever is passing as their brains at this point. The girl is a badass. She's not afraid of shit and wants to, as she says, score. She's a girl who wants it all as far as what all is in her world which really, when you come right down to it, isn't all that much. The camera zoomed in on the two kids on top of each other, but then white feathers started to float down on their asses and when the snow-ish stuff cleared, guess what? The girl is now a swan, a Big Bird kind of swan, which is to say not pretty by any stretch. She's transformed from a fine-boned, if badass human, to a tough old bird, thick in the middle, stubby scaly legs, webbed feet.

Who would opt for that look? She's hysterical. What's happened to me? The guy flips. Who is this freak I've been fucking? Falls into the water and that's the end of him."

The woman unbuckled then re-buckled one of her gloves, which had a fair amount of hardware on it, then left to stretch her legs. The crowd was restless, out of the movie's spell. People around me became ordinary humans, eating popcorn, calmly milling about, no longer, at least not for the moment, believers in the screen's horror.

Crack returned with a couple of drinks, and we settled down on the grass to watch the rest of *Swan Lake Ness Monster*. Much of it was shot on location in Horner's Landing, Crack learned, and isn't that something? If there had been a boat back to the town and the train, I would have left immediately. If there were Pike Runners, renegade unauthorized boats, this far north, I would have been gone as soon as I got off the train and the noddie wore off. It had been a long shot and had wasted hours, and newsflash, Crack, I didn't have a lot of spare ones to throw out the window. I felt like I was in some kind of suspended house arrest with no choice but to watch the end of a movie I'd never heard of.

Odette was under a spell, but then being a demon seemed to be who she really was. There was no remorse, no inner struggle, no attempt to resist the desires implanted in her. Swans may be associated with grace, but they are nasty, aggressive animals with powerful necks and beaks that can kill. Psychopomp nincompoop, she stalked the kids out on the lake, fueled by bitterness, because the sensation of bare skin touching bare skin was one she would never have, and as an indiscriminate hunter, her prey numbered couples of all kinds: queer, straight, trans—no one, I mean no one, was safe from her. The movie was very clear about this.

And then I saw her: Singe Laveneer up there on the screen standing in front of a house on a street that looked like the one that ran parallel to the river and the train platform, McMurdo Street, Horner's Landing. She was meeting

Jim, an investigator with a camera, determined to capture the creature where everyone else had failed. Jim, you could tell, served a certain purpose, like Arbogast in *Psycho* or Dick Halloran in *The Shining*, the well-meaning problem solver, potential rescuer comes from the outside world who you know is going to collide with an ax or the bottom of a staircase. Singe played a long-necked skeptic who was also a bit of a numbskull, the kind of character who, in her obtuseness, never sees what the audience does and pays for her stubborn what-you-see-(so far)-is-what-you-get pragmatism with her life. It was a small role, little more than an extra with a few lines. Out they went in his rented skiff in twilight, heading towards the center of the lake.

They were going to die. I grabbed Crack's arm. There wasn't going to be much more contact between us than the grasped arm when a pair of curious idiots go out on a lake at night with movie music telling you something bad is going to happen. The arm was not offered but better than no arm, but even the extant limb, warm and able to move, has its limits. It's a source of comfort as long as there could be a creature in the lake, but as soon as the people in the boat disappear, for whatever reason, human warmth recedes, no longer needed.

Someone yelled out, "Don't go into the lake, moron!" Yeah, bad idea.

Odette was sort of like a vampire in that she killed some of her victims and transformed others to be junior versions of herself. The criteria for why some women, and not others, were chosen was never made clear, but it didn't really matter to the story, at least so far. For those chosen women who were thought to have vanished, no corpses were ever found, and they struggled, trapped in swan bodies. They were miserable, horrified at their reincarnation, but then they flew out of the story to wreak havoc someplace else. Lake Ness was Odette's territory. Singe's character was not transformed; she and Jim became birdfeed. Odette must have been incandescent with rage at these interlopers. It was a very bloody scene.

The first explosion came too late to save Jim or Singe's characters. How would blowing up the lake solve the problem? Odette would just go somewhere else. But the explosion wasn't on the technicolor dark blue movie lake. People on the edges of the amphitheater to the west of us were screaming as body parts flew around the structure that housed the bathrooms, but when the second blast occurred, the picture on the screen was still of the lake, placid and dark as it had been before Jim and Singe were attacked. I felt their panic and the pain of metal piercing flesh and bone. The detonations had been on the island, not Lake Ness. Had someone wandered off the path? Was that what set off the old explosives? Pugilist Ninja shrugged and told me that the area of the movie screening had been cleared years ago. It was well-traveled. Any explosives remaining would have gone off long ago.

Lights went out, and phones went dead, the blasts became multiple and calculated. Terror, mine and those of the crowd, accelerated in unison as the post-Dormazin hyper-wake-up chain of molecules grew alarmed. It was time for them to party, as if the inventors had said, we'll put you to sleep, then *boom* if a panic response is triggered: caffeine rush, adrenaline, you name it, it's all yours. Down the hill in front of me, no one was standing, and it looked like a lot of people lying on the ground. What I did absorb was the terror of the people around me. I was frozen with it and stuck to the ground under my feet as if bound by an active electrical current, but then the crowd started running, I followed everyone in motion and direction. The injured were closer to the screen, and therefore further away, so as I ran the feeling of torn and wounded bodies receded.

I tripped over someone, but there was an explosion at the entrance, where so many had fled, without knowing that they were actually rushing toward more peril, as more explosions could be heard. I froze again until the ninja pulled me in the opposite direction, but in the chaos, I lost Crack. I kept running until the anarchy was behind me. In a wooded area I wasn't on any path, there was no path to be found, just short stretches that were slightly more clear of trees and underbrush. I expected one foot after the next to set off a blast of some kind, but all the ground under my feet remained solid and going forward seemed like a better idea than staying in place. I didn't know the exact time, but I could make out a grove of birch, white bark more visible in the moonlight, and the spiky outlines of tall firs and pine.

The sun was just beginning to come up in a half-assed way, but overcast and raining in bursts, there was enough light for me to determine I had wandered far from the main ruins and was in another part of the island. Still moving quickly, fueled by post-noddie-induced jitters, I could hear the river close by and must have arrived at some further edge of the island. The remains were corroded, abandoned industrial structures, very different from the Romantic Gothic arsenal, though originally a component of the same enterprise. For this area of the island the utilitarian was unadorned, form equals function. Suspended between two defunct electrical transmission towers was an aluminum capsule, an abandoned #18 train, a vehicle meant to travel underground, now aerial. A recording was blasting from it.

Who wouldn't want to look inside a thing like that? No electrical wires were visible, so I climbed the creaky steel lattice to look inside, with the hope that from that vantage point I might discover a way to leave the premises with all my limbs intact.

Only one door was open for easy entrance and exit. Subway cars had four doors on each long side, and one on either end, but the other seven had been sealed, so the car, from the inside, had continuous walls. The partition between the conductor's station and the rest of the car had been removed, the control panel left intact, so the car took on the affect of a spaceship, or the idea of a rocket module, though it wasn't flying anywhere. A hammock was strung at one end, a *Not an Exit* sign at the other, and there was an old record player on the floor as well as the scattered remains of a takeout meal from Reel News. From a window, I could see old transmission towers on the edge of a cliff. The site below, along the shore, contained a dock and a couple of similarly converted subway cars, though these were on the ground, propane gas tanks attached. That people lived in these wasn't a surprise. Someone must have gotten the #18 trains from railway salvage, so they were spared the fate of being sunk into the channel and used to seed oyster beds and coral reefs as some of their confrères had been. How they'd been transported to the island was another question. The cars were adorned with vines of brilliant purple morning glories. In fact, there were morning glories all over the place. Stacked alongside the subway cars were crates of metanine, a chemical used in the production of Dormazin. A man ran up to another fellow loading packages onto a boat, pointed to the shore, and hit the other man on the back almost affectionately, an I-told-you-so, we're-A-okay kind of gesture. Both men were wearing goggles and gas masks, but my eyes began to burn from a smell of ammonia. People did live on the island, and they were running a street noddie lab. Morning glory seeds were ground up and added for their hallucinogenic properties. The petals were used for an imperfect-but-close-enough purple-blue dye.

The illegal Dormazin business was tolerated to a certain extent, though people who engaged in it were occasionally busted, and likely disappeared at such times. Shortages of the legit stuff led to a market for the off-the-books stuff and also to price increases when the supply chain had its problems. The Dormazin underworld was left alone to eat its own tail until the body count became too high to sweep under the rug. The system of garage labs and networks of distribution were too entrenched and generated too much revenue, though the genetic propensity for addiction had allegedly been greatly reduced. Anyone who still presented with addictive tendencies, it was felt, would be eliminated eventually by the nature of the world they inhabited. I separated the housed addicts in my life from the nodding-out denizens of the street, from the criminal classes, but it made me suspect that the numbers were far higher,

As an Adjudicator I had cases that involved Dormazin consumption and distribution. I once had a case where the plaintiff claimed his son's addiction was caused by Pangenica. This was tricky ground, blaming negative behavior on us, because Pangenica's litigators had a host of laws in their arsenal, and there was a history of wins. No one would attempt the folly of such a case, except one father who felt he had nothing to lose. His son was found dead in his house, no sign of forced entry, but the house had been robbed, stripped bare. It turned out to be the handiwork of the son's supplier. The son was not only a user, but an integral part of the supply chain for that part of the city. All involved were arrested, convicted, sentenced, and never seen again, but by then the plaintiff himself was deceased of natural causes. Pangenica paid no settlement, though fault was found. The tentacles of Dormizin use, both legal and not, were more ubiquitous than Pangenica was willing to admit.

The sun was coming up and the scene below looked sweet, floral, and the boats were sort of cute in their ramshackle, improvised way. One of the men wore a paisley shirt that was faded to the point of looking nearly uniformly gray, and you could tell his pants were so threadbare, it was a good thing, the raincoat he put on covered his ass. This did not look to be a high-end operation, in fact, the reverse, and I was a witness who wouldn't be allowed to just walk away.

TWENTY

If they took the sleeping part out of the Dormazin and sold only the hallucinogen, they could well be doing a brisk business among the movie-goers. Laced noddies, or noddies minus the Dormazin, caused intense dreams, real visions, Crack had told me, and the altered consciousness during these trips presented itself as solid fact. You couldn't fight the hallucinations with logic from some half-remembered time. If consciousness mediates the day-to-day, street noddie consciousness taps you on the shoulder and says, not so fast, there really are diamonds in the sky. Stars are made of carbon; diamonds and graphite are allotropes of carbon. I was not convinced by his explanation.

Tacked up on a wall of the subway car was a poster from Psychedelicatessen, a storefront of some kind from another century, located in the City of Love, which sounded as hopeless a concept as it was utopian. Maybe that's what Pangenica was all about, too, at least they had promoted themselves as such: Creating people can only generate love because there are no more inherited problems. Love, love, love, love is the only thing you need. That was one aspect of the theory behind the company, one that hadn't always worked out so well, as any Adjudicator would tell you.

The needle was stuck in a groove and kept repeating the same line from "Fly me to the Moon" over and over again until I lifted its arm from the record. It was a gesture I made without thinking, really stupid, because in a few minutes I heard the whining sound of old metal groaning in the wind, but it wasn't the wind, rather the weight of footsteps on the steel lattice. Someone was climbing up to the subway car. The side doors were sealed which meant there was only one way out, the way I came in, which would land me face-to-face with whoever was on his way up, but when I pushed aside the *Not an Exit* sign on the far door and unhooked the chain, that door opened. Almost nothing but air all the way down. It was a reach to the first accessible steel bar, and as I hung over the edge tentatively stretching one foot toward the highest bar, the door slammed on my hand, whether from the wind or due to a hostile person I can't say, but I let go, toe to bar, caught myself, then climbed down as quickly as I could without ever looking up. Once I hit the ground I ran without looking back. This could never be achieved without the adrenaline push from the Dormazin aftereffects, and I have to admit, it was a nice accelerating feeling.

The edge of the island, close to the shore, was rocky, but I was able to run along it, assuming the other dock would appear sooner or later. The island wasn't that big. Hills along the opposite coast, the river's mossy black surface, all looked peaceful and quiet, no evidence of humans anywhere, and you could pretend you were in the far western foothills, a preindustrial, prelapsarian wilderness, if you were so inclined to imagine backwards, but I didn't run in silence. Maybe twigs snapped due to a deer or some other animal, but I interpreted the echo as human footfalls, at least I believed that's what I heard, so I ran faster.

When the dock came into view, it was in a state of mayhem. SWAT teams in helicopters circled overhead. A bomb detection unit complete with specialists in hazmat suits with dogs and robots was beginning its inspection of the island. Small as it was, it still would take them more than a day to cover in its entirety, if they were going slowly, scouring for ordnance and evidence of who did what when. At such time when they reached the farthest edge, there would be consequences for the noddie lab: morning glories uprooted, metanine confiscated, abandoned subway cars left to rust and become overgrown with invasive plants and burrowing animals.

Ambulance boats lined up at the pier, and emergency personnel poured out, wheeling oxygen tanks and IV drips. Some of the non-injured tried to jump on the medical boats and were pushed back, even into the water, after being shouted at: Overloaded ships will sink. One more won't make that much of a difference, a man yelled back as he struggled to get on, but then others shouted him down. You're able-bodied, the EMT workers yelled back, wait for a non-emergency conveyance. Stretchers lay in rows on the dock and along the shore. I saw the couple who had been next to us during the screening huddled under a silver blanket with others in shock, but I did not see Crack among the injured or the unscathed who were milling around waiting to get off the island.

I tried to text him, but neither my phone nor anyone else's was working. While speeding on the aftereffects of Dormazin, I tapped my foot and fingers on a railing in agitation. Unsteady on my feet, I grabbed my left arm, which, though attached and not sustaining so much as a paper cut, throbbed with the phantom pains of those around me. My knees buckled, and I fell to the ground, my legs collapsing as if they were no longer there. An emergency first responder knelt beside me, then said in disgust, WTF, there's nothing wrong with you, don't waste my time. She walked over to a real victim, who was bleeding and unconscious, carried them to the dock by medics, then turned, whispered to one of her colleagues, and pointed at me. I struggled to my feet. I had to get out of there.

Among the non-injured was a group demanding a refund. You could only buy roundtrip tickets, which included the cost of the entertainment on the island, but they claimed the second movie had been interrupted. They were being evacuated, they argued, not leaving as planned, and hadn't been able to enjoy the advertised moonlit night, listening to the wind in the pines, and so on. Instead, they had to endure catastrophic circumstances, unplanned and disruptive in the extreme, and were therefore entitled to a refund of half their ticket price which amounted to $10.75. They cornered the captain of the hydrofoil, now lined up along with the medical boats, ready to take passengers back, and he told them he had no authority to issue refunds, it was someone else's job, but who that person might be, he had no idea. He just operated the boat. He had neither the cash nor an ecash app, nor the connectivity to distribute refunds in any case.

The group kept shouting at him, even as he prepared to cast off. They didn't accept that the hydrofoil was completely full and certainly didn't feel like waiting for his next trip. Why should we wait? Unacceptable! The woman in the ripped skirt, the one who'd explained the movie to me, was standing at the stern and extended her hand to pull me onboard, infuriating the people nearby, but I had my reasons for needing to be on that boat, for getting to shore as soon as possible. As I reached for her hand, another woman grabbed my ankle and tried to pull me off, shouting, she got on, what the fuck! The boat was stronger, as it pushed out into the river, and I thought I'd be torn in two, or have to let go and tumble into the water, but a man yanked her off. Some people on deck ignored me, while others stared, commenting on my insolence for adding to the overcrowding. My former neighbor from the movie paid no attention to any of them, saying to me, we were just watching a bunch of swans, minding our own business, what could go wrong with that? Right? She didn't appear to be injured, and I didn't ask how she got on the boat, just thanked her for pulling me on board.

I inquired if she was from the town, though I didn't think she was, and she shook her head, no. She worked for the Parks Department in the city and was assigned to check out night event crowd control and safety for which the team on Horner's Island would get an A for Abysmal. Sure, this was a one-time rare occurrence, but prepared they clearly were not. Arrival time of emergency personnel was subpar. Evacuating the area in a timely fashion left a great deal to be desired. And those ding-dongs on the pier who wanted what they wanted when they wanted it needed to be informed of basic protocol. The Parks official registered no concern for the traumatized around us. Although she had pulled me onboard in a gesture of goodwill, it seemed whatever the nature of her temperament—chilly or just blind to the agony, discomfort, itchiness of others—it was the opposite of mirror touch, and I could imagine the reasoning of her parents when filling out their Pangenica forms. Such a trait might support survival instincts. You would remain calm and figure out the best way to walk out of a calamity unscathed, which this woman seemed to have done. I'd asked my mother, only one time, why she'd requested mirror touch? It wasn't something you could ask for, was the answer. Even at a young age, I suspected as much, so she certainly hadn't noted it in the fill-in-the-blanks, multiple choice, or in any of the essay questions. It was something that just happened to happen, she'd said, and best not to talk about it.

People were hanging over the hydrofoil's railing, pushed by the density of the crowd behind them. The railing was slippery, and rivulets merged to form streams, making the deck treacherous. You move your hand, and the rest of your body moves. Messages are sent from your brain to your fingers, other cells are working invisibly, you have no control over them, and these microscopic busy bees exist in the millions. Rain falls on your head, you move your hand over your wet hair and stare at more rain making divots on the surface of the river. Pangenica was good at isolating movement, cutting and pasting pieces of nucleic acid and proteins as if they were measuring and making a pattern for a suit, found flaws in the material, but then wait, there are workarounds. There is no isolated gene for eye color, the trait is interconnected to a thousand other traits, and it was once thought impossible to just change this one thing without a host of other alterations, then it became possible. But still, my mother had her doubts and used to say, look at old-time rhinoplasty photos, ultimately those diminished noses look out of whack, like they don't fit with the rest of the person's face. (She had access to these images via Chromatin.

Say a client wanted the nose of a twentieth-century somebody, and she'd say, but that person wasn't born with that schnozz, honeybunch. It was "done.") Over time you get anomalies in the code, and maybe altered consciousnesses is just one of those things. The system needs constant monitoring and adjustment. The woman in the torn skirt taps on your arm, and says, hey, we're here, finally, what a night, and you never see her again.

The walk from the dock to the train station, little more than a platform, tickets came out of machines, was short. It was a good thing Crack had bought roundtrip tickets, otherwise I'd be stuck in Horner's Landing forever, but the train, running on a Sunday schedule, wouldn't arrive for another two hours. I sat on a bench in the drizzle and tried to read *The Shadow Prince*. There was a reproduction of a painting of his mother, Countess Olympe—receding chin, head shaped like a lightbulb, though she was painted as Athena, sword and shield in hand. Within reason, symmetrical faces and bodies are the norm now, but still, even after generations, some people just want their kids to look more or less like themselves, which means nothing but turtles all the way down. We learned that in the past, everyone's idea of perfect varied according to culture and geography, so I could accept the fact that Olympe didn't look like a beauty to me, and it didn't really matter. And besides, that was the way life was before tailors of DNA were making perfect clothing.

The Shadow Prince detailed her machinations, her tricks to ensnare the king, falling in and out of favor back and forth for years until her exile. I had trouble with the idea that her uncle, Cardinal Mazarin, had no ancestors that he would recognize. That threw me for a loop, but mainly, I had trouble imagining the deformed prince Eugene whose brain was so out of sync with his body, even though the book provided pictures of him. Liselotte of the Palatinate, a chronic diarist and relative of the Sun King, wrote that Savoy was "a dirty and debauched boy, who gave no promise of being any good. He had a small, snub nose; his eyes were not bad, and showed intelligence. His mouth was always open. He was fairly small for his age and sedate." What I knew of the pre-Pangenica era: Nixon looked like who he was, supposedly, character equaled physiognomy, all shady and shadowy (as in five o'clock). Handsome mass murderer Ted Bundy did not. What a time to be alive. Did no one question the precarity of the genetic crap shoot? Rain was spotting the pages, so I shut *The Shadow Prince* and put it back in my bag.

The first buildings of the town were only a few blocks from the pier, and there were already clusters of reporters and camera crews jostling to get on the boats going to the island. They'd driven up, wanting their piece of the action, elbowing emergency crews aside, if they were able to. A woman asked to interview me, what had it been like, but I didn't want to stop to talk to her, so she moved on to someone else. There were plenty eager to talk, to describe what they'd experienced in great detail, as if talking would verify what had happened, and who can blame them for feeling that way? As the panic and aftereffects of the Dormazin wore off, absorbing this level of real or imagined trauma would render me unable to speak—a torrent of other people's testimony, so I hurried past them. On the first corner, after the station, there was a Donuts of Distinction, and I stared through a window at people drinking coffee and eating breakfast. Sitting at a counter among them was Crack, biting into what looked like a sugar-syrup-glazed piece of cloudy heaven, after a night on Horner's arsenal depot, even an ordinary doughnut glowed with an inner light.

He didn't notice me walk through the glass doors, but the stool next to him was empty.

How did you get off the island so fast? He jumped, surprised to feel my hand on his back, and told me he had searched for me among the survivors, but then boarded a boat, assuming I'd left before him. He must have elbowed a place on the first boat to leave and couldn't have spent much time looking, but I let it go. He was too-much-coffee jittery, so I was now becoming jittery, too, but I didn't have time to waste, and the jitters could have been self-summoned. Full-on mirror touch, welcome back. I informed Crack that I needed to borrow money since Chester Louie had cleaned me out. I intended to eat breakfast, then be on my way.

"I can put the money back in your account." Crack held out his hand for my phone. If he had the skills to hack Chester's banking information and reverse the clean-out, it was news to me, but I wasn't about to question him.

"Why are you telling me this now? You could have gotten my money back hours ago."

"Once Chester realizes his account has been depleted, your identity is his to reveal, so you might want to wait until you walk into the office Monday with enough to close the case. Tell Adjudications, look, I found Singe. In the meantime, order whatever you want. It's on me."

So I did: Distinction Eggs with Chilis and Shrooms (the word was printed in bubble lettering reminiscent of the Psychedelicatessen poster) and the red cheddar the region is known for. Donuts of Distinction, though a chain, encouraged franchise owners to use local elements to individualize each restaurant to a certain extent.

Our server, wearing the customary uniform, a top hat and a T-shirt printed with a tuxedo jacket, took my order and set my spot with silverware and a placemat, then poured fresh coffee into a Distinctions mug, available for sale at the cash register.

The eggs came with a side of what Crack called old-school special sauce shit.

"Why do you have to call it that?" I asked. "It's my special sauce, and now I'm not going to want it. You eat it, then."

"Look at the placemats."

The placemats were illustrated not with the traditional happy guy dapper donut about to break into a soft shoe routine, but with an abbreviated pictorial history of the town that could be followed in a clockwise direction. Beginning at twelve o'clock, an artist's rendering of indigenous figures had a camping ground on the island, relics had been found on the western edge. Not a surprise, the river had been a rich fishing area long before volatile organics so easily vaporized were dumped from an upstream plant known for manufacturing high-voltage circuits and electrical transformers. Somewhere around nine o'clock, Horner moved his family to the island to live in a Petit Trianon style domicile. He believed the risks were minimal, or so he said, but this turned out not to be true, which begged the question, not aired on the placement, had Horner deliberately put his family in harm's way? Was the blast intentional? Or was he like the backers of the *Titanic* who swore the ship was unsinkable, and therefore, scrimped on the lifeboats? The placemat offered no illumination on this point, except to make clear that the Petit Trianon structure was no longer extant, and no one has lived on the island since. The captain had also declared, in no uncertain terms, that the island was, and had always been, uninhabited, with the brief exception of Horner's family. Of course, the noddie business was not represented in the pictorial history. And if the captain had a stake in it, he would have an interest in promoting ain't nobody here but us chickens, deliverers of noddie nod-outs not.

Crack asked the waitress if she was from the town, and when she answered that she was, he asked if there was anyone who knew things. We needed to find someone who used to live here, and we needed to find, you know, a busybody, the kind of person who is always looking out their window or sitting on their porch, who knows who comes and goes, that kind of person, or maybe a local historian, figuring such an encyclopedic individual might remember Singe who had a small part in the movie when the production came to Horner's. This person, a longtime resident, might recognize her face, have some information. The waitress told us about a guy, Jason J. Kent, who used to do satiric drawings, comics, political cartoons for the local paper when it was on paper. He was the oldest person in town that she knew about, but he was a recluse. Did we want refills?

I did, but Crack shook his head and paid the check, even though I wasn't finished, as if I didn't know time, too, was being eaten up. I took a final bite of a mushroom, but ate it slowly for maximum irritation. The man lived in a house behind a shuttered barbershop, Slick & Dapper High Class Cuts.

People in booths or at the counter began looking at their phones again, a signal connectivity had been restored, but mine was only partially working. The logo of a landline phone receiver popped up to indicate a voice message from the Director sent in the middle of the night. His message was clipped. The labs were working on the samples I'd sent, but this didn't mean that Singe's DNA wasn't needed, on the contrary. In a staccato tone he went on: it was. Urgent. Send updates, or I'll assume you're coming up empty and will proceed accordingly. Altner had disappearachniks on auto-dial. There she is. Nab her. My mother's phone went straight to voicemail.

Following Crack out of the D of D, I said nothing about what I'd just listened to, and as we walked up the street looking for the cartoonist's address, I kept turning my head to be sure the commuter train hadn't come and gone. There was plenty of time, it wasn't due for an hour and a half, but the image of being stuck in Horner's while trains came and went with no way out was not a happy one.

The part of town that was near the center had a few storefronts, especially common here were nail salons with names like Princess Akiko, Atomic Cocktail Nails, Telltale Nails (logo was a heart), and Nail Me. Their windows were arrays of colors, mostly in the red and pink range, and inside you could see hundreds of little glass bottles and displays of glue-on nails in an infinite variety of patterns. If you landed from Mars, saw women in surgical masks bent over the hands and feet of other women and men, you might wonder what ritual, religious rite, or sacrifice was about to occur; faces were serious, work was done in silence, concentration absolute.

There were also a number of businesses that offered bodywork, though it wasn't clear exactly what bodywork, under the circumstances offered by these storefronts, might be. Certain kinds of activities and behaviors had been reduced to a murmur, but then returned, becoming loud whispers in small towns that, as Mr. Horner discovered, were good for hiding things. No one was sure why addiction and a predilection for sex for hire came creeping back. Cutting and pasting DNA for disinterest in mind-altering substances, and foregrounding longings for only standard desires, easily fulfilled, these alterations required far and wide across populations, made a dent in these businesses, but only a dent. Normalcy is generally dominant when it comes to sex, Pangenica asserted. Fringe stuff was called *fringe* for a reason, and easily made almost obsolete, rare though not completely unheard of. In its early days, Pangenica had an expanding lexicon of what was considered perversion, what should be dumped in the trash of undesirable proclivities, and once gone, these inclinations were supposed to be really gone, but sometimes that which had been thought to be extinct returned. If there's money to be made from something, money will be made.

The bodywork storefronts beckoned with the idea you could relax on a table and things would be done to you, hands laid on, healing of a sort, they claimed, reinforced by the orientalist hodgepodge arranged in display windows: waterfalls cascading over pieces of jade, brass hookahs, scimitars, calligraphic scrolls pinned to folding screens, pots of bamboo. I was mesmerized by the decorative waterfalls meant to convey peace and tranquility when my phone pinged with a text. It was from Chester.

$$$$+

But you took everything

From your bank account yes. What about savings retirement stocks and bonds other financial vehicles and products?

That's all I have

Really? Yr answer stretches my credulity

Well you're stretched then

You have 24 hrs

Then he sent a short film beginning in an elevator, tracking down the hall, going into Adjudications, coming to a stop at my empty cleaned-out desk. There was no sound, but whether the footage was deep fake or real I couldn't tell. It looked real, as if, like the Invisible Man, Chester had slipped into Pangenica and filmed my path from the entrance to my desk. When I showed the film to Crack, he said turn off your phone, as if that would be the end of it, don't bother me with your ghosts and tremors, but it would not be the end of it. Chester meant business. As an Adjudicator, you are sometimes like a blind gambler, I suppose. You know some things, but much is beyond your abilities, and turning off my phone would achieve nothing. Chester was a drone embedded in a bird or a dragonfly, following me everywhere. Crack was walking fast, a block ahead of me.

We found the shuttered Slick & Dapper and followed a path of broken concrete that led to a two-story house overlooking the river, and as soon as we stepped into the yard, a dog who was chained up barked in anger and frustration, baring his teeth at us interlopers. I'm not afraid of dogs, and like them even, but this one was on edge, wanted to sink his teeth into someone, lunging continually and never figuring out the leash would only jerk him back. He was chained to the concrete base of a garden gnome that had been painted over so the conical figure appeared to be permanently screaming, mouth painted wide open, eyes bugging out.

We rang the bell and were met by a man not old enough to be Jason J. Kent, but it was his nephew and caretaker, Jason J. Kent, Jr. Stepping into the hall, I thought I would explain who we were and what we wanted, a version of our actual motives, but not necessarily the whole truth: We were looking for a woman who appeared in a movie shot in Horner's Landing, and we were hoping Kent Senior might know her, or something like that. Before I could open my mouth, Crack jumped in saying he was an animator and had long been a fan of his uncle's cartoons. I doubted Crack had ever seen one of them, but he laid it on thick about Kent the virtuoso, adding that we'd come all the way from the city, spent the night on the island, survived the explosions—oh, you didn't hear, didn't know? It's on the news, look. Crack held up his phone. Something was up with Kent Jr. He was repressing the urge to scream, but this made no sense. Why would the appearance of two admirers, though strangers, cause a hysteric reaction? I pressed my lips together to stifle what he was trying to repress, then it felt like he was trying not to burst out laughing. I looked at Crack, trying to focus on him, but was unaware of what I was mirroring and just blathered on.

Step back outside, Junior said.

I thought that was the end of our chance of meeting with Jason Kent Sr., but Junior explained. I have to be careful who I let in. Open your bags. Crack complied. Take a look, buddy, you can search me and my partner. We have nothing to hide. Except our Pangenica IDs, but Jason Jr. only indifferently pushed papers around with the end of a pencil and didn't think to look in our wallets. Some guard. He never even asked to see any form of identification. Either he was new at the job, or visitors were rare.

Junior told us he'd give us five minutes, that Jason Senior went in and out of lucidity, and if we got five lucid minutes, fine, if not, tough luck. Also, Senior couldn't talk, he typed on a screen.

Junior worried me. He shuddered and I shuddered. There was a particular out-of-controlness that troubled me, like epileptic seizures. No one was born with epilepsy, but seizures could be the result of a brain injury, for example. I'd seen a film of someone having a seizure; my eyes rolled back, and I fell off my chair. I needed to find a window to look outside, to calm myself, but none were in evidence, so I tried to control my/his anxiety, while Kent Junior led us down a cluttered hall lined with bookshelves full of comics and books of cartoons. There were framed cartoons on the walls, some were signed *J. Kent*, and they featured a repeating character, an earth marked with latitude and longitude lines, as well as the outline of continents. And the earth was portrayed with a variety of expressions, depending on the situation: horror, terror, disgust. There were other framed panels signed by twentieth-century cartoonists: Eisner, Stan Lee, Feldstein, Schulz, Bretécher, Simmonds, a page from an early Superman. They must have been worth a fortune. Sections of the shelves were organized according to geography of origin or genre.

Then we entered a large back room that had once been a drawing studio, and there, glowering and blinking in a rocking chair buffered by pillows, sat Mr. Kent. I felt his atrophied muscles, his difficulty breathing. He wasn't angry, as PomPom had been, but I can't say he'd made his peace with his body not working as it once had—the hand tremors, the failed brain and voice connections. Barriers melt, dissolve, must be re-established, and I tried to feel my own body, a couple of mosquito bites on my legs, an irritated eye, nothing like what the elder Kent communicated. My diversion tactics weren't working very well. Kent Jr. asked me what I did for a living, a strange archaic phrase "for a living," an expression an old man like Kent Sr. would use, and like Kent Sr., my hand started to shake. Junior asked, what's up with her? You need to leave. Now. Crack: she'll be okay. She just blacks out occasionally. He grabbed my arm and squeezed very hard, so I would feel the pain and focus on his fingernails digging into my skin. Veins, tendons versus dirty nails. Okay, Kent Sr.'s failing body backed off.

Jason Senior looked about one hundred years old. His parents must have emphasized longevity on their forms, but forgot the health necessary to go along with old age which always wins in the end. There's nothing even Pangenica's labs have been able to do about this. He appeared miserable, an aged boy in shorts, knees like potatoes, enormous glasses, quivering hands that would never hold a drawing pen again, and he knew it. Hooked up to an oxygen tank, he was stuck with his own personal Chester, in the form of his nephew, perfunctory and irritable, fitting the role of the caretaker waiting for the old man to kick, so he could grab the money and run, though maybe that wasn't the story, not entirely. Everyone Kent Sr. had known or loved must have been long dead. The house could only have been his own private Penrose without the ocean views.

There was a problem with the oxygen tank, and the old man coughed and gasped for air while Junior Kent tried to fix it. I turned away, and took a few steps down the hall, so I, too, wouldn't gasp for air, I was already experiencing Kent Sr.'s achy joints, and used this pause to take a look at a shelf of comics at the corner where the hall ended and the room began. I wasn't searching for what I did find there on the blond wood shelves identical to all the others in the hall; it was just what was closest, at eye level, and spines out, titles didn't necessarily signal content. It was the pornography section, and I looked. What I discovered in those minutes should have been obvious: drawing has no limits. Drawn people can do things not humanly possible in real life and in places actual people may not have access to, or may not even exist, and you don't need to get signed statements of consent. Some of the comics were very old, yellowed, brittle, well-handled. Others appeared to be new. Mr. Kent would not have been capable of buying the newer editions himself. Were they acquired at his request? Who read them to him and turned the pages? His nephew? Or were they the possessions of Junior Kent, just mixed in with everything else? Crack walked over, glanced at what I was thumbing through, then pulled me away, giving me a *what the hell do you think you're doing, do that when we're alone and I'm watching, otherwise the effort is wasted, act like you're here for a reason*—that kind of look.

When the oxygen was flowing again, Crack launched into some cockeyed story about not only was he a huge fan, but also, oh, by the way, wanted to find this woman. He tried to make a connection between a cult horror movie and Kent's cartoons, a mangled cat's cradle of associations, one shape turning into the next, then back. Kent Junior said they had no knowledge of any movie shot in town or on the island, but they were reclusive, and there was no reason why they would have known, necessarily, about the filming, but Crack wouldn't give up. She used to live here in this town, right? We heard you've lived here a long time, so we thought you might know her. Do you have any information about her? Do you know where we could find her? Crack was bulldozing his way through, and I wished he'd taken some time before we knocked on the door to let me work out a reasonable identity. A fan, that was good, but it wasn't working. He was talking too fast, trying to tie too many unrelated pontoons together. He wasn't skilled at being someone else, and had the affect of an amateur. The old man looked catatonic. Perhaps he hadn't heard or understood what Crack had said. He showed him the picture of Singe, and once again the man in the chair began to cough even more violently, turning bright red, eyes watery from irritation.

Kent Jr. said, see, you're done. Time's up. Scram. He pointed to the door.

Not so fast. Kent Sr. came to life, reached for his screen, and began to type, slowly at first, then in a frenzy of tapping and his own raised eyebrows. We were supposed to know his biography if Crack was such a big fan, but the tapping on the screen proceeded as if we knew nothing, an assumption older people often make: You are an idiot. You know nothing. I was someone of importance and should be still.

Earlier in his life, Kent had drawn cartoons poking fun at the potential failures of genetic design. RNA messengers fell off their bicycles, tripped out on Dormazin, created a race of criminal supermen. Phytosack workers went on strike, or the materials used for making them ceased to exist, became super-rare, extremely expensive, and therefore only obtainable by a few, difficult to procure in the quantities and level of purity required, supply chain blockages, terroroticas blowing up bridges, and before you know it, no more humans, at least not in their present format. In other words, his cartoons commented on what he saw as potential bedlam caused by a variety of unintentional but irrevocable mistakes, but even these cartoons were tolerated until he drew Pangenica making malign decisions, the progenitors of chaos.

Though Kent had an underground following, he began to receive death threats and had to hire a bodyguard. After about a year on the job, he was like family, so when an earotube delivered to the house exploded, Kent had to live with the consequences of having escaped unharmed, while the guard was killed instantly. Was any cartoon worth a human life? No, Kent answered his own question, but he kept working and kept pissing people off. There was nothing else to do, and he wasn't going to capitulate to a bunch of basement lodging thugs carrying poison water for the tower dwellers of Pangenica. People don't know who their enemies are, Kent spoke with finality. The earotube had cost him personally. Kent Jr. lost an arm.

I hadn't noticed. Kent Jr. had access to better bionics than Daphne of Dometop. He held up his left hand, rotated the appendage and bent it back at the wrist in a way a biological hand never could. It boinged back. Senior continued to type. Father and son looked alike, but something was off about Kent Jr, his transparent anxiety, his graying translucent hair. If I was a snoop I'd check in with Vy in Admissions to look at his file. It might make for interesting reading.

Remembering what Dinah had said about Singe's use of her bathroom, I asked if I could use theirs, not because I needed a hair sample, but this is a room where you can find things residents would prefer you not find, though also I had to go. Kent Jr. directed me back down the hall and up a narrow flight of stairs, comics stacked on some of the steps, photographs of Kent Sr. as a young man at his drawing table on a stage accepting an award, leaning over a table holding a martini glass. There was a framed high school yearbook picture from a time when Jason J. Kent's name was Jacob Kadish.

The medicine cabinet contained generic painkillers in extra-large-size economy bottles, razors, a plastic comb that was missing a few teeth, and several bottles of Dormazin, labels faded, out-of-date prescriptions no doubt from a time when the old man had deadlines, probably, but also bottles of street noddies, purple-blue, their trademark color of being a little off. I pocketed a few, as many as I thought would go unnoticed because you never know when they could come in handy. The bathroom window looked out over the river at a neglected pier. The river was shallow here, but wide, and further out were a few falling-down fishing shacks. Not much to do on Horner's for a youngish but no longer that young Kent Junior, except to trip his brains out from time to time with a locally sourced noddie or two.

My mother hoarded Dormazin. Some I found, but no doubt there were other stashes unknown to me, and perhaps forgotten even by her. I was her supplier, so these reserves were either old or she had some other mail order source, delivered by drone. Their potency, while diminished, wasn't zero. Had she started a binge right after I left? I think, in her loneliness, that was her pattern. A stranger disembarks from the *Jolly Sandhog* to find her asleep, and then what? He leaves the way he came, nothing to do here, boss. Or he throws her comatose body into the waves. She never wakes up. I panicked. It was as if I was in another century when you only got someplace by putting one foot in front of another; Penrose was at that kind of distance. Again, I thought of Shackleton's men stranded on South Georgia Island. It took several months, but eventually a boat came for them, right? I stared at the river, so far north, Penrose was the moon.

Down the hall were the bedrooms. Kent Sr.'s had to have been the one with the hospital bed, so of course I went in. There was a loop of porn running on a large screen, a kind of human interaction that had become alien to him, an old man living off the books for some years, as if under house arrest, a far cry from the glamor of the past life depicted on the stairs. The desire to view, this was supposed to have been eliminated, but curiosity—everyone had that. So the standard images on Mr. Kent's inset screen were known to be everywhere, watched by everyone, though in secret. The film was low budget, the kind shot in middle-class bedrooms in which you see the everyday objects of the characters' or director's or whoever's lives, the dollar-store crockery, the lamps found on the street, paintings of matadors, calendars from a dry cleaner. It was easy to watch, hard to turn away, and I spent too much time wanting to see what would happen next, but I did finally turn away because I didn't want to start responding in that way Crack liked to watch. The room was dark, shades drawn, but then on the wall were tacked pictures, drawings. They were cartoons of a woman, limbs made of glass pipes and metal joints, a green lens on a retractable telescope extended where one eye would be, the other eye was humanoid, but though Chimera-like, the creature had the unmistakable features of the woman who for a few years thought she was one hundred percent PomPom's mother. Unclothed, she moved from frame to frame on the track of a character who was part *Homo sapiens*, loosely, part stovetop parts, a blind art thief with canceled eyes, lensless periscopes. She hung out in a vaulted lair made up of mechanized chambers sliding in and out of view, but packed with paintings, figures of deities from all over the steampunk universe (Shiva with arms made of catalytic converters, for example), objects as massive as sarcophagi and as fragile as tin weathervanes. These drawings revealed an obsession with detail not visible in Kent's other work, but the hand had clearly been his. I was unpinning one of the drawings when I heard footsteps on the stairs. It was Kent Jr. looming in the doorway within seconds, while I stood with the framed picture in hand.

My phone vibrated with a text.

90 more minutes

"Downstairs." Kent Jr. shoved his face in front of mine. I hadn't heard him coming and now absorbed his indignation and anger.

Still holding onto the drawing, I made my way downstairs to face Crack and Kent Sr. I tried to project my own rationale, but only absorbed the Kents' what-the-fucks, do you want me to call the police, no, yes, no, then I asked Kent Sr. outright, you knew her, please explain.

His mouth twisted, straightened, twisted, thin old lips in a tight line, as if not to let the words out, and he motioned to Kent Jr. to hand him a screen so he could type. His hands were shaking, his whole arm had tremors, but he managed to tap across the screen.

ISOTOPE
KILL YOUR MASTERS

If you could have seen Singe Laveneer standing on the steps of the National Cathedral of Art explaining her theories of return and replace to a handful of people who stopped on their way into the museum, then the camera follows her as she stands in the main hall handing out leaflets criticizing an exhibit of the drawings of the incarcerated, children's drawings were even included, how aestheticizing anesthetized. Something in her crusade inspired me. I was just one more *alte kaker*, old gent, visiting the city while I still had legs, I knew that. What could I do? I could do what I've always done. I used her face as a model for a cartoon character. Isotope Comics hired me for a series, and I was stuck, needed money, and the deadline was fast approaching, so I used her, sort of. It was meant as a tribute, an act of love, but she didn't see it that way.

She found out years later that I used her face, but still, and though no insult was intended, in fact I had only admiration for her, she was not amused and threatened to sue me. She wanted her face returned to her, in effect. She wanted me to destroy all images of her, which wouldn't be possible even if I had wanted to, and I didn't want to. Death threats from the henchmen of genetico gigantico were a badge of honor, but hatchets thrown by a fellow outlier crackpot I was in love with from afar? I was horrified, offended. Why sue me? She looked at me as a revenue source. Do I look like someone with deep pockets? No one would hire her. She was broke. Is this my problem? I'm her solution? So, no, I don't know her address or even that she ever lived in Horner's. But my nephew has reported seeing her. Kent Junior had seen her in town. He saw her on the pier, and later, when he saw her in his rearview mirror, he believed she was following him. She would appear in his mirror several more times, or he saw her in town, but she never knocked on our door. By then I was housebound. I'm living in my own private Faraday cage.

Heartbroken, Kent seemed to shrink in his chair. He had fallen in love with the idea of Singe, since they'd never met, apart from the random sighting when she was protesting, but the mention of her name was enough to send the old man into a tailspin, a mass of nerves and ramblings. He muttered strings of phrases: volts, amps, isolation. He was waterproof and flame retardant, barely audible. He pointed to his nephew and rasped out that he was a handsome fellow. He used the word *fellow*, not man, not guy or bloke or poor devil, as if he was afraid his nephew was poised to rob him of the woman he loved. After the outburst, he gave the appearance of sleep or some kind of loss of consciousness, mouth open, eyes half shut.

Kent Jr. let us know it was time for us to leave, and though he didn't say so outright, as soon as the door closed behind us, he would return to his cabinets full of painkillers and out-of-date Dormazin.

Junior followed us and once outside, pointed to the brickwork on the right side of the door that was lighter than the rest. These had replaced the ones that had been shattered. The black burn streaks, shadows of the explosion around the door—I hadn't noticed earlier. See that? Kent Jr. ran his bionic hand over a halo of singe marks before waving us away. That's where the letter bomb went off.

Were the Kents reclusive because of the cartoons Kent drew? He was fully aware of the risks when he put pen to paper, knowing when printed, those images would make him, if not a fugitive, if not arrested in the middle of the night and disappeared, then a transgressor with a reputation for being a pain in the ass, which was worse because it meant you didn't matter all that much. Or did he become subversive because of his coding, maybe gone a bit haywire? Was he designed that way by dreamy parents, who like all parents, imagined the best but really had no idea? I could see parents stressing, oh, we'd so like, you know, an independent thinker. Okay, sir, madam, no problem there. Yes and an artistic talent with a comic streak. Well, alright.

Well, alright. Anything you say, the customer isn't always right, but yes, you can order that. Then what was supposed to be just a streak steered him into dangerous satire. Who knew that would happen? Kent Jr. told us some filming had been done on McMurdo Street, two blocks that way then take a left. That doesn't mean she lived on the block where they shot, but take a look if you want, you have nothing to lose.

We walked through the alley back to the street, then made a left as the storefronts gave way to two or three family frame houses, then one-story ranches. The woods were beginning to take over. The town was close to the city but on a different clock, and there was evidence of family life: bicycles, inflatable kiddie pools on lawns, sounds of arguments and music, people staring at us from their porches. Parents and their children, all silent advertisements for the skills of Pangenica, or so it appeared. Crack had transferred a picture of Singe Laveneer to his phone, and he looked at it from time to time as we tried to find what might have been her address. I wondered if he was becoming as spellbound by her as Kent Sr. and the easily lovestruck Waxman had been. Was that why he seemed as intent on finding her as if he were an Adjudicator whose life depended on it? I couldn't ask him, but maybe I should have. Then we saw the house.

Number 9 McMurdo Street, the house that had been featured in *Swan Lake Ness Monster,* was half-stone, half-redwood, a riverfront property, desirable but prone to flooding—don't store valuables in the basement. Ghosts of cameraperson, gaffer, key grip, costume and wardrobe personnel, catering trucks—you could imagine them lined up. But the street was its quiet Sunday morning self, unglamorous; the river smelled of distant things rotting. No investigators of swan myths knocking on doors, only the sidelong glances of citizens, gloom creeping on because in a matter of hours, sundown, sunup, they would be boarding commuter trains headed for the city to get to jobs, appointments, meetings. We walked up a flagstone path to the front door and rang the bell. No one answered. What did you expect on a Sunday morning? I asked Crack if he really imagined Singe would be waiting by the door. Here, I just made you a fresh pot of coffee. I'll spit into a tube, here's my DNA, sorry for the fuss, I'll drive you to the station, you don't want to miss the 11:05.

So we walked around the house, which was sealed tight, skirting clumps of daylilies, a hibiscus, an eye sign indicating the presence of a neighborhood watch group. No one had mowed the lawn or clipped hedges of mountain laurel and hawthorn in a long time. There was a sound of rustling in the grass, and I thought it might be a snake, but more of the grass was pushed aside, and taking a closer look, we found a snapping turtle eating something that at one time had feathers.

It looked at us with a don't-test-me stare. The tiny close-set nostrils were more alarming than her possible bite, holes the size a small nail might make, air intake just enough to be efficient, to keep the chomping machine going, but was there a consciousness in there, somewhere? Billions of snapping turtle brain neurons exchanged electrical impulses and released chemicals that interpreted our appendages as both food and danger. How fast could it put one clawed foot in front of the next? I imagined speed—faster than you might think. One clawed foot suspended in slow motion, jaws snapped, a sign of combativeness. Maybe she'd laid eggs nearby, or maybe the turtle was just trying to get by, just being itself, doing what turtles do. You can pick them up by the thing that protects them (though it's no defense against cars or alligators).

A boy running through his adjacent backyard stopped at the snapper, and told us it was his pet, Arabelle, and it had been ill. What's sick for a turtle? He was barefoot, and he hit the shell with a stick. It wasn't crapping. They knew that? Yes, we took her to the vet. He took an X-ray, and inside was a small plastic turtle that the living one had swallowed. The only way to get it out was surgery.

He was very talkative and told us clutches of snapper eggs can number between eighty and one hundred, and if all were to live to maturity, that would be a lot of animals. There are species that can grow to be as big as saucer sleds, and this was something he wanted to see, though Arabelle was probably as big as she was going to get. Snappers can bite through, in succession, an ax handle, a pineapple, a substantial chair leg, followed by a whole watermelon. Each quick snap of powerful jaws can be seen in slow motion on clips recorded by amateur terrapinists. They're more docile in water, but we weren't on water. Close to it, but not on. While talking, he kept hitting the animal with the stick. There was something wrong with the boy; his parents may have ordered a child with empathy for animals, and what they got was a savant who talked to strangers. Behind the closed doors of Horner's Landing, there could be many such people with mild defects, not enough to be eliminated, but kept somewhat out of sight, a place where Singe might have temporary haven. Crack told the boy it was a myth about them being slow, and the turtle could amputate his toes in a second. The savant scrambled away, disappearing into his yard.

When he was sure the kid was out of sight, Crack took off his Pangenica hoodie and wrapped it around his hand and arm. I thought he was going to approach the snapper and asked why. Leave the thing alone. But then he turned and slammed his fist through one of the panes of glass in the back porch door, put his hand through, unlocked it and motioned me to follow him into number 9.

It was a small house. We entered in the kitchen, walked down a hall to a front room, which had a fireplace made of the same flagstones as the pathway, a couch, some chairs arranged as if people used this room to sit and talk, watch whatever was on the screen. There was a setup of Warhammer figures about to battle on the low hearth, each group of Chaos Dwarfs, Necrons, and Tyranids stood in carefully arranged opposing battalions. Half a donut and an empty coffee cup sat near the battlefield as if the potential weapons of one side or the other. There was a person in a swivel chair facing away from us. She spun round so we were eye-to-eye. Even from the back I should have recognized the greenish-blue hair, growing out brown. It was the woman we'd seen at Mr. Levant's, and she was aiming a gun in our direction. I don't know much about firearms, but what she aimed at us looked like an old police gun, short-barreled and snub-nosed, an artifact from another century, still capable of inflicting injury.

Crack put his hands up and said something about the door being left open and a snapping turtle on the threshold, we were only looking out for whoever lived in the house, as if she wouldn't have heard the shattering glass, that's why she was pointing a gun at us, as if anyone would believe his vicious animal bullshit.

"Singe Laveneer?" I asked.

"She doesn't live here."

"Who are you?"

"Masha." Masha was a mash-up of Singe.

Crack started to describe the murder scene on the lake, how we'd seen her in front of this very house just before they went out onto it, lake scenes obviously shot somewhere else, but the woman interrupted, moving the gun to her other hand, as she pushed glasses up her nose.

"Don't try to find Singe. You can't talk to her."

I noticed a newspaper dated a few years earlier on a table beside a phone studded with faceted green glass, stand-ins for emeralds. Did Singe also have an affinity for bling?

She told me I looked like I'd just seen Frankenstein. I said, no, it's the gun, which is real. It actually wasn't the gun, so much as the woman's fear which I was absorbing. Her affect was cool, but her breathing was rapid. Masha asked if I knew Dr. Frankenstein was slang for Pangenica? Crack's hoodie! He'd put it back on, and she'd seen the logo. This was a mistake an Adjudicator in the field would never make. Ha, ha, Frankenstein, that's a good one, but it's inaccurate. We didn't try to reanimate dead tissue; we engaged living cells with known results. Randomness can have dire consequences, which is why Pangenica's aim was to eliminate chance.

"Beneath the chaos of reproduction and natural selection there is a system, and beneath the calculating determination of the corporation is the potential for total bedlam." I rattled off Pangenica's policy for defending its actions, ready-made texts referred to in order to mute criticism. I felt stupid repeating basic handbook blah blah blah, but it was a way to deflect what the Singe double was feeling, which was heading toward acute fear and panic.

She looked at the old gun as if it could speak and give answers, then put it down. There were very few living opponents to Frankenstein, as far as I knew.

My phone vibrated.

Don't see the $$$ yet. 45 minutes

Somewhere in the city, Chester Louie was glancing at the time, checking his bank account, fingers tapping on his screen.

The boy from next door ran through, asked for some other child who turned out not to be home, but he nonetheless moved a couple of Warhammer figures into a different battle formation, then exited the front door, ignoring the gun balanced on the arm of the chair, as you might not even notice it if you grew up in a house with guns, just a thing that was often laying around like a kitchen knife or a set of drill bits.

Sirens blared outside, and for a moment I was startled, but whoever came to her door would do so unheralded and in silence, no flashing lights, no loudspeakers. The ambulances or police cars were headed to the island. I asked Masha who she was, and to my surprise, she put down the gun and said she would send me an earoscript that would self-destruct a few minutes after it was opened. She had picked up my address as soon as my phone crossed her threshold.

Eaeroscript

I was a mistake that wasn't supposed to be. You know women used to get pregnant accidentally all the time, in an era of panic that no one remembers, but like everyone else, I was created in a lab, yet still came into the world via accident. This is what happened. A lab technician, whose identity is unknown to me, endured the insults, outbursts, and worse from her department director, and she worked out a scheme to cause him to lose his job. I don't know which department she was working for, but she deliberately mixed a batch of wrong kids, random mismatches. Once discovered, the man, whoever he was, had the-buck-stops-here responsibility for any missteps, and he'd take the fall. More like revenge than prank? Maybe. Most of the collage blastocysts were detected in the transfer from Petri dish to Phytosack, but not all. Why had I survived, and got past through no agency of my own, because I had none, while the others were dismantled? For this I have no explanation. At birth I was pawned off on a couple who'd given imprecise answers on their forms. My parents were suspicious, but I was partly what they ordered, and they weren't litigious people (what the hell, she's ours), so I grew up in a fairly loving but distant household, messy and disordered, everyone had their own concerns and obsessions. Nobody talked about the fact that I looked only vaguely like them, and there were some similar personality traits. In a moment of doubt that I overheard, my father reminding my mother that I was good at spelling, which they did remember ordering—all their children were crackerjack spellers. When I was eighteen, I rescued a kid on an inflatable raft that was being swept away during a flood. The river here can be fast and unpredictable, but there was a motorboat with the keys left in the ignition, docked at the pier just upstream but within my range of vision, so I jumped in, headed into the current, and grabbed her. To this day, I'm not sure why I did it, I acted on impulse more than anything. There was a problem and a solution at hand. If there had been no boat, or a boat less sturdy, I wouldn't have tried to rescue anyone. Singe Laveneer saw my picture in the paper and set out to find the person in the photograph who so resembled herself at a younger age. Little gestures were more telling than a page of facts. We both tucked our hair behind our ears in the same way, had similar speech patterns, the same walk. People who are like you can turn up in unexpected places. It happens. Similarities can be partial, not exact, but there's enough to make you feel you're not alone in the universe. You see someone in line making faces before a camera, you pass them in the street, and see a similarity, but then they're gone in the crowd.

“Did you have a DNA test?” I asked as the script pixelated and disappeared. What secrets lay or were evaded in Vy’s Admissions records?

“There was no need. How she learned the truth of my origins, I can’t tell you. The technician, I discovered, vanished shortly after her prank was revealed. No surprise there.”

“Was this before or after PomPom?”

“Following PomPom’s accident.”

“PomPom is sort of like your sister.”

“No, I’m more of a clone.”

The highly placed lab technician had access to Singe’s DNA, made a copy or copies, and then used some for the prank, but this opened up the possibility that there could be other Singes in the world. The woman insisted that she was not an offspring or a family member of any kind. The imaginary universe populated with people identical to everyone who’s ever lived isn’t on some infinitely distant planet, she was saying, it’s right here.

Singe was in hiding, but she was Singe’s voice box, her periscope. I could sense her growing agitation that maybe she had already told us too much, but I had my doubts, too. Was I misreading? My mistakes in the past had been embarrassing. Crack was not in love with me. He just looked at me a certain way when he clicked on porn, and said okay, let’s watch this.

“I could spit in a tube, your job would be done, and you could be on your way, but I’m not going to do that.”

If the double existed, then her DNA was archived. (She hadn’t had a meeting with a disappearchnik yet, obviously. She was sitting before us.) It was used to create her, mixed in with some other bits and pieces, but this case could be resolved without DNA, because, as Dot said, Singe already knew the answer. She wanted the burden of proof to be on Pangenica.

“You can access it without finding her. Clayton’s will be there, too.”

“I can’t get into the archive without clearance.”

She took out her wallet, opened it, and held up an ID card, a holographic *T* catching the light; an invisible *Q* would be in the upper right corner.

“You have it now. It will work until tomorrow morning.”

Not everyone is who they claim to be, Altner had said, and Adjudications was based on this truism. He wanted more than DNA. The case demanded up-to-date (as in the last five minutes), in-person collection from verified humans, but the Singe double insisted Adjudication’s argument was nonsense. DNA = DNA. It’s all in the climate-controlled archives. I was beginning to suspect that the Director of Adjudications was using me the way sandhogs were sent into underwater caissons to dig out rocks and mud in order to construct bridge foundations. Some died in the process, but no one remembers them, and now look, you got a nice bridge.

She told me where the ID came from. Why not? She had nothing to lose. While Crackhour was talking about vinegar consciousness and the impossibility of experiencing what a bat experiences, the fellow from Crafted Identities was sliding an envelope across the table. Maybe, like the Singe double, he, too, was another prank that got away. Maybe he was the original prank baby.

At a glance, the ID looked perfect, with its globe logo hologram in oil slick fluctuating rainbow colors, but it was timed, and it was only a temporary green light. She had planned to use it to get her file and destroy copies of it that could fall into curious hands, but if I was willing, she would give the ID to me. In return, I could do the job for her. The ID was laminated, yet made so the coating could be peeled back, and the panel for bio-identifiers could be replaced by someone else’s biometrics. This was genius on the part of the fabricator, taking advantage of a design flaw the company hadn’t caught. IDs could have been solid but were layered and therefore vulnerable. She removed the panel, as tiny as a SIM card, folded it so as to be unusable, then picked up a lone Space Marine from the battle arrangement and turned it over. Underneath, a spare blank panel had been hidden, and she handed it to me to take an iris scan. Space Marines, Adeptus Astartes, are genetically engineered blue combatants in the Warhammer universe. They have super strength, and they are monks, standing as all Warhammer figures, about an inch and a half high, give or take. Their stands were plenty big enough to conceal an ID panel. I held it up to my eye for thirty seconds, and it recorded the web pattern, the brown cork-like threads that make up my iris.

TWENTY-ONE

15 minutes

Chester included a graphic of a car going over a cliff, over and over.

Crack was dismissive, what could the guy do? There were all kinds of things he could do, but Crack had stopped listening to me. To deflect anxiety, I opened *The Shadow Prince,* the final pages would disturb me so much, I would leave it on the train.

In London in 1712, Mr. J. Baker at the Black Boy in Paternoster Row published an account called *Prince Eugene, Not the Man You Took Him for or a Merry Tale of a Modern Hero.* The biography was written after Savoy's death in Vienna due to unknown or undiagnosed causes and because any memoirs, journals, or notes Savoy might have kept disappeared or were destroyed shortly after his death, Mr. Baker, staying up late filling page after page as if his life depended on it, could use hearsay, gossip, truth, and fiction to his heart's content.

J. Baker had an investment in writing a book that would turn a large profit. Only a story of suspense and character assassination would save himself from debtor's prison. The bailiff was at the door, and so he needed to sell many copies.

1712 was a difficult year for J. Baker, of whom little else, including his real name, is known. Racing between composing his popular but somewhat slanderous biography, betting on an income that may or may not ever materialize, and the demands of his creditors kept the lights burning in the Black Boy. The more urgent his situation became, the more he invented, although there were a few grains of truth in his book. He accused Eugene's mother of the murder of thirty-six people of both sexes, the worst French sorceress, he wrote, since Joan of Arc. In spite of the powers he attributed to her, he acknowledged that Olympe died in poverty. He denied that the duke participated in any of the battles he claimed to have won. The accounts, particularly the reports of the carnage at Zenta, he was convinced, were all libelous inventions. He didn't believe the prince was any kind of soldier, but like his mother, appeared at times only as a specter or shadow, though as a shadow of whom or what he did not say. The duke eluded any attachment to women and suffered a weakness for boys, and in France was known as Mars without Venus. This Baker did not invent, yet these revelations were included with the intention of boosting sales, if nothing else. The book could be purchased for sixpence. One copy of *A Merry Tale of a Modern Hero* can be found today in the British Museum. It was, in its own way, though full of misinformation, a very influential book. A journal attributed to Savoy would appear in 1809 and a collection of letters written by the duke was published in 1811.

In these, he allegedly wrote:

> *The unbounded licentiousness authorized by the example of the monarch and his court produced a species of crime, which struck terror into France and filled all Europe with astonishment and horror. The use of poison as the instrument of vengeance or avarice began to be introduced.*

Accusations had long been heaped on his mother's head after her death, and so Savoy, too, was transformed into a fantastic demon, a creature who performed great deceptions and had an unquenchable appetite for what were called *perversions*. The character behind the rib in the curtain, the boy spying on his mother and the king, continued to mystify, even when he was an adult and a conquering hero. He was never the man you took him for—that much might have been true. Savoy's queer identity and his identity as a man of war was masked and unmasked at various stages of his career and after his death as well.

To the Austrians, there was no doubt he was a hero, a man of erudition and culture, military skill and humanity. Both mother and son generated as many myths about their intrigues and proclivities as they did facts, and so their actual personae are left somewhat obscured and open to interpretation. Savoy was a portrait of contradictions, but he safeguarded one city, Vienna, as truly European, leaving Sarajevo to absorb the blows that came from being positioned as an outpost of the East. J. Baker of Paternoster Row did profit from scandal mongering, saving himself from the Marshalsea Debtors' Prison by making the man who pushed the Turks out of Europe look like a turtle who saw himself as Jupiter, although it was that same allegedly vain recluse who laid out what some consider a blueprint for the pattern of violence in the Balkans that continues to this day.

On January 26, 1717, Mary Wortley Montagu wrote of him to Lady Mar: "I don't know what comfort other people find in considering the weaknesses of great men because it brings them nearer to their own level, but 'tis allways a mortification to me to observe that there is no perfection in Humanity. Surrounded by acres of landscape paintings and sculpture on allegorical and military themes he rested between plotting battles and expansionist projects. If his troops marched in the mud and ate acorns, so did he, but at home he fed his pets, gibbons, gazelles, orangutans, and waited for another imperial war."

Lady Montagu left Vienna for Istanbul where her husband was posted as ambassador to the sultan. On February 12, 1717, she passed through the battlefield of Zenta in Croatia and described it in a letter to Alexander Pope:

The marks of the Glorious bloody day are yet recent, the field being strew'd with Skulls and Carcases of unbury'd Men, Horses and Camels. I could not look without horror on such numbers of mangled humane bodys, and refflect on the Injustice of War, that makes 'murther not only necessary but meritorious.

The train was half-empty, and I wanted to take another Dormazin, a short intense infusion of knockout drops, then I would wake up in the city alert, like sleeping on a long overnight flight, and when you arrive it's morning, and you're ready to become the person you need to be in whatever place you've arrived at. What I remembered: It felt so good when you woke up—the sharpness, the quickness—and I was anxious for the burst of energy that would nudge anxiety out of the way. I took one of Kent's pills out of my pocket, little blue pieces of heaven. It felt so good. Just one more. The pills were wrapped in a square of paper, hidden in a right-hand pocket. I was sitting next to the window, Crack right next to me on the aisle. I didn't think he could see me take one out, but he did and grabbed the tablet from my hand.

I had no time to sleep, apart from the duration of the train ride but also feared that sleep, if I didn't take a Dormazin, would either overcome me for eight hours, or on the other hand, remain elusive. The lights would always be on, thoughts repeating, agitated, looking for solutions: visions of cut-and-pasted DNA, of a blackish-greenish dried-out old sea anemone of a Phytosack laying on top of half-shredded papers, coffee cup with a face drawn on a white plastic lid because those indentations made it look like a face already. Sleep, in such a state, was unattainable, until just when I needed to be most alert and focused. Then I'd conk out.

I need it, Crack. I won't get hooked from just one weekend's use. Just one, just one more, right now, come on

Crack. Who made you panjandrum majordomo? I have less than twenty-four little hours.

You swallow one of these, and you won't just sleep, he said. You enter a tributary of altered consciousness, turn off your mind, and gently float downstream. Also, since these are street noddies, dosage is iffy. Should the chemicals give you a bad trip, say the juice has turned—who knows how long Kent left them in the cabinet? It's fermented, so let's say you take one of these, someone has to keep watch, and that someone will have to be me, which means I can't take a Dormazin because, as I just indicated, someone has to be the designated driver.

I offered to trade him. Give me one of your legit noddies, and you can keep everything I stole from the Kents. When the time came, I would need to be more awake than he did. At the very least, I required concentrated sleep now, and I held up the ID, as if to prove it without saying anything more.

But here's what Crack did. He pulled down a tray table, took out a Swiss Army knife, and cut one of the street noddies into quarters. It was a dry scored tablet, unlike those whose enteric coatings came in a spectrum of blue hues, or the sapphire gel caps my mother used to take because those glittery high end Dormies were covered by enviable health insurance. (Chromatin had an interest in Dormazin and made money from every prescription.) I swallowed the quarter as if it was no big thing, but felt the desperation of its chalky texture. All of it—the train's torn upholstery, the smeared squoval windows—was desperate, last chance, holding on for dear life, and I waited for sleep.

While the noddie dissolved in my stomach and prepared to do its work, I looked out the other side of the train. For a few miles, the tracks ran along an isthmus, but the water on the eastern side had turned to swamp; it was so choked by algae bloom eutrophication, which led to aquatic plants and reeds prematurely aging the water body, turning it to land in places. So, while the river rose on one side lapping at the tracks, fists of land accelerated their mass, spongy then solid, though how solid, I wouldn't want to test personally.

The train passed a former prison that resembled a ruin from an old war movie. It was unused, and had been for some time, but the structure remained impenetrable; concertina wire still threaded walls and fences. Sailboats and motorboats gave way to garbage barges headed for the landfill. Houses yielded to grand mansions perched in the hills. Slowly there would be more houses, then apartment buildings, warehouses, industrial sites of unknown purpose, power plants close to waters that became ferociously tidal, the further south and closer to the city you traveled.

Why wasn't I sleeping? Or maybe I was.

Was the Singe double the only cell cluster to survive? An unnamed lab assistant plots to get rid of her weinepstrump level boss by mixing DNA headed to Phytosack rejuvenation, but the scheme backfires, and she's the one the disappearachniks come for. All embryos were eliminated but one which contained the troublemaker Singe's coding. Thanks to oversight, she got through. How sad for Singe that she actually had a daughter out there, more of a clone to be honest, but still, perhaps more like a daughter than the bitter, acid-strafed PomPom. The Singe double grew up feeling as if she never belonged anywhere, not with her assigned family, and it was hard to rejigger her story, so, oh yeah, you won't believe this, but Singe L. was mater-matter. The fake ID was going to burn her bridges, if I would do it for her, and I'd thereby be killing two birds with one artificially engineered stone. She was doing me a huge favor, after all.

If there was a Singe double, how do I know I'm not sitting next to a Crackhour double? The hothead Crack, who sped out of the Pangenica parking lot, shared a corporeal self with the detached arctic underwater swimmer, but there was also the calculating noddie man, and they all seemed to live in parallel universes. Was one only a diluted version of the other, indebted, drained of blood, but a survivalist nonetheless? How to read Crack's face? Once in a while, his expression mirrored mine, it really did. Sometimes it was the Great Barrier Reef, even in an eroded state. Or it was like watching a very slow movie, real-time 360-degree pan around a big room, or it was an action-packed shootout, expressions changing so quickly I couldn't keep track, and even then, mirror toucher that I am, I wasn't sure if the expression on his face was a guide to what he was thinking, or exactly the opposite.

What happens when you have a body that doesn't cooperate with your desires? You could be a brain in a glass jar, but still want to be touched, though all but neurologists shudder and back off. If a living, pulsating brain could be constructed to be the size of a house you could walk through and see the neurons, dendrites, and axons reaching from the hippocampus to the cortex, attic of memories, would you, as you rounded a particular corner, find the neuronal correlates of consciousness? You wouldn't see thoughts, only the mechanics, how the plumbing and electrical systems work, but there are memories I'd take a sledgehammer to, and desires I'd chainsaw out of existence. Or what if you could shrink a person to the size of a single cell—organelles pulsing so they could walk or swim through the rooms, stairways, closets, cabinets of the actual, normal-size brain—and do the same as above, looking for stimulated, irritated tissue without becoming absorbed into the house itself? If so, the danger: What if you fell into a particularly repugnant memory that you, as a cell-sized but complex creature and still you, had to relive over and over? More synapses than stars in galaxies. Impossible. Brains look identical but people are all different. Disease treatment is the same for different people. What if there is an epigenetic aspect to consciousness? The word is like throwing water on a witch, facing a vampire with a garland of garlic. The ghost of Lamarck saws at the foundation of Pangenica. According to company protocols, the giraffe, whose neck stretched generation after generation to reach higher leaves, needed to be safari shot out of existence, the molecular potion structures were broken and reverted to poison.

TWENTY-TWO

Why wasn't I sleeping? Perhaps Kent Jr. had stockpiled defective products for a rainy day when he would take them all at once, including these stolen pills so long past their expiration date as to be ineffective unless you take a fistful.

Just when I wanted the train to go faster, it slowed down, coming to a crawl as we arrived at a bend in the river, then came to a stop at the base of the Narrows Bridge, one of the longest in the world. You could still hear birds in the trees. I looked up at the web of suspension cables. There were two people at the top of one of the towers. It wasn't exactly legal to be up there, but urban explorers had been known to make the ascent, recording and posting how they accessed entry points, climbed interior pylon ladders, and came out so high on the bridge, you could see the curvature of the earth. There were two figures. They appeared to be doing a tango on top of the tower, swerving and moving around each other. People film themselves on precipices all the time, music in the background, you concentrate on your breathing, maybe don't look down, but watch your step, if possible. When does swing dancing look like a struggle? With no sound available, impossible to interpret or know for certain one way or another. Then there was only one.

Did I hear the sound of a body hitting the water? I think I felt the air rush, flapping jacket, spinning head over heels, then hitting the water as if on a hard surface. From that height, water is unforgiving. My face stung from the slap, as if shocked by an electrical current, then the feeling was gone in an instant. The body was too far away for me to have a sense of whether he was pushed or jumped and what different fears he would have felt in the seconds before he fell in either case.

The train didn't move. Rescue crews arrived, needed access across the tracks, so the train was stuck. How thoroughly just one pill, when it did kick in, grabbed neurons and hypnotized them into cooperating. The blue of the upholstered train seats turned midnight, then neon blue; the opposite shore was still wooded, and the trees turned into cotton balls of green. Aquatic plants looked like neurotransmitters searching for receptors.

Then we were approaching Central Station, main city island. I was wide awake and felt as if I'd drunk rocket fuel and was ready to run to the end of the island then swim the channel if I had to. Tunnels under the station were dark except for sculptures made of fluorescent tubing dating back to the twentieth century that ran intermittently along the passageways in long narrow bursts of light as the train snaked its way along, taking one fork and then another. The light tubes had been replaced many times, and so was it the same installation if all the parts were generations removed from the original, none of which remained? (Was Kent's steampunk Singe, made up of replaceable parts, the same Singe over time anyway?) We climbed an unmoving escalator and walked out the ground floor and into the street. The storm had picked up again and left the city with a partial power outage.

A lone shawarma truck was parked on the corner, engine running and fueling the vehicle's electrical system, so that its white and green lights wreathing the service window kept blinking, and even from a distance, music could be heard coming from a battery-operated cassette player sitting on the counter.

Well, I came home so late last night
Looked but found no one in sight
Guess that I'll investigate
Who's been keeping my baby out late

The cook was singing at the top of his lungs. He wiped down the counter, poured oil onto a grill, and sharpened his knives to the rhythm of the music. Was some personal heartache tied to the song? Impossible to know. That song speaks to me, people say, but the cook was smiling as he sang, making his voice low and deep, as if he only had an audience of one.

Eating burnt toast
and drinking black black coffee
I'm eating burnt toast
and drinking black black coffee

His voice followed us for a block, at least until we got to an avenue that led directly downtown, and then my phone vibrated, this time a voicemail from Captain Ada. She had called when I was in the tunnel, so I'd heard nothing until reception was returned, and even then, registration of the message was delayed, as if my phone wanted to be sure I was really above ground.

Hey, Loew, you asked me to send up a flare when I got a passenger for Penrose. A man came on board who wanted to go to your island, but only told me so after I'd pulled out from the second-to-last island on my route. Waters were choppy, the storm's coming back, so I had to concentrate on navigation, but then, the guy decided not to disembark, said he only wanted to look at the last island before open sea, so he didn't get off at Penrose, anyway, just thought you might want to know. At first, I thought he was an inspector from the Guard, checking to be sure I stopped at every island, like they do even if there's no passengers, and no one was waiting on a dock of any particular island. That's my job, I always followed the letter of the law, and my score is always A++. But now I don't think the man was an inspector, because as I pulled away from the Penrose dock (in fact, it was still in view), the man unzipped his pants and peed over the edge of the boat. No inspector would ever do that, even undercover. To be honest, when he first unzipped, I reached for the gun I keep under the control panel, because it was just me and him on the boat. I don't know his name, just that he had a ticket. He got off where he boarded, main city island.

I needed to get to Penrose, and the end of the block seemed to stretch further and further away the more I tried to run towards it. Crackhour caught my arm, how was I going to get to the island without taking a Sentinel Guard boat? With the storm and outages, Captain Ada had likely done her last run until Monday morning. Well, there were ways. Pike Runners, if you could find one. They took their name from the extinct fish that would eat everything in a pond until there was nothing living left. These small leaky boats had been used by human traffickers to run refugees. These now piloted the same vessels like private taxis, and they would go to the city islands, off hours and very cheaply, often overcrowded, but for a price they would also go far out to the channel and oceanic islands. The boats were illegal; they used disabled radar transponders, and nautical police, for a fee, turned a blind eye to them, but every once in a while whoever was navigating those crafts would go haywire, crash, and sink, bodies washed up on islands near and far.

I have to try to get there. Let's go.

We can't.

Why not?

Relax.

With the blackout, the only way to get to the lower end of the island was to walk, and there was still some daylight left. None of the traffic lights were operational. Cars, both abandoned and moving, filled the streets, but every other intersection seemed to be blocked by either intractable gridlock or the wrecks of crashes. We walked past Dometop Insurance and through the window could see a man watching a screen, feet on the counter. This wasn't Daphne's shift, apparently, or she had the day off. A few blocks away The Barrel of Monkeys was closed because without electricity, there was no refrigeration, and Ice Unlimited, without a backup generator, had become a rink of slush, Zamboni mired, spinning its rollers. I checked my phone. No messages from anyone.

After walking for over an hour, we made it as far south as you could go before main city island ended in piers and ferry terminals. Waves crashed against pilings, against yachts and painted kayaks alike, and given the severity of the storm ahead, Crackhour offered to travel to Penrose with me. Extreme seas presented an environment he was familiar with, but nobody meets my mother, ever. My ex only met her once. New faces were unbearable for her, and people didn't know how to talk to her. She was unpredictable. Everyone tried to say the right thing with no idea what that might be and ended up embarrassed. Thanks but no thanks, I'd go alone.

I looked for the legit ferry, the *Jolly Sandhog*, but all city and state voyages were canceled, boats in lockdown. I hoped to at least find Captain Ada hanging out at a bar or a dockside D of D, as she sometimes did. If her passenger to Penrose had an electronic ticket, data on the man might still be available and accessible. Hidden in the scanner were numbers that would point to financial sources, how the ticket was bought, locations, wisps of identities, and if Ada had it hanging from her belt, still, that information could be clicked into life. If the scanner was locked up in the ferry berthed and inactive, tossed by waves and wind, hatches battened down, then she could unlock those hatches and even, for a price, set sail. These were leftover shreds of noddie dreams. Ada was nowhere to be found.

We walked from one pier to the next, but not even the most bug-eyed fifteen-for-eight noddie-addicted Pike Runner was out on a night like this. It was, by now, early evening, fog was rolling in, and there was little hope of finding a way to get to Penrose Island. We sought shelter at a bar where I thought I might find Runners and others boozing it up before a trip, but apart from a stuffed great white suspended from the ceiling, the bar was close to deserted; the shark wasn't talking. It was a dark, narrow room. Crack had a beer, but insisted I drink only water, because the Dormazin would still be lingering in my bloodstream. A lone bartender was watching the news on a rare battery-operated screen as long as it lasted. Without electricity, the city descended into an earlier century. You find you can manage, sort of, having no or little electronic connections to others. It wasn't intuitive, but not impossible either.

The explosions on Horner's Island were getting major news coverage, but there was no mention of any noddie lab. The bartender was listening to our conversation, I could tell. Like any somewhat informed conspiracist, he suggested the noddie-ites were government protected, as were their bombing antics. Hadn't we heard about the gang that blew up the subway station in Slavtown Ciudad Medina? Of course we hadn't and never would. It was covered up by the Department of Foundational Media, which I'd also never heard of. Follow the money, he whispered. Who benefits from this commerce? But then why was he confiding in two perfect strangers? I wanted to get out of there, but Crack winked at the guy, one those tired if-you-know-you-know winks that seriously put me off. Bombs were set by noddie-makers to scare people off the island, of course. Crack tapped the side of his glass in time with the musical background for an ad for weed killer, then he concurred and posed the question, so what other covert activities weren't represented on the D of D placemat? Noddie-ites were a cover for what?

What did I think? I had nothing to contribute in terms of how to tie, say, the existence of a prank clone to extreme weather, so that their connection could add up to a cool conspiracy, an—improbable but when you think about it and that's the beauty of it—logical kind of scheme. I picked up that Kent Sr. was the kind of old gent who referred to himself as an old gent. The stuffed shark still had pointy teeth, and its glass eyes, close up, reflected rain bouncing off the bar's aluminum awning. So close to the ocean, but completely out of reach and unswimmable for the dead fish anyway.

The story of the explosion on the island was followed by the report of a body found near the Narrows Bridge, determined to be that of a thirty-seven-year-old man, floating face down among (close-up of) the plastic bottles, clamshell packaging, chemical patterns in rainbow-colored paisleys and archipelagos on the surface of the water. The camera backed off. There was a picture of the body as it was pulled from the water wearing a mustard-yellow jacket, black pants, pink plastic gloved hands. No face was shown, but I had seen those clothes before. I was so sure I asked Crack to hack and do a quick cash transfer from Chester's account back to mine.

"It may already be too late. Use Ecash or FoundSwap. Do it now. Please."

"You think he's dead?"

"Of course."

"Okay, I'll see what I can do. Why don't we start with ten percent of the original amount he took?"

"No. Why don't we start with a hundred percent? And why don't I take a little interest from Chester as well, while you're at it?"

If that was Chester face down under a bridge, his bank records would be examined by the coroner's department whether or not the death was suspicious. Investigating bodies would note: why this activity in the last twenty-four hours of the man's life and then just post-demise? How could he make a transfer when he was no longer breathing? Not possible. The alternative was that I was, and would remain, completely broke, and I saw no reason to leave anything behind to be frozen, seized, or distributed to an unknown party or parties.

"I'm going to need old-school cash for the Pike Runner." My phone told me there was a lone working ATM near the docks, the only one for miles around. Its slots would be corroded by salt water and age, but it was still working.

Crack reminded me there was no hope of finding a boat to Penrose that night, that no one could get to the island, and so my mother couldn't be in a safer location. He'd get his car from the shop, a twenty-four-hour operation, and he'd meet me back under the shark at half past midnight, then we'd drive to Pangenica. His face showed no emotion, no exasperation, not even stubbornness.

So I mirrored him. I want my money back. Immediately. Crack took out his phone, complaining that his battery was low, and once it died, who knew when he'd be able to recharge, all stated as if I was making a completely unreasonable request that was costing him, personally. I couldn't see what he was doing, his fingers skated up and down the screen, tap dancing and gliding. A visitor from a past century would think he was some kind of Tourette's driven obsessive playing with a handheld black mirror. I had no idea it could be so easy to hack fiduciary institutions with their sand traps and detonators. In ten or fifteen minutes he was finished, but told me it would take a couple of days for the money to appear in my account. In the meantime, he opened his wallet and gave me cash, not much, but most of what it appeared he had. Paper money, legal and viable but rarely used. The bills in circulation were very old, worn, looked like vectors for communicable diseases, bearing portraits of long-forgotten presidents, inventors, explorers who seemed to float against a background of hard-to-reach terrestrial environments. One could only guess who they had been, if anyone even bothered or cared. The bills had been known to be used in artwork: background for the portrait of a hedge fund manager terrorotica guru, glued to the pedestal of a statue of an excavator thief of ossuaries, drifting down from a stock exchange balcony during a performance piece. Now I possessed a small stack and didn't even know where to put them.

Crack left to get his car, and though I agreed not to go anywhere and to wait for him, I had no intention of staying put—it was a time risk calculation. Crack would eventually return in his SunbirdDodgeDartPontiacGremlinPinto, and if I was here, fine; if not, I could find another way to get to Pangenica. The image of the man found near the Narrows Bridge was paused on the bartender's screen while he wiped glasses with his back to it.

Though it was early for Pike Runners to be out, I wanted to start looking, but as I stood to leave, I glanced toward the back and saw the glowing end of a cigarette. It was Waxman sitting in a booth, and he smiled in my direction. He was unmistakable, looking battered, but the cigarette waved for me to join him, and I didn't really have a choice. While my attention had been on Crack or the news, I hadn't seen him come in, or maybe he'd been there all along, a shadow reflected in the glass eyes of a stuffed shark. I sat down opposite him, as if there was nothing unusual about running into him here at this hour. His raincoat was torn and dirt-streaked, though whether the slashes came from a wild animal or a human disappearachnik of some kind whose agency was unknown to me, I couldn't ask. He stubbed out his joint and put it in his pocket, saving it for another rainy day. His joints were self-rolled, not something you see often, and I pictured him selecting weed from an array of glass jars, buying rolling papers, a tall thin man in baggy trousers taking up a lot of room in a small shop, annoying people with his meticulousness, and the care he took to choose, to be satisfied.

"Still looking for our mutual friend? You don't have a lot of time, I know."

He had a gin and vermouth martini in front of him, at least that's what he said it was, but he wasn't knocking it back, and he reminded me of a character from a film I'd seen about the Chernobyl nuclear disaster. A physicist is sitting at a bar, orders a drink, asks for a different glass, presumably one cleaned hours before the core meltdown, so he's guessing the rinse water wasn't contaminated, or not as contaminated. The point was he knew what happened, even if the extent of the danger was supposed to be a state secret, and so Waxman knew what happened in his lab, even if what transpired there were classified events. I put my hand over his glass as he reached for it and asked him about the Department of Neuronal Correlates. What about it? Did his pipette suck out the genetic material for Child #18 and give it to Child #19, then swap out 19's for 18's?

"What did I do in the Department of Neuronal Correlates?" He looked at the screen over the bar showing scenes of water sloshing around lobbies, chairs and empty trash cans floating by. "Not just find consciousness," he spoke slowly, "but try to measure it, and it's hard to measure. You can't quantify consciousness in spoons, mileage, molecules, or cells. We were looking for the off/on switch, the flint, the spark."

He took the glass from under my hand and swirled the liquid in it. I told him I didn't have a lot of time. I had someplace to be. Okay, okay, he nodded, he understood, and he told me a joke.

Astronauts finally land on Mars, they disembark from their spaceship and are met by a group of little green men.

The captain asks the Martian who appears to be their leader, "Are all Martians about three feet tall?" The Martian leader nods. "Are all of you green?" Wondrously, their leader speaks in English, "Yes, everyone on our planet is green. We have no race problems on Mars." The space captain looks the group up and down, then finally asks, "Do all Martians wear so much gold jewelry?" The Martian answers, "The goyim don't."

Waxman opened a pack of cigarettes, cellophane crinkling in his fist, laughed at his joke but kept talking. The joke meant things aren't always what they seem, but sometimes they can be. He kept talking.

Animals don't just have one predetermined stamp: lynx are aggressive, magpies are hoarders, cranes are explorers, ants take risks. They have personalities within the range of their expected predictable behaviors for finding food, mating, migrating. So, what about that? Wouldn't you think there's a connection to consciousness in there somewhere? Within groups there are those driven by capital, the alpha males and females, canny at hunting, finding food, telling the lesser among them to fuck off, get the hell away from that hyena corpse, it's my food. There are crows who share; everybody eats when you come to my house. There are blue frogs who dance on Nile crocodiles' noses, and those who bury in the mud, anxiety-driven octopi who change color and shape at the sight of a predator, females who chuck shells at males who annoy them, and those who are known to eat sharks.

"You were the Director of Neuronal Correlates. You were Teller, Fermi, Oppenheimer, Waxman. You knew the plan."

"I didn't know the big picture. I moved nuclei around. That's all."

Did he really believe that?

If consciousness is a regulator, a negotiating mechanism for the present, I'm not sure how it could have a parking spot reserved on DNA, but if how you experience earthquakes or chocolate is also filtered by temperament, then maybe, okay. A place on the striated rug that is the genome, yes, I guess it could be there. If consciousness is molded by how you remember that cold drink, such as having a fearful or pleasurable feeling that makes you want more or less of something, then genetic figuring is useless, or maybe just weights the dice a bit. A line from one of Crackhour's animations: *The genome is a guidebook for predicting how an organism will navigate or react to the future.* Control of consciousness would be a goldmine.

And then what if you could download consciousness from another century? Hadrian, Stalin, Madame Mao—they're back! Tyrant rogue gene or rogue gene for tyranny. And who's to say this wasn't the case for Pangenica's top brass, those who hold the keys to the kingdom with their disappearachniks and infinite collections of everything?

"If you can switch consciousnesses, you could alleviate suffering." Waxman, innocent and naïve, trying to build a shelter on a toxic dump site. "I needed to find someone with an anomaly, a person who had altered perceptions, who saw numbers and heard colors, someone like my lost never-loved-but-tried misophonist who was disappeared. Where to find such a person who wasn't supposed to exist? That's when, looking in the archives, I learned about you."

Waxman held his breath. I stopped breathing, too. *What are you doing?* I wrote on a napkin. It's a test, he exhaled. I want to see your anomaly in action.

Waxman, reading about hybrid mythological creatures who lived on snow, now you see them, now you don't, and all the while dreaming of a woman he could barely talk to—what made her different, how could he see her more often, what would he do if they were alone? I didn't want that woman to ever be me, and I don't think I was a replacement in that sense, but she led him to me, he'd seen my paper file. I hadn't seen it myself, never clicked on links, attachments, turned pages I had no access to anyway, but assumed mirror touch wasn't referenced. If so, I wasn't supposed to be standing on two feet, so was such information really in my file? (Or here's a theory: did he go drinking with Crack one night, ply him with promises of high-quality Dormazin, then oops, secret leaked? Crack hadn't wanted to leave me alone with him, as if he knew, and this was unusual for Crack, to be defensive of me or of anyone. He was a solo diver, but if there were others, he was more of a you-go-into-the-cave-first-I'll-follow kind of guy.)

"But you didn't find me. Thanks to Altner, I found you."

"The Director used you, a talented Adjudicator, skilled at unearthing and unmasking, he used you to locate me. Dropping out of sight causes alarms to go off, no matter how careful you are. The Director of Adjudications wanted to leverage the Singe case in his favor. On the other hand, I needed to ensure she couldn't be found, and I wanted to know who had used my lab to create these two children." Someone had gotten the Singe Laveneer ConSwitch file before him, before it even had a name.

"Altner wanted the file resolved. If Singe were disappeared, it never would be. If a claimant is disappeared, the case is in limbo, unsettled, questions unanswered. It's not a cold case, it doesn't go away."

Waxman didn't believe me, but he didn't know how Adjudications operated. The death of one party doesn't necessarily signal the end of an investigation. The Pike Runners would be assembling on the docks looking for passengers, for the highest bidder for their services. I didn't have time for a conversation that was going nowhere and needed to make it to the edge where the water met the road, before the only Runners left were so noddified, you wouldn't hire them to cross a puddle.

"But you didn't want me to find her." She never lived in a water tower or anyplace that Waxman could describe to me accurately.

"I did not."

"That's why you told me she was radioactive."

Waxman took a swallow from his glass, the first time I'd seen him drink since I sat down. He looked uncomfortable but he often appeared uncomfortable. How to sit in a chair? How to walk between tables without knocking off beakers and test tubes? A man who sat around puzzling over connections between dinosaur bones and capital, a man who could cast his eyes around a room like a jewel thief casing a diamond dealership while dreaming of a woman who looked at him as if he were no more than a grating noise. I realized Altner only saw the man who was ill at ease in his body, and therefore didn't know who he was dealing with. That awkward pencil-man Waxman was only part of the picture.

Waxman finished his drink, and though he wasn't going to answer my question, his anxiety was added onto my own. The clock was ticking. I told him I had to leave. I had to check on someone on an outer island.

"Whoever controls consciousness is the ultimate puppet master. If you lose your bearings, your identity, you run the risk of living like a consciousness-less drone. Who needs Artificial Intelligence when you can turn humans into robots? You need to feel agony and pleasure, but if you don't, you can be manipulated should anyone choose to do so. Singe had the capability of unmasking an arms race, not of explosives or germ warfare or other toxins, but a war within future bodies, a war within ourselves. The Director of Adjudications felt he would get a surplus of credit for finding her. I have a daughter out there somewhere. I don't want her to believe I'm the architect of ConSwitch. It needs to be destroyed; its tracks have to be swept away. Must be urgent, your need to get to another island tonight."

"It is."

"I'm hungry." Waxman looked at the bottom of his glass. "I'll walk with you a bit."

I wasn't sure what he wanted from me, maybe he just needed to confess to someone, and he followed me out of the bar. An exile, a refugee who never quite figured out the place where he found refuge, so he does everything wrong, misinterprets, doesn't see consequences, doesn't read social cues, retreats to his corner of Pangenica. Once we'd walked out from under the awning, he unfurled his umbrella. It was small, like a toy that didn't ever offer protection for his own body, much less anyone else's. It's just water, I said. Waxman didn't offer to share the umbrella in any case. A few Pike Runners were starting to cluster near the whaling ship, smoking, gazing at their phones, drinking from cans or bottles hidden in paper bags, looking around, careful about eye contact but predatory, if you did catch their eyes.

Within sight of the whaler was a kebaburitto truck. Waxman ordered two, both for himself, explaining he didn't know where he would find his next meal. The woman working the grill asked if he wanted a little extra something on a night like this. Waxman had already taken extra hot sauces, napkins, forks. Was she offering a quick something with her in the back of the truck? She leaned on the counter and extended her hand, folded into a fist, then opened her fingers, one by one. Nestled in the palm of her hand were two noddies. "One for you. One for your friend. You got some things you need to do tonight?" She looked at me and winked. "But you gotta sleep, too. Monday morning is coming up fast. Peoples has to go to work early."

I told her thanks but no thanks. On the train, perhaps, I had been susceptible to Crackhour's cravings for noddies, having once tasted them. I'd never felt the desire for Dormazin in the past when I was near him or my mother or any other addict. Now, away from Crack, I no longer cared one way or another. From under the truck awning, I could see more men and women now congregating right under the ship's giant keel nestled in a lift dock, so the planks of the hull could be replaced as needed. I was impatient and felt stuck in place, an innocent bystander compelled by Waxman's appetites. My phone pinged with a text from Crack that his car needed more work than he realized—spark plug replacement, faulty clutch, all going to take longer, no choice but to wait for the mechanic. I skipped over the details, whatever he wrote, it was a gift of more time, but still I needed to get going. I'm leaving, I said to Waxman, I don't have time.

But he kept up with me as I crossed the street, and I could see them as we got closer, men and women in hoodies bearing logos from sports they may or may not care about, torn rubberized jeans, running shoes or boots that matched if they were lucky. A few looked glazed over, listening to trance music or motivational speakers, but most Pike Runners sized up potential customers as keenly and as cautiously as clients looked at them—both sides feeling last-chance desperation, whether their anxiety was about if they had enough pieces of In-God-We-Trust to pay for a next meal, or from the need to get somewhere you weren't supposed to go and to get there quickly.

One of them had broken into the ship and climbed the rigging, on the lookout for police. To mingle in a crowd like this made you feel like you were in league with low-tech felons who would throw you overboard for a bag of nickels or noddies, or a warning that Marine Sentinels were bearing down on the starboard side.

The whaler smelled of new wood, white oak and yellow pine, and again, I wondered if you could say it was still the same as the original, if most of it had been replaced, like the Dan Flavin sculpture made of fluorescent light tubes installed in one of the subway tunnels during the twentieth century. Over time, the tubes burnt out and had to be replaced, so eventually none of the original remained. At the bow was a new figurehead, Poseidon—forked beard, holding a trident, painted a lambent gold, a beacon that glowed under a tarp. And there I saw a familiar face: Daphne from Dometop, shouting that she was fast and silent, gesturing at those milling around or passing by that her services were for sale. Whether she was moonlighting as a Runner or maybe that was her main job and she moonlighted at the insurance agency, I had no idea, but I walked over to her, as she balanced on a rocking skateboard with three wheels.

Before I could say anything, she asked where Crack was. Sorry, you're stuck with me, Daph. As at Dometop, she was direct, asked what she could do me for, and I told her where I needed to go, that I needed to leave immediately.

"You don't have to tell me your business on that island. My job is only to dump you there." She scratched the shoulder of her good arm. Depending on the storm, I needed her to wait for me, then ferry me back to the main island, but she was noncommittal. It might well be a one-way trip.

This version of Daphne was all business: knots, wind calculations, nautical miles, a wave pilot sense of the movement of water that would be inches under our feet. Hearing the edge in her voice, a few others came over. Often Pike Runners compete, offering lower prices than the mate standing next to them, but I waved off stragglers. Better a Runner you know than taking a chance on random Dormazin enthusiasts, but Daphne was expensive. On a night like this, to leave straight away upped the price. There was regular basic sunny day service, she said, but was there such a thing as standard calm seas under a golden sun regular service for illicit navigation? She offered, in her calculations, a ten percent discount because she knew me. This, too, I believed, was a made-up thing. She didn't really know me and offering a discount on something as ambiguous and inflated as Pike Running came out of thin air. We finally reached an agreement, and I handed her a wad of paper money which she counted, licking a finger of her prosthetic hand as she did so.

I followed Daphne down past the whaling ship and a bunch of fragile-looking sailboats to her motorboat—small, old, painted black, but she assured me it was fast and quiet. I caught a glimpse of one side, decorated with a figure of a pirate, telescope held up to an eye, but then I realized this was no nod to Pike Runners' ancestors. The decal was small, hard to see, but it was Kent's glass-limbed Singe. No doubt others owned this boat before Daphne, but I asked her if she was a fan of Isotope Comics? She nodded in a noncommittal way. Dometop night shift could be slow. She read a lot of stuff. Waxman paced back and forth a few feet away. A pile of punctured life vests, bright orange, and tangled yellow netting washed ashore, and someone began to move pieces of it aside, shouting that there was a body in the heap. Daphne stepped away from us to take a look. Clusters gathered on a nearby dock to stare while others rifled through the remains to see what could be scavenged. I looked away. Waxman was agitated, but the commotion around the body and the shouts from onlookers was all just background noise for him.

"Before you leave, Loew, there's something else I need to tell you—" He grabbed my arm and whispered in my ear, like this was what he'd wanted to tell me all along, but hadn't been able to cough out the news. "Your file exists in two places: It's digitally stored, as all are, but also as a paper file, as some are, and I've seen both. The paper version contains an interesting date. Your DNA should have been registered nine months before you were born, but yours was registered on your actual birthday. Who made this error? Who did this? I was curious. Who wouldn't be? So I dug deeper to find the identity of the person who registered your DNA, sourced from a sample of your blood obtained after you were born. This person was the Director of Adjudications." Waxman paused, looked at me, but as far as I was concerned, he was speaking Martian. "He's a very careful man with his work, but he made a critical slip-up. The date matters. The reason it wasn't registered properly is because nine months earlier it wasn't available. No Phytosack with Zedi Loew's name on it ever existed. The records of you originating at Pangenica were registered after the fact to make it look as if you had been hatched like everyone else. The Director of Adjudications had his careless moments, but he's good at what he does. Until I came along, I don't think anyone ever knew."

It was the hallucination of a man who tracked Sasquatches and lived on Zagnut bars. The Director of the Department of Neuronal Correlates needed a way to explain my synesthesia.

"I have no memory of any birth canal, sorry."

"No one ever did."

"So, you're saying Altner is my father? We look nothing alike."

I didn't believe him. If Dot had had me the old-fashioned way, neither of us would still be standing, therefore I had to have kicked my way out of a Phytosack like everyone else. Spring, no snowman. Snowman, no spring, like the children's book, and I'm not melting, am I? Waxman, apart from the picture of the Sasquatch print in his abandoned apartment, lived in a world of demonstrable, observable facts and conditions. That Waxman could feel anything as soupy or sappy as love for another human was difficult to imagine. It was easier to picture him grasping at the ephemeral nature of the one he lost.

"Not at all. I've seen his archived DNA, and you're no relation whatsoever. Your mother couldn't tell you, I'm guessing. You were hiding in plain sight, like the love of my life." He looked defeated—a fugitive, cornered and ready to turn himself in, no shadow prince who knew about the existence of a tunnel a few feet away, a passageway he could disappear into, bar the door behind him, and come out the other end in another city miles away.

"Do you want to come with me or what?" Daphne returned, impatient to get going. The storm at sea was only going to get worse. "An additional passenger will cost you extra. If not, say your goodbyes now or my initial offer will go up based on added risk assessment. Also, added weight." She looked Waxman up and down. "I don't have all night. If you're not ready to push off, fine, say so. Don't waste my time. I got other paying customers."

She didn't actually, but Waxman shook his head. He wasn't going anywhere, and it had nothing to do with cash.

He handed me a couple pages of typing paper folded into quarters.

I climbed into the unnamed boat, she checked a toolbox, moved plastic crates to the back, untied the boat, and prepared to push off. When I turned around, Waxman had disappeared into the night, wiping hands on dirty raincoat, gone.

She released the throttle and headed into the waves that picked up the farther out we traveled. Too late for a change of plans. Pike Runners weren't known to give refunds, and it was unlikely Daphne would be an exception. As if an afterthought, she tossed me an orange life vest but didn't wear one herself. There was only one. I'll clamp it onto you, she said, and if you do drown, it'll be easier for me to hold onto your body, floating along like cork. She wore a green rain slicker, chameleon-like, visible on a city street, but if she went overboard at night, that would be the end of her.

Captain Ada navigated using an Automatic Identification System that showed her land and other boats, represented by a symbol to indicate size along a velocity vector to denote how fast and from what direction the craft was heading your way, especially important if paths were set to collide. I'd seen her click on a ship, get its name, classification, course, and speed. Everybody flies by wire, so if little boats don't have AIS, they are at peril, just like swimmers, kayakers, jet skiers. Daphne's boat had nothing but her. It was like driving on a highway, but the highway was moving, and I wasn't sure she could brake in time, or if she could steer fast enough. If another ship appeared in the storm, it was only a question of her eyeballs and reflexes.

Once we were out of sight of land, I asked why she was moonlighting as a Runner? She held up her artificial limb. If it came undone, if the motor died and she was alone, she would be traveling in circles all night.

"You lost your arm on a job, but you're still navigating." I was asking but didn't want to sound doubtful of her skills on the open sea.

"That was the story."

"There was no shark?"

"There are sharks in the water. Have I met one? Do I look like a seal to you?"

Warmer water brought an abundance of seals, which in turn brought sharks as what they saw as meals swam further south and closer to the city's outer islands. They also bit people, but Daphne indicated that wasn't what happened, though she didn't say what did.

"So, you were born with one arm."

"No one is born with one arm." She shouted into the wind so loudly that if anyone had been listening, they wouldn't have heard her clearly, but her tone of voice was unmistakably sarcastic, as if to say, yes, I was born this way, figure it out. I didn't know what to believe. She was Kent Jr.'s lost twin. There was no letter bomb any more than there had been a shark.

"Did you notice a similarity between the character painted on the side of your boat and the woman we were looking for?"

"First, you asked if I read Isotope Comics, then if that's her, the woman who rammed into your partner's car. . . . Is that her painted on the side of my boat? No, I never noticed a similarity. Yes, I read all kinds of whatever when I'm sitting behind the counter at my service job and wish I was anywhere else. Wouldn't you?"

Adjudicators were trained to ask questions, but to make the questions seem like they're just part of the conversation, to draw people out before they realize what's going on. I was having trouble with Daphne. Even if I hadn't been anxious about the trip, she was quicker than I was.

"Your limp got better overnight," she noticed. I ignored the observation. "Years ago, I gave a ride to a guy who drew for Isotope. He wanted to go beyond the outer islands just to see what was there on a nice day, but I knew what he was looking for, and I said, yeah, I'll take you. I know there are those unexplainables like the Devil's Teeth Islands that moved an inch a year up or down a coast, but I'm talking about pieces of land that come and go, lava flows hurled up by underwater volcanoes that cool into islands. They collect soil, plants grow, birds build nests, small mammals arrive, but the ocean is relentless. After a few years, maybe even twenty or thirty, the island gets waterlogged and sinks. Maybe a few get a reprieve for however long and do not disappear. It's risky to say okay, I'm moving here, but it's been known to happen. What's good about these floating islands is that they're off most navigational charts, too small not to fail, sometimes picked by satellite, but no one really gives a shit, so if you or a loved one thinks you're about to vanish beyond the horizon, that there's a cell in an Orientation Site with your name on it written in chalk, easily erased with the back of a hand, these islands could be for you. I'm just enlightening you; I know where they are. I could tell the old guy was on a scouting mission, but I don't say as much to him. In addition to paying, he gave me the decal you saw on the side of the boat, he had a bunch of them in a bag, like someone giving out freebies at a Comic Con. Nice enough guy, but I never saw or heard from him again."

An island whose bedrock was pumice didn't seem like much of an option to me. Sometimes staying where you are turns out to be okay, you may not get vanished, but then again, you might.

"Some are sinking desert death traps, and some certainly are not. I'm talking about the latter, the ones where you might have a chance."

Robinsonade stories number in the hundreds: Crusoe, the Swiss Family, cartoons of a bearded man wearing leaves, just enough space to circle a lone palm tree, all shipwrecked, launched by a storm to make it to the limited kind of shore presented by a small wild island. Get away from civilization only to reproduce it, if at all possible, in some form or another, build houses, domesticate animals, and if you encounter another human, make him your servant. Sounds good to me. Where do I sign?

"Thanks, but not interested. No need."

You nibble one side of the mushroom, and you rid yourself of the fear that when you're alone, you're not as alone as you think. Hello, satellite drone, or some other eyes and ears device. The other side of the mushroom affirms you're utterly alone, and no one will hear you sing along with whatever device you have whose battery hasn't run out, and no one will save you as you sit Amelia Earhart–style and stare out at the ocean from the crash site of your tiny island.

"Okay, friend, just trying to be friendly. Let me add, let me just tell you, I never noticed the similarity between your Singe and anybody or anything. To tell you the truth, I don't look that closely at the cash payers. The paying entity could be a box turtle. Whoever pays the bills, what do I care?"

She revved the motor, increasing speed, so the boat seemed to be in a slapping contest with every wave, and the bow was like a porpoise half out of the water. "So you found her? That woman who looks like a glass robot? You got things sorted? Your boss, he got some kind of vehicle to do his airport pickup? You know flights are going to be canceled on a night like tonight, or was it last night?"

I didn't answer, which is easy to do in a gale when trying not to be washed overboard. By the time we approached the first islands, it was so dark there was no horizon, no place where you could say here's where water ends and sky begins. I felt the same loss of gravity pilots have reported, a condition of spatial disorientation. They can't tell up from down, sky from land or clouds from sea, all are mixed up, either at night or when haze obscures the horizon.

In the face of strong winds, no longer able to shout above them, we huddled beside each other, though I can't say I felt any affection for Daphne, nor did she for me, but she put her prosthetic arm around me and in a whisper repeated, without eye contact, that one of the things she did as a Runner was to ferry people to islands that were out of reach, erratically charted, evasive of satellites, sometimes they were and sometimes they weren't mapped, and if I ever needed to go to one of those fly-by-night destinations, I would know where to find her. Her rates were decent, she added.

The sea didn't get calmer, but I got used to the rhythm of the choppy waters and constant spray. I don't know how Daphne navigated, charting by stars that weren't easy to see, but when she said, we're here and turned the masthead light on the rocky base of Penrose, where the dock had been, there were only a few planks floating in the surf.

My worst fears were confirmed. Dot would look over the edge, realize no boat could dock, then what? A sense of claustrophobia under the big sky because there is no exit, 360 degrees of nothing but sky and water, weathering the storm curled up on the first floor, or looking out from the top.

My mother's addiction may have been so acute, she wouldn't be conscious of starving to death. Which would she run out of first, Dormazin or food? And in the scheme of things, food was just an inconvenience, fuel to get to pills when you were in the final stages of withdrawal. It is rumored that Amelia Earhart did not crash in the Pacific, but she landed on an uninhabited island. Earhart wasn't addicted to Dormazin, and she would have been aware of what would happen to her. Would Dot? Depends where she was on the spectrum of cravings at that moment and what her stash looked like—what had expired, how many of what strength might she take at one go. Talking, singing to herself until demons can't be kept at bay, would she swallow rat poison and get it over with? I hated feeling her terror, desperation, calling out for me, maybe knowing she'd never see me again. I hoped she'd overdose, fall into blue oblivion, to be found many years later.

The splintered pilings stuck above the surface of the water like a bad haircut by an addict barber. I had imagined her death many times. The imaginings began as soon as the ferry left Penrose. Her grip on the laws of gravity was so precarious, and her everyday life could go haywire at any time. She clung to her isolation, handling every problem with Dormazin as I stared at the rocky cliffs of her exile. Maybe that wasn't such a bad thing, making that choice to step away from the demons via sleep.

Daphne said, I don't think you'll be getting off here. I'll have to charge you for a round trip. She saw no need to linger, but I asked her to wait a few minutes. Staring at the snapped pilings, I said the prayer for the dead as my mother would have said it, just mouthing words silently, even though Daphne had no knowledge of the language I was using. Kaddish radish brackish Tiffany Haddish.

Daphne was faster than I would have thought, either despite the storm or because of it, but it was after midnight when we got back to shore. I thanked her and shook hands, but she was already looking for her next passenger. Still, I wished her well and crossed the street. As I approached the bar, Crack could be seen at the counter, one hand in a pocket of his Pangenica jacket, the other around a full glass, so perhaps he hadn't been waiting long. The shark swayed slightly in the wind when I opened the door.

I tapped him on the shoulder. He didn't ask where I'd been, and I didn't tell him, nor did I say, oh by the way, I don't know if my mother is dead or alive, I don't know if the dock was demolished in the storm, it wasn't in great shape, but it would have held, I think, or did someone toss a grenade from the bow of another Runner's motorboat? No need to actually get off the boat and end the days of a half-cracked Dormazin addict. Just blow up the dock, and isolation will do the job for you. Nobody's coming out to check that ceilometer.

I kept those thoughts wrapped up tight and out of sight as he left his drink and held the door open for me. We walked to his car in silence. The SunbirdDodgeDartGremlinPinto looked exactly the same, but when I got in, the back seat had been cleaned, and there was a pine tree air freshener hanging from the mirror. We drove the few blocks to the inter-island tunnel. Lower island streets still followed the curves of the original geography, hills and groves long ago flattened and paved, unlike the uptown grid that dominated to the north. We followed the coastline, even driving the wrong way on empty one-way streets until we saw the lights and stonework of the entrance to Tunnel A.

Inter-island tunnels were a problem. The one we needed connected the main city island to the island where Pangenica was headquartered, and flood water had been pumped out, but there were no lights, so driving in the dark was limited to emergency vehicles only. All but two of the tubes were shut down, leaving a single lane going out (Tunnel A) and a single lane going in (Tunnel B). We were not an emergency vehicle, but Crack had prepared a story. He would tell the sentry he had to deliver a small but critical number of medical supplies, travel-size tanks of Phytobase fluid, for example. He would offer to open the trunk, and hope they wouldn't say, okay, show me. I pointed out there was no such thing as travel size. Embryos in Phytosacks didn't go anywhere, but he was undeterred.

Rain streaked down the Guard booth while two barely visible souls in uniform were inside, bent over screens, playing games. They took their sweet time putting on the plastic sheets that were their raincoats, ambling to the car, hands on their guns, because who but troublemakers would be out in this typhoon-made-landfall kind of storm? They weren't happy about being roused, you could tell, but one, at least, was interested in the peculiarities of Crack's car: the Slant-Six engine, the PontiacSunbird body, Mercury dash, Lamborghini shield ornament soldered on the hood, off-center. He wanted to look in the trunk, not because he was suspicious of Crack's story about emergency medical supplies, but because everything about the car was fascinating.

He walked around to the back, put his hand on the trunk, and asked Crack to pop it open. Crack said, of course, no problem, he would have to find the key, get out of the car, and come round to unlock it manually. Wait a sec, let me find an umbrella, there's so much stuff in the back seat. The other guard, who was in charge, was more interested in going back to playing the first-person shooter game they were both engaged in, searching bombed-out buildings, going house to house, dodging snipers, parkouring from roof to roof, occasional hand-to-hand combat. His impatience mixed with the other guard's curiosity about the car was a diabolical combination. The latter really really wanted to test-drive the car, was intrigued by its multi-hybrid construction, and could have lingered over it, examining every screw and gasket for hours. Once the trunk was opened and found to be empty, we'd be arrested on the spot. I couldn't tell which of the two guards was going to get his way and concentrated on the gamer, hoping he'd prevail.

"Come on, nothing in there." He motioned for his colleague to get out of the rain, not to make unnecessary work for them, not to waste time, in effect, and after looking longingly at the car's body, he complied. Maybe it was the downpour that finally persuaded him to let us go.

Crack was all smiles as if they were fellow soldiers who had toughed it out together somewhere, now returned stateside, they shake hands, thanks, officer.

"Keep your brights on, buddy." The remaining guard waved us into the darkness that was Tunnel A. Crack put the car in gear, and we headed into the mouth of the passageway.

Once in, there was no space to turn around and go back. That was it. If the guards at the other end had, in the low visibility caused by the tempest, confused A and B, and a car or truck came headed toward us in the opposite direction, we'd be flattened. If I knew how long it would take, I would be able to time the distance. I'd know okay, seven, six, five more minutes to go. It had never occurred to me to do this before. Traveling at the speed limit, did it take five or fifteen minutes to drive under variable traffic conditions? I took the train to work and had never timed the part of the trip that was under water. I just looked out the front window as ribs of the train tunnel sped past.

Despite high beams, we descended into a featureless black hole, and it was easy to imagine we weren't traveling to a specific place, an industrial park, flagship Pangenica, a site I knew well, but were actually driving down to the center of the earth. Palms sweating, imagining hurtling toward some kind of molten core that would eat you alive, but Crack was calm, so I concentrated on him. He told me to stop staring. I just need to absorb some serenity now. You know how it works.

There wasn't a light at the end of the tunnel, eventually it just got a little less dark and then we were out. Commuter tracks ran alongside the highway, and we passed local ghost train stations that had been eliminated to focus on express service. City to industrial park, few stops remaining for hapless residents who lived between those two destinations. Solitary ransacked train cars sat at abandoned stations here or there, and they were lit, though how or by whom was unknown. No one seemed to care enough to rout out the renegade users. Power was mostly extinguished, so these beacons of sporadic light marked the possibility that someone made a home out of the gutted cars, or found shelter in them, stationary shadows of their former selves.

When we arrived at Pangenica, I would go in alone. The ID would work for me, but Crack's would set off alarms. It was still the weekend. Regular IDs for weekday employees were reset remotely, so they couldn't be used to get into the buildings until six a.m. Monday. Crack couldn't get in if he wanted to. The labs ran round the clock, and there were people who did work on weekends, but he was not one of them.

There were few cars in the lot, the parking attendant booth was empty, and this made sense because non-essential weekend employees had been furloughed due to the storm, only critical personnel were required to come into work, so Pangenica was mostly dark, but not entirely. The complex had a private power plant, but the facility wasn't invulnerable. The Phytosacks needed to keep pulsing, being fed, and to continue to grow on an hourly basis. If the power went, if there was a total blackout, the Phystosacks would no longer receive nutrients, oxygen, temperature control, and deaths would be total, no survivors. It would be a catastrophe of unheard of proportions, there was always a source of back power, so some floors glowed and seemed to float in space. In the dark or semi-darkness, even someone familiar with the complex would have a difficult time knowing what was where. Crack said he'd wait for me here in the parking lot right in front, possibly swallow a three-for-one Dormazin, and I'll be awake when you run out, engine revved, ready to go.

TWENTY-THREE

I walked through the first series of doors, just as I'd done so many times. My image on the security cameras set off no alarms. The guard, a man I'd never seen before, barely looked up when I tapped my ID on the turnstile. I was in.

Archives and Records occupied its own wing in a structure that looked like it was made of glass waffles, the perfect material for a building that needed to appear transparent and available when its function and contents were anything but.

The waffle house was accessed via a skybridge on the tenth floor that connected it to the main building. You went in on the tenth floor, then worked your way down, but this also meant the only way out was to go back up to the tenth floor. The idea of being trapped on one of the lower floors induced waves of claustrophobia, just thinking about the rows of potentially unstable metal shelving, lights blinking, power going out. I hoped I could find the Singe file quickly, exit just as fast, and that Crack's car would start the instant I slammed my butt into the passenger seat.

I opened one set of doors, and as I crossed the tenth-floor skybridge, I tried not to look down, just straight ahead at the series of sliding glass doors. A voice told me to tap my ID on the sensor to the left of the door. I tapped, but nothing happened. While starting to back away, the sound of the doors I'd just passed through shutting and locking behind me made my toes curl inside my shoes, as if clutching an invisible rope, last-ditch and futile attempt to reach nonexistent safety. It was possible I couldn't go back the way I came. Entrances and exits were timed and controlled by an electrical system that was erratic. I tapped a second time. A siren sounded briefly, and I expected to be arrested on the spot, but this shoplifting alarm blared whenever the doors opened, and stopped after a few seconds. It was as if the system was a slow brain that took a few seconds for the legitimacy of my ID to clear, as if high security was designed to be nervous, constantly on a hair trigger of high alert, it assumed guilt. Then I did look down the ten stories to the flooded pavement below. The glass floors could induce vertigo, but I risked it, and looked. No human presence could be detected, as far as I could see.

After a few minutes, the set of doors slid open. I didn't have to worry about someone seeing me in the archive. Someone already had. Sitting behind the front circulation desk, the only desk manned by a human in that particular wing was Vy Sapper, wearing Jane Ames' orange shoes, and she let me know she had seen me first, when I was still on the skybridge, and I couldn't go back now.

"Hey, Loew. Nice to see you, and I know it's you, but I'm going to have to run your ID."

No problem. Of course. I handed it to her along with my phone (none were allowed in the facility) and prepared to go through the metal detector.

"So, you got switched here, Vy? Weekend shift?" I tried to make time-filler chat like Crack at the guard house, if you want to look in the trunk, be my guest, thanks, sure, no big thing.

"Just short-staffed for the moment. I don't mind filling in." She scanned my card. "I see you got Q Clearance. Good for you. Must have been urgent, what you needed here. Usually it takes weeks to get Q." She had a black and red taser gun that she spun on the countertop, and she saw me looking at it, so she explained that the guard whose shift was customary at this time had a family emergency in the storm. His house was rapidly flooding, wife and children were clinging to the roof, and so he'd left the taser with her, taking his automatic with him, adios, but don't worry, Vy, old chum, who's going to barge into the archive on a night like tonight?

Who builds a house so close to a river? Vy said to me. So, why are you here, again?

I told her I needed the Laveneer file, which she might remember I was looking for from the last time we spoke. I expected she'd look it up, put in a request, then I'd be escorted into another room where the file would be brought to me. "The Director of Adjudications decided to levitate off his chair and got my status expedited." I tried to joke, just wanting to get in and out as quickly as I could. I held my hand out for the ID.

"Lucky you. The truth is, Loew, I never leave."

Really? I didn't know what to make of the concept of never leaving. It couldn't be literally factual. With overtime, it could feel like you never left, but Vy meant what she said. She explained she slept in an alcove in Admissions, an assemblage of soft chairs salvaged from a library. Offices had mini-fridges. The cafeteria was open twenty-four hours, she showered in the Pangenica gym, located in an outer building. Vy was unhoused.

There were places you could live rent free: disused water towers, junked aircraft, commuter train domiciles, and arboreal subway cars, but Vy said she couldn't live as a squatter in these places, and my suggesting such shelters showed how little I knew about anything. Despite all the advances in engineering, it was impossible to one hundred percent eliminate violent tendencies. Women were vulnerable to assault from roving citizens here and there, and that was just one reason it was safer to make a home, or the idea of a home, in Pangenica.

"It may come as a surprise to you, an Adjudicator with a good salary and a roof over your head, but no one will rent or sell to me because I have a record."

This is what I thought: Vy shoplifted candy, cigarettes, small electronic devices, embezzled petty cash. These were the kinds of crimes for which one wasn't disappeared, but once convicted of minor offenses committed serially—that might be enough to make you a semi-pariah, denied housing at every turn. But these kinds of misdemeanors occupied a very short list. I might have read about middle ground infractions in law school, but it wasn't my area of expertise, and therefore couldn't recall the sequence. It didn't matter. Vy told me what she had done, and it was none of those things.

"I used to work in the labs until I did something one night that I had my reasons for doing, but it landed me in a deuce of a pickle—a tight spot, you might say."

In an old screwball comedy, this is where I would respond, you don't say? And Vy would answer, I do say.

But she didn't shift her face into the exaggerated frown that's a hallmark of fake theatrical concern. The eaeroscript was taking a long time to write, time I didn't have, but what could I do but watch hands tick on an analog clock that hung on no walls and wait while she typed, knowing that when all that industry arrived, it would vanish within minutes as if written on one of those Etch-A-Sketch toys. Write something across the screen, shake it, and the lines are gone. She returned my phone to me, so I could read what she'd written.

Eaeroscipt
Vy Sapper

In the lab I worked in, the manager had a habit of putting his hands on my arm or back, lingering too long, more aggressive than the word lingering would imply, and sometimes his hands moved up and down like windshield wipers. What's the problem? Don't overreact, right? He showed me pictures of his daughter, saying wasn't she hot? Who'd have thought I'd have a kid like that? Which was supposed to be a cue to say to him that he was kind of hot, you could see it, even if, in fact, your revulsion knew no bounds. The tobacco and skunky weed smell, it was permanent with him. If later you said anything about the incident, his answer would always be, is that a crime? I worked in a miasma of is it or isn't it. He was so confident, so sure of himself and his position in the company and in life itself, it was disarming. He often stood too close in what must have been choreographed moments, because you'd have nowhere to step back to without colliding with tanks of Phytobase, knocking into spectrographs, or mobile Phytosack storage units. There were the usual rumors about groping and walking in when assistants were changing, sometimes explained away as accidents, or something imagined that didn't really happen.

Who knew what was true? I didn't get the worst of it. He spoke to me as if I was three years old, an idiot who constantly gets it wrong, who can't tell RNA messenger from a thymine molecule. I made mistakes. I confess, in case you didn't already guess, I'm a recovered noddie addict, but that slow condescending voice was persistent, and what could I or anyone do to stop him? So, I was prepared when he told me I'd lose my job unless I did him. Let it be said, I had a fair amount of revenge drive. I wanted to fuck him up.

I gave a lot of thought to how I would prank him, not drawing-a-moustache-on-the-Mona Lisa kind of prank, but more like "there's Richard Nixon giving a speech from the back of a train, and Dick Tuck signals the engineer to pull out and keep driving." I needed a roorback, a piece of slander intended for sabotage, but I wasn't interested in slanderous language, I wanted action. Even if it backfired, the risk was worth the outcome, so I thought.

There are surveillance cameras in the lab. I knew that, and that my activities were tracked, but I also knew guys in security, and I knew the footage from the vast network that is Pangenica wasn't watched 24/7. How could it be? They play games on their phones half the time. I was willing to risk it, and that night it was like I threw a bunch of balls in the air not caring where they landed, because it was impossible to lose. You'd think that application forms were inseverable from DNA destinations—but there is a moment when the tether is untied before it's retied.

I'll explain it this way, fast, simple, without violating my NDA. Trust what I'm telling you. Imagine an astronaut working outside a station. For an instant, he becomes unhooked and doomed to float off into space, his very survival comes down to minutes, maybe seconds. But then another rocket comes along, is fantastically close, and he clamps on. Hatch opens, another berth is secured. The odds of this happening are less than microscopic, but not zero. Remember biohackers? Those antique and glamourous cowboy criminals who worked out of garages, potting sheds, and storage lockers, had gone extinct.

It was thought to have been a crime committed with mail order supplies, a centrifuge made of blender parts and spring-form pans, test-tube racks made of flip tops. Don't mix your smoothie in the same pitcher that once held fluorescent bacteria. Nobody was expecting me or anyone else to present as a reincarnation of those forgotten bio-renegades. I thought that was in my favor. I figured the odds of my being caught were infinitesimal, but this turned out not to be true. I was arrested in the morning.

He knew he would have been blamed for the disaster in the lab, but it was me—the ex-addict he'd given every chance to. He claimed everyone loved him. Everything was always consensual.

What I did, they said, was suicide-bomber level, not just targeted at one victim, but my action had the potential to affect many, like contaminating a food supply, that level of high-risk interference. You were after one person but risked the health and welfare of many in order to achieve your goal. And yet you had no anxiety, no sense of cause and effect. What gives? You aren't a child. You knew what you were doing. I was given a choice that wasn't really a choice: there's a cell waiting for you, or you can be studied.

So, I accepted to be the subject of experiments, and it was quickly determined I was neither mutation nor anomaly, which baffled them even more. Nevertheless, blood was drawn repeatedly, as well as X-rays, CAT scans, MRIs. This was many years ago, but it continues still. I'm notified and I have to go, and since I have to be readily available, they gave me a sleepy, nothing position in classified Admissions and sometimes elsewhere, such as here in Archives and Records, almost a no-show job, but whether working in Admissions or Archives, I learned things. Maybe it wasn't a smart idea to park me there, but they did. In any case, I don't have a home to walk off to. My home, such as it is, continues to be where I'm experimented on.

They wanted to study me because the propensity to take risks can be a desirable trait. Risk-takers discover new things, but a certain level of dicey behavior can be too much. How can such a thing be calibrated?

When I thought about risky decisions, I imagined things like precarious investments, like putting money into a life-saving medication that also had serious side effects, or the financing of a colony on Jupiter or Mars, so hobbled by inhospitable conditions whose partial solutions were fantastically expensive, and not really viable, those kinds of gambling, high stakes, winner take all or lose all situations. If the risks of being studied were physical, that could mean something like jumping out of a helicopter in a Rocket J. Squirrel suit or driving a truck full of volatile chemicals down a winding mountain road. Faulty brakes and a compromised steering column—sorry about that.

At first the tests were just medical—exams I was subjected to, but could not control the results of. Then they became more physical, like testing my reflexes, muscle resistance, and then the tests grew more complex still, testing things like impulsiveness and self-control. The tests were never painful, sometimes they were even pleasurable, and it was often interesting to be the subject, to be part of the analysis of results: How is one typical, how atypical, how unique? All in all, it seemed like I'd been let off easy.

Then, at one point, I was abruptly taken from my post, hooded, forcibly led out of the building. The hood was made of rubber, no weave you could potentially see bits and pieces through, so I had no clue where I was being taken. Though guided, I had to step up to get into a vehicle. From the feel of the seats and the sound of sliding doors and lock clicking shut, the creaking of a man sitting behind me, the weight of others on either side, from all of that, I imagined I was in a Stasi van like one I'd seen in a museum when I was able to travel—a past life. It had looked so innocent: a white van like a milk truck with a print curtain. Butter wouldn't melt in its mouth, if it had one. There was nothing even pretending to be benign or cute in my situation, as far as I could tell. From the urgency, the hustle, the blinding, surely I was about to be shot. Driven who-knows-how-long, taken out, up steps into a building, then into an elevator that seemed to be traveling down, but I couldn't be sure. It was possible I'd been transported some distance from Pangenica, or could well have been driven in circles, and I was back in the building.

When the hood was taken off, I stood facing three men in military uniforms in a windowless room, and it was that kind of quiet where I sensed there was nothing but earth all around, but I really had no way of knowing. One of the men pushed me into a chair in front of a screen, and I was asked to watch hours of convoys driving across a desert, images recorded via drone. That was all. Then I was returned to Admissions. This happened a few more times, but eventually the footage changed to streets of a ruined city, not entirely deserted. The following week, the camera, using night vision, went even closer into the ruins. I was told this was live, real-time, and because it was real, I didn't think it was part of an experiment. I played a lot of combat simulation computer games, and I was good at it. My handlers, if you could call them that, knew I had skills. We would talk about shooting games from time to time. Looking back, I was being led by the nose, totally manipulated.

So that day, the camera went closer and closer, broadcasting voices in languages I didn't understand, and were not translated for me. Then the atrocities began, and I wasn't allowed to look away. I knew the recording was sent from a part of the world in which conflict couldn't be reduced to two or three tribal peoples who didn't get along, who had their own disputes, but factions were many and allegiances difficult to sort out and keep track of. Also, there were big players sitting in offices in other countries, untraceable and unthreatened by anyone. It's a war zone without a war, a landscape of hostility and confusion where genetic monitoring isn't as refined, though there are wealthy enclaves. The men in uniform standing behind me communicated the idea that by watching I was doing a service, and I had been recruited for this for a reason. They spoke with finality and confidence.

After months of watching, I was told to direct the drone-bomb into buildings that were empty, but used by snipers. My job was to reduce their cover to rubble. Drones never lie, right? The uniforms assured me there were no such things as mistakes, so I flew around structures that looked like little more than piles of bricks, remains of walls, openings that had once been windows. I did what I was asked to do. It was like a computer game—emptyish space at night. No actual lives lost. Next time, a different building, the same command was issued, and I was made to believe this was a life-or-death situation, bad actors needed to be routed out. I complied, sure I had no choice but to pull the lever, but that time when I hit the fire button, out of the smoke, a small figure appeared, running from what was left of the shelter. Was it human? Had he or she been alone? I'll never know. Now I swiveled, eyeballed the uniforms behind me, hoping for a clue that I was part of a staged experiment and not some elite citizens drone attack troop. Was the shoulder braid slightly askew, military decorations made-up nonsense, signs they had been rented from a costume library? Did an actor crack a smile when I wasn't looking? I wasn't able to turn around fast enough to catch one or look closely enough. The concept of theatricality, a performance only, presented itself to me like a province of safety, if I could just get over the barbed wire and electrified fence. The truth was, there was no elite group involved. It was just me.

After that bombing incident, there was a lull, and I thought maybe all the tests and experiments were done with. But then they resumed. Once again, hooded, taken somewhere—a different room, different men in uniform. I was commanded to watch a train snaking its way through what looked like steppes. The train, so I was told, was carrying a weapons-grade biotoxin that was so dangerous and uncontrollable, that once unleashed, the contagion would spread globally in a matter of days. The lethal toxin should never be used, and it was about to fall into the wrong hands. To a cell of terroroticas, or hard-headed gang bangers with global ambitions, or unknown shadow boxers for a cartel, a megalomaniac . . . It didn't matter except none had any idea how unstoppable these organisms were. If launched, millions would be killed.

But many innocent people on the train will die if you do blow it up. I was shown photographs, clips of some of the passengers enjoying life with families and loved ones, just so I'd have a sense of the human beings who were, unknowingly, about to be sacrificed. I was scared and didn't know why they were demanding I make some kind of decision. In the ruined city, I didn't know if innocent random people were being killed. Now, they were telling me that the casualties would be high, and most would be passengers who had the unfortunate luck to be traveling on that train at that moment.

Wouldn't the explosion only further disperse the microbes? No, the intense heat would kill them. Was I being told the truth? Possibility:

There were no biotoxins on the train. My trust in authority could be a joke. Maybe it was all a set-up to make it look like one thing when the actual goal was something else entirely. For example, the train needed to be destroyed in order to annihilate the one person they wanted to assassinate—like the drug king pin who exploded a plane full of passengers just to murder one man—who it turned out hadn't boarded the plane at the last minute. In any case, why leave the decision up to me? I'm a nobody—but maybe that was the point. I won't tell you if I pressed fire.

The next series of experiments were enforced close-range voyeurism, and I had to watch while people endured a spectrum of experiences from extreme pleasure to pain, all presented in a variety of psychological, emotional, and verbal abusages. These were local settings, up close and personal, no mediating screen, not events that occurred in another part of the world under circumstances of outright conflict, duress, guerilla warfare. The situations snuck up like hidden bear traps. The ground is ordinary: grass, moss-covered stones, a few weeds, low flowering perennials, but it's only cover, below is air, then a spike-littered pit. I had to watch subjects eat a great meal, engage in cornball conversation about being reunited after a long time, kissing then passionate fucking, but I never knew when sex could suddenly become weaponized.

This time, I was hooked up to machines measuring my responses. I began not to fervently hope but to seriously suspect the subjects I watched were actors, though of course, I could never be one hundred percent sure. The actors could have been prisoners or semi-prisoners like myself who had to do what they were told. There was no way to know for certain.

The next phase was constructed to give me a little more control of the degree of pain or pleasure. I got to move pieces around the board, to decide levels, to construct what the voice coming from a speaker called the mise en scène. It wasn't like okay, now you're free to do whatever you want, pleasure for everyone. Pleasure is always high stakes, that is to say, it comes with a price. I was given guidelines, perimeters that I couldn't violate. The enactments, if that's what they were, took place in a black box theater with me behind a one-way mirror, though sometimes there were outside locations, and I was positioned in a small house like a sentry box or booth, an aedicule. Its windows were black glass. I could see out, but no one could see in. The voice that instructed me was always the same: male, authoritative, pretentious accent. I referred to him as my director.

Throughout all these years, there's something critical they left out. What if I was asked to watch someone I knew? If the tormented subject was someone I was a) close to, b) I knew medium well, or c) I knew only slightly, like a former classmate not seen in years, or d) a near stranger, say, someone I once sat next to on a plane but still remember, what then? Variations: it is the tormentor who is a friend, but I didn't know they were torturers as a side hustle. What then? I was asked to be judge, jury, and executioner, but the element of social connection was left out. All were strangers to me.

Lines of typing vanished under my thumb. I mouthed *Waxman*, and Vy nodded. She had known enough of his work to fiddle with it and had made the switch. There had been no file in the garbage. He'd known all along, and he wanted me to find Mrs. Laveneer before anyone else did, just as Altner wanted me to find him.

Vy was no longer Vy. She wasn't the person I thought she was, but someone who hid her own personal phantom limbs and scarification. She didn't ask me what I thought of what I'd just read, but only turned up the collar of her jacket and buttoned it all the way to the top. The archives were kept at a cold temperature for the preservation of materials, and it felt like it was getting colder, the effects of the electrical grid gone haywire. The silver nail polish on her fingers as they moved up and down, looked like metal caps. She shoved her hands in her pockets so hard, coins fell to the floor. Vy, who had accidentally both created the Singe double and switched the consciousnesses of PomPom and Clayton, something her tormentor Waxman (who also tormented himself) had been trying to do himself, she was someone who still had coins.

A Dormazin wouldn't be a bad thing to have at that moment, a nodding-out distraction, a way to displace anxiety, to not think about what Vy might or might not have done: fast sleep, wake me when all this is over. My kingdom for altered consciousness, take my consciousness, please.

I felt a compulsion to rewind back to every memory I had, an impossible task, to look for a black window, an anonymous structure, like a house but not a house, a building that could easily pass unnoticed. Penrose was the only place I could imagine that would be safe from some kind of mobile watching unit. If there had been such a structure, who was being watched, and if it was me, what was the experiment? Vy handed my ID back, typed some more, then turned her screen around, and showed me that when she typed in *Laveneer*, a message read that there were no entries under that name.

"Listen, Loew. Last night I decided to have dinner in the ground floor café. Given the general power outage, I thought the few guards would be on high alert, but they clumped together, talking, distracted. Someone they worked with had been run over by a subway. Can you imagine? When one of them did notice me eating day-old muffins and melted ice cream, I just said, oh, working late, don't mind me, but then I was called for an experiment, and when called, I have to go. I took the elevator to the basement as instructed.

"I was met by a man in a white lab coat, nothing unusual about that, and he led me to a chamber where I was told to sit in front of a simple control panel, just a dial, really, with an arrow that could point to a series of ever-increasing numbers as it was turned. Through the one-way mirror I could see a woman strapped to a chair."

The lights flickered, came back on, and then strains of music, *eating burnt toast and drinking black black coffee. . . . Yeah, that's all she left for me* could be heard from the stacks, as if the electrical system had gone haywire. Vy's phone rang. She looked at it but didn't answer.

"I'd like to show you something. Recordings of my participation arrive within hours of each experiment's completion. Sometimes it's not so bad to watch them, but mostly watching is to be reminded of the brokering of pain, and refusal isn't an option. I make silent bargains with myself. If I do *x*, watch in a straight unreactive way, then *y*, the subject will be released, will be the result, with the possibility of *z*, a reprieve for me in some form. They can tell if I've watched. Also, the files are undeletable, and can't be dragged to the trash bin."

Vy clicked a link, and a recording of the experiment filled a screen. The woman in the chair was Masha, the Singe double.

"I knew what would happen. The woman would be asked questions by someone in the room, someone I couldn't see. I couldn't hear her answers, but the man in the lab coat who was wearing headphones could, and when she refused to answer—I could see her shaking her head—he would ask me to deliver ever-more-powerful electric shocks. This was an old experiment that I'd read about, meant to demonstrate obedience to authority even if authority is despotic and advocates the administration of pain in a variety of ways. I was sure the woman in the chair was a paid actor because that had been the case in the original experiment, though the person at the control panel hadn't known it at the time. So, because I had a demonstrable record for defying authority, I complied with what I was asked to do, which is to say, I increased the power and frequency of the shocks—I believed none of it was real, and if I proved myself to have become blindly obedient, maybe the experiments would stop. There would be no more point to them."

The image corresponded to Vy's explanation. When Masha shook her head, refusing to answer, she received a shock. I felt the shock as well and hoped Vy didn't notice when the jolt of electricity made me wince and lose my balance. I held onto the edge of the counter, so as not to fall to the floor.

"Can you turn up the audio?"

"No. I can't."

I didn't know if it was true, that there was no sound. What I think was true: Within twenty-four hours, I'd led Pangenica to the double, and maybe that had been the plan all along. Masha was unbuckled from the chair and either lifeless or unconscious, fell to the floor. Impossible to see if she was breathing. Her body was carried out, and the recording ended.

"The woman in the chair wasn't an actor," I said to Vy.

"No, she *was* an actor."

What was Masha doing when the knocking on her door at Horner's Landing began? Disappearachniks don't break down the door unless it's necessary to do so. They hope you'll just let them in because there is no point to do otherwise. The double was a suspicious person who had her reasons. She might have fled out the back, though they'd be standing around on the patio flagstones, too; there was no exit, only a waiting van. Another possibility: She opened the door straightaway, thinking it was the boy from the neighboring house coming to play with the unseen child who lived with her, her son, of course, and I felt the floor give way under my feet. Vy clicked the file closed.

If Vy needed to believe that no one was harmed by her decision to ramp up the voltage every time she was told to, that the woman strapped to the chair was an actor, not a real person whose existence, from the moment she was just a bunch of cells, was Vy's doing, I left things as they were, not tampering with stories she told herself. I didn't tell her about the armies of Space Marines carefully arranged by children she had no knowledge of.

On the other hand, I was a trained and licensed Adjudicator, I discovered and reported—that was my job—but in that recording, I was undone, a dupe, a fraud, nothing in my work mattered in the way I thought it did. When the file was here, when it existed, Pangenica knew what was in it. They knew about the switch. They didn't need me to prove anything, and now it looked like by finding the double, they may have found the location of the original.

"I was supposed to be putting the pieces together."

"No, Loew, you're not that important. Others do that and they have the best interest of the company. This was a sweep-up operation, nothing more. You're just a screw in a Zamboni, it's the machine in toto that has an identity, smoothing the ice, so it's perfect—no slurry ridges, no grooves, no coded messages etched into the surface. The screw is nothing. Nobody cares. Can I see your ID again?"

"Why?"

"Just give it to me. I want to show you something."

I handed it to her.

"It's a fake. Look. But you know that."

"No, it isn't. I got in, didn't I? My authorization was expedited," I insisted. "If it was a fake, I'd still be outside."

"The ID didn't let you in. I did. Look. IDs with Q clearance have electronic watermarks on the lower right corner. Your counterfeiters neglected this detail or didn't know. They have most Q ID information correct, but not that."

"It was all for nothing, anyway."

"No, it wasn't all for nothing. There's something in this for me. You're going to give me the keys to your apartment."

"Why would I do that?'

"I can call security right now, and by tomorrow at this time, your remains will fit in a can of beans. Give me your keys."

"No, Vy, I'm not handing my apartment over to you. I'm already half-disappeared."

"You're right, that's true, more than half."

She turned her screen around and typed in my name. Nothing. I'd already been erased. I'd never been picked up from a Pangenica waiting room, yelling and screaming, wrapped in a pink blanket anyway. "No Phytosack" didn't even exist as a box to be checked, but there I was, standing, soon-to-be not standing. Waxman was right. The snowman was melting, as it inevitably would. I tried to focus on Vy, heart beating just a little faster, a touch of bitterness. Even that was better than what I was feeling, a loss of everything, every particle of identity, and the person who could answer my questions never would. A disappearachnik had his job for the day. Later he'd have dinner with co-workers or pick up his dry cleaning or walk his dog and think about where he'd have lunch tomorrow.

"Give me your keys, and I'll show you a way out of the building."

"I know my way out of the building, and there is no point."

"Another way out. No guarantees but at least you'll have a running start."

Vy in my apartment, opening cupboards, throwing out expired jars of pickled mushrooms and containers of olives, trying on rhinestone starburst earrings, Madridische red lipstick, paging through acting manuals, finding photographs of Dot and me as a child at the beach, screaming on a Tilt-a-Whirl, my wedding pictures, and wondering what happened to the man who was putting a slice of cake in my mouth? Trying to look me up, what had she not known—

But then, oh, yeah, Zedi Loew, she's over and done with, that's why she's sitting on my bed in my apartment, main city island.

I didn't have a no-choice-what-the-hell feeling about it, nowhere near it, but I put the keys to my apartment at the base of her screen, made a show of acting like okay, it's your funeral, Vy. When actually, it was mine.

Looking down through the glass floor and rain, the figure of a man could be seen, arms full of folders walking one way, then backtracking like a bee caught in a flooded hive. Or maybe I was the trapped insect caught in something sticky, soon to harden into a low-grade contaminated amber. Somewhere in the waffle house hive below lay the file of whoever hit PomPom with their car or minivan or ice cream truck, then drove away.

Somewhere in the stacks, if you looked in the right place, you might find the identity of an Adjudicator so obedient that they pushed a boy through thin ice. To do this, their consciousness would have to be commandeered from an early age, from conception, and this person or persons would travel the city like one possessed, a creature who could be made to do just about anything. No clue who this might be or might have been—not Altner, not the Adjudicators whose desks and offices were adjacent to mine, a department soon to be absorbed into the Department of Disappearachniks, or D of D.

This is the key to the front door, this is the top lock, the only one I use. Counterintuitively it turns counterclockwise, the light under the ceiling fan doesn't work, the fridge hasn't been cleaned in a while.

A User's Manual poured out of me, and then the man who'd seemed lost in the lower floors appeared at the top of the stairs, a short distance from Vy's desk. Holding a cup of coffee in one hand and folders in the crook of his elbow, he smiled as he walked toward us. It was L. J. Morris, the junior archivist, up in everyone's business, animated, confident in his schemes, and pretty happy for someone whose boyfriend had dumped him a few hours before. His smile was smirky, but then it often was, and if he was fueled by bitterness, he was good at hiding it. Fuck Around, Find Out, people used to say, and perhaps Morris had learned this lesson that night. I tried not to mirror his smile.

Vy said, Mr. Sunshine, you can't bring liquids of any kind into the archive.

"The librarian who was stationed before you waved me through." Morris held up the paper vending machine cup and shook it a bit to imitate waving. Some sloshed to the floor.

He wondered what I was doing in the building on a weekend, in a wing that was off limits for most employees. Morris's jacket was a size too small, and his laminated Pangenica ID was pinned to a narrow lapel, just under a pin in the shape of a dial phone. It was easy to imagine the smiling face in the ID photo talking on just such a rotary phone, offering advice, voicing critical commentary, letting things slip, hand over receiver, to whisper to someone actually in the room. He repeated his question.

Technically, I was Morris's superior, but he was mosquito-like in his ability to bite, regardless of his size, and he knew it. He could ask in a friendly, benign, just curious kind of voice, as if conspiracies lay waiting for him to be unearthed.

I'll show you, Vy said, and turned her screen around, so he could see my ID where she'd scanned it a few minutes ago. Morris put his coffee on the edge of her desk, appeared to squint, frown, concentrate while Vy explained, Adjudicators sometimes need special, timed access. Cases come along that require emergency service. A young woman claims to be the lost child of family X. Some details check out, others don't. The dying mother wants to know for certain, does not want to be fooled. Not a lot of time to resolve. A man develops late onset color blindness. He's a pilot and can't do his job. Is it the company's fault? He has no savings. He demands a settlement, pronto. Vy was a rapid-fire cannon of emergency cases. All those years of working in Admissions, she'd learned things. It was smart of her to display the scan, so I wouldn't have to show Morris my flawed ID, but then Morris grabbed the mouse that was within easy reach and began to circle around the screen, distracting Vy, who I could tell was trying to squelch ripples of anxiety. He wanted to take a closer look, and leaned in, clicking on an icon of a musical note to see what Vy listened to, then clicked on a camera to look at her photos, None of it interested him, and Vy made a move to grab the mouse, but he brushed away her hand, clicking on a movie projector that would access Last Played, and the screen filled with footage, now sound included, of Vy and the torture of the Singe double.

Morris's eyes bugged out in mock shock, and in full-on ratfink voice he said, what have we here?

All Morris had wanted to know was: What's Zedi Loew doing in Archives and Records? It was an innocent question. He probably didn't even suspect Vy was making up fly-by-night seat-of-the-pants baloney about Adjudications protocol. Unleashing the genie that was Last Played, clicked just out of curiosity, because Vy tried to grab the mouse back, so was hiding something, and bingo, he got way more than he bargained for.

In Masha's screams, Morris couldn't have known exactly what he was looking at, only that it was bad, and that he never encountered facts he couldn't use. With the air of a conspiracy entrepreneur, the Junior Archivist could link a file from Accounting to election fraud to a sex tape from the era of VHS tapes that still had currency to affect the lives of the people sitting next to you. A hoarder of facts he could weaponize, spin into counter-semi-or-barely-facts, and now, just because being a nosy Parker was his stock in trade, he'd hit a jackpot.

Vy knocked his hand away, and in the violence of the shove, the cup fell, and then the files fanned out of his arms and into the pool of coffee. He bent over to collect the papers, but before threats were out of his mouth, Vy was tasering him all over his body at close range. He dropped unconscious, or at least appeared unconscious, perhaps he was only paralyzed with pain, belt buckle making a cracking sound as it hit glass tile. For a moment, I felt a kind of pulsing sting, like an electric shock, but was able to shift my focus to Vy who seemed so sure of what she was doing.

The files were in flame-retardant folders, but nothing protected the papers from liquid damage. Physical paper wasn't invulnerable, but it was known that when planes collided with towers, lives were lost, but pieces of paper survived, floating in the air currents, fragments landing on other islands carrying still-legible evidence of offices and transactions of all kinds. Pangenica folders, translucent green, embossed with the company's globe logo, fanned out on the floor. I picked up a file labeled *Heckle and Jeckle* about experiments with magpies who, with beaks or claws, scratched off yellow stickers when subjected to the mirror test, but black stickers that blended in with their feathers remained unseen. Mixed among *Heckle and Jeckle* was an envelope that had the Director of Adjudications' name on the outside, and had nothing to do with magpies.

Subject: T. Altner, Director of Adjudications
To: [redacted]
From: [redacted]

The Director of Adjudications was relocated from the Ciudad Medina office with a background in identifying cases of fraud, and in this he is considered a leading expert in a specialized class of criminal conduct. He once had the reputation of an ace Adjudicator in the field, and came to us as a top-notch administrator.

After arrival, we had him employed as a spy at one of our competitors, and in this role, he also excelled, notifying us of pending patents, trademarks, biotech engineering innovations, AI potential in the field. When the company went bankrupt, we moved him to the central office.

Questions about the Director first arose when discrepancies were observed between known income and escalating expenditures: a landmarked upstate summer house, new cars, vacations, not the kind limited to an outing to the local Wonderville Amusement Park, expensive dinners, shopping sprees at high-end shops, a penthouse apartment on the main city island. Flagged by the Accounting Department, there were some questionable uses of the Adjudications Department credit card, but not for the reasons initially suspected.

What was not known at the time: Altner had a betting scheme, though in truth, he was an amateur in areas of gambling. However, as a Senior Adjudicator, he was a superb actor. It began as a side hustle, but he was good at what he could do and was also skilled at appearing to work as Director of Adjudications. Over the years what began as a part-time sideline took over more and more of his focus. No one ever met him face-to-face or even on a screen. He would lure investors in, throwing around terms like high-yield investment programs, off-shore products and vehicles, as well as hedge futures trading, but he was just a script, not a corporeal entity.

Promising towering returns, producing false statements, sometimes generated by use of

Adjudication computers, he did nothing with the money he was meant to be investing but spend it. When someone wanted to make a withdrawal, he discouraged them, saying he offered even higher returns if they kept their money in. Things were good and only going to get better. When too many of his "customers" wanted to withdraw funds, he needed cash fast and began to gamble on Adjudication case outcomes, of which he did have considerable insider knowledge, though he kept the nature of his exact job a secret as required. It began with the close community of expats from Slavtown, an insular group that trusted their fellow former citizens, but when word got out that Altner was the OTB of Pangenica cases, there were plenty eager to take their chances with him. Even still, it was not enough to cover the demands of payments that were starting to landslide in. He began to dip into his expense account. It wasn't nearly enough either, and such behavior began to set off alarms.

Altner needed a case that would be a sure thing. He needed a big win, and he put all his cash and assets on the Laveneer case. The in-house trumpeting of his success, his problem-solving gymnastics, saving the company millions in actual dollars and millions more that would have been required to mop up bad publicity and win back the public's trust, all that would be enough on the positive side of the ledger for his irregularities to be overlooked—possibly—and he could pay off some of his investors.

But in truth, this case cannot be aired publicly, and so does nothing to scrub away his misuse of company monies. What Altner didn't realize is the Laveneer file should never have been investigated, should have been left as the cold case it was. While it is true that he is a man who could clean a mess so thoroughly and with no leftover questions to the extent that you would never know litigation, or potential litigation, was ever even whispered by the petitioning parties, our feeling at this time is the Director of Adjudication's termination should be enacted immediately upon receipt of this memo.

Who was the report addressed to and where had it originated? All were blacked out. It was someone's job to be censor, the Redactionator who redactionated, who was known as a redactionary. I held a few of the papers up to the light, but what was opaque remained opaque. What was he doing with this file? It was possible the Junior Archivist was just doing his job, moving papers from place to place, and this was only the historic copy. The original would have made its way to the department charged with acting on its demand. But this was a volatile copy, and whether Morris was deliberately moving it somewhere or was removing the report for his own purposes, I would never know, and maybe it didn't matter. Vy pulled at my arm, you need to go.

But wait, hadn't Altner assigned the case to me because I was an Adjudicator who he knew could find people, who would just do a job and not ask too many questions? But if it was Waxman who put the file on my desk, Altner saw a goldmine in this case, and decided to hum along as if it were just another job. The initial goal was for Singe to have been buried, lost under a mountain of data, but I wasn't sure. She was radioactive; the woman who knew too much. The Director needed her to be found. There were others in Adjudications, some were more skilled, more talented actors than I was, but a few were most certainly slower, ham-handed in their impersonations, sluggish in their assessment reports and resolutions, known for not sticking to the facts.

Vy motioned, come on already. You have to get out of here.

She motioned I should follow her around her desk, then through a door that led to a stockroom and a narrow elevator.

"Take this one floor up. That's as high as it will go. From there you'll be able to access the roof, and you can jump from this roof to the roof garden of the main administrative building. The gap between buildings is about four feet. Once in the garden, take the espalier escalier down as far as it goes. The drop at the bottom, the distance between the end of the last tree and the ground, is a few feet. It shouldn't be impossible to fall without injury. If the main entrance and all other entrances aren't an option, this is the only way out."

She was right. Archives and Records had no independent entrance. It was only accessed via skybridge from the core administrative building. All entrances and exits to the administrative building were locked and/or guarded in a variety of ways, both human and mechanical, and an architectural dead end on its own, A & R had no links to any other building or facility in the complex.

"A lab chimp was known to escape this way some years ago. Chimps weigh between eighty-eight and one hundred thirty pounds. You're in that range, and my guess is some limbs will hold, and some won't. You'll have to feel your way down. Put a foot on a branch, slowly put your weight on it. If it feels like it's going to give, don't put all your weight on it, but remove your foot, and try another branch."

Some roots were thick, others the size of threads, but they clung to stone and a staircase-like series of trellises screwed into the wall, not buried into the earth. Squirrels, even a large scurry of squirrels, scaled the wall with impunity, but an adult human, even one who was fairly small, would pull the whole structure away from the wall just by stepping onto it. What if all reachable limbs were tested and none would hold, then what? I'd be stuck, Spiderwoman in a glue trap.

"You've done this yourself?"

Vy shook her head. Her strategy was that of an untested amateur, and not only did it make me nervous, I absorbed Vy's anxiety for me. I looked around. Would it be possible to make a home among the moveable stacks and piles of paper? There were a couple of screens overhead; one had a security cam feed. The grainy figure of a man entered the lobby, pushed a button for the elevator.

It was Crack. He hadn't taken a Dormazin, it very much looked like. No way he had been asleep in his car. I hadn't been in the building that long. The guard glanced at his ID and waved him through. Crack did have weekend access.

"I wouldn't get a ride anywhere with him, if I were you," Vy said, as she pushed the button again.

The elevator, used for transporting documents, arrived. It was narrow, like a vertical coffin. I paused before I stepped inside. If there was a power outage, I would be caught in a black, silent box. No sensory information coming in, nothing going out, but even in total silence and complete darkness, I would still have consciousness. I would be screaming, and to lose consciousness would be a blessing, because I really shouldn't be screaming, letting it be known exactly where I was, and once my position was ascertained, maybe they would leave me in the trapped black box. Security guards, wherever they're sitting, slap hands one against the other, then wipe them on their pants: Well, that's the end of her, no muss, no fuss. The facilitator of my own private disappearing trick, I stepped over the threshold and into the car. What choice did I have? Vy said, good luck, press the up button, I'll take good care of. . . .

She held up my keys as the doors closed.

TWENTY-FOUR

The elevator opened on the top floor, a small room that housed a ventilation pump, scattered screwdrivers, pliers, a lug wrench, and other tools left behind. A metal ladder led to a landing and a latched door that opened onto the roof bulkhead. Barely making a sound when hook was lifted from eye, the latch was a simple pre-Industrial Revolution mechanical solution in a sea of high-tech security. Someone must have thought no one would ever be up on this part of the roof. When I pushed open the door and poked my head out, the sky was beginning to lighten over the ocean, and I could hear the soughing of trees. Still, I was glad for the light that the glass panels provided. It was raining softly, enough to make the roof slippery. I stepped back as far as I could, then ran, thinking of the skaters, how they bent their knees before they sprang into the air. I sprinted, then stopped, skidding to about a foot before the edge. You only get one shot, and if you miss, you become a body in the narrow alley between two buildings, soon-to-be waterlogged, maybe not found for days.

You can do it, Loew.

It was Crack.

He was standing on the opposite roof, the one I intended to jump to. The wind and rain had turned gentle for a moment, the dawn was promising, a scene of rescue, except none was possible. There was nervous static in the background. Crack spoke in a low tone, as if he thought I would have to be spellbound by the sound of his voice, about how he got past the entrance guards, and how he calculated the only way out, for me, would be this way, via the roof. There were only a few feet between the buildings, so he didn't even have to shout. It was impossible to stay where I was and a bad idea to be on the other roof.

He reached out his hand. I didn't take it.

The door to Archives and Records on the roof flew open and hit the side of a wall, banging in the wind. No one was following me, yet, that I could see, but they would be soon. My legs were shaking, while Crack appeared cool, and so I tried to absorb his sense of certainty, the solidity with which he stood on two legs seemed genuine, a perception of being anchored, but I turned my back on him and whispered into my phone to check what was in my bank. Drops of water magnified pixels into rainbow patterns on the screen, but the balance was clear: *zero, zero, zero*. There was still no money in it, and there never would be. Now that I was erased, it would be impossible to transfer funds, even if Crack was so inclined, and I guessed that he was not. I had a date with the on-the-clock disappearachniks who would leave no trail, and no evidence of who I had been. As an Adjudicator, I knew the company was thorough in its traditional practices.

If my foot slipped on the corner where roof meets wall, that most perilous of ninety-degree angles, what difference would it make? Now or later. You can blow this or you can blow that. Opt for later is the prevailing instinct. I backed up a few feet, so I wouldn't be near him when I landed, if I landed.

He moved, too, like a basketball guard. It was difficult to read his gesture: I'll catch you, or I'll push you into the space between? Which would it be? Impossible to know.

Visualize floating, a parabola from here to there, trick motor neurons into imitating those skaters, imagine horizontal velocity, change the center of gravity, and go. On impulse, I reversed direction, made the leap diagonally, a longer jump, but I took the chance. Airborne for a second, then feet hit the roof, just missing a planter of snakeweed—medicinal, poisonous, yellow flowers battered by the storm.

I'd like to say my alighting in one piece caused Crack to reel back, King Kong style, stung by the diminutive wasps that were the wind-up airplanes of his time, but no shock was registered, my reception was matter-of-fact, tipping a hat, if not extending a handshake. How are you? Not bad and yourself? Nice to see you. Nice to have you onboard.

So what was it all about, Crackhour, when you sort it out? The rush to get to Waxman's apartment, to Horner's Landing, to talk to the Kents, his unease when the man from Crafted Identities was sighted behind us at Mr. Levant's? (Did the man who made fake IDs know something I didn't, or was he just as oblivious as I was?) Crack made up a drama featuring salt-and-vinegar consciousness, and all I'm left with is burnt toast and black coffee.

"You're wondering why I'm here when I should be waiting in the car. It's not what you think."

"I'm dying of curiosity but pressed for time."

Chester (monetizing a chance opportunity) and Debonis (aggrandizing his miniscule fiefdom) thought they were so clever, but they'd just gotten in the way. Crack didn't have to do a thing. Others tied up loose ends for him. He stepped back to sit on a bench, as if our being on the roof was like any other rainy morning, drinking coffee, putting off going to work, looking out at the ocean.

"Let me explain."

"I'm all ears, but I'm on the clock."

"I was at a party on an island near Hellsgate, the part of the bay where rivers merge and the currents are strong and unpredictable. Not easy to get to, but quite a few people made the trip; none that I knew, as it turned out, and striking up conversations with strangers at parties leaves me feeling like a pitch-altered recording of myself, so I planned to leave after one drink, if I could get a ride back. Standing on a terrace lit by paper lanterns, looking out over the water, I was trying to figure out how to leave, when a woman approached me, stood right next to me on the terrace as if we were old friends, though I'd never seen her before. Her skin was the color of maple syrup, blond hair pressed into waves, her nose looked like it had been in a couple of fights, not squashed, just asymmetrical. She had an accent that sounded as if her words were figuring things out at the back of her throat before they were allowed past her lips. Words formed slowly, carefully, subject to in-house censoring service, so syllables were a little bent by the time they got out. We stared toward the lights of a farther shore, not making eye contact, and she asked me if I thought it would be possible to swim to the next island downstream, or would you be swept out to sea? She leaned further out, not a smart idea—the brick was crumbling, already fallen away in some places, and she gave the impression like maybe she intended to dive in. I pulled her back."

Prince Achmed, silhouette animation paper cutout, was pretty much rescue-driven. That was his story, pinned up in Crack's office behind a screensaver of a dolphin entertaining itself by blowing bubble rings—a sign of intelligence, of consciousness, the ability to alleviate boredom when stuck in Sea World. Crack shadowed his ex-wife, but she had zero interest in any kind of reconciliation. Go away. Leave me alone. He was left by the side of the road holding his phone, which only got him into trouble. The stalker was a Crack I didn't really recognize, but evidence suggested he wasn't the only Crack who had been unknown to me.

"We got high, drunk, I don't remember exactly. We found an empty room, no one was around, and while we were together, though at what precise point I couldn't nail down, she decided she wanted to leave, but I wanted her to stay, so I told her an interesting story about a woman I watched watch movies. Dormazin, just a half a street noddie, plus alcohol, affects speech centers and triggers an over-firing amygdala. I wanted to impress her, and it worked—she was intrigued, she stayed. I never wanted anyone to stay with me in that way. It had been a long time, and I felt I would do or say anything, but when I was feeling around, I reached into a pocket of her dress made of sharkskin, like a mermaid who doubled as an espionagist, an infiltrator, a solver, and my hand grabbed her ID. That's how I knew who she was, but it was too late. I said what I said."

Crack hadn't informed on me to just anyone, but to a woman who worked for the Department of Evolutionary Engineering.

"The next time I saw her, it was in a very different setting."

"I'll bet."

"Loew, listen, I fought to keep you alive, argued that you were worth keeping an eye on, you were good at your job, maybe your anomaly was worth repeating."

His ex-wife wasn't the only one he'd been stalking. He had informed on me for a handful of slow blue death. The Dormazin addiction created a sinkhole Crack covered with planking, but his escalating cravings were very much still there, doing what empty holes do, the cover fools no one. If he was lucky enough not to have a meeting with his own personal disappearachnik, he would soon be kicked out, his possessions, including the Zoltar, piled into a shopping cart, forced to live in a subway station or a perch above an abandoned parking lot. He needed the money they paid to inform, because he was done and he knew it.

Crackhour got up from the bench and walked to a far end of the roof, standing in such a way, so he blocked the few feet that led to the center of the espaliered trees, the strongest part of the escalier. If I was to leave by the vegetational back stairs, he had to move. He reached over the edge, picked a storm-resistant apple from the top of the wall, and took a bite. Their skins were salty, but the flesh inside was tart, difficult to eat uncooked. The apple was small, and he took one bite, then tossed the core over the rim. Even if the seeds germinated, they wouldn't produce the same tree as the parent. The ground was littered with useless fallen apples. Nobody cared.

"You could make it," Crack said. "You should try now before the wind really picks up again." He stepped to one side and gestured. This way, be my guest, please. If I fell, then the wall would have done his job for him.

I put one foot over the ledge and onto a branch. It held my weight, and I swung my other leg around and onto another limb. These were thinner, near the top, but they held. I began my descent. It was more of a ladder than a staircase. Trees and vines were tied to the support structure, but the question was how strongly they were attached to the building. It could all peel off in a wave of plants and trellises. There was no way to know whether the espalier escalier could withstand climbing, apart from trying it out.

Two stories down, the branches began to wobble and bow, as if being shaken from the top. I looked up—a better idea than looking down—only to see that Crack had begun to follow me. It was unlikely the escalier would hold both of us. What better way to make a permanent exit than to topple and take me with him. I picked up my pace, even as some branches snapped underfoot. Slipping, grabbing, I inhaled the smell of wet stone and snapped boughs, and tested their strength more rapidly.

My feet hit the ground. The parking lot was still an empty stretch of asphalt, I didn't look up to see how far above me Crack was on the wall, or how quickly he was closing in. A stack of palettes wrapped in plastic lay beside a boom crane truck that should have been parked in one of the many loading bays, but had been abandoned. Running behind a row of pines, I was able to reach the truck door, which was swinging in the wind, and climbed into the cab.

A twisted side mirror provided a view to the front of the building, and bursting into its curved edge, I could see Crack make it to the ground. One of the guards rushed over to him; they talked and gestured for a few seconds. Are you alright? Yes, I'm fine, and then they walked in the direction of the truck. Did Crack really need any help? Couldn't he do this by himself? I wasn't going anywhere, but they stopped a couple of yards away, and I could hear Crack tell the guard to check the power station behind the pines. His voice was loud, and it carried. Pangenica's private power plant was a series of silo-like structures surrounded by a chain-link fence and barbed wire. Ordinarily, it was locked, but in a storm such as this one, with the continual possibility of blackouts, the station needed to be accessed by people who might not have entrance codes. Cavernous and dark, if you knew where to walk and had a flashlight, it would be a decent place to hide. The guard took off in that direction while Crack walked to the other side of the truck and opened the door.

TWENTY-FIVE

Then I was in Crack's car, and he was driving. Sometimes causes and effects aren't neat, and you're stuck with the person who made your life miserable. You've heard or read stories about the lieutenant who ordered a village massacre then went back home where now stateside, he managed a jewelry store in a strip mall, or the death camp guard who lived down the hall from one of his victims, or the guy who claimed he shot in self-defense, but there he is out mowing his lawn, or the person who was only a follower, but still administered electric shocks, and there she is getting takeout sushi like anyone else.

Why did I get in his car? Because I had nowhere else to go. The drying thread of hope: Some people evade capture, they release the security locks on tiger cages, hide in plain sight on lesser islands, mingling with those too impoverished to pay for Pangenica's services. The lifelines tossed might not turn into pythons with hearts in their eyes and just might be a length of rope, more or less. There might be fifty out of a hundred reasons not to get in the car, but then maybe the fifty reasons to lift one foot, and the next edge towards fifty-one, so you get in.

Crack, who took an interest in an old man's archive of comics, in the consciousness of two unknown children, one of them dead. Crack, who was ready to turn me in for the promise of a lifetime supply of noddies one minute, and then offered a path out. Get into my car, and I'll take you, the next. Did Crack look like who he was? I had thought so, and this was a misstep, but here I was sitting in his car, not leg against leg, almost on the brake, but pressed against the door.

Dot used to say in tales you get rich by finding treasure in concrete material non-crypto form: gold, jewels, etc. If you don't find capital, you may acquire it, not exactly working and earning, but by answering riddles, marrying royalty, performing some kind of world record feat: grow your hair tower-height long, feel a pea under tower-height mattresses, hold your breath under water for hundreds of years. Almost none of this is realistic except maybe marrying money. It's great to say fuck you, to say it and mean it with all kinds of absolute reasons, but if you're hungry and have nothing but zeros to your name, you say fuck you, but still get in the car and drive. The word that means less than zero, unless you're Captain Ada saying it into a radio, then she gets a whopping fine, but everyone says it all the time, and it has all the power of hard old gum spots on the sidewalk.

Dot didn't save my Phytosack—she who saved everything. Because there was no Phytosack. Waxman knew I was born in an unspeakable obsolete way, not even untimely ripped. Traits just out for a generational stroll, contributed by a ceilometer inspector who came and went. It was all spelled out on the pages he'd handed me, my paper file. I tore it up and tossed the pieces out the window. Crack asked what I was doing letting the rain in, and I reminded him that if I felt the rain, I wouldn't feel others, i.e. him.

Keep driving, Crackhour.

He drove fast, but sooner or later, he would reach the end of the long cigar-shaped island that was Pangenica's locus. At that end point where there was a narrow land bridge, partially washed out, a town blinked its lights on the other side.

I could become Fentster, the cartographer, who had to travel constantly, from high chaparral to high littoral, not just mapping the present, live maps of such conflict zones as still existed, migration of exiles, deportees, guerilla movements, seismic activity, but also anticipating the future, spinning data into shapes, overlaying continents with population densities and weather patterns to come, revising topographies as land masses build up and erode. Okay, Crackhour, get over this isthmus and let me out on the other side. As Isla Fentster, I knew a few places that might still be out of reach.

Maps, with few exceptions, are based on facts, not emotions. You might say maps are factories of facts, facts of the moment, subject to change, even to distortion if the creator or the person who's paying so desires. This was a decent place to hide or hide out.

Heading into the unknown—there were maps for that, too. I'm not talking about the earth balanced on the back of a turtle, balanced on another turtle, nothing but turtles all the way down, but maps that depicted a flat earth, *hic sunt dracones*, written in the air, a warning: don't go there, dumbass. Boom. You'll fall off. So, would I fall off, too? We talk about the map of the brain, but not the map of the heart made up of chambers, or the stomach full of microbiome-sloshing acid and who knows what, or the lungs, just air, then not. Waves met at the center of the strip of land, then retreated back to the ocean. If a junky car could make it across, you could hear music blasting from midnight food trucks, even from this far away, somebody over there, myself included, was going to need a map to the ends of the earth.

END_

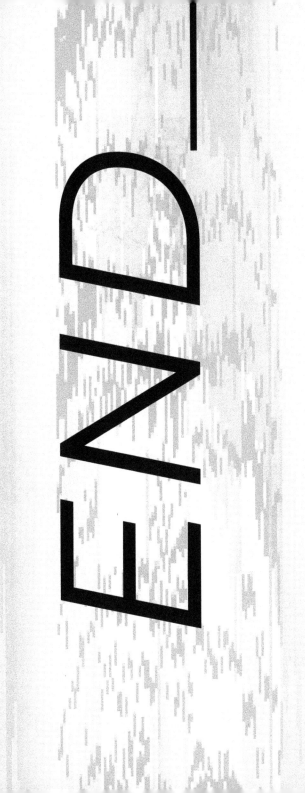

ABOUT THE AUTHOR

PHOTO BY JOHN FOSTER

Susan Daitch graduated from Barnard College and attended the Whitney Museum Independent Study Program. She is the author of six novels and a collection of short stories. Her short fiction and essays have appeared in *Guernica, Tablet, Tin House, McSweeney's, Bomb, Conjunctions, The Norton Anthology of Postmodern American Fiction*, and elsewhere. Susan's work was the subject of a Review of Contemporary Fiction, along with that of David Foster Wallace, and William Vollman. Her first novel, *L.C.*, was a recipient of an NEA heritage award and a Lannan Foundation grant. *Fall Out*, a novella, was published by Madras Press, all proceeds donated to Women for Afghan Women. She has also received two Vogelstein Foundation awards and a Fellowship from the New York Foundation for the Arts. Her novel, *Siege of Comedians,* was listed as one of the best books of 2021 in *The Wall Street Journal.* One of her essays was listed as a Notable in the Best American Essays 2022. Her work has been translated into German, Spanish, and Italian.